Palindrome

Palindrome

E. Z. RINSKY

WITNESS
IMPULSE

An Imprint of HarperCollins*Publishers*

EPub Edition JUNE 2016 ISBN: 9780062495488

Print Edition ISBN: 9780062495471

10 9 8 7 6 5 4 3 2 1

To Mom, who taught me to keep showing up.

Palindrome

Palindrome

Prelude

SAVANNAH AWOKE TO the sound of a faucet dripping somewhere over her head. She felt groggy and her mouth was dry. Couldn't quite remember where she was, and the thick darkness offered no clues.

Her butt was numb. She tried to shift around in the wooden chair she found herself sitting in. Frowned as she realized that she could hardly move. Fingers tingling, mind foggy. She felt drugged, detached from her body, like she was floating above her own head, looking down on herself below.

She took a deep, worried breath, and as the smell of the cellar rushed into her lungs—rank, like damp soil—her heart sank. She remembered where she was. A ninety-pound dumbbell bound to her ankles had kept her prisoner to this chair for what felt like weeks, submerged in the complete darkness of this basement, flitting between terrible dreams and this cold, stale reality.

But something had changed since she'd last been awake. Her face. The skin on her face was burning, like she'd had a harsh chemical peel.

Savannah reached a finger to her cheek to inspect the burns and recoiled in pain.

She gritted her teeth as she lightly brushed her face to inspect the damage. Unfamiliar grooves ran down her cold cheeks, over her forehead and chin. She bit her lip and shuddered as she traced the fresh lines with her fingertips, trying to figure out what had happened to her. She imagined her face looked like the surface of some lonely moon, covered in deep canals and craters.

She dropped her hand as a door slammed somewhere off in the distance—from the same direction as the faucet? Heavy footsteps clomped down stairs, then the door to the cellar groaned open, the ancient hinges protesting the intrusion.

"What happened to my face?" Savannah asked as her captor slammed the door closed. She was surprised at how weak and grainy her voice sounded. Her captor ignored her, was fiddling with what sounded like tools in a plastic bag. "Wait," Savannah realized. "Did you turn on a light? I can't see you. I can't see anything. I can't see."

"I know." A deep, rumbling voice from across the room that reminded Savannah of a lawn mower engine.

"I'm also very thirsty," Savannah said, her voice sounding small and pathetic coming from her parched lips.

Her captor dropped something on what sounded like a tabletop. Clanking of metal on metal. More ruffling of what Savannah definitely recognized as plastic grocery bags. Heavy breathing.

"Can I please have something to drink?" Savannah said.

Her captor ignored her again, now occupied with what sounded like a socket wrench. A pipe gurgled over her head. This was the first time this person had lingered here, done anything but drop food or water on her lap. The first time that she recalled, anyways; it felt like her memories were buried in the bottom of a deep well, and every time she tried to summon one, the bucket came up empty.

"Are you feeling totally awake? Alert?" her captor finally asked.

"I . . . guess."

It sounded like items were being taken out of the plastic bag and dropped onto the tabletop. A cold draft from somewhere ran through her hair. Clicking, and the sound of metal on metal—a gun?

"Are you going to kill me?"

"Yes."

Savannah was surprised to find that this answer brought neither fear nor relief. It was simply a procedural footnote in the saga that had been the last few weeks—or months?

"Today?"

"In just a few moments."

"What did you do to my face?"

No response. She settled deeper into the damp wooden chair that she could hardly even feel beneath her anymore. She'd long since given up any hope of moving the dumbbell. Her captor muttered something that Savannah couldn't make out, then stepped close to her. She could feel warm, stale breath on her lacerated cheeks. She struggled to remember what this person looked like, wasn't sure if she'd ever actually seen their face.

"Okay."

There was an unmistakable anticipation in the voice today. Until now it had always been bland, cold, methodical: *Here is your water. Here is your food.* But today her captor sounded almost nervous.

"I need you to listen very closely to my instructions. If you don't pay attention, this will all be for nothing."

4 E. Z. RINSKY

Savannah bit her lip so hard she tasted blood.

More heavy breathing. Her captor's breath smelled not unpleasant. Like cinnamon gum.

"I was able to locate your sister."

Savannah's heart fluttered to life for the first time in ages.

"I don't have a sister." The listless lie left her dry throat quivering.

"Her name is Greta. She lives in Manhattan. In a studio on 86th and Amsterdam. She is a financial analyst for a large bank and owns a German shepherd."

Savannah couldn't contain her whimper. The helplessness she'd felt the first days of her captivity—before she'd resigned herself to her fate—returned. She raised a weak hand in an attempt to slap or grasp the captor she couldn't see, but caught only air.

"Please don't hurt her," she gasped.

"I won't touch her if you follow my instructions. Do you agree to follow my instructions?"

Savannah inhaled sharply. "Yes."

"Do you swear to do exactly as I say?"

Savannah lowered her head. "Yes. I swear."

"Good."

Something shuffled near her feet, and again she heard the crinkle of a plastic bag. A wet sound of smacking lips right next to her ear, then a tender whisper:

"When a person dies, their soul departs their body instantly. At the moment their heart stops. They are here one moment and gone the next. But that isn't going to happen to you, Savannah."

It was the first time she'd ever heard this person say her name. It sickened her. The last syllable hung in the stale air between them for a moment. Her captor was panting in her ear like an expectant dog. The faucet in the distance continued to drip.

"Why isn't that going to happen to me?" Savannah finally asked.

"Because of what I've done."

A cold hand suddenly brushed the scars on her face. She could sense a sort of affection in the way her captor traced the lines around her eyes, down to her chin. "My guess is you will have three to five minutes in between."

Savannah's mouth was dry and sticky.

"I don't understand."

"I want to understand where we go after we die. You will die, but you will be tethered, anchored here in physicality. We can only fool them for a few minutes, but that should be more than enough."

Savannah's voice cracked.

"Enough for what?"

The voice seemed surprised. "For you to tell me what's happening."

She heard some fidgeting as the voice backed away from her ear and moved directly in front of her face. Savannah heard two clicks. "This is a tape recorder. Everything you say while your soul is tethered will be recorded. As soon as you see something, anything, start speaking. Describe it. Describe everything you see in as great a detail possible. This is the most important thing. Do you understand?"

Savannah shifted in her chair.

"Yes."

"And if you disobey me, if you intend to spite me by keeping silent, by keeping the secret to yourself, then I will find your sister and kill her also."

Satisfied, her captor rose and shuffled around. Savannah heard what sounded like the clink of glass.

"Please don't hurt my sister," she heard herself saying. "If I don't say anything, it's not because I'm not cooperating. It's because, maybe, because it's not working. Hurting her won't do any good."

No reply. The silence deepened as the faucet in the distance was finally turned off.

Her captor again moved in close and said, "I'm ready. Do you understand your instructions?"

"I . . ." Savannah was crying. She felt very strange. "Yes. I understand."

"Do you have any questions? If you do, please ask. It's important that you understand."

"I . . . Will it hurt? Dying?"

Her captor made a sound that was almost like a light chuckle. A click as the tape recorder was switched on.

"You tell me."

PART ONE:

Play

"LISTEN TO YOUR breath. Inhale all the way, fill your lungs, and then let it out, *Hmmmm*."

The wood-paneled studio is filled with the exhalations of two dozen spandex-clad students—nearly all women, all of whom are either younger than me or just immaculately preserved by years of "practice." The ten-year-old reason I'm here is crouching on the mat next to mine, her eyes closed in fervent concentration, stick-thin arms stretching toward opposite walls in her miniature warrior. At least *she's* enjoying herself. My white V-neck is soaked in sweat, my knees and butt are screaming in pain, and—as anticipated—I feel way more stressed than I did a half hour ago.

" . . . down into the tabletop position, and then you're going to slowly touch your left knee to your right elbow."

The instructor folds herself up into a pretzel like it's the most natural thing in the world. The blond woman next to me is a fucking contortionist; they'd burn you at the stake in the Middle Ages for moving like this. I try to jerk my knee up to my chest, forcing it, gritting my teeth, and instead of any sort of profound insight, I'm rewarded with a shooting pain up my back.

Sadie has no problem with any of the poses. Little kids' bodies are like putty, plus they don't really have any awful realities lingering in the back of their skulls while they're trying to stretch: unpaid utilities bills, looming root canals, sexual dry spells.

I'm more or less collapsed now on my mat, wheezing like the little engine who couldn't, almost certainly the person in this room who needs this the most and is enjoying it the least.

" . . . We're going to bring it back to downward dog now. Bend your knees if you need, and remember we all have different levels of flexibility and strength . . ."

I'm sure the instructor is addressing this directly at me, but I'm too ashamed to meet her gaze. Instead I focus my attention on my daughter, effortlessly arching her lower back, swanlike. It seems impossible that we share genetic material.

As something snaps in my lower back, I curse the parents of her school friends. Who introduces their kids to yoga in fourth grade? Last week when I picked Sadie up from school she started begging me to take her to a yoga class because all her friends are into it. So I gotta choose between being the stick-in-the-mud single dad who they whisper about at PTA meetings, the one whose poor daughter is missing out on all the opportunities afforded by your conventional healthy-as-fuck nuclear family, or exposing her to this indoctrinating witchcraft bullshit—smug, slender women who think they're the only people on the planet who know how to breathe.

Finally we're doing the only position my creaky body is qualified for: lying flat on your back, chilling. But even now, as we're supposed to be clearing our minds of karmic toxins, I'm thinking about last night, combing through the jacket pockets of a corpse someone threw in a Dumpster behind a Chinatown deli. Hoisting 180 pounds of deadweight onto my shoulders and tossing him facedown onto the cold cement, cutting a line down the back of his sweatshirt with my ceramic knife, other hand clasped over my nose to keep out the smell. Pulling back the fabric with a gloved hand to reveal the end of a two-week-long investigation: a splotchy brown birthmark the shape of a ketchup bottle. Snapping a few pictures to erase any doubt in the widow's mind, then flipping him over onto his back, writing his name, address and phone number on an index card. I call the cops from a pay phone, tell them where they can find the guy, then head over to his widow's house both to deliver the bad news and collect my fee—*I promised to find your husband, sweetheart, didn't say anything about what condition he'd be in.*

Not my fault that he was a bad high-stakes mahjong player but didn't know it. Or at least didn't figure it out till he owed enough to buy a small house in the Poconos.

"Dad, come on. It's over."

Sadie is standing over my heaving form, her pink face expressing both gratitude and sympathy. I sit up with a grunt. Around us, flushed coeds roll up their mats and talk about which juice bar to go to.

"Did you like it?" she asks as I follow her to a wall of wood cubbies and squeeze between a skinny woman who's positively glowing and a sweaty man in a wifebeater to retrieve our clothes.

"It was alright," I tell Sadie as I hand her her coat. Before handing Sadie her backpack, I covertly remove my Magnum from the side pocket and tuck it into my waist. Was starting to feel naked without it. "A lot of it hurt, to be honest."

"That means you need it!" she says seriously as we get in line to exit. No way to avoid the instructor, who is standing by the door with a tissue box for donations. I force a smile and drop in a five—if I just think of these classes as a self-serve S&M dungeon, I guess it's sort of a bargain.

I hold Sadie's hand as we walk down the staircase, past a flurry of glistening women too young for me to even think about in a sexual way. At this point it's just painful. They do smile at Sadie though and even grin at me when they realize the nature of today's masochism session. I'm no longer a creepy, groaning, forty-five-year-old guy in their eyes. I'm a daddy.

"Can we get ice cream?" Sadie asks as soon we burst out into the brisk January afternoon. St. Marks Place is momentarily jarring after the calm of the studio: teens loitering in front of head shops and tattoo parlors, impatient taxi drivers honking to no avail, tourists taking pictures of storefronts I've never even bothered looking at.

"It's too cold for ice cream," I protest, even as Sadie's tiny gloved hand pulls me toward an admittedly enticing dessert spot across the street. The line extends all the way outside. Better be good.

"How can it be too cold for ice cream if I want it?" she replies.

I drop her hand to inspect the dwindling contents of my wallet and curse to myself. Costs twenty dollars just to leave your apartment in this city, triple that if you have a kid. I have only four bucks left after that gouging at the yoga studio. They better take cards. I look up, and Sadie's already sprinted across the street and gotten in line.

"Sadie!" I say and barrel after her, squeezing between the bumpers of two taxis. I wedge beside her in line, ignoring a dirty look from the orange-faced guy behind her. I grab her shoulders and stare into her wide eyes. "You can't do that. There's too many people around here. I could lose you."

She shrugs and looks away, cranes her neck trying to get an advance view of the selection of artisanal flavors.

"I can't see," she complains. "Pick me up."

I grip her skinny hips through her puffy green coat and, with a grunt, heave her up onto my shoulders so she can see over the line. My first involuntary thought: how light she is compared to last night's dumpster corpse. I try to push that from my mind.

"See anything good?" I moan, my shoulders and arms still shaky from the yoga.

"I don't know. I don't know what they taste like by just looking."

I roll my eyes and lower her to the ground. Within moments, Sadie is rocking back and forth impatiently. The line is moving glacially, each client appearing to take at least six or seven samples, nodding seriously as they taste, mulling each one over, discussing the flavors with their companions like they're philosophy dissertations. Sadie looks tormented.

"How was school today?" I ask, trying to distract her.

"Fine," she shrugs, not taking her eyes off the distant dessert counter. To her it must seem we're an eternity away. Everything is so black and white at her age. Right now she's in hell—is there anything worse than waiting in a stagnant line? And once she gets the ice cream: total, unadulterated bliss. Maybe it's silly, but I envy that feast-or-famine mind-set. Certainly better than middling in the neutral nether-zone. If my life were a food, it would be bland grey pudding, sweetened only by a touch of Sadie and the rare occasion when a client pays me on time.

"Fine? Did you learn anything cool? Besides what all your friends are doing?"

"Nah."

The line inches forward as a satisfied young couple peels off from the cashier and leaves the shop, sharing a grotesque mound of chocolate ice cream piled tenuously atop a waffle cone. Another man a few spots ahead of us throws his hands up in exasperation and storms off, giving up.

"What are you gonna get, Dad?" Sadie asks, jumping out of her skin.

"Nothing. I told you, it's too cold for ice cream."

"I think when you see the ice cream up there you will change your mind," she says.

"Nope."

"You don't know. You don't know what you'll feel like when you see the ice cream."

"Yes I do," I say. "I've been around ice cream before."

Sadie rolls her eyes and sighs, like *I'm* the child.

"You think you know everything, Dad. You know a lot, but not everything."

I'm probably not supposed to let my daughter speak to me like that, but then, I probably won't be winning any parenting medals anytime soon either.

It takes fifteen minutes to reach the pearly gates. Saint Peter is a slightly overweight redheaded boy wearing his corporate baseball cap backwards. His pitiful rebellion. He stands slouched behind his array of gourmet offerings, his vacant eyes not exactly conveying pride in his work.

"Next customer," he grunts wearily.

Sadie takes a moment to scan the brightly colored flavors until she fixates on a bucket of pink.

"Can I taste the strawberry oatmeal cookie?" Sadie nearly shrieks.

Glassy eyed, the boy diligently scoops a tiny sample onto a plastic spoon and hands it to her. Her eyes go wide when she sticks it in her mouth.

"I want that!" she declares.

"Are you sure you don't wanna try anything else?" I say. "We waited so long."

"Nope. I like that. That's what I want."

"You heard the lady," I instruct the employee. "A small strawberry oatmeal cookie in a cup."

"Cone!" insists Sadie.

"No. You'll drip it all over yourself. Cup," I assure him.

I stare at Sadie's exuberant face as the boy readies her dessert. She looks like she's gonna burst.

"This is the best part," I tell her. "The anticipation. It's always better than the actual thing."

"No it's not."

"Six bucks," says the boy, the cup of pink ice cream visible beside him behind the glass display.

"You take cards?"

"Cash only."

"Jesus," I mutter to myself and open my wallet, pantomiming surprise when I discover my four pathetic singles. How the hell is that not enough for a small cup of ice cream? I summon an exasperated look—it doesn't take much—and hold out the four pitiful bills.

"I have four," I say. "I'm sorry. Is that alright? I'll come back later and bring you another two."

The boy looks confused. "It's six," he states.

"I understand. But I only have four. I'm sorry. I'll come back later with another two."

Sadie is wearing a mask of horror as the possible implications of the situation become clear to her.

"There's an ATM across the street," he says.

"Alright. Can we just have the ice cream now though? I don't want to wait in line again. Then I'll run across the street and get the cash."

"Uhhhh . . ." The boy's mouth is open slightly; this sort of decision tree analysis is way beyond his job description. "Sorry, it's six bucks."

Sadie's upper lip is trembling. Jesus. I bite my lip and lean in close to him. My daughter is not leaving here without her ice cream.

"Listen to me carefully, you shit stain," I whisper. "I want you to look down, through the glass, at my waist."

Confused, he obliges, and first squints, then recoils when he understands. The silver butt of a .38 Magnum is protruding from my belt line.

The color drains from his face.

"W-w-what the fuck, man?"

He nearly shoves the cup of ice cream at me.

"Take it, man. Fucking *nut job.*"

I smile and hand him the four dollars.

"Thanks, we'll be back in a second." I give the cup and a plastic spoon to Sadie and watch her face light up as she takes a monstrous bite. The boy is still staring blankly at me, terrified.

"That's fucked up, man," I hear him mutter.

Maybe I should write a parenting book.

I take Sadie by the hand and pull her out of the ice cream shop into the busy sidewalk before the kid can gather his wits. It occurs to me that while I fully intended to bring him his money at the time, it would be really awkward at this point.

We walk to Washington Square Park and find a park bench where Sadie can plow through her ice cream with abandon. I can't help feeling a little satisfied.

The case of Frank Lamb and the overpriced artisanal ice cream: closed.

My phone starts vibrating. Must be the widow. Probably can't accept the finality of last night's revelation and wants me to play therapist.

Nope. Blocked number.

"Hello?"

"Is this Frank Lamb?" It's a woman's voice, but not the widow. Deep and silky.

"Last time I checked."

"I'd like to hire you," she says as Sadie scrapes the bottom of the cup.

"Let's talk. You're in the city?"

"Yes."

I try to imagine what the woman on the other end looks like and have a hard time even getting started.

"Whereabouts? I could swing by your office or home or whatever."

"I'll come to you."

I sigh. "That's fine. I should caution you though, I work out of my apartment. But I assure you I'm the consummate professional when it comes to—"

"I'm actually calling because I hear you have a tendency to be unprofessional."

Oh boy.

"Alright. 247 East Broadway. I can be back there by five. That work?"

She's already hung up.

I'M A PRIVATE investigator, but that's vague. My job is getting things for people. It never fails to surprise me how many people want things: A woman wants a gold watch—an heirloom—back from her estranged brother. An insurance company wants evidence of fraud. A dirtbag wants the money another dirtbag owes him, plus maybe the dirtbag himself. A lawyer wants a reason to disqualify a juror. A half-senile man realizes he threw out papers with his Social Security information, pays me three grand to follow the trash, protecting an identity that's not worth stealing.

I never ask why they want it; I just get it for them and collect my bounty. This has nothing to do with professionalism. I'm simply not interested. I have my life with Sadie and my job as a retriever, crawling through the grease that lubricates the gears of society to recover ideas, objects, evidence, people. I usually loathe my clients, but it's a loathing born of fear—that if I crawl around in this muck too long, I'll be absorbed by it, dragging Sadie down with me.

I used to think more about how I ended up here—examining Dumpster corpses, snapping pictures of adulterous trysts, manipulating the truth out of low-ranking drug mules—but it's proven to be an exercise in masochism. Looking back, it feels like I never had a choice, like the river of fate just pushed me here and I never bothered resisting the current until I was in too deep. I went to law school because people always told me I'd be a good lawyer, but I took leave after a year and a half, when my mom got sick, and never went back. Worked as a bartender for a few years until someone offered me an entry-level marketing job. Was promptly fired after deciding I was smarter than my boss and explaining my reasoning to her, sprinkling in some admittedly unnecessary commentary on her appearance for flavor. Went back to bartending and started taking night classes at cop academy, figuring at least I wouldn't have to work in an office. I figured wrong and spent a miserable four years filling out paperwork and biting my tongue in the 21st Precinct. Then Sadie fell into my lap, and I saw an opportunity to make a move: private sector. Be my own boss, work my own hours, make a name for myself.

It took three months before I got my first job, a referral from a detective I was friendly with. An insurance fraud investigation, fairly basic PI stuff. A Wall Street quant's Upper West Side town house burned down two months after he took out a well-above-market policy on it. Smart guys think they can get away with anything.

It didn't take long for things to get ugly. Turned out he stopped showing up at work shortly after the "accident," and not even his wife knew where he went. Comes out he had a real bad coke problem. Burned through a six-figure salary, then started buying blow on margin. Give the guy credit—he had the foresight to see where this was headed, and the patience to wait two months before torching his home and ditching his wife and three kids.

Took me a week to discover that the quant was still in touch with one of his coworkers, a weak-willed man who broke down as soon as I asked if he knew about the fraud before it happened, which would make him complicit.

I found the poor quant in a motel room upstate, shades drawn, shaking under the covers, thin streams of blood pouring from his nose. Just waiting for someone like me to put my shoulder through the door.

When I told him I was a PI, he knew the gig was up. Blew his brains out, coating the still life behind the bed with what looked like Bolognese sauce. First time I'd seen anything like that. I fainted.

That's when I got the first inkling of what I'd gotten myself into. It was going to be an ugly life; that would be the price I'd pay for self-employment. Didn't have the prescience to just get out then. Insurance company recovered the claim and offered me another job, paying me double. I didn't like snooping, but apparently I was pretty good at it.

Most of the time—assuming *someone* knows the location of the mark—my job is comprised of two easy steps: Find the person who knows where it is, and then make them tell you. Sometimes they can't wait to get it off their chest, and sometimes you gotta beat the piñata to get the candy. Every person holds their knowledge behind a combination lock, and in eight years of this shit, I have yet to meet a combo that doesn't consist of some mix of fear, trust and greed.

THE DOWNSTAIRS BUZZER goes off before I can get my place anywhere close to clean. The kitchen is strewn with evidence of last night's culinary fiasco—a "Mexican casserole" I whipped up after paying the babysitter, which Sadie correctly diagnosed as nothing but salsa, canned beans and cheddar poured over corn tortillas and microwaved.

"It's so bad that you're not even eating it!" the little empress said, noting my untouched plate. I just shrugged, didn't explain that the smell of trash-soaked flesh was still in my nose, on my jacket and gloves.

I buzz in my prospective client, then race to my room, rip off an ancient Rolling Stones T-shirt and slap on a wrinkled blue button-down. In the living room, Sadie is on the couch, swimming in one of my old wifebeaters, reading a library book and drinking instant hot cocoa. I should probably be more concerned about her sugar intake.

"Sadie, could you read in your room? I'm sorry, but I'm gonna have a meeting in the kitchen."

"Okay," she says, popping up. "How long? Are you working tonight?"

"I don't think so," I say, straightening my collar. "No open cases. We'll watch a movie or something, alright? Your pick."

"Okay," she says, ducking into her room: a section of the living room I paid someone to wall off a few years ago. She's got enough room for a twin mattress and a dresser, that's about it, but she probably won't mind for a couple more years at least.

A firm knock on the door. My guest scaled those steps pretty damn fast. I quickly assess the apartment as a prospective client might: the mess in the kitchen, clothes coating the carpeted living room floor, Sadie's schoolwork all over the dinner table. If she wants unprofessional, she's come to the right place.

I begin my apology before the door is even open.

"I'm sorry about the mess. Fridays are cleaning day, I swear we have a system—"

My sheepish grin freezes as I pull the door back to reveal a jarringly beautiful woman. I'm rendered momentarily speechless as I drink her in. Just south of six feet—about two inches taller than me. Auburn hair trimmed to a length that only truly beautiful women can pull off. Wide green eyes, flawless, sharp cheeks. A body with the gentle hills and valleys of a rolling Scottish countryside, evident beneath a tight black turtleneck. She's wearing black leather gloves and red silk pants that hug a breathtaking pair of hips. Her rigid expression reveals nothing more than the fact that she's likely impervious to stupid flirtation, *so don't even try, hotshot.*

"Frank Lamb?" she says, her low voice immediately recognizable as the one I heard on the phone.

"That's what it says on the buzzer." *Jesus, Frank. Stupid, stupid.* "Please come in. You don't have a coat?"

She ignores the question. I beckon her to the dinner table and bid her to sit down in the most comfortable chair I own: a plush art deco number that Sadie and I found on 5th Street. She sits stiffly upright as I sweep Sadie's math homework to the side. There's something almost robotic about this woman. If she notices the mess, she's doing a great job of hiding it.

"Hi." Sadie has come out of her room to size up our visitor.

"Sadie." I turn and force some oomph into my voice. "I asked you to stay in your room and read until we're done."

"It's okay, she doesn't mind, right?" Sadie beams a grin at our guest, the one that usually charms any woman within fifteen years of birthing age, but this target's icy exterior is surprisingly impenetrable.

"Actually, I think it's best if I meet with Mr. Lamb in private," she says.

I give Sadie a glare like *sorry, but you're gonna have to scram, kid*, and she reluctantly retreats back into her room.

"Sorry," I say. "That's my daughter. Like I said, I don't usually meet clients here."

"I love children," she says emptily. "You're married?"

"No."

"Where's her mother?" The question catches me off guard.

"Not in the picture."

"Not in the picture?" Only her sharp gaze tells me it's a question.

"This is getting pretty personal, considering you haven't even told me your name yet."

She frowns, as if she's displeased with herself, like this is a mistake she makes often and is working to correct.

"Of course. That was rude. My name is Greta Kanter."

She doesn't offer me her hand. Her gloves are still on. She's not showing a sliver of flesh below where the crest of her tight black turtleneck hugs her neck. I'm thinking, if she's a leper, then sign me up for leprosy.

"Nice to meet you, Greta. Well, first things first. If you don't mind, I must insist on seeing some photo ID and knowing who gave you my name. Both are kind of standard."

She purses a pair of creamy lips and wordlessly plucks a green leather wallet from some fold of her pants, hands me a driver's license. I copy down the info—taking a little longer than I have to so I can admire a DMV photo that could pass for a glamour shot.

She says, "I got your name from Orange."

Ugh.

I was hired about eight months ago by a Columbia linguistics professor to gather proof that her loser husband was having an affair. She was all but sure he'd been cheating on her and didn't want to give him a penny when she divorced him. It only took two days to figure out that whatever he was doing, he was doing it behind an incredibly sketchy-looking metal grated door on West 59th Street, nestled between an old Polish restaurant and Laundromat. The husband stops a couple times a week in the early evening, buzzes in, then leaves four or five hours later. I figure, too much time for sex, plus I never see women coming or going. Must be drugs or gambling. Finally, after watching this guy for a week, I buzz in myself and wave to the little CC camera. A voice tells me to wait, and thirty seconds later a grotesque fat man in a tan suit materializes from the darkness, huffing from what must be some steep steps, followed by two dudes in sweatshirts, each about two heads taller than me and looking straight out of a Ukrainian mail-order meathead catalogue.

The fat guy is pale, with black eyes sunk deep into his rubbery face. He's built like a 350-pound teapot, and his face bulges and bloats in all the worst places. Gives me a greasy handshake, introduces himself as Matty Julius, but everyone calls him Orange.

He's doused in expensive cologne, and I catch the monogram on his silk pocket square. I think he puts in a lot of effort to draw attention from the parts of his appearance he can't change. I also think he might be wearing a toupee.

He explains he's seen me out here taking pictures of his facade over the last few nights, and if I'd be so kind as to turn those photos over to him, he'd be happy to offer double whatever my current employer is paying me. I casually note the size of the rocks on his stubby fingers, think I could probably ask for triple and he wouldn't blink, but explain that I already signed a contract—I'm an investigator, not a mercenary. But he needn't worry; the pictures will never be seen by anyone but my client.

He nods, satisfied, impressed even. I can tell he's one of these guys who takes a lot of pride in being a man of his word. Unbelievable how many dirtbags consider themselves men of honor. He's about to sidle back into his nether-lair when he stops and asks if I have a card, says he's actually in need of a snooper. Especially one he knows won't sell him down the river to a higher bidder.

Matty "Orange" Julius calls me two weeks later. He and his goons pick me up in a black Escalade and drive me around town while he describes the job. He wants me to hunt down a pair of Italians who sold him what he claims is a fake Rembrandt. I say I don't know jack about art, and he replies all I have to know is how to track down shitbags. Cuts me a check for the down payment right there in the car, catches my smirk when I see *Midtown Fitness, DBA* in the upper left-hand corner, and then I'm off, Orange never clueing me in to the precise nature of his apparently very well-decorated subterranean operation.

It was two months before I busted in on the Italians in their recently acquired Miami penthouse, brandishing my Magnum and screaming to drop the prosecco and kiss the fucking carpet. Finding them had required less blurring than straight-up mauling of certain laws. Notably: those against breaking and entering, aggressive interrogation techniques, and whichever amendment preserves an immigrant's right to not be knocked unconscious, bound with duct tape, and hauled back to Manhattan in the trunk of a rented Hyundai with very bad shocks.

"Look," I tell Greta, handing her back her license, "you should know that's not my usual purview. I got caught a little deep in that mess and ended up doing some things I'm not proud of. If you're looking to hurt someone, I'm not your guy. Hurting happens incidentally, but I try to avoid it. And if you want someone *killed,* I'm going to advise you to just turn around, as I'd be legally obliged to report that."

In the silence that follows, I find myself desperately hoping she doesn't take my advice. I really need the work. I try to keep my gaze level with hers, but it's like looking into the sun.

Finally she licks her lips. It's subtle and quick but doesn't escape my attention.

"Nothing like that, Mr. Lamb." She interlocks her gloved hands in front of her on the table, still sitting straight as a flagpole. Maybe she does yoga. "I want you to find something for me. And Orange Julius spoke very highly of your tracking abilities. As for the legality of the methods you employ, I couldn't care less. I care only about results."

I swallow hard. I've never met a woman like this. She's beyond gorgeous, sure, but something about her unnerves me. Her skin is *too* perfect, her wide, unblinking green eyes coldly calculating. It's like aliens created a flawless synthetic human from silicone. She's like a parody of beauty.

"Alright," I say. "I'm listening."

She reaches a gloved hand into her black leather handbag and removes a thick folder. She's about to open it but seems to think better of it and looks at me. The dying January day seeps in from the window behind me, casting half her face in pale, orange light. Her eyes are locked in a subtle—but fierce—glare that, with a little imagination, could be construed as sexual. I try to force that thought out of my head; I've seen guys crush on their clients, and it never ends well. Sure, Sadie could use a mom, but Greta doesn't quite strike me as the nurturing type.

"The first and most important thing to understand, Mr. Lamb, is that I value discretion. Nothing I tell you can be mentioned to anyone, even if you don't decide to accept my case. Is that clear?"

I've already lost control of this situation. Usually I'm the one laying down the ground rules, telling the flustered client how it's gonna be.

"That's actually very standard with PIs," I say, trying to sound authoritative. "If you'd like me to sign some type of nondisclosure though, I'd be happy to."

"That won't be necessary," she says, then reaches back into her purse and pulls out five crisp hundred-dollar bills. She drops them on the table and slides them toward me, her tightly gloved hand dragging sensuously across my shitty Ikea tabletop. "But I'd like you to have this in advance, as a way of thanking you for not sharing this with anyone."

I can feel my forehead crinkling of its own volition. Five hundred bucks just to keep this quiet? Must be plenty more where that came from.

But I slide the bills back to her.

"I haven't agreed to work for you yet, Greta. But I assure you that nothing you say to me leaves this room." With a smile, I add, "Again, unless you ask me to kill someone."

She frowns but leaves the bills out in plain sight, as if to remind me that they're there if I want them. Then she hands me the folder, grimacing like she's giving up her child for adoption. It's a police report, at least three hundred pages thick, stuffed with typed memos, glossy pictures and court documents.

The front page says simply, *Savannah Kanter. Homicide. 7/21/08.*

"Your . . ."

"Sister," she says. I shift in my chair. Before I can express my condolences, she clarifies: "I'm not asking you to investigate a murder. The case was closed two weeks after her death. The murderer turned himself in and has been incarcerated ever since."

"Okay." I make a triangle with my fingertips and try to ignore the way her chest slowly expands and contracts beneath that tight turtleneck. It's weird that she has a copy of the police report. Detectives' offices will usually give relatives a copy eventually if they ask for it, but the last thing most families want is to dwell on the grisly details. "Then . . . ?"

"I need you to find a by-product of the murder."

By-product?

"Let's start at the beginning," I say. It feels like a feeble attempt to take control of this dialogue. Her unblinking eyes, low breathing, rigid posture . . . She's like a magnet, sending my usually trusty compass spinning. I've never met a person who carries themselves like she does. "What happened to your sister?"

She hesitates, like she's summoning the strength for whatever's about to come out of her mouth next. She's so fucking beautiful. I'm trying to not imagine kissing her but can't help myself. Imagine sliding my hands down her hips, the weight of her heaving form on top of me—

"My family was on vacation. Me, Savannah and our parents. We rented a beach house a few miles south of Bangor. Maine. I was twenty-eight, Savannah was twenty-four—"

This was five years ago, so she's only thirty-three now? I had her pegged for early forties.

"We'd been there for three days, the four of us just relaxing. Swimming and lounging on the beach during the day. Playing cards and drinking at night. We hadn't been together for a while. My father's job requires constant travel, and he and my mother are always in Europe, Asia—"

"What does he do exactly?"

"Journalist. Writes international news for an English periodical. On day four of our trip we went into town. We got ice cream on the boardwalk and sat down on a picnic bench. Savannah handed me her cone and said she was going to run to the bathroom. She never came back."

She pauses and gazes at the back of her gloved hand. I make a mental note to mention this to Sadie as a cautionary tale—*this is why you always hold Daddy's hand in public.*

"Are you alright?" I ask. "Would you like a glass of water?"

Yeah, that will fix everything. Idiot.

She ignores me anyways:

"For twelve days, nothing. It still seems impossible, given the scope of the search, that we didn't find her. Every hotel in the state was emailed her picture. Police barricades on all major highways stopped cars at random. My father got on the local news and offered a half-million-dollar reward." She smiles emptily. "My parents had money. The police took it very seriously. They found some of Savannah's hairs in a parking lot about a hundred fifty feet from where we were sitting. There must have been a struggle while she was forced into a car. That was all they had to go on."

I'm struck by how impassively she describes all this; the same detached tone in which one might read a dense legal document or narrate a documentary on indigenous Indians. It's been years, so maybe she's just recited this so many times that it's become rote, devoid of emotion, the facts no longer resonant of the horror she must have gone through.

"No eyewitnesses saw her being shoved in the car?" I ask.

"No."

"Identifiable tire tracks near the hair?" I ask. "Anything caught on camera?"

"No," she shakes her head. "Gravel parking lot. Too vague. And we're talking about rural Maine. Not cameras on every corner, like here."

"Okay, so then?"

"Twelve days later a man approached a traffic cop in Portland and said he killed Savannah. He showed him a Polaroid of her corpse and told him where he could find the body. It was there. In the cellar of a cabin seven miles south of the boardwalk."

"Just a second," I say and quickly jump from my chair to stick my head into the living room, making sure that Sadie isn't eavesdropping on this. Kids should learn about murder the right way: on television, when their parents aren't around. I return to my seat. Greta's face is unwavering.

"Why her?" I ask, figuring the answer is that she was as beautiful as her sister.

"The police thought it was because she was small, much shorter than me, and skinnier. She weighed around a hundred pounds.

She would have been relatively easy to drag back to the car." She pauses, and then, as if anticipating my next question, adds, "She wasn't raped."

"I don't have much experience with homicide, but I imagine that's unusual."

Greta's nostrils flare. "That is perhaps the least unusual part of the whole thing. She was asphyxiated," she continues. "In court, he explained that he tied a plastic bag around her head until she stopped breathing."

I'm suddenly seized by an overpowering desire for a drink. There's a bottle of rye on the bookcase, visible over Greta's right shoulder, but it's not even dark out yet, and I'm pretty sure that day drinking isn't the kind of unprofessionalism she had in mind. From the window behind me I hear somebody on East Broadway screaming in Spanish and what sounds like the clattering of a metal trashcan.

"I don't understand what you want me to do," I say, imagining an iced double shot burning its way down my throat.

"You're not very patient, are you?" she asks, without the slightest hint of flirtation in her voice. She speaks slowly and deliberately, mechanically, like someone keeps pulling a drawstring on her back to trigger prerecorded phrases. Images of her in the throes of passion keep trying to burrow in through my ear and nest in my brain, and I keep mentally swatting them away like mosquitoes.

"No, I'm not," I say. "I seriously might have ADD. I hope that's not a deal breaker."

Again, she ignores my pathetic attempt at humor. This reminds me of every bad first date I've ever been on.

Greta grabs the folder back from me. She flips through it for half a minute—I desperately want to ask her about the gloves but resist—and finds a photocopy of an article from a local Maine newspaper. I scan the first paragraph.

"Silas Graham. Even sounds like a murderer. He pleaded insanity?"

"Yes. And it held up."

"Because he turned himself in?"

"There's more. He also confessed to killing his parents twenty-two years before and told them where they could find *those* bodies. Their decomposed bodies were buried in a scrap yard in rural Alabama, identifiable only by dental records. But indeed, it didn't take long to discover that the two of them were declared missing when Silas was around eleven. Silas was taken into foster care shortly thereafter. It took less than two weeks of court time to determine that he was likely a paranoid schizophrenic, and he was committed to an institution for the criminally insane."

That bottle is looking better and better. I'm no prude, but this kind of shit—kidnapped and murdered girls—isn't exactly my wheelhouse.

"I was on the force for a few years before going solo," I say. "In my very limited experience with this sort of thing, the 'criminally insane' verdict is usually indicative of little more than an expensive team of lawyers."

She smirks ever so slightly and flips a few pages deeper into the folder. "Not this time. Look at his face."

I inspect the grainy black-and-white photo she's pointing at for a moment, then recoil.

"Oh my god." I have to look away, the picture is making me a little ill. "Are those burns?"

"Tattoos. All over his face."

Greta continues flipping through the folder and stops at a full glossy. She stares at it a moment, taking in slowly what must be a picture of her sister. She breathes deeply, then rotates it in my direction. What I see makes my stomach tingle with cold. Savannah lying faceup on a coroner's slab. Her face has the exact same tattoos as her killer.

"Jesus," I gasp.

Greta nods and mercifully flips to another page.

"What the fuck?" I ask. "Why would he do that to her, then kill her?"

Her green eyes seem to be staring at something very far away. A siren screams down East Broadway and then fades.

"I've long since given up trying to understand," she says, her words sounding weighed down. "But here's the important thing." She flips to another article about Silas's trial and points to a circled paragraph. "Read," she says.

. . . *next to the body was found a Sony tape recorder, a model discontinued in 1992. Throughout the brief trial, Mr. Graham displayed an exceptional willingness to cooperate. The only exception being when asked about the purpose of this device, to which Mr. Graham repeated only, "I made a tape. I made a tape of her dying." When pressed as to the nature of this tape, Graham showed uncharacteristic reticence, shaking his head and occasionally appearing close to tears . . .*

I look up into Greta's glowing eyes.

"I want you to find the tape," she says.

I can't contain a snort. "The guy was nuts. He probably didn't even know what he was saying."

She stares past me, out the living room window. Not much of a view beyond the brick co-op towers across the street.

"He knew," she says.

What little willpower I have evaporates. I shoot out of my chair, return with two lowballs and the bottle of rye. Pour myself four fingers.

"Want any?" I ask.

She purses her lips. "No."

I shoot down half of it. Instantly I'm hit with a little hazy relief, and lean back in my chair.

"Alright, so let's pretend you're right. It exists. What do you want with this alleged cassette tape?"

She doesn't respond. Stares unblinking over my right shoulder.

"Greta, if you want me to find this—"

"On the last day of the trial the verdict was read," she starts. "Life in an institution for the criminally insane. I remember his face when this was announced. He seemed relieved—or pleased perhaps. Don't ask me why. As they were leading him down the aisle, out of the courtroom, he stopped at the front row, where I was sitting with my parents, and leaned in close to me. He was so close I could smell his breath—his teeth were rotting brown, and it smelled like he hadn't brushed them for years." The first traces of emotion I've heard from Greta so far. Voice wavering slightly in anger. "And his tattoos . . . he didn't even seem human. His voice was so awful. Throaty and raw."

She stops and looks at me for a painfully long moment. I shiver involuntarily. She seems to be deliberating whether or not to continue.

She says, "He leaned in close and whispered, '*It was worth it. I got what I wanted.*'"

I polish off my rye and have to tuck my fingers under my thighs to resist a refill.

I say, "Like I said, he's crazy."

"He made a tape of her dying, Lamb. That's what he said."

I raise an eyebrow. Greta's face is cracking slightly with emotion. Yet there's something about the way she's telling this story that doesn't quite ring true with me. It seems rehearsed, though that could just be because she's gone through this so many times. But I can't shake the feeling that she's omitting crucial details. And why hasn't she taken off those gloves?

As the light fades outside, Greta's pale skin seems to turn luminescent, glowing like a jack-o'-lantern filled with blue ice.

"Sure you don't want a drink?" I ask, my left leg fidgeting uncontrollably.

Greta doesn't seem to have heard the question. I suddenly remember poor Sadie, sitting alone in her room all this time. She probably doesn't even mind. I got her a bunch of good stuff from the library last week. But she'll probably guilt the hell out of me once Greta leaves.

"So . . ." I finally say, leaning in closer. I can smell her expensive perfume and minty breath.

Greta purses her lips, like she's swishing her next words around in her cheek; tasting them before releasing them.

"I told all this to the detectives on the case. They didn't care. They found the killer, that's all that mattered to them. Why should they care about some cassette tape?"

I shake my head slowly, mulling over the implications of what Greta is telling me. "But . . ." I swallow a laugh of disbelief. "I mean, surely you have to agree the most likely scenario is that it simply doesn't—"

"It exists, Lamb," she spits. Then she suddenly starts rubbing viciously at her upper cheeks, rubbing until I understand that she's scraping away a thick layer of makeup to reveal dark blue circles hanging beneath her eyes. "It's all I can think about. It's out there somewhere. Savannah's last words. And I can't make peace with this until I have it back. The thought of some sicko out there listening to her . . . I haven't really *slept* for five years."

Another long, empty pause. Another siren screams down East Broadway.

"Isn't it possible you misheard?"

"No," she growls, and the sudden shift in her voice makes me jump slightly out of my seat, then try to compose myself. She's growing heated, her face starting to glow pink. "And either he still has it, or he stashed it somewhere before he was arrested. It's mine, Lamb, you understand? He has my sister's voice. Her dying words. Nobody should have that but *me*."

I'm not quite sure I *do* understand.

"Okay. So suppose I agree to try to find this—"

"You'll start by talking to Silas. He's housed in the Berkley Clinic—a mental institution a hundred miles north of the cabin where my sister was murdered. I'll give you ten thousand up front. And three hundred thousand when the tape is in my hands. Cash. And I'll be able to tell if it's the real thing, because it will be Savannah's voice."

A three-hundred-thousand-dollar bounty for something other than a briefcase filled with five hundred thousand in cash is nearly unheard of. This is it. The holy grail of snooping. This is the stuff PIs dream of. But I summon my best poker face, act unimpressed by her offer.

"I'm guessing Silas isn't going to be thrilled with the prospect of cooperating."

"That's where your unprofessionalism comes in," she says.

"There are guards, no? Loony bins are basically prisons."

"For three hundred thousand dollars, I suspect you could get creative."

This is a lot to process. While my gears are still turning, she sits back in her chair and conveys something with the slightest upturn of her lip that may be flirtatious but reads more likely as disgust. Her smudged makeup does nothing to mar her beauty. On the contrary, the imperfection gives her the slightest air of vulnerability. She glowers at me and lowers her voice.

"And once I have the tape," she says, "you will have me. However you want."

Her face is completely deadpan. Betrays no hint that this is something she would enjoy in any way. It's just another part of the generous compensation she's offering. My poker face is wilting, my heart screaming, pushing blood to every corner of my body. Controlling myself is taking every inch of concentration. Both legs are shaking. She frightens me.

"Ten thousand up front, but another five for expenses," I practically squeak. "And make it three fifty. Only half of that is for me. I'm going to need help."

She weighs this for a moment. "Who?"

My mouth is dry. I can't tell if this thing seizing me is lust or terror. Either way, I suddenly want her out of my apartment, away from Sadie. I clear my throat.

"I had help on the Orange case, never could have done it alone. Courtney Lavagnino is the best tracker I've ever worked with. Honestly, he's a genius."

"Courtney?" She spits his name out like it's bitter. I catch a glimmer of fiery orange in her eyes. "That's a man?"

"He was the brains behind finding the forgers," I gush, eager to change the topic. "He's brilliant. Speaks like seven languages. He once found a ninety-year-old Nazi hiding out in New Zealand, based only on a water-damaged black-and-white photo of him from the war. He worked briefly for the DEA, gathering evidence against drug moguls, but quit because he needed to work at his own speed. He was hired by a hot sauce manufacturer to find a pepper seed—a single fucking *seed*—rumored to grow into the hottest pepper known to man. He found it. If you're serious about getting this tape back, you'll pay for both of us."

She runs a gloved hand through her hair. I want to say she's calming herself down, but really she never actually flipped out. Did she ever even raise her voice? She's able to project this terror just with her eyes.

"Then give me his information. It sounds like he's the one I need, not you."

I shake my head. "If you want to find a truffle, you can't just hire the pig."

She raises an eyebrow. I clarify: "For Courtney, it's all an intellectual exercise. He's a pure tracker—not always a man of action. If you want someone to locate the tape, hire Courtney. If you want someone to *get* the tape, you need both of us."

Greta mulls this over. I sense the additional fifty grand is inconsequential to her if it means a higher chance of her holding the tape in her hands.

"Where was the seed?" she asks.

"In the safe-deposit box of a South American dictator. Courtney wouldn't tell me which one. He was apparently a connoisseur and collector of peppers, bought it on the black market for millions. As I said—he *found* it. I believe he was working with someone like myself, who figured out how to actually steal the thing."

If I'm underselling Courtney's competence in the field a bit, it's more than offset by failing to mention his occasional interpersonal gaffes. He almost derailed our search for the forgers by growing impatient with what turned out to be a key witness, pointing out inconsistencies in that poor, confused girl's story with the callous logic of a poacher doing his taxes. Nearly broke her, and it took me hours of comfort and coaxing to finally extract what we needed out of her.

Greta reaches into her purse and removes a large wad of hundreds. Counts them out and plops them on the table.

"Well this time, locating it is not sufficient. I want you to hand it to me. Here is ten thousand up front, plus five for expenses. After three days call me on this number"—she scribbles it down on a page in the police report—"and report your progress."

"Don't you want to sign—"

"No contracts. Just get me the tape. Call me sooner if you discover anything important."

I can hardly stand up to let her out. My legs are trembling, and the tips of my fingers are numb. By the time I manage to pull myself up, she's already out the door, the click of her black boots receding down the staircase. I stare at the pile of money on the table and try to remember if I ever actually agreed to this.

I PICK UP Sadie from school the next day, and we walk to the coffee shop a few blocks from our apartment to meet Courtney Lavagnino. We spot him sitting in the darkest corner he could find, a mug in his hand, eating lentils out of a Tupperware container and reading a thick Russian paperback. Sadie and I walk to the counter to order. Courtney is so wrapped up in his book, he doesn't even notice us entering. Some detective.

I order a red-eye and scone for me plus a bran muffin for Sadie. The barista has a pierced nose, and the tattoos on her arms make me shudder, thinking about Savannah's face up on the slab. The barista blinks when I try to pay with a hundred.

"I don't have change for this," she says.

"So keep it," I say. "We come here a lot."

I pull up an extra seat at the small wooden table, and Sadie and I sit down across from Courtney. Far from startled, he sets down his novel—appearing disappointed by the interruption—and takes a smooth sip of tea. He still has that hideous ponytail. My theory is he knows it's stupid but keeps it as a tribute to the freedoms of self-employment.

"Hey champ," I say. "Thanks for coming down to my end of town."

"Hi Frank," he says warily, like he's expecting bad news. In fact, his entire pale, horse-shaped face looks like it was designed specifically to react to unpleasantness: skeptical eyebrows, wide, sad eyes, and a thin mouth that tends to default to a dour frown. Eventually I learned that the frown just means he's lost in thought, but anyone who sees him pouting on the subway, lanky arms crossed across his sunken, flannel-clad chest, corners of his mouth pointed at the floor, probably takes him for a miserable hipster. Irony is, I doubt he even knows what *hipster* means.

I guess he's the closest thing I have to a work friend. We only worked together for seven weeks on the Orange case, but during that time we hardly left each other's side. Unlike me, Courtney seems to have made a deliberate decision to be a snooper. He's certainly smart enough that he could have done anything he wanted. Ponytail aside, he wouldn't look out of place in professorial tweed, lecturing about Camus. Or he probably would have made a hell of a beat reporter.

We haven't spoken since wrapping up the case for Orange Julius over half a year ago. I'd considered trying to get in touch with him since, just to hang out, but had no idea what to invite him to. He doesn't drink alcohol or coffee, so what do I ask? If he wants to meet up for a round of putt-putt?

And besides, contacting him is itself an ordeal. He doesn't have a phone or computer. He's accessible only by email, which he checks two or three times a week at a library in Harlem. He has some sort of weird paranoia about technology, which he explained once while we were on the road. Being reachable 24/7 is part of it. He says he can't read, think or sleep knowing that someone could call at any minute. But also, all his time spent tracking people has made him aware of the digital trail we all leave in our wake, as conspicuous and easy to follow as elephant footprints. He doesn't want anyone to be able to find *him*. Hiring him for a PI job is like trying to get a reservation at a fancy restaurant. But he seems to have enough of a reputation in the right circles that suitors will put up with the inconvenience.

"You must be Sadie?" he asks my daughter with a weird smile. I've never seen him around kids, but I'm starting to suspect he's one of those guys who treats them like little adults. He sometimes seems like he learned how to interact with people from reading sociology textbooks.

Sadie nods slowly.

"Your dad talked about you a lot when we were working together. Here, I got you something."

With a flourish, he produces a little silk sack from his pocket and hands it to her. Sadie glances up at me.

"It's okay," I say. "Probably."

Sadie tentatively reaches out to grab the bag then pulls it close and opens it, her forehead crinkling first in apparent confusion, then her eyes widening in awe. It's a handblown glass vial that glows royal blue even in the dim light of the coffee shop.

"What's it for?" Sadie asks, the colors seeming to swirl and shift as she rotates it in front of her face.

"I'm not sure exactly," he explains proudly. "I found it in a Moroccan market. It was just so beautiful that I had to have it. You can keep anything in it: jewels or spices or pearls. Whatever secret treasures an adventurous young woman like yourself happens upon."

"Awesome," she whispers.

"What do you say, Sadie?"

"Thanks, Mister, uh—" she says, still staring at it, mesmerized.

"Just Courtney," he says.

"Yes, thanks, Courtney," I say. "That was very thoughtful. Alright now, Sadie, do you have a book with you?"

"Yeah."

"Could you go read your book at a different table? Courtney and I need to have a private talk."

"Okay."

She scampers off and sits down on the other side of the tiny café. There's only a young man on his computer between us, but he's bumping to whatever is on his headphones; I'm not particularly worried about being overheard.

"What are you drinking?" Courtney asks.

"Red-eye. Black coffee with two shots of espresso."

The corners of his lips turn down.

"I thought you said you were going to cut down on caffeine once we finished that job. That's disgusting. And terrible for your heart."

"You must have misheard." I take a big gulp just to piss him off and smack my lips. "So where did you really get that thing? You know what that is, don't you?"

"What?" Courtney looks confused. "What do you mean?"

"You bought that in a market in Morocco?"

"No, I said I *found* it."

"Where, in a drug den?"

Courtney's face drops.

"That's a heroin vial," I say. "Although I suppose in a cinch it could also be used to hold cocaine or meth."

Courtney's face contorts. "I'm so sorry, Frank, I had no idea—"

"It's okay." I wave dismissively. "You washed it, I hope?"

He lowers his head into his palms, and his fingers dig into his scalp. "I'm so sorry, I was just trying to do something nice—"

"Listen, forget it." I take a big bite of scone and, with my mouth full, ask, "What were you doing in Morocco?"

He glances over at my daughter playing with his drug paraphernalia, shakes his head in disbelief. Finally sighs and explains:

"This was right after the Orange job. I was following fifteen pounds of top-shelf ecstasy—tipped off by an old friend. He told me that the DEA had been trying to get this guy for a few months, then he fled the country, and they gave up. I found his operation in the back of a dried fruit stand in Tangier but didn't get anywhere close to the drugs. As soon as I figured out I'd found them, a gentleman was kind enough to break my jaw and hit me in the kidney.

"They dragged me to some hotel room where a guy asked me questions in Moroccan Arabic and kicked me a few times in the face each time I answered, apparently displeased with my dialect. I learned Arabic from a Lebanese woman—totally different language. Then he stabbed me in the thigh and left me bleeding on the hotel room floor. It's a miracle I managed to crawl to the phone.

"I spent a month in a hospital in Tangier—not an experience I'd recommend. No AC, in the middle of a North African July. And that's to say nothing of the quality of care. Anyways, I finally got back to the city with nothing to show for my efforts but a few nasty scars and that interesting little vial, which my assailant left behind. Must have fallen out of his pocket during the beating."

I click my tongue. "Tell me, how can someone who has *worked* for the fucking DEA not recognize a heroin vial?"

Courtney shrugs. "Finding drugs is just like finding anything else. I don't need to know anything about it except that I find it, tell my employers where it is, maybe take some photos, and am paid handsomely. Except with drugs my efforts take it out of circulation, maybe even save a few lives."

"You're a regular Mother Teresa."

Courtney raises an eyebrow—his equivalent of a smile—but it's gone in an instant. And then the time for small talk is over.

"So." He taps his long fingers on the rim of his mug. "What have you got?"

He slides out of his jacket and lets it sink behind him on the chair, as if expecting the excitement of a new job to get his literal blood flowing. With the jacket goes the illusion of physical normalcy. His long head is perched on top of a body that looks like a bunch of twigs sewn together and draped in flannel. Whenever he stands up it reminds me of a praying mantis rearing before it kills something.

I summarize my encounter with Greta for him—omitting only her physical description and the enticing offer I'd been unable to get out of my head all night, thinking maybe Courtney will accuse me of only saying yes as a personal favor to my shlong. But either I'm a bad liar, or Courtney is incredibly perceptive. Probably both.

"She's beautiful, isn't she?" Courtney says, depositing a forkful of lentils into the slot between his scraggly mustache and what could only generously be called a beard.

"What?" I act surprised and turn to check on Sadie to avoid making eye contact with him.

"She overpowered you with her beauty, obviously. If she weren't beautiful, you wouldn't have let her walk out of there without some more answers. Don't even bother denying it—it's written all over your face."

"Fuck," I mutter. "Yeah, she's gorgeous."

"Do you have the case file?"

I slide the thick folder across the table to him. He flips through it. I can tell when he hits the full glossy postmortem, because a deep, distant sadness fills his large, wet eyes. He shakes his head.

"Oh my. Tattooed face," he says. "This is pretty ugly. I'm not sure I want to get anywhere near this."

I smile to myself. He's trying to convince himself, not me. This is sick, sure, but he's seriously intrigued. Time to reel him in.

Casually, I say, "Three hundred fifty grand is the bounty."

He physically spasms, jerks up from the folder, and stares at me, as if trying to figure out if I'm serious.

"Already gave me fifteen for upfront and expenses," I add. "Cash."

He blinks a few times. His face says *that's life-changing money.*

"But . . . You mentioned that you don't totally believe her story. If she'd lie about what happened, how do we know she'll pay?

Should we set up a managed account with a lawyer to make sure the money's there?"

I shrug. "She'd never agree to that. I can tell. And besides, it was just my gut feeling. Felt like she was omitting things. Maybe she just didn't think they were important."

Courtney stares at me. "Start second-guessing your gut feelings about people, Frank, and you'll cripple yourself."

I roll my eyes. "Thanks, Mom. Look, in all likelihood it doesn't even matter. The tape probably isn't real, or it's ruined or trashed. We'll just get paid $15K to confirm that."

Courtney takes a long drink of tea and pokes at his dwindling lentils.

"You don't believe that," he says.

I glare at him. "Did you bring your own lentils here in Tupperware? You can't fucking do that."

Courtney grins. And the only time he ever actually smiles is when he knows he's right about something. It's absolutely infuriating.

"If you really thought it didn't exist, you wouldn't have brought me on board. Doesn't take two of us to tell her we didn't find anything."

I tap on the edge of my mug and shake my head. "I'm just trying to be realistic. This is probably a wild-goose chase."

Courtney inspects the depths of his tea for a moment then looks back up at me, brow knitted thoughtfully.

"Why would someone tattoo their victim and then record them as they died?"

"Because they're nuts. That's why."

Courtney doesn't seem to hear me.

"Reminds me of something I read recently. They found an Egyptian mummy, from around 700 AD. Also a woman. She's presently on display in the British Museum. What's most interesting about her, Frank, is a tattoo on her thigh of an angel and the name 'Michael' written beneath in ancient Greek. Michael is the most powerful of the angels. They think the tattoo was meant to protect her in the afterlife."

I finish off my scone, glance over at Sadie to make sure she's doing fine. She appears to be buried in her book, but I wouldn't be surprised if she's been eavesdropping a bit.

"You're giving this guy Silas too much credit, Courtney. He's a nutter, plain and simple."

"I don't see why you'd assume that. Thoughtfulness, subtlety and patience. These are an investigator's greatest assets. I don't see why I'd commit to work on a job with someone who displays such—"

"Alright, alright. Forget it. Thoughtfulness, subtlety, whatever."

For a moment we are each preoccupied with our respective drinks.

"Seems like there's no reason not to spend a few days checking it out, right?" I finally say delicately. "If the trail is too cold, or we get a bad feeling, just have to let her know. Maybe even give her five grand back so she doesn't smear us around town. I don't know about you, but I don't have anything better to work on right now. I closed out my last active case two nights ago."

Courtney fiddles with a long raggedy hair protruding from his chin. He's clearly still trying to talk himself out of this.

"I don't generally like to jump into something with so many questions still up in the air. For one, why did she wait five years to hire someone?"

I don't want to admit it, but that thought never occurred to me. "Maybe we're not the first."

"Why is this worth three hundred fifty thousand to this woman?" Courtney fires back.

"Obviously, money is no object to her."

Courtney polishes off his lentils.

"But you're right," I say. "I guess we should probably speak to Orange. That's how she got my number. Try to figure out what the hell Greta's deal is—what he knows about her—before we get too deep into this."

Courtney flinches at the mention of Orange. He points a knobby index finger at me, his face stone. "I refuse to deal with that hunk of human excrement again. If you think—"

"That doesn't sound very *patient*, Courtney."

He exhales loudly through his nostrils. I can imagine the conflict waging behind his pale half-moon forehead as he replays our last encounter with Orange.

After my schmooze with Orange in the back of his Escalade, I called another PI I knew, asked if he could recommend a good tracker to help me find these Italian forgers. He gave me Courtney's email and assured me that he was the absolute best he'd ever worked with. When I explained the job to Courtney, I was totally honest: I didn't know exactly what was going on behind the iron grate of Midtown Fitness, but I suspected two of the usual suspects: gambling or drugs.

It was only after we found the two Italians and delivered them—duct taped and not in the best spirits—to Orange's place of business that we understood exactly what we were dealing with: Orange was a pimp. Worse than a pimp, actually. He ran a sex dungeon in Midtown, and all of the poor girls were Korean and Chinese immigrants who'd undoubtedly been brought to the States under false pretenses. The reason I never saw women coming or going? They were never allowed to leave. They lived down there.

Courtney had been so horrified at discovering the true nature of our employer that he'd refused to accept any payment for our seven weeks of work. Drug dens were one thing, he said, but he didn't do business with men who kept girls in cages. I didn't feel great about it either and apologized profusely for my naiveté, but I couldn't end up working seven weeks for free, dirty money or not.

"Court. We need to know what he knows about Greta." I'm by no means an Orange apologist; he's an unequivocal piece of garbage. But pieces of garbage won't open up if you're going to ride in on your high horse, making demands.

Law of interrogation: Prisoner is infinitely more likely to talk if he trusts you. Surest way to earn his trust is to have an actual open mind, to not prejudge. So when I'm dealing with a scumbag, I try to fixate on one positive aspect about them.

In Orange's case, it's that I feel a little sorry for the guy. Last time we saw him, I realized he is totally miserable. Intensely lonely, horribly bored, his only passion is the art and artifacts that he collects to class-up his palatial sex dungeon. Crazy as it sounds, I felt like he really wanted to be friends with me. And when Courtney refused payment, he seemed weirdly betrayed.

"I am *not* dealing with him," Courtney repeats, shaking his head into his tea, again trying to convince himself, not me.

"But if anything, doesn't that experience reinforce how important it is to do our due diligence on clients?"

Courtney frowns into the grain of the wood tabletop. Then looks up at me.

"Didn't you promise Greta confidentiality?" he says. "That you wouldn't tell anyone she hired us?"

I pick up my coffee to hide a smirk. Courtney's will is weakening. I can hear the airy resignation in his voice. It's just too much money to walk away from. It's like throwing away a lottery ticket before scratching it. Get in that habit and you won't be in this line of work for long.

"Yeah but . . ." I say. "We gotta figure out what her connection to Orange is. If we take this case, we gotta talk to him."

"Ugh . . ." Courtney rubs his temples with the pads of his index fingers. Too much money, and I'm making too much sense. He wants to say yes so bad. Though truth is, I knew I had him once he started talking about mummies. "You're right. There's too much that's weird about this whole thing. What's with the gloves? And the cash? Even if her family is fabulously wealthy . . . She walks around with fifteen grand in her purse?"

"She knew that cold, hard cash was what it would take to get us on board." I smile. "I mean, you're on board, right?"

Courtney flares his nostrils and polishes off his tea.

"Yes. I suppose I am."

I drop Sadie off with the Feinsods, a sweet family who lives right down Grand Street in a co-op building. Sadie and I met Tammy Feinsod and their son Ben six years ago at some kind of toddler convention in a Lower East Side community center. Sadie and Ben have had playdates scheduled weekly ever since, and they really hit it off. It's gonna get weird when they hit puberty.

I tell Tammy I'll be gone at least a week and try to pay her. She refuses adamantly. I insist, telling her at least take two hundred for food and stuff. She won't take it.

"I'll try to call every night," I tell Sadie at the doorway.

"You still haven't said where you're going!" she says.

I can feel my lips squirming. It's my body expressing how much it hates having to lie to her. I'll actually be in the city at least another day, while we find Orange and ask him about Greta. But things might get involved, messy. Don't want Sadie waiting outside school for a dead-beat that's too busy getting some complimentary chiropractic work from Orange's pet gorillas to pick her up.

"Courtney and I need to check some stuff out up in Maine."

"What kind of stuff?"

Tammy's expression is a little expectant—like she's curious to hear the answer too.

This is why I don't have many friends. The people I work with are generally idiosyncratic loners, and the people I *don't* work with I have nothing in common with.

Tammy is a manager at some skin-care products company, and her husband, Greg, is a programmer. When they first asked me what I do for a living, I told them I was just doing a few freelance projects—technically not a lie. It would be too much of a production to explain the whole thing; I work and live in a world they don't even know exists. I kept answering in vague half-truths until Tammy and Greg got the idea and stopped asking about my professional life.

"A freelance insurance investigation." I smile sadly. "Boring stuff. But really I'll call whenever I can, okay? And you can call me, too, whenever Mr. and Mrs. Feinsod say it's okay."

Sadie crosses her arms and puffs out her chest. "You and Courtney weren't talking about insurance."

I sigh and shrug at Tammy like *kids, what can you do?*

"I'll give you two a minute," Tammy says and disappears back into the apartment.

I take a knee and look Sadie directly in the eyes. "I'll tell you all about it when I get back, okay, sweetheart?"

"Are you working for that tall lady?"

I grimace. "Yes."

"She was a bitch."

I scratch my neck. "I didn't really like her either, to be honest. But don't use that word."

"You think she's pretty, huh?"

Do I have it written in pen on my forehead?

"Yeah. She's pretty." I sigh.

"Don't be stupid, Dad. You don't have to work for everyone that asks you."

"I have to try on this one, sweetie. She's paying me a *lot*. We can go on a long vacation if I can figure this one out."

Sadie eyes me dubiously. "You're bringing Courtney with you, right?"

I nod.

"You should do whatever he says. He's smarter than you."

I kiss her on the cheek and hug her.

"I know," I say. "Much smarter."

A HALF HOUR later I meet Courtney down the street in Seward Park. I've got Orange's number cued up but try to get in the right state of mind before I dial. Every client deals with a slightly different Frank Lamb, depending on their needs. With Orange I err on the side of aggressive and no-nonsense; show any weakness to Orange and he'll exploit it.

"Just call, it won't get any easier," says Courtney.

"Respect my methods," I say. "Unless you'd like to call yourself?"

He grimaces at the phone like it's some kind of bomb.

"That's what I thought," I say. Take a few more deep breaths then hit call.

The phone rings only once.

"Midtown Fitness."

The words are low and muddy. I can just tell the guy on the other end is four times my size.

"I wanna talk to Orange," I say, trying to match his baritone and sprinkling in a little Brooklyn accent for flavor. Next to me on the park bench, Courtney rolls his eyes.

Orange goes through these charades like making you arrange an appointment through one of his cronies—as if he doesn't have time to take calls himself. Best I can figure, he rarely leaves his dungeon. And he's running a brothel and gambling den, not a hotel; it's not like he's burdened with paperwork and managerial tasks.

Why the games? I'm guessing because Orange's whole operation is a lie, in the sense that he's not the kind of guy who should be a pimp. After combing around a bit, I found out he inherited the biz after his dad died in an ice fishing accident over a decade ago. Orange's natural curiosity, haughty eye for culture and propensity for sitting would have served him well as a film or food critic. But circumstance has thrust this hideous specimen into life as a crime lord, so he wastes away playing the part.

I suspect that in some tiny corner of his psyche he feels guilty about the girls. But what can he do? Can't *ever* show that weakness to his employees. Problem is, his insecurities don't make him less dangerous. Quite the opposite really. Never fuck with someone who feels like they have something to prove. I've heard stories of him beating his girls to the brink of death and of having one of his goons dismembered for doing a side job for a competitor. Probably the only reason Courtney was spared the same fate after insulting him by refusing payment was because Orange didn't want the reputation of hurting private contractors, whose services he employs occasionally to hunt down debtors.

A pregnant pause on the phone.

"Who is this?"

Gotta play his stupid goddamn game.

"Tell him it's Frankie. Lamb."

A click as the phone is set down. I breathe on my hands to keep warm. Courtney is wearing a bright red duck-hunting hat, a ratty grey scarf over a thick flannel shirt, and tight blue jeans that hug his tiny thighs, wrapping them up like blue taquitos.

Little kids are everywhere. Running around with a basketball, no hoop in sight; crawling up and down the freezing metal slide; hanging on the monkey bars, T-shirts pulled up to reveal their tiny midriffs. Lots of giggling and screaming—next time I'll choose a tougher-sounding location to call a gangbanger from.

I snap to attention as the goon picks the phone back up.

"Orange wants to know if you're still working with the skinny-ass guido."

I glance up at Courtney, and we lock eyes. He can tell something's up.

"What's the difference?"

"Hold on." The phone is set down again.

"What is it?" Courtney whispers, concerned.

I put my hand over the receiver. "Your lucky day. I think I'm gonna have to go there alone."

He looks relieved.

The dude picks the phone back up. "Orange says he'll talk to you, but you gotta bring your guido friend in with you. Orange wants an apology from him. Come at six today. Bring a towel. We don't have them here."

Then he hangs up.

"So?" Courtney asks eagerly. "I'm off the hook?"

I stare at the cold pavement and click my tongue.

"No. I misunderstood. You gotta come too. Sounds like Orange won't talk to me unless you come with and apologize first."

Courtney's frown extends until the edges of his lips are nearly touching his neck. I think I see a vein popping in his forehead.

"We gotta talk to him, Courtney," I say.

"He probably wants to lure me there so he can kill me."

"If he was gonna kill you, he would have done it last time you were there. He's just prideful. Wants you to grovel."

"Can't you do this over the phone?"

I hand him my cell. "You're welcome to try."

He shakes his head emphatically and then, with an air of resignation, stands up from the bench. He has absolutely no hips or butt; his pants are held up only by a fading rawhide belt that clings desperately to his concave stomach, like it's terrified that if Courtney misses one more meal, it will tumble into the abyss.

"Will you come with?" I ask.

Courtney shakes his head slowly in disbelief, staring distantly at the kids on the jungle gym.

"Seems that if we're working together on this, I don't have a choice."

"Good man," I say, standing and clapping him on his boney back.

"Words won't be enough," Courtney says, watching some kids squeal, coasting down a twisty metal slide. "We gotta bring him something if we want him to talk. A token of goodwill."

"Best Buy gift certificate?"

"How long do we have?"

"We gotta get there at six. So three hours. He likes artsy-fartsy stuff. Something that flatters his intelligence and worldliness would be good. Maybe a painting or something?"

Courtney scratches at his stubbly cheek.

"Cake. Everybody likes cake."

It's ALREADY GETTING dark as I hit the Midtown Fitness buzzer. To our left, a waiter from the Polish diner next door is writing the dinner specials on a chalkboard. I think I catch him shooting us a disapproving look. He must see enough sleazy-looking fellows buzzing in here to get the general idea.

Courtney pulls his scarf tight around his pencil-thin neck as I wave to the camera above the door. Five long seconds later there's a buzz and the grated metal door clicks open. Courtney hesitates before stepping over the threshold.

"Come on," I say, starting down the metal staircase carrying a white Styrofoam box containing Orange's present: a $40 slice of cake encased in a glass cube, with a phony certificate of authenticity from a guy Courtney knows in a Soho antique store. Case is sealed, so Orange won't be able to inspect it closely enough to tell it's fake; Courtney's friend assured us no collector would ever open the case and risk the specimen disintegrating. "We're already late. Orange hates tardiness."

"He's so principled," mutters Courtney as he comes in after me. Midtown Fitness is accessible only via a poorly lit metal staircase—slippery and wet from people tracking in snow—that takes us twenty feet below street level. The staircase turns right into a dank corridor, peppered with heavy doors marked only with rusty combination locks. Behind each door is at least one drugged-up sex slave. The last time we were here, bringing Orange the forgers, I witnessed a client sheepishly ask the guy at the gym desk for a "personal training session" and slip him some cash. In return he received a slip of paper with a door number and combination, plus a hearty enjoinder to enjoy his "workout."

"I really could have died happy never coming back to this place," sighs Courtney as we follow the weak light down the hallway. Orange keeps it dark. Maybe for mood lighting. Or maybe his clients don't want anyone to see their wretched faces.

"But you have to admire Orange's entrepreneurial spirit," I chuckle.

"He's truly loathsome."

On cue, a stifled moan echoes from behind one of the doors.

"Loathsome, sure. But honorable in certain ways. Paid us on delivery. More than you can say for most."

Courtney snorts.

"Honorable," he repeats. "Yeah, that's the first adjective that comes to mind when I think about doping up fifteen-year-old Korean girls too."

"Get it all out of your system now," I say.

The corridor terminates in a glass door: the entrance to the gym. Inside, it isn't lit much better than the hallway. The bald guy at the front desk on the other side of the glass isn't even bothering to keep up with the fitness charade today, just munching on a Snickers while he gazes blankly at a closed-circuit TV. I knock on the door, and he looks up at us.

"Open," he yawns.

Behind him is a dingy, whitewashed room housing a sorry collection of dumbbells, mats and benches. There's a single stationary bike and a dusty treadmill that I don't think is even plugged in. There's one guy working out: a crew-cut employee grunting in rhythm with his bicep curls, dark sweat stains on the chest of his Michigan State sweatshirt. We tread over water-stained carpeting to the reception desk.

"Welcome to Midtown Fitness," the bald guy grunts in a thick Russian accent, seeming to resent the interruption.

"We're here to see Orange," I say.

"Got an appointment?"

"Someone told us he'd see us at six."

The steel-jawed concierge swivels and shouts to Crew Cut. "Orange expecting anyone?"

My chest tenses for a moment. I've never come here asking for anything. Asking a favor is an entirely different animal.

"Uh-huh," Crew grunts between reps. "Orange said to send 'em into the *shvitz*."

The front desk dude nods, satisfied, then slowly stands and comes around the desk. Towers over us.

"Weapons?" he asks, like he's bored.

"Yeah," I say, handing him both my Magnum and ceramic knife. Courtney shakes his head no. The dude places my weapons on the desk, then gives us each a halfhearted frisk with hands the size of bear paws.

"What's in the box?" he asks, jutting his chin at the taped-up Styrofoam box covered in a bunch of "fragile" stickers we slapped on for effect.

"We brought something for Orange."

He raises an eyebrow.

"You can open if you want," says Courtney calmly, "but I suspect your employer might not appreciate that."

He stares first at the box, then at me, then at Courtney. You can practically see the rusty gears cranking inside his thick skull. Then he nods and slowly meanders back around the desk. Sits back down, exuding a sense of urgency similar to what you see in overworked DMV employees.

"Change in the locker room," he sighs, and points to an ominous, filthy doorway on the far side of the room. "You got towels?"

Fuck. Forgot.

"No."

He shakes his head at us, displeased.

"Nobody told you to bring them?" he says, implying the impossibility of such a clerical error ever occurring on his watch.

"No, someone did. Just slipped my mind."

He sighs heavily and checks under the counter.

"We are not fucking Equinox," he mutters, then surfaces with two ratty cloths, one brown, one that perhaps used to be white. "These are from the lost and found." He flashes a sick grin that carries the import of these words—nobody was exercising with these towels. "So I will need them back. After."

I can hear Courtney breathing beside me. I don't need to look at his face to know he's trying hard to suppress his horror. I grit my teeth and snatch them from the attendant.

"No problem," I say, then grab Courtney's shoulder and pull him toward the locker room.

"He wants us to go in the *sauna* with him?" Courtney whispers, panicked, once we're out of earshot.

"Worse, unfortunately," I reply. "Unless I'm mistaken, *shvitz* is the steam room."

The locker room is floored in grimy white linoleum and smells like armpit and onion.

"Don't think about it," I advise Courtney, noticing him taking in his surroundings like one might a prison cell. "Just strip."

I throw all my clothes into an open locker. Crosses my mind that I probably could have smuggled my knife in my shoe if I'd wanted. Not that I'm anywhere near stupid enough to try to hurt Orange in his lair; I'd sooner pistol-whip a menstruating rhinoceros.

I wrap the brown towel around my waist and turn to see that Courtney is standing over his towel, totally nude, as if he just can't bring himself to touch it. The guy is built like a Somalian scarecrow. I can see all his ribs.

"You can go in in your birthday suit if you want, champ," I chuckle. "Don't wanna give Orange the wrong idea though."

"You know this rag is probably coated in *semen*," he hisses, like it's some sort of curse.

I shrug. "You want glamour, you're in the wrong line of work."

Courtney takes a deep breath and shudders as he wraps the white towel around his emaciated waist.

"Please shut the door." The source of the voice is invisible, shrouded by thick clouds of swirling steam. "You're letting it all out."

I was in a steam room a few years ago, tried it out when someone brought me into their gym as a guest, but I definitely don't remember it being as unbelievably *hot* as this one. It feels like I just turned the oven to broil and stuck my head inside.

"Gentlemen," the voice says, "*please* close the fucking door. I'm trying to exercise in here."

I hear Courtney obediently pull it shut behind us. He's panting as badly as I am, shocked by the heat. It feels like I'm being repeatedly smacked in the face with a scorching-hot damp rag.

"You two *pooftas* just going to stand there?" Orange's mocking laugh rumbles like a tractor. "Come on in."

It's impossible to determine the dimensions of the room. I stumble forward blindly, groping ahead like a zombie. My hand meets something soft, and once I realize what I've done, I retract in horror.

"Well that's one way to say hello," Orange laughs joylessly. This is like the sick analog of small talk before an important business meeting.

"I'm sorry, Orange, I couldn't see."

A hand the size of a catcher's mitt grabs me by the shoulder and yanks me forward, pushes my butt onto a hard tile bench.

"Frank?" I can make out Courtney's form a few feet in front of me, writhing frantically, like a dying fish.

The enormous form next to me emits a low, throaty laugh.

"Sit down and let's get on with it," Orange says, then extends a meaty arm and pulls Courtney onto a sliver of bench on the other side of his circumference. As my eyes slowly adjust, Matty "Orange" Julius's form begins to take shape: a mountain of wet flesh rising from the mist, folds and creases that remind me of a brain in formaldehyde. I note that our host is not wearing a towel.

"Frankie and Courtney." Another low rumble that resonates in this tiny chamber like a subwoofer. "What do you want? I have a French lesson in a half hour."

Neither Courtney nor I speak. A sharp hiss of steam somewhere by our feet.

"Here for a girl?" Orange asks. "I'll give you an hour for half price. I recently acquired a new Thai beauty. *Very* flexible. And she has this delightful routine where she cuts a dime-size hole in the top of a banana and sucks the meat out, leaving the peel untouched."

He's baiting us. Testing Courtney, daring him to disrespect him again in his own lair, and asserting his dominance when Courtney stays silent—*if* he stays silent.

I close my eyes and clench my teeth, praying Courtney sees this for what it is: establishing the pecking order here as a precondition to any sort of negotiation.

"First of all, I'd like to apologize for disrespecting you by refusing payment," Courtney says softly from the other side of Orange, and I exhale in relief, even though the disdain in his voice is obvious, anger at being forced to submit before this tower of flesh. I imagine that the heat in this room is being generated by Courtney's blood boiling. "Please understand this was never my intention. We came here today because we need help. I hope we can put my uncouth behavior behind us."

"Interesting," Orange says. I know he'll at least hear us out. If there's one thing you can bank on with Orange, it's curiosity. He's bored. It's to be expected from someone who spends most of their life in an underground gym. He is, after all, sitting alone in a dark steam room at six on a Saturday evening.

"We brought you a gift," I say hastily, before Courtney can retract his apology. "It's in the locker room. An actual slice of cake from—"

"—the Treaty of Versailles," Courtney interrupts. Clearly doesn't trust me to get the details right. "Eaten in Paris in 1919. Immaculately preserved. Worth a small fortune. A true historical artifact. We thought you'd appreciate it."

"Mmm," he grunts. "Do you really think so little of me? That I can be *bribed* into forgiving you, Courtney?" He breathes in and out a few times.

I'm already entirely coated in sweat.

I try to make eye contact with Courtney to decide how we're going to go about this, but before my eyes is only meat and steam. I suspect, however, that I'd better do most of the talking. If Courtney keeps talking, Orange is gonna keep provoking him. And if Courtney cracks—not going ape-shit like I do sometimes, but just getting seriously *irked,* his downturned lips twitching, hinting at the carefully controlled disdain behind his eyes—we're not going to get anything out of Orange. Hell, we might not even get out of here with all our fingers.

"We wanted to ask you about someone," I say. "Greta Kanter. She hired us and said you referred her."

Orange Julius takes a moment to rub his hands through the slick fur on his belly. It sounds like someone squeezing the life from a juicy peach.

"Greta Kanter," he repeats slowly.

"Yeah," I say. "How do you know her? What's her deal?"

"Greta . . . I'd forgotten about her . . ." Orange makes a sound that's somewhere between a chuckle and a groan. "Of course that's why you're here. I suppose I do owe you an explanation, Frankie. Her deal, as it appears to me, is simply that she's a gorgeous kook with more money than—"

Orange is seized by a wet cough that doubles him over and makes the bench I'm sitting on quake. He spits something at his feet, takes a moment to recover, then continues.

"Excuse me. More money than God. She arrived at my door a few months ago on some kind of quixotic quest. She wanted to pore through my collections, but for what she wouldn't tell me. Ordinarily a nonstarter, obviously, but the vixen softened my heart with twenty grand. Cash. Just to look for an hour! So I let her, why not? I had cameras on her anyways in case she tried to steal anything. She came up empty, and as she stormed out, huffing, I thought to give your number, Frankie. Told her maybe you could find whatever she was looking for. Thought I'd do you a favor. You saved me a pretty penny by retrieving those forgers. Never would have hooked you up if I'd known you were gonna share the wealth with this one though." Orange nods his globe of a head in Courtney's general direction. "If you two want my advice, I would milk her a bit before *politely* cutting her loose. I met her briefly, but her aura was singularly off-putting."

The steam fires up, and I realize that my heart is pounding and sweat is pouring from my forehead. I don't know how long I can handle this; it must be close to two hundred degrees in here. Also Julius's leg is practically on top of mine, and I'm sitting only inches from his armpit, which smells like there was a chemical spill at the synthetic garlic factory.

"You didn't ask what she was looking for?" Courtney asks.

"I've told you all I know about her, and truthfully I have no interest in discussing Ms. Kanter further," Orange replies calmly, then takes in a deep breath of steam. "I was hoping you two had something more interesting for me. But I'd now like to resume my bath in peace. Thank you for the cake and tactful apology. You can show yourselves out."

We are in his place of work, surrounded by his employees, unable to breathe, shriveling up like a pair of clams—we don't exactly have a lot of leverage here.

"That cake is worth five figures," I say.

"I told you what I know," he says.

"I could throw in another three thousand dollars for you to think about it a little harder."

He just laughs bitterly and continues rubbing his paws around his belly and chest, as if confirming that every pore on his body is oozing rancid perspiration.

"Five thousand," I say. It sounds pathetic coming from my mouth.

"I'm not holding out on you. I told you all I know. Good day, gentlemen. Frankie, best of luck. And Courtney, if you ever interrupt my private bath again, I'll feed you shards of glass. Leave the cake at the front desk."

I can see Courtney's form shoot up and make for the door, clearly relieved to end this exchange.

I stand up, admittedly pleased to leave this smelly hellhole, when something clicks. *Why did Greta think the tape was here with Orange?* I turn back to him.

"What do you know about a cassette tape?" I ask.

Even through the wall of steam between us, I can see Orange's form jerk to attention. For a moment he says nothing. Courtney stands behind me, itching to burst out of here.

"What kind of cassette tape?" Orange says slowly, carefully.

"Maybe one that . . . well we were speculating it may contain something related to . . . life after death."

The glare of Orange's small black eyes pierces through the steam.

"Tape . . . That's what she was looking for," he wheezes. "That . . . *whore.*" The sudden tremor in his voice is terrifying. "Courtney, Frankie, sit back down. We're not done here."

I bite my lip. This is a side of Orange I haven't seen before. I sit back down beside him on the bench.

"What's going on?" Courtney says, slowly reclaiming his seat beside the perspiring giant.

Orange doesn't seem to have even heard Courtney. "Egnaro's tape . . ." he says, half to himself, half to us. "What did she tell you? What does it say?" His voice picks up intensity. He's breathing heavily through his bulbous nose. "Tell me everything you know. And if you lie to me, you two leave here in little pieces. I swear it."

The steam fires up again. My face is tingling, bordering on numb. I'm sweating so much that I wonder when I'll simply dry out. It's getting really hard to concentrate. How much do we tell Orange? How much does he already know?

Courtney says, "Greta approached Frank two days ago to find this tape. She said she heard about us from you."

Orange chews on this a moment. "Keep going," he says.

"She said she'd pay us three hundred fifty grand to find it," I add.

Orange smacks his wet lips and cracks his knuckles. "Keep going."

"I . . ." I try to probe my boiling brain for details that I want to share with this blob. "She wore gloves the whole time, I thought that was weird—"

"Yes, her gloves," Orange says, rubbing his sweaty tummy impatiently. "What else?"

"I don't—"

"Tell me what's *on the fucking tape!*" Orange roars, the echo of his rage seeming to linger for full seconds, dissipated only by the returning hiss of the steam.

I'm about to mention Savannah and Silas when Courtney speaks up:

"That's all you get, Matty. Not until you give us something back."

Orange growls something indecipherable. For a moment I'm sure he's about to simply lunge at Courtney and try to beat the information out of him. I picture myself wrapping my forearms around Orange's slick neck from behind and trying to yank his amoeba-like form off my partner, the whole thing rendered moot because there are undoubtedly cameras in here and Orange's goons would arrive the second I laid a hand on their boss.

I realize I haven't breathed in about two minutes. But the fact that Orange hasn't snapped his fingers and had us both flayed by his Ukrainians means we have more leverage than we thought: He *really* wants to know about this tape.

Orange traces some kind of design on his belly. Coughs a bit but manages to contain it this time.

"*Sensible,* Courtney. You may be an ungrateful, smug little self-righteous guido, but you *are* sensible. So yes, I'm a fair man. Let's make a deal." Orange clears his throat. "I'll tell you everything I know about the tape. But in exchange—"

"I can't do the banana trick, if that's what you're thinking," Courtney says.

Orange pretends he didn't hear. "In exchange, if you find it, I want to hear it first, before you give it to her. I understand that she hired you first and you two gentlemen are too honest to drop her, even if I could match her price. So I won't even try. My request is humble. One listen. Fair? It's your guarantee that I'll tell you the truth, because I have a vested interest in your success."

I exhale. Doesn't seem we have much of a choice here.

"Okay," I say. "That alright with you, Courtney?"

"Fine," he spits.

Julius abandons his belly and leans back on the tile bench with a groan. "Okay *pooftas*. Here's what I know about the tape—"

"Orange, um, any way you think we could talk about this in a less humid environment?" I feel close to passing out.

"Little much for you, eh?" Orange Julius's booming laugh echoes off the tiled walls of the steam room. He grunts and rises slowly from the bench, less standing than oozing upright. He reminds me of a flowering tea ball gradually diffusing in a pot of boiling water. "I suppose now that we're in business together again, I can accommodate that. I'll tell Monsieur Reneé we'll have to reschedule."

"THIS CAKE IS a hundred years old?"

After rinsing off in Midtown Fitness's communal shower—walls stained with rust, drains clogged with what looks like years of accumulated black hair—the three of us retire to the lounge. The innocuous door marked Supplies in the corner of the gym opens into an impossibly unexpected space a world away from the locker room—a palatial room even more lavish than I remembered.

Orange must have accumulated some more crap since we dropped off those forgers: A beautiful globe as tall as a man hangs from the raised ceiling, suspended between glimmering crystal chandeliers. Bookcases stretch to the ceiling, filled with ancient-looking volumes that I doubt anyone here ever opens. Three young Asian waitresses in tight black leather attend to a couple of men gathered around the poker table, the girls' six-inch heels sinking into the rich red carpet like quicksand.

Orange reclines on a chaise lounge; an enormous brown leather piece that looks custom made to accommodate his giant cheese ball of a body. He's draped in a fuzzy pink bathrobe big enough to pitch a tent under but still stopping short at his girthy upper thighs.

He holds the glass case up to the light of the chandelier to inspect the vanilla cake that was baked this morning. Courtney glued it to the base of the box then carefully painted it with green-tinted frosting and egg whites to make it look ancient and brittle.

"Nearly," Courtney says. "Imagine. The other pieces were eaten by Woodrow Wilson, Georges Clemenceau . . ."

"Mmm," Orange grumbles. "Next time bring me something I can eat." He hands the case off to a Chinese girl who can't be much bigger than Sadie. She carries it over to a bookcase and deposits it between some other antique curiosities, where it will surely remain untouched for years. Then she returns to his side, cuts a cigar for him, sticks it between his teeth, and lights it for him. She kisses him on the cheek, and as she retreats to the minibar to fetch us some drinks, Orange winks at us. I bite my tongue and force a smile. Beside me on the shiny black love seat, Courtney does a remarkable job of swallowing his disdain.

The waitress returns with a tray bearing three tumblers filled with ice and a bottle of fifteen-year scotch. Pours one for Orange first, then sets up a folding table in front of Courtney and pours one for each of us. She avoids our gaze the whole time—probably instructed to just stare at the floor. I grind my teeth and think about my Magnum sitting up at the front desk.

"Could I actually," Courtney says to the waitress, "get an ice water?"

She nods obediently, still staring at the floor. I doubt her English extends beyond drink orders and sex commands.

I greedily suck on the smoky scotch, and it goes straight to my head. I must be badly dehydrated.

"I first heard of the tape maybe four years ago. There was a guy who showed up at the front desk out there," Orange says, puffing on his cigar. "He was short, midforties. Prematurely grey. Bushy lumber-jack beard. He had awful dark circles beneath his eyes—every time I saw him he looked the same, like he'd just chugged three energy drinks and was going to vomit. I could tell he was a first-timer."

"First-timer?" I ask.

"Never paid for a girl before." Orange puts a fat finger to his lips. "They're easy to spot. They've usually been agonizing over the decision for weeks. They feel like they're crossing some thresh-old from which they can never return. The truth is much more benign, really. My father gave me my first girl when I was four-teen. Birthday present. Nothing changed."

Courtney rolls his eyes. Orange pretends not to notice.

"So this client, I arranged for him to liaise with a cute little girl I found in K-town. Don't worry, Courtney. She was nineteen. Usu-ally first-timers are nervous, come in under a minute. But she told me later that he was the complete opposite: lay down naked on the bed and just stared at the ceiling for an hour. Took her twenty minutes just to get him—*ahem*—primed. Then she rode him for a half hour, and let me tell you, this girl knows what she's doing—but *nothing*. The guy lays there like a corpse. Never comes."

Orange continues, swirling his tumbler, sucking pensively on his cigar, like he's waxing philosophic.

"Okay. That's weird, but I've heard weirder. But then, first thing in the morning, he's back again. I had to call a girl and wake her up to come in. He started showing up here *every day*. Sometimes twice a day. Hemorrhaging money, but he didn't seem to care. Each time I saw him he looked a little thinner—not quite like you, Courtney, but still. It was clear that he was emptying his life savings. The only request he made was that it be a different girl every time, which started getting tricky. Had to make calls to some friends to get some fresh meat in here just for him. Had to charge him more, but he didn't blink. And every time I talked to the girls after, they told me the exact same thing: He just lay there, never said a word. Never came. After an hour, he zipped up and left. Then he'd be back, maybe that afternoon. He'd spend *hours* here sometimes waiting for another girl to show up. Would sit down right where you're sitting there. Never said a word, except asking to make sure he was getting a different girl. Once I accidentally gave him a girl he'd had before, maybe a month before. He took one look at her and said, 'No. I want someone new.' And that was it."

Courtney looks sick to his stomach. I go bottoms up on the scotch to hide my grimace. The waitress immediately materializes to give me a refill. She hands Courtney an ice water with lime and smiles an empty smile that makes my heart quiver.

"So." I take a deep breath. "How long did this go on?"

"About seven or eight weeks, I think."

"Then what?" I ask. Courtney is fiddling anxiously with a few long hairs that hang off his chin like a billy goat.

"I ran out of girls. Couldn't find a single new one in this whole fucking city. I called every contact I had, nobody had anyone new. I told him this, and he just stood up and left. Simple as that. Oh—I forgot. He never wore protection. Not once."

I grind my teeth. "That seems ill advised, so to speak."

Orange looks hurt. "My girls are clean. I take care of them."

I can feel Courtney struggling to suppress a retort. I put my hand on his boney knee and squeeze: *cool it.*

"Alright," I say. "So what does this have to do with the tape?"

"Wait for it, Frankie."

Orange signals for a refill, and when the waitress approaches he wraps a mammoth arm around her and pulls her in close for a slobbery kiss. Then he spanks her, and she runs off. I wonder if Orange has ever had sex with a woman he doesn't own.

"So when I tell him this, he just stands up and walks out of my gym. I didn't see him again for about a month, when he showed up here at four in the morning, clawing at that glass door, moaning. It's just me and my guy Gussy—all the girls were asleep. We let him in, and he practically collapses on the floor. I couldn't tell if he was drunk or just miserable. Never seen anyone in a state like that. Screaming, moaning incoherently. I just stared at Gussy—neither of us knew what to do with this sack of shit. I mean that—he was a fucking sack of *shit*. Like, he was *empty*. A sack of skin with nothing inside. Then he stops sobbing and looks up at Gussy and goes, 'Kill me. Shoot me in the head.'"

Orange pauses and stares at his drink.

"You know, I've seen some very nasty things down here, but I've never seen anything like this. Never seen a person so far *gone*."

"So you shot him?" Courtney asks, deadpan.

Orange looks appalled. "Of course not. I dragged him in here, sat him across from me at the poker table, and asked him to tell me what's going on."

"How kind. You're like a philanthropist."

Orange laughs deeply.

"Watch it, you fucking guido," he growls. Then polishes off his second drink. "I can't claim it was totally magnanimous. Don't forget, he'd been one hell of a customer. He'd dropped fifteen grand here in two months. Since he'd left I'd gotten some more girls in. Figured maybe . . ."

"Jesus," Courtney whispers. I tighten my grip on his knee-cap. I'm not exactly charmed by Orange's attitude toward women either—but just gotta keep it bottled up until we're out of here.

"So he calms down a little bit. Finally looks at me with these *empty* eyes. I say, 'Why do you want me to kill you?' and he replies, 'I know what's coming. I heard it on a tape.'"

I raise an eyebrow. Courtney clears his throat; his curiosity just overtook his disgust.

"What else did he say?" Courtney asks.

"He kept repeating himself, that he'd heard what's coming. And that he heard it on a tape. I asked him what tape, you know. This guy was hardly even with me, you could see it in his face. He was here, sitting here, but his head was somewhere else, somewhere *far* away."

Orange reaches toward the red carpet, and his massive hand finds a hidden drawer in his lounge. He removes a bag of what appears to be chocolate-covered macadamia nuts, pops a few in his cavernous mouth. Doesn't offer us any.

"I ask him how he knew the tape was telling the truth, kind of indulging him, you know. And he freaks out a little, almost screams at me, 'I heard it. *I saw it.*'"

Orange chews another couple of nuts.

"Kept repeating that. That he knows what's coming, that he heard it, saw it. Finally he says one other thing. He says, 'It's the same backwards as forwards.' I ask, 'What, the tape?' and he nods really hard. I can tell I'm sort of losing him. He's losing the ability to really even convey himself through speech. He's stuttering, and when he can get words out, they're slurred. A few things he says are just plain gibberish. Then he shoots up out of the chair and starts motioning like this." Orange pantomimes writing. "He wants a pen. So I get one, a pen and paper, and hand it to him. And he starts writing. It's like crazy person writing."

"What did he write?" Courtney asks.

Orange hesitates. "We're in business, right? We have a deal? I get one listen, right?"

We both nod vigorously. Orange sits up slightly and licks his lips.

"Don't cross me on this," he says.

"You have our word," I say, unsure how much I believe myself. Courtney nods in enthusiastic affirmation.

Orange's nostrils flare. "Follow me."

He grunts and sits up. Takes a moment to collect himself, then catches his breath, heaves himself to his feet, and motions for us to follow him. He leads us past the bar, past the poker tables. We follow him through a curtained doorway, brushing past a different girl heading back out with a few drinks on a tray. Orange gives her a halfhearted smack on the ass as she passes. We follow him up a narrow staircase; if he was any fatter, he wouldn't have been able to squeeze his way up. As it stands, his pink bathrobe scrapes against the whitewashed walls.

At the top is a locked door, which he opens with a combination, and then we're in what must be his office. Not particularly spacious, set up like a CEO's might be: polished mahogany desk, potted plants, more artwork. Packed wall to wall with glass display cases containing assorted trinkets. Notably missing are windows (since we're underground) and any pictures on the desk. No family photos. I'm surprised he doesn't keep portraits of his favorite whores.

Courtney and I sit down in two armchairs on the customer side of the desk while Orange digs through his desk drawers until he finds a key ring. He waddles to a lone green file cabinet in the corner of the room. Unlocks the bottom drawer—exposing us to a voluminous, bathrobe-garbed backside—then returns to his seat holding a single laminated page, which he puts down in front of us.

"Did you show this to Greta?" I ask.

Orange shakes his head. "I haven't shown this to anyone until now. If I'd known she was after the *tape,* I wouldn't have let her in the front door."

He wets his thick lips.

"I'd long since given up hope of finding the tape. More or less assumed it didn't exist. But now you two come in here and tell me someone else is after it . . . She must have heard that I was looking for it years ago and wanted to check if I had it in my collection." Orange shakes his head. "And she was desperate . . . feverish. It wasn't just money she offered, you know. She told me if she found what she was looking for . . ."

"What?" I ask.

"She said if she found what she needed in my archives I would 'have' her. You know. Fuck her."

Courtney gives me a sidelong look, like *she said that to you, too, didn't she?* I try to hide my burning face from Court. Feel like an idiot for assuming I was the first to receive that particular term in our agreement. Should make me want it less. But it doesn't.

"But she didn't tell you what she was looking for? And then left empty-handed?"

Orange nods his head.

"I just gave her your number, talked you up to get her out of here. She was making my skin crawl. I appreciated the offer, of course, but . . ." I can't tell if Orange is blushing or if his blubbery face is still glowing from the *shvitz.*

He's *definitely* never had consensual sex in his life.

Orange bites his lip and pushes the laminated paper over to

us. We stare at it. It *is* crazy person writing. The central text is surrounded by squiggles that are half letters, half something else. And the words in the center of the page, though clear, are written dysgraphically, in square box letters. No curves. Only straight lines; his *o* is a square. It's also rife with misspellings. First is a single word near the top of the page:

Sexes

Then, beneath it, what looks like some kind of confession:

Orange,

Same plaid backwrds. Evry Second. I saw wat happns. Thatz why we did it. Beulah twelve. Im twelve.

Live not on Evil

Then he seems to completely lose it, degenerating into nonsense:

Evlewt mi evlewtha ...

His letters become unreadable until the end. Signed:

Egnaro

I click my tongue. Guy was nuts. Like Silas. Probably not worth reading too much into this.

"What happened after he wrote this?" I ask Orange.

"He ran out in a panic. Like a madman. We watched him on the cameras. He raced from here, faster than I've ever seen anyone move. I tried to hunt him down. Asked everyone I knew if they'd ever heard of an 'Egnaro.' Nothing."

"Sounds Hispanic," I muse.

Courtney is still staring intently at the laminated page.

"But if Greta is paying you to find it, she must know something I don't. It must really exist," Orange says, squinting at the paper in concentration, forehead wrinkled like a salted snail. He clearly doesn't know anything about the tape's connection to Savannah's murder or that Greta is her sister. "So what do we know?" Orange squeezes his fat cheeks. "Obviously the tape is intimately connected to the Beulah Twelve . . ."

"What's the Beu—" I start, but Courtney suddenly grabs my thigh and digs his nails in deep, so deep that I almost squeak.

"Obviously," replies Courtney, cool as a Frappuccino. Great liar. A million times better than me. I've seen mannequins with more tells than Courtney. But my lips must have squirmed, because Orange looks up and inspects us, correctly ascertaining that we're holding out on him.

"What else did Greta tell you?" he asks.

Courtney taps my thigh with his index finger. We're both thinking the same thing: Tread very carefully. Give him enough info that he believes we're on his team, but not so much that he could hire his own team to track it down before us . . . *If* it's real.

"Greta believes the tape contains the dying words of a young woman who was murdered," I say. *And now feed back to Orange what he already knows to be true.* "In which she reveals the nature of the afterlife."

"And of course she knew of the Beulah Twelve connection," lies Courtney. "Though obviously didn't have access to the same level of detail as you."

Orange's black eyes are glowing. I'm involuntary reminded of the look on Sadie's face after her first bite of ice cream the other day but am instantly sickened by the comparison.

"A girl's dying words," he says, "telling you about the world to come. Imagine if it exists! A tape that tells us what happens after we die! Is there a more fantastic treasure anywhere on earth?" Orange's breathing approaches *shvitz* levels. His eyes alight with wonder—he can't wait to get his grubby hands on the thing.

"Why?" I say. Orange and Courtney turn to stare at me. "I mean, seriously. So what? Say this thing exists, and it really—somehow—tells you about what happens after you die. What's gonna change? You're going to start going to church on Sundays?"

The look Orange gives me in response sends chills shooting down my spine. For just a fleeting moment, I think I'm privy to decades of aggregate, deeply suppressed suffering. Countless hours spent in this subterranean prison he's built for himself. Self-loathing the likes of which I can hardly fathom. Burying himself among his ever-growing hoards, like a pharaoh already in his sar-cophagus, just waiting to move on.

"I suppose I shouldn't be surprised that you can't relate," Orange says quietly. "I can't speak for others, but for me to know that there's another life, one without this, this . . ." Orange glances down to his pink-clad girth, shaking his head as if still in disbelief of his physical form. "This *burden* . . ." He lowers his voice to a strained whisper. "My friends, if this is what Egnaro and Greta think it is, it's worth much more than whatever she's paying you. Its value is beyond material wealth. To hear this tape . . . to know what no man has known before, to be privy to the secrets of the universe, to perhaps understand *God himself* . . ."

Hot breath pours from Orange's nostrils. I'm thinking the guy knows that at best he's wasting his life, at worst he's hurt a lot of people. In his mind, here's a chance for redemption. All his sins can be offset by this groundbreaking metaphysical discovery.

There's no way he listens just once then hands it back to us.

"So there's two questions," Orange says. "Where is it? And what does it say, exactly? How could any audio recording *prove* such a—"

Courtney suddenly slams a thin hand onto the desktop. "Julius. You're an idiot."

Orange raises an eyebrow. "Oh yeah?"

"His name isn't Egnaro. *Egnaro* is just *Orange* spelled backwards."

Orange furrows his eyebrows in concern and snatches the sheet back, as if to confirm this.

"Palindromes," Courtney says softly.

"Palindromes?" Orange asks, still staring at the signature.

"Words or phrases that are the same forwards as backwards. *Sexes* is a palindrome. And then see, he started writing this message to you, telling you about the tape. Then 'Live not on evil' is itself a little palindrome. Then he tried to finish the letter by just writing it backwards, but must have kinda lost it."

Orange's eyes scan the sheet, muttering to himself, confirming what Courtney said.

"Son of a bitch," he says. "I *am* an idiot."

"So . . ." Courtney muses to himself. "So what he wrote is a palindrome. So what?"

Courtney purses his lips and strokes his thin mustache. Orange and I watch him in silence, not daring to interrupt his train of thought.

"What about this," Courtney finally says. "What if the tape is literally the same played backwards as forwards. Like you play it in reverse and it sounds exactly the same. This explains two things: why the killer used a tape recorder, because another medium like digital could be doctored to provide this effect. And it also explains how it's proof. Because, essentially, it's impossible."

"You mean . . ." Orange is positively giddy. Leaning over the desk on his elbows, excited like a little kid who has to pee. "Like you play the tape and you hear the girl saying something. And then once it finishes you have the tape player play it backwards, and you hear her saying the same thing?"

Courtney nods. Orange's jaw is unhinged, palms on his cheeks. Happy as a pig in shit.

"But like you said, that's impossible," I say.

Courtney smiles. "Exactly. That's the only way the tape could prove anything. If it did something impossible. If something physically impossible could happen, maybe something else *impossible* could happen. Like heaven."

"But if you're weak, like this guy," says Orange, gesturing to the laminated sheet, "encountering such a thing really could drive you completely mad."

"But mad how? What would you do if you knew there was an afterlife?" Courtney asks Orange. "Why would that make your client go on a sexual rampage?" Courtney leans in close and lowers his voice seriously. "Now it's my turn to add another condition to our deal, Matty Julius."

Orange grows pale. He tried to make Courtney his bitch, but now there's no question who is in control of this situation.

"You're a human stool sample, and no cassette tape can change that. Your operation here is beyond unconscionable: exploiting underage girls, selling their bodies to diseased perverts in exchange for an opiate drip and just enough spending money to replace the clothes that your clientele rip off of them in their animal frenzies . . . It's much too late for you, Matty. But you can at least spare a few poor souls the torture you've inflicted on thousands of others. If we bring you this tape to listen to, and it proves what we think it does," Courtney says, "no more girls. Keep the gambling, the *shvitzing,* the drugs. But no girls. You send them back to wherever you got them. Back to their families. With cash."

Orange grows very still, then manages to nod dumbly.

"Okay," he whispers.

"It might tell you something you don't want to hear," Courtney says. "Is it heaven? Hell? Or most likely, something you've never even considered. No matter what it tells you, you send them home. Do I have your word?"

"I . . . Yes," he nods queasily, and I'm pretty sure he means it.

"So you still want us to bring you the tape for a listen?" I ask him.

"Oh yes," Orange whispers. "More than ever."

PART TWO:

Pause

IT'S AFTER TEN at night, and Courtney is at the wheel of our rented Honda Accord, speeding north on I-95. There's a drizzle of freezing rain.

The plan is to check out the murder scene first, since it's on the way to the institution housing Silas. We should get to Bangor by one, then we'll check into a motel. Murder scene has been cold five years, one more night won't make a difference. I've got my phone in my hand, am staring blankly at the screen.

"Orange isn't *just* a filthy idiot." Courtney is babbling; he's been unable to settle down since leaving Midtown Fitness. "He's also a narcissist. And that's his mistake: He thought he could figure this all out himself. Never bothered to ask for help," Courtney chortles. "All that time thinking somebody named Egnaro was the key to finding the Beulah Twelve . . ."

I lean back in my seat.

"Can you please explain what the fuck is the Beulah Twelve?"

Courtney shakes his head like he's disappointed in me.

"I'm sure you've heard of them. Must just not remember. It was huge news for a week a few years ago. Beulah is this tiny little town in rural Colorado. Twelve upstanding male citizens kidnapped a boy of seven. They brought him to the leader's house—his attic had been converted into some kind of crazy church. They killed the boy on an altar. Very sacrificial, ritualistic. Any of this ringing a bell?"

"Maybe," I lie.

"And *then*." Courtney grins. "The twelve men disappeared into thin air. They left the boy *flayed* on the altar, got in their trucks, and *disappeared*. A few weeks into the investigation it turns out all twelve of them were seen in Chicago, plus they used their credit cards there. Maxed them out, I think. But besides that, no trace. Ever. They never found any of them."

I'm feeling a little too tired for this. I watch the windshield wipers furiously smack away raindrops.

"Okay . . . so?"

"So clearly Orange's client—Egnaro— was one of them. He was going nuts about how they 'did it'—that must mean killed the kid, right? But what if *Savannah's* death was related to the Beulah Twelve? What if—" Courtney is as animated as I've ever seen him. And instead of gesticulating with his hands, he seems to be taking out his excitement on the gas pedal, accelerating to punctuate every revelation. "What if Silas was part of the Beulah Twelve!"

"Let's not speculate." I sigh. "Patience, thoughtfulness, subtlety, right?"

"Absolutely." Courtney nods furiously. "Absolutely."

"So bottom line, this Beulah Twelve shit—which frankly I think is just that. This guy probably read about the Beulah Twelve on the news just like you. I guarantee this dude's freakout happened when this was big news—but this shit doesn't really change anything. We still gotta check out the crime scene, and we still have to get in to talk to Silas to figure out where the hell he stashed this *alleged* tape."

"And," Courtney adds, "you still need to call your friend."

I've been staring at my cell phone for the last half hour, trying to psyche myself up to call a girl. I feel like I'm back in high school.

"You're being ridiculous," says Courtney.

"You don't understand human relationships, do you? It's been ten years since I've talked to her. I didn't even have Sadie last time I saw her."

"Well we need her help. We still know almost nothing about Greta Kanter."

And so here we are, blazing through what's evolving into a torrential sleet storm to the scene of the murder, me trying to psyche myself up enough to buzz an old flame that I kind of screwed the pooch with. Helen Langdon. A colleague from my days at the NYPD, who's since been promoted to Detective Second Grade. She could run a background check on Greta—is it just a coincidence that the deceased girl's sister is a total screw job?

"Call," says Courtney.

"Maybe we could have gotten a little more out of Orange about Greta's visit if you hadn't run your fucking mouth back there, genius," I say. "What happened to patience?"

Courtney shakes his head, still peering out into rain-stained, inky darkness. "I think he appreciated someone being straight with him."

I snort. "Are you a sociotard? One of those people who can't pick up on subtle cues, like how someone threatening to force-feed you glass means they aren't happy?"

"Call," says Courtney.

"I will. Hold your horses."

"Call now."

I stare out into the dark night through the rain-streaked windows. Can just make out silhouettes of pine trees and highway signs. "I was such an idiot," I say. "I'm so embarrassed. It makes me cringe just thinking about it."

"What happened?" I know Courtney couldn't care less. Just knows that indulging me is a necessary precursor to getting me to dial.

I breathe out slowly. Courtney cranks the speedometer past 100 to pass a red minivan, executes it with the precision and impassivity of an electric can opener.

"I sorta cheated on her."

"Sorta?" Courtney cocks his head in amusement but doesn't take his eyes from the road for even a moment.

"She was working a night shift. I went out with some old law school friends after work. I got trashed and hooked up with some floozy I met at the bar."

"How did she find out?"

"I told her," I sigh.

Courtney actually seems impressed. "That's admirable."

"That's exactly what she said. But also that it meant I must not really want to be with her. Subconsciously. We'd been dating for about three months then. I told her she was wrong, that it was just a stupid mistake, that she was the best thing that had happened to me in a long time. It was true. She was a real fucking gem. A hard-ass, a real tough cookie, that's for sure—you have to be to survive as a female officer. Especially in the city. But a gem once you dug beneath all that. Anyways, she didn't cry or anything. Just looked at me real hard and said, 'I guess that's it.' God, I felt so ashamed."

"So you're upset that you told her? Or that you did it."

"Shut up." I open the glove compartment and root around for the trail mix we bought at the last gas station.

"Upset that you weren't thoughtful and patient enough?" Courtney asks, unable to contain a note of glee.

"Go fuck yourself."

"Call. I listened to your stupid story, now call."

My heart is pounding. I enter what I sort of hope isn't still her cell number—I've switched it to every new phone I've gotten. I Google her once in a while, too, just to see what she's up to, if she's married and so on. Best I can tell, she's not. I hit call and pray nobody picks up. Two rings.

"Hello?"

Shit, shit, shit.

"Hi."

"Who is this?"

"This . . . is this Helen?"

"Who is *this*?"

My chest heaves. I put a hand on the dash to steady myself.

"It's Frank. Lamb."

A long pause. Courtney looks at me like *so?*

I bite my tongue. I don't know where she is, on the other end, but I know what she's doing: She's got a pen out, doodling little geometric shapes on a pad of sticky notes. I never saw her answer a phone without her pen and pad ready, breaking from the drawing only to chew thoughtfully, desperately, on the end of the pen, like it's leaking some vitamin she's deficient in.

Just when I think maybe she's hung up she says:

"Frank. Wow. How are you?"

"I'm fine. Okay, I guess. How are you?"

"Same."

Another pause. Courtney gestures: *Come on!*

"Um, look I know this is a little weird, but I need some help. On an investigation."

I'm a little relieved to hear her laugh softly on the other end of the line.

"Help, huh?"

"Yeah. You're still in the department, right?"

"What do you need, Frank?"

"A girl named Savannah Kanter was murdered five years ago. Her sister hired me to look into a little detail of the crime, and I have a feeling she might have a record. At the very least, something weird is going on with her." I clear my throat. "Her name is Greta Kanter. K-A-N-T-E-R. Also, obviously, anything about the crime itself would be just super."

Another awful silence. The splatter of the rain on the windshield picks up a little.

"Frank, I can't."

"I can pay you."

"Stop it. You know I'm not supposed to do that. I could lose my job."

"Just think about it," I plead.

I can hear her huff. I hear a click that I know is her tapping the end of her pen against her front teeth.

"Was it in the city?" she finally asks.

"No. Rural Maine. Outside Bangor."

"That means I'd have to call and request files—"

"I know. Look, if you can't do it, fine. Just know I'm desperate here. This woman walked into my office and gave me $15K up front. *Cash.* The bounty is huge. I don't know a damn thing about her. What would you do?"

"Not tell an NYPD detective, for one thing," she says. "What do you think the chances are that that money is clean?"

She's not making this easy, that's for sure. Courtney has had one hand fiddling with his ponytail since he realized this wasn't going well. I think he's also picked up the speed. Rain crashes down in sheets on the windshield.

"Can you at least run her driver's license?" I ask.

I hear her breathing on the other end and consider saying something to evoke the magic we had for at least a two-month stretch, an inside joke or something.

"Goddammit," she sighs. "I'm not gonna make you beg me.

Just a sec. Lemme get into the system remotely. I'm at home. What's the number?"

I respell the name and feed her the license number. Hear the distant clicking of her fingers on the keyboard. Are they painted? She used to paint them bright colors; a weird habit that always seemed incongruous with her otherwise tough exterior.

"Okay, Greta Kanter . . ." She hums to herself. "Got her. Ready?"

"Yeah," I say, switching to speaker so Courtney can hear.

"Record totally clean. Not even a traffic violation, but she lives in the city, so she probably doesn't even drive. Six foot, green eyes. Here's a picture of her. Very pretty."

I cough uncomfortably. Courtney raises an eyebrow at me.

"Is she?" I say into the phone. "I didn't notice."

Helen continues, "Address on 83rd, Upper West Side, thirty-nine years old—born in Sheepshead Bay, so probably Russian parents."

"Anything coming up about her sister? And the murder?"

"I told you, I'm not gonna get anything like that without requesting files from the people who handled it. All I could find is public news clippings, same stuff you have access to."

I lick my lips. "Alright, so everything looks clean and normal on her?"

"Yes. And you know what it's like: If there's something weird, you can usually spot it right away."

"Sure," I say. "Thanks, Helen."

Awkward pause.

"No problem," she says. "Is that it, Frank? I'm pretty busy right now."

"Oh, of course. No, no. That's all, I guess."

"Alright. I guess I'll talk to you in another ten years or so. Have a good night."

Click.

Courtney avoids eye contact with me. Wish I'd taken the phone off speaker for that last bit.

"Well that went about as well as expected," I mutter and close my eyes.

"To be fair, you probably could have exchanged a few more niceties before—"

"Jesus Christ. I called, okay?"

"It wouldn't have killed you to be a little more patient. That's all I'm saying."

Blood rushes to my face. "Aren't you a fucking virgin? Don't act like you know fucking anything about women or relationships, alright?"

"I'm not a virgin."

"You *love* this, don't you? You act so fucking high and mighty and smug. '*Wouldn't have killed you to be a little more patient.*' Are you serious? Who do you think you are? Jesus? You're a wiry vegan with a ponytail, so you figure you're qualified to dish out advice like Doctor fucking Phil, huh?"

I'm enraged to see that Courtney is smiling.

"What's so goddamn funny?" I growl.

"Nothing," Courtney replies.

"If you weren't driving right now, I'd strangle you with that goddamn ponytail."

Courtney doesn't respond, just stares out into the dark rain. I pull the lever that makes my seat recline and pull my jacket over my eyes. I listen to the roaring of the Honda's transmission, protesting mildly as Courtney directs her through the constant staccato of freezing rain. I think about Sadie, imagine us on a beach somewhere on the Mediterranean. Maybe there's a woman lying next to me in the sand. Maybe it's Helen. Maybe it's Greta Kanter.

And fuck it, Courtney can come too.

WHEN I OPEN my eyes it's still dark in the motel room. That's where we are, right? A motel? Don't even remember checking in or passing out. I'm on my back on top of a starched sheet, thick darkness swimming above me. I have to pee.

Can't hear Courtney breathing. He must be down in the lobby working.

I reach for the bedside lamp and twist it on, but nothing happens. Burned out.

I throw off the thin blankets and sit up in the darkness. It's cold in here, I realize. Really, incredibly cold. Maybe the power went out because of the storm? No electricity, no heat? I grope for the blanket and rip it off the bed, wrap it around my shoulders, stand up. My legs feel wobbly, like I'm drunk or something. I shudder. I don't like this. Something's wrong. Where's Courtney?

I try to feel my way to where the bathroom should be, unable to even recall the layout of this room. Can't even remember going to sleep here. And shouldn't this room be carpeted? Instead I'm standing on freezing . . . dirt?

Breathing fast. The wet air is so cold it burns my lungs.

"Hello?" I say. My voice echoes like I'm in a space much bigger than a motel room. It's damp in here and smells like mold. I wrap the blanket tighter around me. My bare legs are shaking.

And then, out of the corner of my eye, I see something yellow. Something glowing. I jerk to face it, but it seems to move, staying only in my periphery.

"Hello?" My voice shaking. I'm shivering with cold. The light dancing in the corner of my eye. Freezing wet dirt between my toes. I jerk again to face the light, and this time it stays put. My heart stops.

It's a girl, dressed in an amber sundress. Blond and short. Beautiful clear skin. I recognize that sad face. It's Savannah Kanter, without the horrible tattoos.

I try to speak but my mouth won't cooperate. She's looking at me, eyes wide with urgency. I take a step toward her, but she takes a step backwards. Again I step toward her, and again she steps backwards.

"Savannah?" I whisper.

She responds with a word I can't understand. It's warbled. Reminds me of someone speaking underwater.

"Why are you here?" I ask.

She makes a pleading sound, words that mean nothing to me.

"Do you want to tell me something?" I ask.

She nods fervently, but there's something wrong with the motion. It's glitchy or jerky, like she's coming through on a bad internet connection. She seems frustrated. Desperate.

"Tell me," I whisper.

She starts speaking, but again it's indecipherable.

"I can't understand," I say, but she doesn't seem to hear.

Her brown eyes are wide, imploring. Hands wrapped in tight fists. She's telling me something important, but I can't understand a word. It's not quite gibberish though. It's real words, but almost like another language. Another language spoken underwater.

And it's only as I start feeling very tired, and this glowing girl begins to fade beneath the weight of my heavy eyelids, that I realize she's speaking backwards.

MY BACK ACHES when I open my eyes. There's sun behind the thick white curtains of the motel room. I blink a few times. On the wall across from me is a painting of the most drab landscape I could imagine. Whoever plopped down their easel in that marshland should have kept driving.

I sit up slowly. Courtney's bed is empty.

I try the bedside lamp. Lightbulb switches on.

I draw a hot shower and replay what I saw last night. The details seem too vivid to be a dream: the soft contours of Savannah's cheeks, the grit of cold dirt between my toes. I remember them clearly, as if the dream has been seared onto a cross section of my brain. I shudder, thinking how real the cold, stale air felt in my lungs . . . her wide, pleading eyes.

I linger in the shower, as if the water will wash away the image of Savannah. I've never been a vivid dreamer and am just fine with that. Could always count on six hours a day off the clock. If my clients start regularly intruding on my nightly headspace, I might have to raise my rates.

I dry off and make it down to the cramped dining room of the Howard Johnson. Hard plastic chairs. Cheap, coffee-stained foldout tables. Courtney is the only person here, sitting in front of my laptop, a half-eaten apple in one hand.

"How long have you been up?" I ask, sliding in across from him.

"All night. Couldn't sleep," he says, his eyes scanning the screen.

"Did the power go off last night?" I ask.

Courtney looks up from the monitor. "No," he says, frowning. "Why?"

"Nothing. Never mind."

He stares seriously at me for a moment, like to let me know that he knows I'm lying to him, then lets it go.

"So I guess I'll drive today," I say. "You can nap in the car."

"No need. I have plenty of energy. Found a market around the corner that sells kale. I ate like two pounds of it."

I snort and drag myself over to the dreary continental breakfast station. Minimuffins, Froot Loops and Apple Jacks. I fill up a bowl with Apple Jacks and skim milk, drown a flimsy paper cup in a torrent of weak black coffee, and return to Courtney.

"What you looking at?" I feel like an impatient kid nagging *are we there yet?* Courtney finally looks up from his computer.

"Read every article I could find about the murder, about Silas. Everything Greta told us seems to be true. Silas turned himself in and was committed to the institution she mentioned. And I found a mention of the tape. Just one. Check this out."

Courtney rotates the computer to show me an archived article from a very poppy-looking news outlet. Headline reads, *Creepiest video you'll see today.* And there's a paragraph explaining what we already know: This is the creep who turned himself in with a Polaroid of Savannah's body. I shudder, thinking about last night. Try to put it out of my mind.

Courtney hits play.

It's a video taken on a cell phone, obvious because it's a little shaky and grainy. Must have been taken from the jury box, illegally. It takes a few seconds to recognize Silas, sitting between two men in suits, wearing a shabby suit himself. It's more than a little surreal in light of his mutilated face, which is much more grotesque and intricate than the black-and-white photo Greta gave me indicated. It's impossible to discern the precise images from this clip, but the patterns are brightly colored and deeply engraved. His face and shaven head (also tatted) look like an Oriental rug.

Silas is talking to someone we can't see. The judge? He's stammering.

"You won't understand," he says, shaking his head. His wrists are cuffed to the table in front of him. He's almost writhing as he speaks, like there's an animal inside of him trying to escape.

A disembodied voice that we can't discern replies, but whatever it says irks Silas into shaking his head even more adamantly.

"You won't understand," he says.

The off camera voice insists gently, "Why did you kill her, Silas?"

Silas squirms.

"I don't remember," he mutters. There's muted shuffling in the background. It's getting hard to hear exactly what he's saying. Fortunately at this point someone started putting in subtitles.

"Remember that the acceptance of your insanity plea is predicated on your full cooperation."

Silas licks his lips, eyes still downcast. The courtroom is pretty much silent.

"It was an experiment," he practically whispers.

"What kind of experiment?"

"Like science. Like a science experiment."

"What was the nature of the experiment?"

"I . . . I wanted to see where she'd go."

"Can you elaborate on that?"

Silas shakes his head.

Someone else asks, "What did you find, Mr. Graham?"

Silas opens his mouth to speak, but nothing comes out, like there's an invisible hand muting him.

"Mr. Graham? What did you find?"

End of video.

I sit back at the table. My stomach feels a little upset. The Apple Jacks are getting soggy, but I can't bring myself to take a bite. I reach for the coffee but find myself looking at an empty, brown bottom. I frown at Courtney. He looks tired, kale notwithstanding.

"Wow," I mutter.

"Yeah."

An elderly couple enters the dining room. They appear excited by the minimuffins.

"I watched it almost twenty times," Courtney says.

"And?"

"Well . . ." Courtney touches a thin finger to his eyebrow. "Obviously this is like a twenty-second clip of a two-week-long trial. A drop in the ocean. So maybe not wise to read too much into this. Probably someone was secretly recording intermittently all day, and this was the most compelling clip, the one they thought could fetch the most if they leaked it to this site. So first thing to remember: We have no idea what comes before or after this."

"Greta does though," I say. "I mean, she was there, right?"

"Right." Courtney nods. "But she doesn't seem to feel like telling us much more than she already did: Silas says that Savannah's voice was recorded onto this tape, and on the way out of the courtroom Silas told her that he 'got what he wanted.'"

"He doesn't seem *totally* nuts, as one might expect," I say. "If you ignore the tattoos and the a priori knowledge that he strangled Savannah and killed his parents when he was ten with a hammer . . . He seems more scared, frankly, than bonkers."

Courtney takes a bite of apple and with a full mouth says, "I agree with you on that."

I lean back in my chair. Close my eyes for a moment, and there's Savannah again, glowing, warbling at me.

"I need more coffee."

Courtney closes my laptop and hands it to me. He tosses his apple core into my slimy Apple Jacks milk and strokes his raggedy cheeks.

"Get it to go. I'm eager to get to the cabin."

I walk to the trash and dump out my untouched cereal. Get a refill on my coffee. It's doing nothing for me. Might as well be drinking hot sewage water.

We check out at the front desk and carry our bags out the back of the motel, into the parking lot.

"Wouldn't he probably bring it with him?" I'm dismayed to find that it's still drizzling outside, and the sky is the color of dirty glass. The Howard Johnson sits just off the highway. Across the highway is a sad system of low, industrial-looking buildings and what looks like a mini-golf course. "Why would he leave it at the cabin, then go turn himself in? Doesn't make any sense."

"Well why he turned himself in is itself confounding." Courtney picks what looks like kale remnants from his teeth. "But assuming that he knew he would, it makes sense that he'd stash the tape somewhere rather than have it be seized and put in an evidence warehouse forever."

"He's not in a proper penitentiary though. They might let you bring some personal possessions in with you."

"Yeah, but he didn't know he was gonna end up there."

"Fine. So why does he turn himself in?"

"Maybe it's like he told Greta." Courtney shrugs. "He got what he wanted."

We're a few feet from the Honda. I stop suddenly and look at

Courtney. I don't like the way I'm feeling right now. This whole morning—since waking up from that too-vivid dream—I've been gripped by a distinctly unpleasant sort of foggy-headedness. If I had to describe the feeling more precisely, I would call it the sensation of impermanence.

"You don't really believe that—you know—that this guy Silas actually found something, do you? If there *is* a tape, it's just gonna be Savannah talking. It's not like . . . You don't actually believe what you said yesterday at Orange's, do you, about it being a palindrome, proving something about an afterlife?"

Courtney frowns and scratches his head. "I'm keeping an open mind. I don't see why you'd dismiss anything out of hand."

"Well," I snort. "Can't we dismiss the outcomes that are *impossible*? I've already dismissed the possibility that Silas is a Martian. Is that too closed-minded for you?"

Courtney narrows his eyes. "A lot of people believe in life after death, you know."

"Do you?" I ask.

"Undecided. Like any good detective, I'm waiting for more evidence before I make my assessment."

I shake my head and walk to the car. Courtney tries to take the driver's seat, and I snatch the keys from him.

"You're tired. Plus, you believe in heaven. So you don't have an incentive to drive safely."

Courtney heads around to the passenger's side.

"Maybe we'll find something at the cabin to change your mind, Frank."

FINDING THE CABIN where Savannah was killed takes longer than we expected. I can't help feeling relieved by this. Driving around is helping me wake up a little, shake off the images from my encounter last night.

We start at the boardwalk that Greta described, the one where she'd last seen her sister walk to the bathroom and never return. It's off season, and the boardwalk is empty. All the shops are shut down for the winter, metal grates pulled down over their facades. We linger on a soaked wooden bench in silence for a few minutes, staring at the angry sea, letting the frigid, wet wind sting our cheeks.

Behind the cluster of closed shops, we walk past the bathrooms, back to our Honda. It's the only car in the parking lot. Gravel. Just like Greta said. I get in the car and turn on the heat. Courtney stands outside, scanning like a hawk. He kneels, and I watch him comb a boney hand through the gravel. He winces as a gust nearly whips his scarf off, then hurries into the passenger seat.

After we've gone another hour north on I-95 and taken the exit prescribed by the built-in GPS, our technology fails us. The cell reception gets so spotty that Google Maps on my phone is an exercise in masochism, and the car's GPS is either thrown off by same, or these roads are just too poorly mapped for it to navigate. We have to pull over and ask directions to the cabin—33 Rutgers Lane—four times. Nobody has heard of Savannah Kanter, or maybe they just don't want to talk about it. We don't say much as we drive. I know Courtney is also imagining Silas driving down this road with Savannah in the backseat, probably tied up and shrieking. Or was she already unconscious by then?

Outside of a Texaco, we find someone who remembers the crime: a yellow-toothed woman built like a bear, filling up her rust-colored pickup. She tells us that she, like most people who live around here, went to check out the cabin once all the fuss died down. Turns out we've overshot the place by a mile and a half.

"There's a green mailbox with the number on it," she says. But as we retreat to our car she suddenly calls out, as an afterthought, "But you shouldn't go there."

Courtney and I both swivel in place. She's staring at us, shaking her head.

"Why not?" Courtney says.

Her wrinkled face contorts like she's sucking on something sour. "Just . . ." she says, then shakes her head, turns away.

We take a few steps closer to her. A click as her tank fills up. She starts climbing into her truck, but Courtney digs into his coat and pulls out three hundred-dollar bills, jabs them at her.

"Tell us everything you know."

She turns and stares at the bills, then exhales and climbs out of the truck, leaving the door open like she might have to make a quick escape.

"I'm not stupid or anything," she says, "but there's something bad happening at that cabin. Everyone around here knows it. Nobody visits anymore. Kids used to go there and party. Till one night they heard *voices* coming from that place. Not people's voices either. Weird screaming, like a . . . spirit or something. And weird clanking and banging, flashing lights. A few nights later a couple men went back there with guns. From the road they heard the same shit. And then their pit bull started barking. I knew one of the guys, Jonathan Gordon was his name. It wasn't his dog, but he saw the dog take off toward the cabin, barking like nuts. The guys didn't follow. They were *scared*. I heard John talking about that night later, he said the same thing: weird voices, banging, clanging, flashing. He says he thinks it was that girl's spirit trying to escape. The banging is her pounding on the walls."

The woman goes quiet. Stares at the three hundred in her palm, as if wondering if it was worth it. I see Savannah again, staring at me, desperate. My knees get a little weak. What was she trying to tell me?

"What happened to the dog?" Courtney asks.

She shakes her head and looks away. "Someone driving past the cabin saw him the next morning. He was cut open in the middle of the road, guts everywhere. Real, like . . . *deliberate*."

"What—"

"I'm done," she says, steeling her jaw, her eyes starting to well. "You want your money back, fine. I'm done."

"Keep it," Courtney says, and we get in our car, drive in silence for a while, taking it slow so we don't miss the cabin.

It's around two in the afternoon when we find what must be the spot: a dirt driveway distinguished only by a rusty green mailbox marked in fading white paint: *33 Rutgers.* It's so muddy from the persistent drizzle that we decide it's best to park on the shoulder and walk from there. I shut off the ignition but don't move. My butt refuses to leave the car seat.

Courtney is glaring at me.

"What's going on?" he asks.

"Nothing."

Courtney sniffs and stares me down with wet eyes that look as grey as the sky. I can't help squirming under his intense gaze. Then he cracks a tiny smile of triumph.

"You're a terrible liar, Frank. It's one of your better qualities."

I sigh and close my eyes.

"I had a weird dream last night," I say and recount it, omitting nothing. He can sniff out a lie anyways.

He's quiet for a moment. Then opens the passenger side door.

"I wouldn't worry about it," he says, avoiding eye contact as he climbs out. "You were probably just processing some of the stuff you heard from Orange."

"You're not saying that just to make me feel better, are you?" I ask as we walk around to the trunk.

"Of course I am," he says and smacks me on the back. He grabs a red acrylic satchel from the trunk that contains his forensic tools. My own bulky backpack contains the few blunt and crude implements I use in the field. He carries things like tiny screwdrivers you use for eyeglasses and makeup brushes. Most of my tools have existed since the agricultural revolution.

When Courtney hands me a pair of latex gloves to wear, I nearly burst out laughing.

"It's been five years, man. I doubt we're going to disturb any evidence."

But I comply, and we trudge through the thick mud, me wishing I'd worn anything but my tennis shoes, Courtney seemingly prescient in his knee-high galoshes.

As we get close to the cabin, I try to ignore images my brain keeps summoning of last night's apparition. *Try to think about anything else: Sadie, sports, yoga.* I could probably use some fucking yoga right about now. At least it's still light out here. If it was night, I'd be losing my shit.

We stop walking for a moment as the cabin comes into view. No question now. This is where it happened.

It's a one-story affair: dark brown, rotting logs stacked Lincoln style. A crumbling brick chimney protrudes from one end like it's trying to escape from whatever's inside. A fallen branch from one of the surrounding pine trees is still lying on the shingled roof. I squint up at where the branch must have broken off, from a towering Douglas whose base is just ten feet from the north wall of the cabin. Probably lightning.

We abandon the muddy driveway, which continues around to the back of the house, and head for what used to be the front door, now just an empty frame containing a portrait of deep black. Clumps of wild grass, weeds and pine needles crunch beneath our feet like breaking glass. Rotting wood steps lead up to a porch and empty doorframe.

I lick my lips. "Go in?" I ask. "Or maybe, you know, comb the exterior a bit."

In response, Courtney only rummages in his bag for a penlight, then steps inside. I follow.

We enter a dark, narrow hallway. The air is wet and smells moldy. Walls are wet wood that peel away when I touch them. We don't even bother looking for a light switch. On our right is a coat closet, which Courtney opens, flashlight clenched between his teeth. Totally empty besides a few rusty wire hangers.

Courtney pokes his head in and inspects the corners of the closet. With an outdated digital camera, he takes a few pictures that I can't imagine him ever needing. I shift my weight back and forth anxiously and avoid thinking about where we are. Rotting, moldy, evil smells: the scent of death.

"See anything?" I ask.

"No." He pulls his head out. "Let's keep going."

The hallway opens into a living room badly in need of some interior decorating. A little light streams in through two dusty windows on the wall opposite us. To the left is an open door, behind which I can see a toilet gone red with rust. The room smells rank and mildewed. Water drips from the ceiling; in fact there's light coming in from a hole in the roof as well. On the floor of the living room is a soaked, dirt-encrusted mat. Beside it are two metal foldout chairs. There's a bookcase in the corner that's totally empty, save a mess of spiderwebs. The most outstanding feature of the room is a towering pyramid of empty beer bottles, stacked to nearly my height. I pull one out carefully and inspect the label: Black Lab stout. Never heard of it. But all hundred-some bottles are the same. Black Lab stout. A smiling black dog bares his tongue a hundred times over.

Once my eyes adjust to the dim light, I notice that the floor is coated in wet cigarette butts.

"Think the cops were drinking and smoking when they confiscated everything here for evidence?" I ask.

"I'd wager that's from local teens. Like that woman said. Everyone knows the story. They probably hung out here on Halloween for a scare. Or came here to make out . . . before they started hearing voices and someone cut up a dog, anyways."

There are two doors on the wall opposite the bathroom. I have to throw my shoulder into the rotting wood to open the first. There's a yellowing mattress on an otherwise bare floor. Something jumps out of the mattress.

I scream.

Courtney rushes in behind me, just in time to see the squirrel leap through one of the empty window frames.

"Little tense?" Courtney asks.

"Little."

We probe the rest of the square bedroom, Courtney going down on his hands and knees to pull the mattress across the room to check what's underneath. Nothing but mattress stuffing.

"Think this was Silas's bed?" I ask.

Courtney is combing over the surface now with a black light and tweezers.

"No hairs," he mutters.

"It's been five years."

"Still. Stuff doesn't just disappear."

"He was also bald in all the pictures we saw, remember? Tattoos all over his skull. Besides, we're not investigating the murder, champ. Just trying to figure out where that sick fuck stashed this tape."

"And in order to do that," Courtney says, rising to his feet and returning the black light to his bag, "we're going to have to get in his head. Unfortunately, we know almost nothing about the guy. So he turns himself in, okay. What does he do with this tape? Keep it on him? Bury it to retrieve later? Destroy it?"

I stare out the empty window pane. Conifers retreating to eternity, all shrouded in a light drizzle. A sea of tightly packed and drenched pinecones and pine needles.

"If he buried it, we have no chance," I say.

"Agreed."

We leave the bedroom, and I slam my shoulder into the second moldy door off the living room. This room is slightly bigger. Another decaying mattress in the corner, a fireplace and a small kitchenette: propane stove on a metal stool, rusty steel sink, two pans hanging from hooks on the wall. There's also a white mini-fridge, which Courtney opens. Mercifully empty; if someone had left a tuna casserole behind, we'd need hazmat suits to stay in here.

I try the faucet, and there's a hiss of air, then gurgling and finally an ejaculation of freezing water.

Courtney is kneeling at the fireplace, combing through a pile of black ash with what looks like a very fine paintbrush.

"You think there hasn't been a fire in there since Silas?"

"No way to tell really. Ash doesn't age. Looks the same the day it's burned as it does a hundred years later. This is all soaked through from water coming down the chimney." Courtney stops. He quickly fumbles in his pack for a magnifying glass and a pair of tweezers, then bends down until he's practically kissing the pile of black charcoal.

"What is it, Courtney?" I ask.

He doesn't respond, just picks carefully through his pile. I shiver and zip my windbreaker up as high as it will go.

Courtney finally extracts something with his tweezers and stands up, examining it in the glow of his flashlight. Then he grins.

"Take a look at that, Frank," he says proudly.

I squint. It is nothing; a strand of charred white material a quarter the length of a fingernail.

"Congrats, you've cracked the case," I say, rolling my eyes.

"You know what that is?"

"A scale model of your prick?"

"I believe"—Courtney inspects it again with his magnifying glass—"that this is bone."

My stomach does a little somersault.

"Bone?" I stare at the little sprig. "How the hell can you tell?"

He tugs it a bit with his tweezers.

"You make a really hot fire, let it burn for *hours,* it looks like the bone has been consumed, but you're wrong. Because bone is surprisingly hard to burn."

"Okay." I grimace. "So it's bone. Whose?"

I pull my jacket tighter around my collar. The rain is picking up outside.

"Not Savannah's, since she was totally intact," Courtney says, dropping the alleged bone into a small Ziploc bag and stashing it in his kit. "I'll bet it belongs to that dog."

I rub my cheeks to warm them up. "Those teenagers must have been having some pretty wild parties."

Courtney traces his thin jawline, doesn't seem to hear me. "What if someone else was here looking for the tape? Scared the locals off by killing that dog?"

I say nothing.

"Pure speculation." I shiver. "Let's get out of here."

"Almost done," he replies, zipping up his bag and walking back into the living room. "Gotta check the basement."

There's no descending stairway or trapdoor to the basement inside the house, so we check the back to see if there's an exterior staircase.

There's more shit behind the cabin than I expected. It's a junk-yard.

Two ancient pickup trucks devoured by rust, both half-buried in the wet ground and stripped down to their skeletons. Maybe they belonged to Silas? From the looks of it, they were here well before he ever showed up.

There's what looks like a disassembled, rusty oven covered in mud; coils of wire; cracked ceramic plant pots just filled with dirt; a few shredded rubber tires; an old coffee machine; a pile of yellowed, soaked paper; and more empty Black Lab beer bottles.

About twenty feet from the back door, there's a wooden shed about six foot square, composed of vertical two-by-fours. A thin pole runs through the roof of the shed, up about twenty-five feet. We wade through the trash to see it up close. It takes Courtney a moment to figure out what it is:

"Solar panels up there, and there must be a generator inside."

"Let's find out for sure," I say and grab my flathead screwdriver from my backpack. I wedge it between two of the wet boards and pry one loose easily; nails glide out of their rotting homes like warm knives from year-old butter. Courtney shines his penlight into the chasm.

"I was right," he says, not bragging. Just stating. "Still running too."

"Think Silas put it in?" I ask.

"Guess so." Courtney shrugs. "Maybe there's no power lines out here."

I pry out two more boards with my latex-gloved hands and poke my head into the shed. The air in here is still and heavy. In the light, I make out something that looks like a giant car battery. And sure enough, a little red light is flickering.

"This looks like a pretty advanced battery," Courtney says, shoving his own head in after I'm done looking. "Storing solar power for literal rainy days is fairly new technology. Quite pricey. Silas must have really needed dependable power for whatever he was doing."

"Tattooing?" I ask.

Courtney just clicks his tongue and makes a sound like *hrmph*. Then we abandon the shed and walk back to the cabin. My hands are numb from cold; the latex gloves aren't helping much in that arena.

The basement is the only room that hasn't been overrun by teenagers and other thrill-seeking visitors. We know this because the entrance has been sealed, presumably by the cops. At least a foot of thick cement has been poured over the doors and surrounding area. That's a new one.

From what I can tell, it used to be one of those two-doored

entrances that protrudes from the ground at an angle—the kind that usually opens to a descending staircase. We've been referring to the area beneath the house as a *cellar* or *basement*, but it's clear that the more appropriate term might be *bunker*.

Something about the cement looks off. I spent a summer working construction in high school—mixed enough buckets of cement to know the way this material is catching the dying daylight isn't normal. While Courtney snaps pictures of the cement-sealed entrance from every conceivable angle, I kneel down to inspect it.

"Court, you have a magnifying glass?" I ask.

He removes one from his bag and hands it to me. Then squats down next to me and raps a knuckle against the grey cement coating.

"Still hard?" I ask.

He blushes and returns his hand to his pocket. Just watches me in silence as I get down on my stomach for a closer look at the grain of the material.

"You ever heard of cops sealing a crime scene like this?" I ask.

"No," Courtney says. "Locals must have really been defiling this place. They didn't want anyone messing around down here, *ever*. Don't know why they didn't just put a padlock on the door. What about trying to dig around the door, Frank? The ground is soft from the rain, and if the foundation down there is soft, rotting wood—"

"It's not," I say. "There's concrete that extends around the perimeter of the house a few inches under the dirt." I scoop some mud away with my gloved hand to show him. "Cement foundation."

"I guess we'll need a jackhammer, then," he says.

"Well that's just it," I sigh, once I've confirmed my initial suspicion. "A jackhammer wouldn't do it. It's not pure cement. It's mixed with some sort of metal alloy. This stuff won't crumble."

Courtney stands up and tries to rub the mud off the knees of his skinny blue jeans but succeeds only in spreading it around into a chocolatey-looking mess.

"So?" he asks.

"I think we'd need an industrial-strength waterjet saw to blast through," I say, grunting as I rise to my feet. "Would cost upwards of ten grand, plus we'd need a truck or big van to carry it up that driveway."

Courtney stares at the bunker, which looks built to withstand a direct impact from a barrage of missiles.

"It would take a full day, at least, and obviously we'd need more cash," I say.

Courtney's face is truly pained.

"What do you think?" he asks. "Do we need to get in there? We have tons of pictures in the police file."

I bite my lip. I definitely don't *want* to get in there. Tough to separate those two. The bottom of the grey sun flirts with the upper tips of the tallest pines. Icy droplets sting my cheeks. I can't help imagining that Savannah's body, impossibly, is still down there, immaculately preserved.

BACK IN THE Honda, I turn on the ignition just to warm up. Unspeakable relief just at putting a mere driveway length between me and that house. Courtney seems emotionally drained too. Feels like we were looking around that cabin for a lot longer than two hours.

I wasn't getting reception at the cabin, but back in the car, my phone tells me I have a missed call from Orange. I get the feeling he's gonna be hassling us pretty regularly for updates. I'll let him sweat it out a bit.

Instead I use my one bar of service to call Greta. Need to show her some progress and ask for money for the water saw. Five rings, then a generic message. I hang up.

"No dice," I say.

Courtney flares his nostrils.

"Leave a message!" he says once it's obviously too late. "It looks professional."

"Nobody leaves messages anymore. If you'd owned a phone in the last decade, you'd know that."

The windshield starts steaming up a little. I feel a weariness in my bones, a tension in my neck and back that I haven't felt in a long time.

"How you feeling about all this?" I ask Courtney.

He blinks a few times, pushes a long breath out through his chapped lips. "I've never dealt with anything like this. A girl killed, you know. Your dream . . ."

I shift uncomfortably in my car seat.

My phone starts vibrating. Blocked number. A little adrenaline shoots up from my gut, my chest tightens. I answer it on speakerphone.

"Did you find it?" Greta's voice is raspy and strained, tingling with desperation.

Courtney stares at the phone in disgust, raises an eyebrow and shoots me a look like *wow*.

"It's only been two days." I try to stifle a nervous laugh. "I'm calling to ask you for cash for an expense. The cellar door to the cabin is sealed up real good. We'll need around ten thousand for a waterjet saw to bust in there. We figure there's, well, not a *good* chance Silas stashed it down there, but we gotta have a look around."

We can hear her breathing heavily into the phone. Impossible not to think of sex; what she'd sound like as I brought her closer and closer to orgasm. I try to force the thought from my mind.

"You don't have to go down there," she finally says. "It's not down there."

Courtney is grinding his teeth, looking at me like *where did you find this lady?*

"How do you know?" I ask, throat dry.

"Because I went down there myself to look."

"Before it was sealed up?"

She lets my stupid question hang in the airwaves for a moment, punishing me by forcing me to replay it in my head a couple times.

"I didn't even know anyone sealed it up," she says. "I went there shortly after the trial."

"But maybe you missed it—"

"You need to ask Silas," she says, her voice firming up like tofu in the fryer. "He's the only one who knows where it is."

Courtney shakes his head, then takes a deep breath and leans over the phone.

"Hi Greta. This is Courtney Lavagnino, the tracker working with Frank on this project. I'm just wondering why you wouldn't tell Frank that you'd already been in this cabin, and already searched the basement. You could have saved us some time."

"I didn't think it was pertinent."

We exchange a look of disbelief.

"Well, with all due respect, ma'am," Courtney says, "we'll decide what's pertinent and what's not. Now, is there anything else you know that you think might help us find this tape for you?"

Again she lets us suffer in silence. I'm breathing harder than I would like. I turn off the heat, roll down my window and suck down some fresh Maine air.

"I found a stack of blank, unused cassette tapes down there," she says. "The police must have seen them but just left them there."

Courtney tugs at an eyelash. "So then—"

"The tape *exists*," Greta practically growls.

How do I not have bourbon? Next grocery store we drive past, I'm pulling over.

"And only Silas knows where it is."

"I understand that—" Courtney starts, but she's already hung up. He stares at me.

"Quite a little ray of sunshine, isn't she?" I smile weakly.

He shakes his head, stunned, speechless.

"You should see her in person though," I add. "Looks like an angel."

I throw the car into gear and, after spinning in mud, catch some traction and ease out onto the empty two-lane highway.

"Where to now?" Courtney asks softly. He seems almost hurt by that interaction.

"You heard the lady. Let's go talk to this fucker."

NEXT MORNING I'M wearing a suit—and not in a courtroom—for the first time I can remember. We stopped at Walmart and picked them up for forty bucks apiece last night. Loony-bin staff aren't paid enough to tell the difference.

Courtney takes the Accord over I-80 down a four-lane highway lined on either side by pines, truck stops and farmland. Courtney swerves around a pickup truck pulling a trailer with two horses sticking their heads out of the back, catching the breeze.

Now I get to make the easiest phone call of the week.

"Tammy? It's Frank. Is Sadie there?"

"Hi Frank! Yeah just a minute, I'll get her."

I gaze out the window. Mist rising from yesterday's rain. The tires sound slick beneath us. My heart feels a little lighter with every mile we put between us and that cabin. Plus, the dream feels a little more distant today.

"Dad?"

"Hey, sweetheart. How are you? How is the Feinsods'? Having fun hanging out with Ben?"

"It's fine but . . ." Sadie lowers her voice into the phone. "She's an even worse cook than you."

"You'll live."

"When are you coming back?"

I suck on my teeth. "Not sure, maybe another few days."

"Is it going okay?"

"I'll tell you about it all when I get back, alright?"

"Alright." I imagine her pouting on the other end. "How's Courtney?" she asks.

"I wish you could see him now," I say. "You wouldn't even recognize him."

We woke up at five to apply each other's disguises. Courtney's thin hair is dusted a light shade of grey, and I chopped off his ponytail and parted the rest down the middle. Then I gave him a clean shave and aged him about thirty years with ultrathin rubber patches that make him look wrinkled. Powder to blend it all together, a few liver spots and thick rimmed glasses, and we have a convincing charade. The frown and blue bags under his eyes are his own.

I admire my work; you'd have to get pretty darn close to Courtney's face to notice anything amiss.

"How's school going?" I ask.

"Good. We're learning about the layers of the Earth. Did you know there's basically lava under everything?"

"I . . . I guess I knew that."

"Cool, huh? You just have to dig and you'll get to lava."

I rub my eyes. "We'll try that when I get home, okay? I'll get us both shovels, and we'll dig till we hit lava."

"Don't make fun of me."

"Okay, I gotta run, sweetie. I'll try to call tonight, okay?"

"Alright. Bye."

Courtney talks out of the side of his jowled mouth. "How's she doing?"

"Fine."

I inspect my own face in the rearview mirror and don't recognize the man staring back. The blond wig set us back four hundred, but a shitty one is too easy to spot. Blue-colored contacts, crow's-feet drawn on with a makeup pencil, and a mustache. Courtney's not as good at applying makeup as I am, so we had to get creative.

We drive in silence for a few minutes. Courtney weaves past a twelve-wheeler. I review the notes we gathered last night.

The Berkley Clinic is located on a 255-acre property that was originally an apple orchard. In 1915 the land was acquired by an oilman named Hugh Brandsworth, who built a munitions factory, as well as a dormitory for the workers. Then, in the fifties, it was converted into a penitentiary, a large percentage of its inmates World War II vets with PTSD. They built a central administration building, put metal screens over the windows in the dormitory, and turned the factory into a cafeteria/common area. Today there are three buildings that house the five hundred-plus inmates (all male): the original, hundred-year-old dorm is low security—guys whose families put them there. Nervous breakdowns, mild schizophrenia, bipolar; *Cuckoo's Nest* stuff. Next up is a newer building, which is home to a hundred or so petty criminals, who may or may not have mental issues. Public nudity, unarmed robbery—mostly first-time offenders.

And then the third building, presumably home to our man, Mr. Silas Graham: the Sachar Center. Place is home to some of the nastiest, nuttiest men in the Northeast; the real sickos who need more care than your run-of-the-mill maximum-security complex can provide. A hodgepodge of pedos, rapists and murderers assigned here as part of their plea bargain. Most of them are serving life sentences—most will die here, and society will be all the better for it. They get a little therapy—both group and individual—plus meds for those who need them, which I'm betting is the vast majority. Visitations are strictly controlled for these perps. That could be an issue.

"Even if we get in there to talk to him, there will be guards around," Courtney says, artificial jowls turned down; this old man look is actually pretty natural for him. "Will you be able to interrogate him if people are watching?"

"If you have a better idea, I'm all ears."

"I still think bribery could work."

I fidget in my seat. My seat belt feels too tight.

"If this goes south, we can always try bribery. I've got five thousand wrapped up in my groin."

Courtney glances at me, like he's sizing me up for the first time. "But you think this will work right?"

"I think this has as good a chance of working as anything else."

Courtney tightens his grip on the wheel.

THE BERKLEY CLINIC is about a hundred miles north of the cabin, smack in the middle of bumble-fuck. It's been four miles since our last Waffle House, and that's saying something. Haven't passed more than a dozen cars in the last ten minutes coming down this road. Then a rust-red brick wall appears amidst never-ending coniferous forest. Courtney slows down, takes a careful left into the front gate. Rolls down the window at the security booth and flashes our phony IDs to a fat, walrus-looking fella.

"We're the guys from the Bureau," Courtney announces. "Someone called this morning? We're here to talk to one of your patients."

I really did call, but I can tell by the way Walrus hesitates before he nods that this is the first he's heard of it.

"Turn around and park outside the gate." He points to a small lot across the street. "Leave weapons in the car. I'll have to frisk you before I let you in."

We don't put up a fight; Courtney doesn't even carry a weapon. After we park, I put my Magnum in the glove compartment and slip my ceramic knife out of my sock and leave it too. We lock up the Honda—plates changed this morning so they can't track us through the car rental company if this all falls apart—and walk briskly, purposefully, across the poorly paved road to the front gate. According to Wikipedia, this is the only break in the fifteen-foot-high brick perimeter besides a freight entrance on the south side of the complex, which is used only for trucks dropping off supplies.

Walrus frisks us with fat, gloved hands. I'm thinking this is probably the first time he's done this in a while. Doesn't even make us take our shoes off; again, I could easily have smuggled in my knife.

Satisfied, the guard returns to his booth, and the gate creaks open.

"Follow the driveway up to the admin building." He points. "I already radioed in. Some folks are coming out to meet you."

Cursory nods and smiles to Walrus, and then we're inside, walking erect and serious enough to connote professionalism but slow enough to convey our age.

Courtney must see me anxiously drumming my fingers against my thigh, because under his breath he says, "Relax. And don't act like yourself. You're too high-strung. Feds are always really calm. All business."

"Courtney. Shut up."

Black tar driveway clicks under our polished shoes. I take in our surroundings.

I find it hard to believe that this place used to be an orchard. The ground is flat and bare, and the only trees in sight are squat and lifeless, caked in frost. In the summer or spring this place might actually look alright, but January leaves it desolate and sterile. Low grey buildings and chain-link fences sprawl over the property, reminiscent of a crappy elementary school. An empty, caged-in basketball court on our left. A few men in scrubs—must be orderlies—are eating lunch on a bench, their breath steaming. The entire fucking complex is enclosed by that rectangular brick wall, topped off with a healthy serving of barbed wire. Plus, there are eight guard towers arranged at strategic points of potential entry.

Nobody has ever escaped from this place, but fun trivia: Twelve years ago an inmate stole a plastic knife from the cafeteria, used it to slice thin strips of cloth from his shirt, and strangled two guards to death.

Courtney says, "Are you sure you want to do the talking? I know the story as well as you."

"I've got this. You just stand there and look ugly."

The driveway leads to a roundabout. We stop outside the central office; a one-story grey building that looks about as inviting as an Ebola quarantine.

I stretch a little, try to work some tightness out of my lower back and the wrinkles out of my shitty suit. Straighten my tie. Two people are approaching us, a pear-shaped man with pink cheeks wearing a drab blue suit and a woman in a white lab coat. They look confused. Before I have a chance, Courtney steps forward to greet them, badge already in hand.

"Hi, I'm Leonard Francis, and this is Ben Donovan," Courtney says crisply. "We're from the Bureau. Someone should have called this morning to let you know we were coming."

I hold out my badge as well, and the man and woman inspect them for a moment, as if they know what they're looking for.

The man says, "Yes, I received that message. I'm Harrison Linton, director here," and extends his hand for a firm handshake, his jowled cheeks and thick lips approximating a smile.

"Dr. Marie Pollis." The woman is small and mousey, with rimless glasses over narrow eyes. "I'm in charge of our mental health program here. How can we help you two?"

Courtney runs a hand through his dyed grey hair. Again I think this is actually a natural look for him; his temperament always seemed strange in such a young man's body. He's got a small pillow taped under his dress shirt to simulate a gut, and he stands with his knuckles on his hips, puffing out his paunch like he's proud of it.

"I apologize for the short notice," I say, stepping up and subtly butting Courtney out of the way. "It's been a very hectic week. But we desperately need to speak to one of your patients. It's something of an urgent matter. We are currently engaged in a manhunt for a murder suspect, a rather grisly case. I can't explain all the details, as the investigation is ongoing, but we have very good reason to believe that this was a copycat incident. And speaking to the original killer, even if he knows nothing about this copycat, could be critical to apprehending and negotiating with our suspect."

Harrison and Dr. Pollis exchange a quick look. They don't get visitors like this very often—exactly what we were hoping.

"Do you have a permit or something?" Harrison asks.

"Of course," I say. "Leonard?"

Courtney removes a document—which he spent hours last night perfecting—from his suit pocket and hands it to Harrison. His big, wet eyes scan it back and forth, like he's watching a tennis match on clay, then they freeze, bulging, riveted like the ball is just hanging in midair. He looks up at us and exhales, his breath an ominous grey cloud that hovers between us.

"Silas Graham?" he asks slowly. "He's been here for years. There's no way he's in touch with anything going on out there." He gestures vaguely to the entrance, as if this facility is the real world and everything beyond its gates a mere distraction.

I nod, expecting this objection. Courtney stands slightly behind me with his hand behind his back.

"Understanding Silas better may well help us to anticipate our suspect's next move," Courtney says. "Maybe not, but more information certainly can't hurt. And again, I stress"—he furrows his bushed-up eyebrows in deep concern—"time is of the essence."

Dr. Pollis shakes her head adamantly. "There's no way you can speak to Silas. Not only is he in maximum security but he hasn't agreed to see a visitor in years. And that's his right."

Harrison seems uncomfortable with this hard line. He's a man who doesn't like conflict. "Listen, why don't you two come in and warm up. We'll see what we can do for you."

Dr. Pollis glares at him, then we follow them up a cement walkway to the administration building, past an American flag waving miserably in the cold breeze. A pair of reinforced glass doors open into a tiled reception room that smells of bleach and lentil stew. It's like a weird parody of a college admissions building.

Behind the desk sits a tired-looking blond woman on the phone. A guard sits in a high chair reading a magazine. A few plants behind the desk do little to warm the aseptic atmosphere of this place. We follow Harrison and Dr. Pollis behind the reception desk into a glass-walled office. Every door, I notice, has to be opened with a magnetic key card. Harrison closes the door and walks around to sit behind a metal desk covered in papers. A family portrait and a few framed degrees hang on the wall; he's a psychologist.

Courtney and I sit across the desk from him as we did at Orange's, like two gay dads here for a parent teacher conference. Dr. Pollis stands awkwardly off to the side.

"So you want to talk to Silas . . ." Harrison makes a clicking noise with his tongue, then looks again at Dr. Pollis. "Even if we could get him to agree to talk to you, I doubt you'll get much out of him, truthfully. What do you think?"

She fiddles with her chestnut hair. "It seems like a long shot."

"Is he responsive, though?" I ask. "I mean, do you think he would be willing to cooperate? We only need to talk to him for maybe a half hour or so."

"Maybe a bit longer . . ." Courtney adds. I shoot him a quick look.

"So somebody else committed a crime that looks like Silas's?" Harrison asks. I grin to myself. Guy is curious. "That's it?"

"Well." I sigh, like this is the twentieth time I've had to lay out all the details for someone. "I suppose I oversimplified it a bit. We think Silas was something of a role model for him—we have reason to believe the two knew each other. We're having a hard time tracking down our suspect and feel like Silas is our best way of getting inside his head. The better we can understand Silas—we hope—perhaps we can gather some clues about our suspect's current state of mind."

"He's on the loose?" Dr. Pollis asks, with strange indifference. No trace of alarm. Guess she has more immediate threats to worry about, working at this place.

"That's right," I reply. Beside me Courtney strokes his faux-wrinkled cheeks rapidly, as he often does when he's thinking hard. I pray the makeup doesn't smudge. "And we're having an unusually hard time finding him. Obviously time is of the essence here. To find him before—God forbid—he kills again."

"If you don't mind me asking—" Dr. Pollis starts.

"I'm sorry." I compensate with an apologetic smile. "I really can't say any more about the crime."

"Well." Harrison spreads his palms. His face is definitely several stages redder than it was outside. "If we can't get you in to see Silas, which sounds like it's going to be tricky, maybe you could at least speak to the doctor in charge of his care. Dr. Pollis, would that be alright?"

Her face scrunches up. I'm thinking he trusts us, she doesn't.

"I suppose," she says.

"Great." Harrison grins. "If you two don't mind, could I get those badges back from you? Just need to photocopy them for our records."

My stomach falls out from under me. I can feel my dick shriveling up into my body. Gig's up. Abort. Maybe we can get out of here without facing five years for impersonating FBI agents. But Courtney, calm as can be, obligingly extends his fake badge, and I, with trembling hands, do the same. And then I watch in terror as Harrison, eyes twinkling, gently plucks them from our grasp with thick, ruddy hands.

"And do you have the number of your central office that I can call to confirm your authorization?" he asks gently. He doesn't suspect anything, that's my only source of comfort. He really does believe us. But of *course* he would do a quick background check. Jesus. Fuck.

"Of course," Courtney replies and removes his wallet from his suit pocket. I smile at Dr. Pollis like *this happens all the time.* She gives me the obligatory tight-lipped nod of two candidates for the same job sharing a waiting room. Courtney fiddles through his cards, frowns to himself, like I did when I pretended I thought I had more cash for ice cream.

"Must have given out all my cards," Courtney says. He removes a pen from his suit pocket and scribbles ten digits on the back of another card, hands it to Harrison.

Harrison wheezes as he rises to his feet.

"Be right back," he says and walks out to the front desk. Dr. Pollis just stands there awkwardly. I lean over to try to conceal my shaking knees. I think I'm gonna piss myself. I stare at the portrait of Harrison's family in an attempt to calm myself, but all that does is evoke images of Sadie in tears as I'm led away from her in cuffs.

I try to catch Courtney's eye, to nonverbally ask if maybe it's bribe time, but he refuses to make eye contact with me. He's just smiling pleasantly at Dr. Pollis, hands on his lap.

"Do you have a restroom I could use?" he asks her.

"Sure. To the left of the front desk," she says. As Courtney rises to his feet, he slips a hand into my pants pocket. I start to recoil, until I realize what's going on: he's snatching my cell phone. Then he strolls from the office with an air of *business as usual.*

Dr. Pollis is leaning against the glass wall, arms crossed. She looks bored.

"So," I say weakly. "How long have you been working here?"

"Nine years," she says. I notice she's not wearing any makeup— looking good might be a liability around here.

"Only men here?" I ask.

"That's right. We have a much smaller sister facility about five miles north of here."

"In Canada?"

I force myself to grin. Dr. Pollis humors me with the most cursory of smiles.

"Not quite," she responds.

I look over her shoulder, through the glass walls. Harrison's nowhere in sight. Did Courtney leave to strangle him or something? Is he hiding the body? Then I spot my lanky partner returning. We should have just given up and left, especially if we're not going to be able to get into Silas's room anyways.

Courtney calmly returns to the office and retakes his seat.

Again I try to catch his eye, but he ignores me. I check my watch; Harrison has been gone seven minutes. Is he calling the cops? The whole scene plays out in front of my eyes. They search our car, find my Magnum, pictures of Savannah's corpse . . . I steel my teeth, start envisioning kicking Harrison in the nuts as soon as he returns and just dashing out of here. Maybe we'll have to take out Walrus at the gate. Also kick him in the nuts. He'll be fine—

Harrison walks in.

"Great, thanks." He grins. Then picks up his desk phone. "Dr. Nancy? Hi, it's Harrison. I have two gentlemen here who'd like to speak to you, if you don't mind. About Silas Graham. Mmm-hmm. Okay, I'll send them right over. Have a good one."

He sets the phone down and smiles.

"No pictures, no recording devices. And I assume you've already handed over any weapons?"

We both nod slowly.

"Great. Dr. Pollis, could you please walk them over to Sachar?"

DR. POLLIS LEADS us back past the flagpole to the edge of an athletic field. On the other side of the field, another low grey building bulges like a bad wart on the face of the earth. Frozen brown grass crunches beneath our feet. Every direction eventually terminates in the brick wall that encloses this place. There are guard towers in each corner, and then four more halfway along each wall.

I get the feeling that the Berkley Clinic has way more land than they need; besides the few buildings and chain-link-fence-enclosed recreational areas, this place is mostly just empty stretches of grass.

At one point Dr. Pollis's cell phone rings, and she steps away from us to take it. I immediately turn to Courtney.

"How the fuck did you pull that off?" I whisper.

"That was close, Frank." He shakes his head. "Gave him your number and answered in a different voice from the bathroom, pretended to transfer him, searched for our records in the computer, then authorized us. Thank God they don't have any experience dealing with situations like this."

"You had my number memorized?"

"Of course. I memorize all my numbers. Don't have a phone to store them in, and it's faster than flipping through a notebook."

"Jesus." My body is still rigid as a board, and there are little marks on my palm where my fingernails nearly drew blood. "Let's just call it quits. If we can't get in to see Silas, this whole thing is worthless anyways. He probably has that fucking tape under his pillow—"

Dr. Pollis returns, shaking her head. "Sorry about that. I'll have to leave you two with Dr. Nancy once we're at Sachar. Suicide attempt in House Three."

"Is that common here?" Courtney asks, scarf wrapped tightly around his neck. No hat; he correctly intuited his red duck-hunting number might have hurt the credibility of his disguise.

"Unfortunately, quite," Dr. Pollis responds as we resume walking. "No metal silverware, no belts, no shoelaces . . . but they still find ways. This gentleman was on gardening duty. Got his hands on some weed killer and chugged it. Just not quite enough, apparently."

"You trust them to garden? Don't they need, like, tools?" I ask.

"Depends on their classification," she responds. "Not the Sachars—the Category Threes—obviously. They don't even get to eat in the cafeteria together. We try not to put them in groups of more than ten, *ever*. That's when things turn ugly. But the Category Ones and some of the Twos are usually just fine with some responsibility. Fine until they aren't, that is."

To our right, about fifty yards away, a group of men in blue shirts toss baseballs to each other while a few orderlies supervise.

"Has Silas ever attempted suicide?" I ask.

Dr. Pollis purses her lips and looks at me over her glasses as we walk. Weighing what she's allowed to say, I suppose.

"Once. A few years ago."

"Not since?"

"No . . . but he's been different ever since."

I notice Courtney's fingers twitching with excitement. Can tell he wants to pick this woman's brain for hours but can't risk her feeling she's said too much. I still can't believe this charade worked. Seems too easy, which makes my stomach churn.

"How so?" Courtney asks casually.

Dr. Pollis quickly checks something on her phone. She walks fast, and we have to struggle to keep pace with her while also affecting the gait of men thirty years older.

"When he first came here he was almost megalomaniacal. Beyond help, beyond control. The other patients were drawn to him; his tattoos and reputation for heinous crime made him a natural leader. And he'd talk about his crimes, brag even. Even to me and Dr. Nancy—who is his group and one-on-one doctor. In his file, we have at least three different records of his crime, as told by him. I thought for a while he was psychopathic, but then he tried to kill himself and I realized this couldn't be the case."

Courtney licks his lips. I stare ahead at the squat two-story building that houses this monster and shudder.

"Why not?" I ask.

"Because I realized that his entire personality, everything he showed to the world, was a facade. One so elaborate that it even fooled me. Just as his face is hidden beneath those . . . *pictures* . . . he had hidden himself beneath this constructed personality—a brazen ass who would boast about his victims, strangle smaller patients in the showers, throw a plate of food at a resident and spit in his face. They just took it. Nobody wanted to mess with Silas, but not because he's physically imposing. He's quite tall, but lanky and thin. Looks like a strong breeze could knock him over. Kind of like you," she says to Courtney.

I swallow a chortle.

Dr. Pollis continues, "He terrified everyone because of his bravado. They all knew what he'd done. But then something happened. He tried to kill himself, and it was clear that he'd erected these high walls to disguise something. Something he was deeply ashamed of."

"What's that?"

"Fear. Crippling fear. He is the most terrified patient— person—I've ever encountered. And a few years ago, the barriers he'd erected around his fear crumbled, and he withdrew. Refused to leave his room for two months, and even when he does now, well . . . It's sad. He's like half a person. Sometimes you get something out of him, sometimes not."

We arrive at a bland building. Stiff grey letters above declare this the Sachar Center. Dr. Pollis checks her phone again and shakes her head, then hands us off to two orderlies at the front door that look like clean-shaven ogres. Key card IDs dangle from necks as thick as oaks.

"Luke, Dennis, take them to Dr. Nancy, would you? I have to run. And when they finish up, you can take them back to Admin to retrieve their badges."

She shakes Courtney's hand first, then mine.

"Best of luck with everything, truly," she says, with an enthusiasm commensurate with her day job. And then she races off, phone in hand.

Dr. Nancy Kramer is significantly more pleasant to speak to than Dr. Pollis. We're in her office, which is like a little bio-dome of pleasantness in what is otherwise, unsurprisingly, a pretty dreary spot. She's cheery; bubbly even. Which is especially impressive considering what her day-to-day here must be like. She's short and a little stocky, dirty blond hair in a ponytail, huge dimples.

She talks about her patients—pedophiles, rapists, cold-blooded killers—like she's their kindergarten teacher. Which is half cute and charming, half superdisturbing.

After Dr. Pollis handed us off, Luke and Dennis led us down a brightly lit narrow corridor, the smell of man lingering faintly beneath enough bleach to make my eyes sting. The hall was lined on both sides with thick blue doors. Men peered at us through their slits of reinforced glass. Some banged on their doors as we passed. Some just glared at us, wide-eyed. One man's pupils were as white as fresh snow, and he was pressed up so close to the window that his eyes were actually flattening against the glass.

Luke and Dennis seemed totally unfazed. Me, I was getting that same sick feeling I'd gotten when my first PI case sent his consciousness bursting out the back of his head, all over cream-colored motel wallpaper. Courtney wasn't digging it either. Tried to stay all business, off-handedly asked the two gorillas which room Silas was in, but they didn't answer. Then up a flight of stairs, through three card-locked doors, and into the employee "lounge" area—though I doubt much lounging truly occurs here. They let us into Dr. Kramer's office and are probably still standing right on the other side of the door with their hands folded across their chests, staring blankly into space.

Now though, I'm starting to feel a little better. I guess that's the idea. Dr. Kramer's got carpeting, for one thing, which makes the whole room feel warmer. A nice, lush forest green. She's got pictures of islands and oceans—landscapes probably being the only thing that won't provoke something fucked up with these guys. We're sitting in plush, plaid lazy-boys, and she sits in her own brown leather chair, not behind her desk like I'd imagined she would but out with us, like we're just having a casual chat.

I recline and let myself relax a little, thinking we're in. Maybe this whole thing won't sour, and in an hour we'll be out of this evil place for good.

I notice she has a goldfish in a bowl resting on her bookcase.

"So, Doctor Kramer, you've been Silas's primary psychiatrist since he checked in five years ago, right?" I say.

"Call me Doctor Nancy," she says. "Everyone does. And yes. I used to see him two or three times a week. But now he hardly leaves his room." She sounds almost nostalgic. "We have to deliver meals to him most of the time."

"What's wrong with him?" I ask, then try to rephrase when Courtney flinches. "I mean, why is he here instead of a normal prison?"

Dr. Nancy nods seriously. Though she's in a standard-issue white smock, you get the feeling that if she had a choice, she'd be wearing a hot pink skirt. And unlike Dr. Pollis, she's wearing a little rouge on her cheeks. But what's the point of looking good when you work in a place like this?

"Paranoid schizophrenic is the official diagnosis. But that's just an overarching label—every person is unique."

Snowflakes and serial killers, am I right?

"But we can't meet him? Face-to-face?" Courtney asks.

Dr. Nancy summons an over-the-top apologetic face. "Unfortunately not. It's a patient's right to refuse visitation. Unless you're accusing *him* of another crime, of course. But it sounds like that's not the case."

Fuck. I fucked up. Probably could have fabricated a story like that. Didn't even think of it. Too late now.

"Alright, so tell us about him," I say.

"Sure!" She smiles. "So he was born somewhere down South—I think Alabama maybe? I'd have to check his folder. He was a very unhappy child. Suffered from some intense learning disabilities, if memory serves. When he was eleven, he killed his parents with a ball-peen hammer and was placed in a foster home somewhere in Maine, about thirty miles from where he'd eventually kill that girl—"

"Thanks, Doctor," I interrupt, "but we already know all this. We have the police report. We're more interested in how he's behaved since he checked in here."

Dr. Nancy blinks.

"His psychological profile," I add, "is our best chance of understanding his copycat."

"Well . . ." She puts a finger on her chin. "When I asked him about it in therapy, he confided that he'd been 'told' to kill them. I asked him if he felt remorse. He said he didn't. That he just did what he'd been told. And then when I pressed him, he admitted that he'd also been told to kill Savannah."

"So he hears voices?" I ask.

"Yes. In fact, though he never really showed remorse for killing his parents, he once broke down here with me. Started sobbing about killing Savannah. Explained that he hadn't had a choice. That he was just doing what he was told. Poor boy. Sometimes I think we're mistreating these men. He's not a bad person, really. He's just lost. He just needs—"

She suddenly catches herself. She was about to say something she didn't want to.

"What does he need?" I ask gently.

She shakes her head, blushing lightly. "Nothing."

Courtney is superfocused. They wouldn't let us bring in recording devices, but I trust his brain as much as any tape recorder. Speaking of—

"Can residents bring personal possessions in with them? Or do they confiscate everything?" I ask.

Dr. Nancy looks confused. "I don't . . . It's not a prison. Most residents are allowed to keep personal belongings in their rooms, assuming we judge them to be conducive to a mentally healthy living environment. And as long as there's no potential to harm, of course."

"Do you happen to know if Silas brought any cassette tapes in with him?" I ask her.

"I have no idea," she says, maybe a little too fast.

Brief awkward silence.

"So he was a real tough guy when he came in, right?" I say. "And then *something* happened, and he tried to kill himself. And now he won't leave his room?"

She purses her lips, like she's considering this for the first time. "Yeah, I guess." She shrugs.

Courtney is growing frustrated and having a hard time hiding it. We simply have to talk to Silas face-to-face to learn anything.

"So it sounded like you were saying that you don't think Silas is actually ill," I say. "Do you think maybe he's lying about hearing voices so he doesn't have to go to maximum security?"

She frowns. A serious mood change just occurred.

"Of course he's ill," she says.

"Dr. Pollis said he hasn't received visitors in a while," I say. "But did he used to? Can you remember anyone coming to visit him?"

"Visitor records would be in his file, but I'm afraid I can't share that with you."

"Can't hurt if you took a look though, right?" I ask, pouring everything I have into a phony grin. "Just to refresh your memory?"

"My memory is just fine," she says curtly. We've pushed a wrong button.

"Seeing that folder would just be so helpful," I say.

"What exactly are you investigating again?" she asks, cocking her head, face suddenly painted with a nasty hyena smile. "Why haven't I heard anything about this before today?"

She stares at us for an uncomfortably long beat, mouth clamped shut, telling me we're not going to get anything else out of her. Dead end. But evidently this isn't yet clear to my companion.

"If we're not going to be able to speak to Silas," Courtney says, leaning so far forward in his chair it looks like he might topple headfirst into the carpet, "then we're going to have to have that file."

"I'm sorry, I can't show that to you," she snaps. "That wouldn't be appropriate."

Her defenses are up. I think I feel the burgeoning beginnings of a headache somewhere in the middle of my brain.

"Neither is fucking your patients," Courtney says, deadpan.

Oh, Jesus. I grip the sides of the lazy-boy. Can't breathe. I stare at Dr. Nancy, still trying to hold it together. Old-man Courtney calm as a Caribbean breeze. Dr. Nancy's hands are shaking. She bites her lip. Nearly bites *through* her lip.

"*Get out,*" she whispers, face going cherry.

Courtney just smiles. "Sorry, is that a sore subject?"

I stare aghast at Courtney. This isn't part of the plan.

She's in a blinding, white-hot rage. Can't even speak, until she manages a shrill stammer:

"*Dennis! Luke!*"

The orderlies burst into the office as soon as they can beep in with their cards, looking a little too excited for my liking. Dr. Nancy can only point a trembling finger at us. I'm thinking they don't give a shit about our badges; they're about to give us the SOP for unruly patients.

"What is it, Doc?" one of the ogres asks.

"Th . . . they . . ."

"They try some funny business with you, Doctor Nancy? Got a little fresh?"

"*Yes,*" she stammers, and it's actually rather convincing, on account of her being in a state of actual shock.

The other ogre grins. "Whaddya think, Doc, Dennis? Should we bring 'em back to Mr. Harrison, file a report? That's a lot of paperwork."

"Obviously there's been some sort of misunderstanding, fellas . . ." I say, my stomach about to bottom out. "You don't want to do anything rash. You don't want any trouble with the Bureau, trust me."

"Actually, Ben," says Courtney to me, but for everyone to hear, "we can't report any of this to HQ. We're not even supposed to be here, remember?"

"Not even supposed to be here?" The second ogre says this as if savoring the taste of it in his mouth.

I swivel to gape at Courtney in disbelief.

What the fuck are you doing?

"Not even supposed to be here . . ." the first ogre echoes, like it's a mantra whose implications become more clear with every repetition. He glares hard at me, like he's wondering which part of me tastes the best. " . . . And Mr. Harrison is a busy man, Luke. I think he'd be pleased if we dealt with this internally. Took a little initiative. That okay, Doc? Want us to deal with these fags ourselves?"

I'm about to point out that were we indeed homosexuals, it seems unlikely that we'd also be trying any "funny business" with Dr. Nancy, when one of them puts me in a headlock. Not sure if it's Dennis or Luke. Not sure if it really matters.

Before I have time to protest, I get a fist to the kidneys. Fire in my chest, can't breathe. Dennis/Luke is grunting something to the effect of, "I'm just getting started, you little homosexual," as he continues pummeling my stomach. Through watering eyes, I see Courtney's not faring much better. So why does it look like that asshole is . . . *smiling*?

We're being dragged out of Dr. Nancy's office in bear hugs that are unnecessarily firm at this point, considering my limbs are sort of moving on their own, spasming like jellyfish tentacles. I try to say something, but it just comes out as an empty gurgle.

I hear the beeps of key cards on doors. We're being dragged down a metal flight of stairs like two sacks of dirty laundry. My forehead clips the corner of the railing, making a ringing sound that I can't tell is inside or outside my skull.

"Guess you two didn't behave yourselves, did you?" my escort guffaws.

"Please. You're making a mistake . . ." I mutter.

This provokes a deep belly laugh I can hear reverberating against my spine.

"If this is wrong, then why does it feel so right?" says Courtney's Ogre.

Mine whispers deep in my ear. "*You* made the mistake fucking with Dr. Nancy. And you fuck with Dr. Nancy, you fuck with me."

They've got a hell of an employee loyalty program here.

"You're in big trouble," I groan halfheartedly.

"Funny," Dennis says. "That's not how it looks from here."

"I wanna talk to Harrison," I grumble, vaguely aware of being carried back past the row of cells. Enthusiastic cheers muffled by thick doors—I must look as bad as I feel.

Beside me I see Courtney hardly struggling. Just staring straight ahead, letting himself be manhandled. No bruises on his face. Smart. No marks.

"I wanna talk to your sup . . . superior," I bluster. Cold air shocks my face once we're out the front doors of Sachar. Then we're being jammed into the back of a golf cart. Our hands are cuffed behind our backs. Dennis and Luke drive up front.

"You don't worry about Harrison," Dennis or Luke says with glee. "We'll let him know that you two got what you needed and politely ducked out."

I command my head to turn slightly, enough to make eye contact with Courtney; convey *what the fuck were you thinking, you fucking piece of shit.* I manage to swivel my stiff neck just enough to witness Courtney swoon and nearly fall out of the cart, saved only by his cuffs.

Guess these goons' job demands a certain dose of healthy sadism. Still, I'm shocked they'd do this to ostensible FBI agents.

Only because Courtney said that to Dr. Nancy! And then that shit about not supposed to be here!

"Court—" I start to mumble.

The golf cart flies over the frozen athletic field; my handcuffed wrists are screaming with every bump. Dennis and Luke wave to some colleagues across the field supervising a group of inmates, who start clapping when they see us in the back of the cart. I suppose this passes for a pretty interesting day around here.

There's a screech of rubber on asphalt as we return to the driveway by the main entrance. My vision is getting blurry, and I think I might puke. Somewhere, distantly, I perceive Dennis and Luke having a talk with Walrus from the security booth.

Here come the dry heaves.

"Courtney," I finally manage to whisper. "I'm gonna fucking kill you. Why would you say all that shit?

"Mmm-hmm," he replies dreamily.

Front gate creaks open. The cart lurches forward and takes this morning's breakfast with it, deposits it squarely on the back of the driver's neck. The cart screams to a halt. I think to myself, as I watch Dennis turn to face me, the realization of what just landed on his neck slowly creeping over his face, that this is unquestionably gonna be the high point of my day.

"*You fucking . . .*"

Rough paws unlock my cuffs. I'm jerked to my feet, and then the world is spinning and black pavement rushes up to meet my face. I taste blood in my mouth and think maybe I just spit out a tooth. Another fist into my ribs.

I've been on the receiving end of so many beat downs, I consider myself something of a connoisseur. And I have to say, I begrudgingly admire these guys' technique.

"We see you fuckers around here again, we strip you ass-naked in the middle of a Sachar cell block and release the animals. You'll be *wishing* for another bashing."

Another kick in the gut for good luck, and they return to their golf cart. I close my eyes and can hear the whirr of its electric engine receding into the distance, along with their whoops of delight.

Lying still, the pain becomes a little more distant. Like, the thing that is hurting no longer seems to be *me*. My body has wisely decided that for the moment, my flesh and whatever constitutes the essence of Frank Lamb are two separate entities.

God. What if Sadie could see me now? The shame would be worse than any sort of pain. This is her daddy's life. His job. Nobody should get the shit kicked out of them after middle school. That's like one of the principles upon which civilization is built. You won't get your ass kicked as a grown adult unless you're asking for it. Today, we were asking for it. Well. Courtney asked for it.

"Fff . . . Frank . . ."

I turn over to face him, and the pain rushes back. This is all his fault. All his goddamn fault. I crawl over to him as quickly as my throbbing limbs will allow me. He's stomach up on the freezing asphalt, staring wide-eyed at the sky, like he's never seen a fucking cloud before.

"You . . . this is all your fault."

I'm nearly on top of him. Raise my right arm as high as I can and try to punch him, but succeed basically in letting my loose fist just slap his thigh.

"I hate you," I say, spitting up blood.

"Frank . . . Stop." Courtney can't even raise his hands to defend himself.

"Fuck. You." I keep half hitting him with limp hands.

"We're . . . we're in the middle of the road. We gotta get off the road," Courtney groans.

Fuck. I hate him most when he's right.

He flops onto his stomach, releasing a guttural expression of pain. And then he's soldier-crawling to the side of the road. To the parking lot where the Honda is. He looks back over his shoulder for me.

"C'mon, Frank," he says. "C'mon."

"Once we're off the road—" I cough. "I'm gonna . . . gonna kill you."

He's into the dirt shoulder long before I am. Better technique: He figured out how to roll like a snail or something. I'm not quite agile enough for that at the moment. It must take me five minutes to collapse alongside him.

"It's too cold out here," I say. "We gotta get into the car."

"Uh-huh."

"And then I'm gonna kill you. Why the fuck would you say that to that doctor? Why would you tell the orderlies we weren't supposed to be there!"

"To get close to them."

Courtney slowly, gingerly, reaches into his torn suit pocket and pulls out a white card dangling by a snapped blue ribbon. I squint.

"Is that an ID card?"

"Yeah. Dennis's. Or Luke's. Whatever."

My brain is having a hard time processing anything right now save the copious amounts of pain emanating from my stomach.

"Why?"

"Because we gotta see Silas," Courtney says. "We're going back inside."

I start to laugh but end up just wheezing. "No . . ." I mutter.

"Yep," Courtney grunts, then he's up on his knees, hauling me up off the frozen earth.

"They're gonna figure out we weren't even FBI agents. You don't think Dr. Nancy is gonna tell Harrison what happened?"

"We're breaking in."

We're both on our wobbly knees now. I stare blankly at him.

"What?"

"And we have to do it soon. That buffoon will report his missing card this afternoon, but it will take at least a few days to issue new cards to the staff and change all the magnetic locks."

I'M CLIMBING DOWN the steep stairs into a cellar, gripping a cold metal pipe overhead for balance. *Hello? Anybody down here?* I wish I had a flashlight. I reach the bottom, and my eyes adjust to the dim light crawling through the windows. A metal table, a wooden chair. It's freezing down here.

And no Savannah this time. Instead her sister, Greta, is sitting in the chair, her form brilliantly alluded to by a dazzling white dress.

Did you find it?

Not yet.

Her green eyes fix on me. She rises from the chair. She's shaped like an hourglass. Her warm, minty breath is on my face, her lips graze my cheek.

I don't care. I can't wait.

Her hand goes under my shirt, initially shocking me with cold—

Courtney smacks my face, and I open my eyes.

"I was worried you'd lost too much blood, but looks like you've got some to spare." He frowns.

I sit up and my body shrieks a protest.

"Where are we?" I groan.

"Motel, about four miles from the center."

"I need coffee," I say.

"You should have water first."

"I. Need. *Coffee*," I growl.

"Suit yourself." Courtney shrugs.

I try to roll out of bed, and everything from my neck to my knees lights up in pain. Courtney rushes to my side to help me.

"How are you in such good shape?" I ask.

"I'm hurting too," he says. "But I was concentrating on relaxing my body as they hit me. Makes a huge difference. You were probably rigid as a board. No shame in that, that's the body's natural reaction."

I'm standing on my wobbly feet. Barely.

"Now you tell me. How long have I been out?"

"About . . ." Courtney checks his watch. "Thirty hours."

"Jesus . . ."

"Yep. What hurts?"

I laugh a little, and my stomach burns.

"Hurts to breathe," I say and wave a hand around my belly. "And all around here."

"Bruised ribs and abdominal muscles, probably," he says. "It'll just hurt to breathe and walk for a week or three. But go pee and make sure there's no blood. Blood means they got you in the kidneys and we'll have to get you to a hospital right away."

"Can you get me some coffee?"

"Want something better than coffee?" he asks.

I raise an eyebrow. "I'm listening."

He leaves me leaning over the nightstand and starts ruffling through his suitcase. My stomach is throbbing slowly, painfully. Zero appetite.

"Think they're looking for us?"

"Maybe, but I'm not particularly worried," Courtney says from across the room. "Harrison called your cell phone, upset. He apologized for his orderlies' bout of pugilism but is also under the impression we made a move on Dr. Nancy. I don't think he suspects the badges and number are fake, thinks we're just perverts. I asked him to email his incident report and assured him we'd have an internal disciplinary hearing. You had still better cancel that number right away though—is it in your name?"

"Yeah."

Courtney breaks from his rummaging to look over his shoulder and deliver a frown of extreme condescension.

"Never get a phone plan under your real name. Cancel it immediately and get a new sim card under a pseudonym."

"Ugh."

"Even if they figure out it's all a sham," Courtney says as he finds what he's looking for and shuts his suitcase, "they'll spend ages tracking that fake license plate. They'll get nothing from those badges, and our disguises were good. Your phone is the only loose end."

Courtney returns to my stooped form, bearing a Mason jar filled with a reddish-brown fluid. Looks like beef broth. In his other hand is a small syringe.

"Bend over the bed," he orders me.

"This doesn't sound better than coffee."

"I promise it is."

I wearily oblige. Courtney yanks down my boxers. I'm thinking, this is rock bottom. Or at least, it better be.

"*Whoa!*" I shriek as he plunges the needle into my left buttocks. Instant energy. Blood rushes to my brain. He's right. Better than coffee. "What the fuck is that?" I say, hastily pulling back my underwear.

"My energy mix," he says, unable to keep the pride out of his voice. "All the B vitamins, plus ginkgo, calcium, potassium and taurine. Delivered instantly to your bloodstream. Nothing better for your immune system."

There's still pain, but I feel a little more empowered to cope with it.

"I think I love vitamins." I grin.

"And *now* you get coffee," Courtney says, tossing the needle in the trash. "Because we have a lot of work to do. And we have to do it fast."

WE'RE SITTING IN the Blue Ribbon Diner, across the street from the motel. In a shopping center between a Laundromat and a CVS. The tabletop between us is a maze of maple syrup stains. The only other patrons in here are a couple of truckers sitting at the bar and a family of four, whom I admire for apparently enjoying their backwoods vacation, which they probably keep telling themselves is *rustic*.

Courtney keeps staring out to the parking lot, as if to make sure our car is still there. It is, with its original plates restored, dull grey exterior the same color as the moody sky.

I pop a few Advil. This is like the mother of all hangovers, even with my vitamin boost.

A wide-hipped woman with red hair up in a bun drops a bucket of coffee in front of me and slams down a sad mug of hot water with a Lipton tea bag for Courtney.

"And what can I get you two gentlemen to eat?" she asks, cheery, unfazed by the cut on my forehead from that stairwell banister and the dark circles under my eyes. Courtney's long face is clear of injuries, but he looks gaunt and pale. The removal of his ponytail and the buzz cut he gave himself in the motel seem to add about five years. He now looks less like a dirty hippie and more like a too-old Brooklyn barista whose heart just isn't in it anymore. He's wearing a checkered flannel and that decaying scarf. Beside him on the table sits his red duck-hunting hat.

"I'll get the Western omelet, plus a side of bacon and a short stack of pancakes," I say.

"Hungry boy." She smiles. "And you, hun?"

"Could I get the Greek salad?" Courtney asks.

The waitress frowns as she records this, like she's unsure if this item is even on the menu.

"Except without cheese, if you don't mind," Courtney adds.

"That it?"

"Yes, thank you."

She sighs. "Gotta eat more than that, sweetie. You're just skin and bones."

"I'll be fine," he says and hands her the menu. She scoots off to the kitchen, probably to ask if the line cooks can scrounge up some lettuce. I take a long sip of coffee.

"So you're proposing we go back to the center in different disguises and break into his cell?"

Courtney shrugs and dunks his tea bag into his steaming mug. "Unless you have a better idea."

"Pretty nuts . . ." I say. "What do you think the odds are that Silas has the tape in his cell?"

"If it exists, that would sure be the logical place for it to be."

I nod slowly and say, "There has to be a tape. There are too many trails leading to it." I stare at the swinging kitchen doors longingly. My stomach is really starting to grumble. "Orange lets us walk out of his den unscathed, only because he thinks we give him a *chance* at a listen. Dr. Nancy totally tightened up when I mentioned it—maybe Silas told her about it in therapy? Greta Kanter is shelling out $350K to have it in her gloved hand . . ." The waitress bursts through the saloon doors, proudly displaying a tray filled with steaming eggs and meats.

"Here's yours," the waitress smiles, unloading the trays in front of me. "And yours, dear. No cheese, like you asked. You want any dressing or anything?"

"I'm fine, thank you," Courtney smiles. "Just some more hot water would be great."

She laughs and moves on to the family.

"Something is weird about Silas too," I hiss. "He kills his parents, and then doesn't kill again for, what, twenty-two years? That's one hell of a hiatus for these voices in his head. I'm thinking maybe there's more victims out there. Maybe even more tapes."

Courtney nods in agreement.

I dig into my omelet and shovel a forkful of ham, egg, Swiss and pepper into my mouth. "Oh Lord. This is the best thing I've ever tasted."

Courtney glares at me.

"Sorry," I say before inhaling a bacon strip. "Does me eating meat offend you?"

"I do find it a little barbaric," he says, toying with his salad, inspecting a rubbery black olive. "But it's your choice. It just confuses me, truthfully. I like you. You're a generally empathetic person, so I don't understand how you can eat another creature with such callous disregard."

"Because they're fucking delicious."

"It's an animal that *feels*," Courtney says. "That was alive. Doesn't that mean anything to you?"

I stop eating and stare at my food, trying to really internalize what Courtney is saying. But I find it nearly impossible to think of my meat as anything but just food.

"Tell you what," I say. "Say we find that tape, and it turns out—I don't know how—but it turns out that we have eternal souls or something. Which means maybe animals do too. If we find that tape in Silas's cell, or wherever, I'll consider becoming a vegetarian."

Courtney puts his fork down and stares at me seriously. "You mean it?"

"Yeah." I crack my knuckles and extend a tender hand. "Shake on it."

"And what if Sadie wants to keep eating meat. Will you let her?"

"We'll cross that bridge when we get to it. At that point we'll probably be vacationing at some remote Italian villa, so that will be a good time for you to bring it up with her."

"Me?" Courtney asks in surprise.

"You're not coming?" I ask in mock seriousness. "C'mon, if we break into that place, get the tape, and Greta pays us what she said she would, or even if she bails and we have to sell it to Orange at a steep discount, the three of us are going to fucking Sicily tomorrow. How does that sound?"

"Fine."

I take a bite of omelet, avoiding any ham on this forkful. That tape could put Sadie through in-state college, or I could open a café to escape from this lifestyle. Just being around people like Orange makes me miserable; reminds me of the depths of depravity to which the human animal can sink. Not to mention, I've taken five serious beatings over the last couple years, including yesterday . . . and I won't be able to keep that up forever.

But there's more. I want to find this thing, listen, and make sure it's bullshit. Because otherwise this little nagging homunculus who came to life sometime this past week—the same voice that's surprising me by taking Courtney's anti-carnivorous criticism to heart—is going to keep wondering if Savannah Kanter really did see something in her final moment on earth. And I'm not sure he'll shut up until he gets an answer, one way or another.

"We can't break into his cell if they know we're there," I say slowly. "Even assuming we could somehow get away from whoever was escorting us, they'd be watching us on camera. Especially now, after 'Ben and Leonard.'"

Courtney listens, rapt. I scratch my chin.

"We'll have to go over the wall," I say.

His eyes go wide and he sits up straight.

"What about the guard towers?"

"We'll go in the morning. There will already be inmates out in the yard for them to keep an eye on, plus hopefully they'll be tired from the night shift. Anyways, they're not worried about people breaking *in*."

Courtney's eyes glow. His thumbs start twitching.

"Over the wall," he repeats breathlessly, unable to contain the excitement in his voice. Bright eyes fixed on me, he raises his mug of steaming tea to his mouth. Recoils the moment the scalding water touches his lips, then nearly drops the mug.

"If we're caught," he says, once he's composed himself, "we'll get much more than a beating."

"True. Though there's not much legal precedent for breaking *into* a loony bin."

Courtney taps his fingers on the tabletop like he's typing up a pros and cons list into an invisible computer.

"You're already thinking too much," I say. "Just gotta do it. Like pulling off a Band-Aid."

I can't tell if I'm trying to convince Courtney or myself.

"So . . . you're in, right?" I ask.

He puts both hands behind his head, leans back and stares at the ceiling of the shabby diner.

"Yes," he sighs. "I suppose I am."

A QUARTER TO seven the next morning, we park the Honda a half mile away from the Berkley Clinic, at the start of a long dirt driveway that leads to what looks like an abandoned farmhouse. Don't think anyone will be disturbing it. Besides, that's truly the least of our concerns.

We're both wearing cheap parkas over our white scrubs and boots for this trudge, with sneakers in our packs to change into for the climb. It's fucking freezing out here; wet, cold wind cutting right to the skin. My long johns—final line of defense—are not equipped to deal with this magnitude of cold, but we wouldn't be able to climb in real coats.

The pale yellow sun seems like he's taunting us, hanging low in the east behind thick fog, like he's still deliberating between showing his face and warming up this barren tundra, or just hitting snooze and pulling the covers over his head for another hour.

I also happen to be terrified, which makes me feel even colder than I am. I've never broken into government property. My joints are still stiff and locked up from the beating. Woke up after a miserable three hours of restless sleep with my jaw sore from grinding my teeth. I'm still taking shallow breaths, because the deep ones hurt my ribs a lot. At least I didn't have any more dreams.

"Seven fifteen we start climbing," Courtney says, mostly to

himself. I feel like I'm gonna throw up every time I think about what we're doing. Just have to keep telling myself that my plan makes sense. And that Courtney wouldn't have agreed if it was boneheaded.

No ski masks. We have to blend in. There are over a hundred orderlies at this place, which hopefully means that nobody will question our presence there. Ideally, this includes Dennis, Luke, Dr. Nancy, Dr. Pollis and Harrison, who saw us in senior citizen gear. I figure we should be in and out in forty-five minutes.

I instruct my feet to keep walking. Don't think, just act.

We arrive at the eastern brick wall—the one closest to Sachar—after a twenty-minute march. The sentry towers are located in each corner of the complex, plus one between each along the four walls, eight in total. We walk until we figure we're three-quarters of the way along the eastern wall: the most distance from guard towers possible.

We move in silence. Courtney unclips his backpack and I do the same. We chuck our hiking boots away and slip on sneakers—what all the orderlies seemed to be wearing. Plus, not bad for running.

Next comes the daisy chain—superthin camping twine that can support like five hundred pounds. Courtney looks around. There are no trees growing close enough to the wall to tie the chain around. That would have made things easier, but he's prepared for this eventuality.

He whips out a minidrill, the kind rock climbers use to secure bolts. My heart tightens as he bores into red brick, the whine of the drill shattering the cold stillness. I imagine the guards suddenly pouring over the walls, a horde of blind rats honing in on the sweet drone.

But then he's done. No guards. I exhale. The only sounds around us are the distant buzzing of cars on the highway, the occasional morning cry of a bird overhead.

I stuff the drill into my backpack, and he hammers a steel bolt into his newly drilled hole, clips on a carabiner, then clips on two lengths of daisy chain.

Looks at me long and hard.

"I'll go first," he says.

"I know. We discussed this."

"Sorry." He bites his lip. "I'm nervous."

"Me too."

Courtney squirms.

"What are we looking at here?" he asks. "Couple months in jail for B and E on federal property?"

"Let's not go there," I say.

He drops the daisy chain and reaches back into his bag. Pulls out two disposable needles and his Mason jar filled with ruddy brown fluid. Fills up the first syringe.

"Forgot to take our vitamins." He smiles. "You first."

I bend over on the wall and wince as Courtney jabs it into my ass.

"Double yesterday's dose," he says as I feel the warmth filling my chest. My bruised ribs and hips seem to be touched with the vitamin's glow. I'm filled with love and confidence. I can do this.

"Now you do me," he says, handing me the second syringe and bending over a little too eagerly. He exposes his pale, rosy, hairless bum to me like a bouquet.

"I really hope we don't die in a few minutes," I say. "Because I'd hate for this to be my last memory."

I shoot vitamins into his boney ass, and Courtney jerks up straight, looking refreshed and flushed.

"Alright!" he says, then clips both daisy chains to his ankle with outrageous enthusiasm and pulls out his suction cups. Two are gloves, two go on your knees. He showed me last night in the motel room: twist right to engage, twist left to disengage. It's not too tough on the hands, but rotating your knees 90 degrees in either direction is pretty fucking hard. Wish Sadie had dragged me to that yoga class a few more times. Courtney breathes in deep, staring intently at the brick wall, psyching himself up. Then he's climbing.

I watch his backside ascend slowly, methodically. Too slow. I shake my leg in agitation.

Left arm up, twist to engage. Right knee, twist to engage. Right hand, twist to engage. Left foot engage, and then disengage the left hand.

His stepwise crawl is distinctly turtlelike, and I can't help thinking how exposed and vulnerable he is up there.

But they can't see us on this side. It's only a fifteen-foot wall, and Courtney is at the top, peering over, in about two minutes.

"So?" I whisper from below. He looks down at me and gives a thumbs-up. Then reaches back into his pack for wire cutters, gets to work cutting a path through the barbed wire.

I dance around nervously like I have to pee, shifting my weight between my two feet. Actually, I *do* have to pee. Really fucking bad, all of a sudden. While Courtney is clipping the wire I pull down the front of my scrubs—no fly—and urinate on the brick wall like a dog. Only as I'm finishing up do I realize that my urine is possibly as incriminating as fingerprints. Guess that will be one for me and Courtney to laugh about in our jail cells.

"Done," Courtney whispers. He tosses the wire cutters down to me, then takes off the four suction cups and throws them down to me as well. I hastily tie on the knees first, then put on the gloves. Courtney gives me a terrified thumbs-up, takes another deep breath, then disappears over the wall. Both lengths of daisy chain go taut, and I try not to imagine him sliding down the other side. Then the chains loosen up. He must have landed. I count to three, waiting for shouting or shooting.

God, I hope they use rubber bullets here.

Nothing.

I unclip one daisy chain from the anchor, clip it into the climbing harness I have on over my smock. Leave the other one attached to shimmy down on the other side.

Close my eyes and take a few fast, deep breaths.

Don't think, Frank. Just fucking do it.

I attack the wall, trying to do just like Courtney did. It should be easier for me, too, since I have him helping me out by pulling from the other side. Gotta hurry. The longer he stands there in the shadow of the wall, the likelier someone is to notice. I'm a scant two feet off the ground and my arms are already on fire. Courtney's jerking me up on the daisy chain like I'm a fish on the line. Five feet up, I try to untwist my left knee and something pops in my hip area. Try to ignore the pain and twist again.

The left knee cup slides off the wall, but so does my right knee; guess I didn't engage it properly. I'm suspended, just hanging by my hands, Courtney tugging urgently on my harness. But I'm not budging.

"Shit, shit," I groan.

I'm breathing hard from exertion, and it hurts like hell. My eyes tear up from the pain in my abdomen and ribs. I simply cannot lift up my left leg to engage again. I'm stuck. Should I just let Courtney go alone?

Not an option. There's no way he can deal with Silas alone. Plus I have the ID card in my backpack. Courtney took the climbing tools, I took the clothes, shoes and any other shit we might need: ceramic knife, notepad, some tools of persuasion, fake ID card for one of us, and the real one he ripped off of Dennis for the other.

Courtney's tugging now seems desperate, like *what's happening over there?* I try again to get my left knee to catch. No dice. I look up. Only like six feet to the top of the wall. Six measly feet. *C'mon, Frankie.*

I slide my feet into a small crevice in the wall between a layer of bricks, disengage my left hand, and reach up as far as I can. Twist back, engage. Right up as far as I can, twist engage. I clench my teeth. I was never good at pull-ups. With every ounce of strength I have, I pull up on my two hands, then instantly slide my feet into another crack, disengage the left, shoot up, engage, disengage the right, shoot up, engage, and then I have my first hand on the top of the wall.

For a second I'm so proud, so ecstatic, that I forget myself. And then I see the guard tower to my right, maybe a hundred meters away. If there's a guard there, he's not out on the balcony looking very closely. Or, I guess, he's looking for people trying to get out, not in. I pull myself up to the top. Not careful enough, though. The suction cup gloves spare my hands from the barbed wire, but the metal tendrils catch my right ankle. It's not deep, but it still hurts like fucking hell. Blood instantly stains the bottom of my white pant leg.

Down at the base of the wall, Courtney is gesticulating wildly. *Come on.*

I unclip the daisy chain that Courtney had been using to assist me and let it drop. Then I grip the one still attached on the outside of the wall and half climb, half slip down as fast as I possibly can.

My butt hits the hard, cold earth at the bottom with a thud. Courtney grabs my elbow and jerks me to my feet. We dash across a stretch of completely exposed yard. I've never felt so vulnerable in my life. No cover, frosty sun, just a seeming eternity of cold, hard grass that Courtney is pulling me across.

Finally we tumble into the shadow of a small shed about twenty yards from the wall. Flatten ourselves against the grey wall. I try to catch my breath but can't, try desperately to gulp down air, but it feels like my lungs can't get full, fingers tingling, like an elephant is standing on my chest.

"Frank," he whispers. "Settle down. You're going to hyperventilate and pass out. It's okay, you hear me? We're in." He puts a hand on my shoulder and taps gently. "That was the hard part. We're in. We're okay."

"Oh my god," I wheeze. "I need to join a gym."

"Concentrate on slowing down your breathing," he says.

He's really gripping my elbow now, looking into my eyes seriously, his long horse-face consuming my entire field of vision.

"You know," I pant, "you really need to pluck your nose hairs."

He shakes his head, rolls his eyes. He takes the suction cup gloves off my hands and unclips the ones around my knees. Then notices my wound, a growing patch of red around my ankle.

"Oh no." He's on his knees, lifting up my scrubs, inspecting the gash caused by the barbed wire.

"I'm fine," I say. "Looks worse than it is."

"We gotta clean this up. People will notice the blood."

"What are we gonna do, launder it?"

Courtney thinks for a moment, then takes a T-shirt out of my pack and ties it around the wound.

"This will at least help it scab and stop you from passing out from blood loss."

He rolls my pant leg back down but stares fixedly at the scarlet splotch, biting his nails. I grab his skinny shoulder and jerk him to his feet.

"Don't think about it," I growl. "Let's just fucking go. In and out. I'm not planning on getting close enough to anyone for them to notice."

Courtney chews on his thumb desperately. Completes a scan of our surroundings like a prairie dog.

"Okay, okay," he concedes. "Let's go. Sachar is right there." He points to the low building we entered two days before to speak to Dr. Nancy. It's about two football-field lengths away. "Then we get to the front gate and just get the hell out of here." He looks at me. "Ready?"

I try to concentrate on my breathing, which has steadied somewhat but is still way too fast.

"If we get caught, I'm gonna try to pin this all on you," I say.

THE PLACE IS dead at this hour. No morning calisthenics or forced marches at dawn. I check my watch: 7:43. Animals still asleep. Guess there's not much reason to get things started early around here. I think about all the psychos still tucked away in their bunk beds. Wonder what they're dreaming about.

We try to stride casually toward Sachar. No question now that the guards in the towers have seen us, but hopefully it's not that unusual for orderlies to be walking the periphery of the property this early in the morning, or for them to be wearing backpacks.

Courtney keeps his hands in his pockets, eyes locked on the

two-story building that houses our man. If I don't say something to shatter the eerie silence, my head is gonna explode. My ankle pulses biting pain. I'm not limping yet because of adrenaline, but each step sends a twinge of sharp discomfort shooting up my leg.

"I wonder if there's a better way, Frank," he whispers. "Maybe we should wait until lunchtime or something when there's more going on to distract everyone."

"No," I say. "We're not changing the plan now. Can't second-guess ourselves. We're here. We're doing this. The longer we stay here, the worse our chances."

We won't have to get through any chain-link fences to get to the front entrance to Sachar, because the fenced-in pen built to contain the tier-three nut jobs during recess is attached to the rear of the building. We walk past the empty cage.

I imagine what the pen must look like around lunchtime, filled with milling psychos. Not much to do in there—a lone, netless basketball hoop, what looks like a rusty bench press, four wooden lunch tables. The ground is hard black pavement with sharp green weeds sprouting out of the cracks. If Silas wasn't nuts when he checked in, he's probably there by now.

We go around the beige, stucco exterior of Sachar. Looks so innocuous from the outside. Could easily be a shitty public library or insurance office. Across endless acres of flat, tired grass rises the old factory, which now houses the Category One dormitory. I can also make out the admissions center, where Harrison works, and what I think is the front gate. Without a golf cart, it's a pretty long walk. Especially with a bleeding ankle.

Front doors of Sachar. Unquestionably cameras on us now.

As if reading my mind, Courtney mutters, "Just relax, Frank.

With a little luck, they'll never even have reason to review any footage."

I grip the ID card around my neck. There's the little magnetized black square to the left of the reinforced glass doors. I bend over and extend the card like I saw Dennis and Luke do for each of the doors inside. Moment of truth. When it beeps and I hear the lock click, my breathing speeds up again. We're going for it.

I exchange a look with Courtney as I pull open the heavy door and step inside, adrenaline firing like a drum circle in my brain. Court's mouth is closed; he's breathing loudly through his thin nose.

We're in the same bland, green-tiled entranceway we stood in a few days ago, but it feels distinctly different this time. I'm more cognizant of how many murderers and rapists we're sharing this building with.

Courtney points his long chin, *this way.*

Down a silent corridor illuminated by caged-in fluorescent tube lights, past those dozens of blue doors.

They can't hurt you through those doors, Frank.

Turn a corner. Another identical hall with more identical fluorescent lights and identical blue metal doors. Pain and fear seem to be heightening my senses, making time move slowly and each square inch of linoleum appear in high-res.

"You remember how to get upstairs?" I whisper.

Courtney doesn't respond, just plows ahead with the purpose of a man possessed. I try to keep up with him. Try to ignore the pain in my ankle and the pulsing fire in my stomach. Turn another corner that I don't remember from last time. Think about my ceramic knife in my backpack, think about how quickly I could have it out if one of these—

I jump out of my skin as a sudden pounding from one of the doors snaps the quiet. It's the same guy from a few days ago, face smushed against the window of his cell, white of his eye as big as a silver dollar and flat against the glass, throbbing red veins, staring at me.

Courtney snatches my elbow and jerks me along.

"We don't know how much time we have," he whispers. "My guess is staff shows up at nine, but who knows."

Half tripping over each other, we jog down the hallway. I'm keeping my eyes straight ahead, ignoring looks or sounds coming from the cells. Ignoring the fragrance of the distinctly institutional cocktail of high-potency cleaning products, very nearly disguising the smells of bodily fluids, rotting food, and man—which will never leave these hallways no matter how long you scrub.

I'm leaving a faint stream of blood; a drop every couple feet, like I've got a light bloody nose I'm not bothering to tend to. Make the mistake of glancing over my shoulder to see the shimmering trail of dried blood leading down the hallway and around the corner, a breadcrumb trail in case we need to retrace our steps.

I rip the ID card off my necklace as we approach the door at the end of the hallway. Clicks open, and we're climbing a metal staircase. I'm pretty sure it's the same one Dennis and Luke carried us down, but in truth it's really only notable for its complete lack of distinguishing characteristics.

Clank up the stairs, trying to keep close to Courtney. And at the top, I buzz us through another door. This feels half familiar, like I've only seen this place in bad dreams. We're into the top level.

"This is right." Courtney pauses to catch his breath, bends over and rests his hands on his knees. "Employee lounge area."

No windows. Beige wall-to-wall carpeting and a collection of heavy blue metal doors, differing from their counterparts down-stairs only by their lack of reinforced glass slits.

I'm moving from door to door, looking for Dr. Nancy's office. Courtney finds it before me and calls out softly. I limp over, leaving a thin blood trail on the carpet, holding the ID card out in front of me like a torch, warding off the evil darkness that's palpable in this place, even so early in the morning.

Courtney holds up a finger to me: *wait*. He raps gently against the door. My heart jumps to my throat. Didn't even consider that she might be in there. He raps again. Nothing. Now he gestures to the black square. I click my card against it and wait for the beep that never comes. The little light turns red instead of green. I try again. Same fucking deal.

"Shit," I whisper.

Courtney's eyes are wide, unblinking, staring in disbelief at the mocking red light.

"Let's just go for Silas," I say.

"We really need that file," Courtney whispers. "Five years of observation. Could be invaluable. What if he mentioned the tape?"

I close my eyes hard, not even sure what I want anymore. No, I know what I want. I want to be with Sadie. That's making this job even harder than it has to be; not being able to unwind with her at night, recover partially from the day stomping on me, grinding me down like a cockroach under its heel.

When I open my eyes, Courtney is kneeling to inspect the lock. This isn't like the cell doors, which only open via key card. This one also has a metal handle and a spot for a real key.

"It's just a big old dead bolt. I can open this."

I kneel beside him. He hands me a penlight from his bag. I squint into the keyhole. It's big, but simple. Standard issue.

"Go for it, boss."

Courtney slaps on a stethoscope and carefully chooses three picks the size of needles from his red bag. He places the chest piece just below the knob, like he's listening for the door's arrhythmia. Inserts the first needle carefully into the keyhole, eyes closed in intense concentration, fingers moving with surgical precision.

I sit down on the carpet and look at my ankle wrapped in a bloody T-shirt. It's not really bleeding anymore, but I'm going to need to sterilize the hell out of this thing as soon as possible. I roll the leg of my scrubs back down so I don't have to look at my wound. Grit my teeth as I watch Courtney, thinking that if I hadn't asked him to help on this case, I probably would have never gotten near this place. Probably would have packed it in after the cabin. Probably would be back taking pictures of adulterers by now. Definitely wouldn't have gotten the shit kicked out of me or gotten my ankle gashed by rusty barbed wire.

It could all be for naught, but that's not what my gut is telling me anymore. There's something Greta isn't telling us, some further reason she's so sure this thing exists. Otherwise why would she risk throwing away fifteen grand in up front and expenses?

Courtney takes off his stethoscope.

"Frank," he whispers. "This is gonna take me a while."

"How long?"

"Twenty, twenty-five minutes. There's a magnetic tumbler I didn't notice. Very tricky."

I bite my lip. "We can't wait that long."

Courtney's eyes are like a raccoon's caught rummaging through the trash. "We gotta have those files," he says.

I breathe in deep. Stare at the door.

"I can get in," I say. "But they'll know we were here."

The terror of indecision flashes on Courtney's face. He reflexively moves his hand to tug on the billy-goat chin hairs he had to shave off for our disguises. Then he says, "Do it."

I pull myself to my feet and open Courtney's bag. Remove the minidrill he used on the brick wall, his hammer, and my ceramic knife. From my bag I take my propylene hand torch. Perhaps my favorite tool. It gets so hot that it could probably just cut through the door alone, but the smoke would set off the fire alarm.

Courtney grimaces at my crude instruments.

"Two minutes," I promise.

First I turn the torch on the keyhole, hold it for forty-five seconds until the metal starts glowing orange. Drop the torch and drill the lock while it's still soft from the heat, savoring the satisfying feel of the hammers being mangled. Courtney winces from the high-pitched whine the drill emits, but it's over quickly. Then I stick my knife in what's left of the keyhole and bash the hilt with the hammer. Once it's in I jiggle it until the door glides open.

The keyhole is totally mangled; they'll definitely review video footage now. But we'll worry about that later.

I follow Courtney into the office. I check my watch: 8:02.

In an instant, Courtney is at Dr. Nancy's file cabinet, furiously combing through paperwork. Psychiatrists and PIs, in my experience, seem to be the two types of professionals who resist technology the most adamantly, hold out the longest. Is it because we prefer the personal scrape of pen on paper, of seeing our notes in our own handwriting? Or because we've seen so much humanity in our work that we've become skeptical and paranoid, unwilling to share our thoughts even with a machine?

I stare at Dr. Nancy's pictures of landscapes. Today, rather than calming me, they serve only to remind me of how many other places I'd prefer to be at this exact moment. Between the pain and maybe getting a little light-headed from blood loss, I start losing myself in a portrait of a tropical beach: electric-blue water licking white sand, palm trees arching in the distance.

"Got it," Courtney declares, frowning, and slams Silas's folder down on Dr. Nancy's desk. I turn to watch him pull a spy camera from his red bag and—in a well-rehearsed motion—flip from page to page, photographing each one in half a second without even looking through the lens. Dr. Nancy's handwriting is messy. That's going to be a pain in the ass. When he gets through all hundred-odd pages, he flips back to the front. Beckons me over.

There's what looks like a typed patient dossier tucked in the front of the folder. Birthdate, weight, height. A black-and-white mug shot of a man I vaguely recognize from the video Courtney showed me. Courtney's index finger settles under a paper-clipped half page that seems to be a kind of summary.

Updated 4/11/12
Steady symptoms of manic depression; delusional and paranoid
schizophrenia, symptoms manifest more severely and frequently
when in company of other patients. Recommend continued
exemption from group activities, including recess and group
meals; meals to be delivered to cell. Additional one-on-one
session per week recommended, to replace group session. Current
medications: 1500 mg Lithium Carbonate, 20 mg Haldol daily—

Courtney's dirty fingernail stops dead:

Recommend continued residency in Western Sachar wing, for
increased quiet, isolation, and sunlight.

"Western wing," he muses, looking at me with his slightly inset green-grey eyes. He licks his dry lips. "That can't be where we were before. Those halls ran along the east and north sides of the building, I think."

He shoves all the papers back in the folder and crams it back into its place in the filing cabinet. We're out of Dr. Nancy's office, back in the hallway of the employee lounge area, and I close the door behind us.

"Which way is west?" he whispers to himself.

I duck back into Dr. Nancy's office to check the direction of the sun, emerge and lead Courtney to a door across from where we entered via the metal staircase.

Courtney raises an eyebrow.

"You sure?" he asks warily.

"Sun rises in the east, right?"

Courtney scrunches his forehead.

"I can never remember," he says.

"I'm like eighty-five percent."

I beep my key card on the western door, and my heart sinks with dread as it clicks open. We enter another stairwell that looks exactly the same as the one across the hall. At the bottom of the single flight of stairs though is a sign that reads *Western Wing*. I click my card, and we enter.

The Western Wing could be described, very roughly, as the penthouse suites of Sachar. There's no hallway. Just a central, circular room the size of my apartment. There's no second floor built over this wing, as evidenced by a circular skylight, which is truly a huge upgrade over the flickering fluorescents of the other halls. Brown-stained linoleum floor.

Six blue doors: the one we entered through and five cells. I check my watch: 8:12. The chamber glows purple under the light of the late January morning that's creeping in through the skylight. Courtney and I move wordlessly around the circular chamber, from one door to the next, peering through the reinforced glass slits, looking for our man. These rooms all have small windows looking out onto the Sachar fields. The view of brick, grass, and chain-link fencing isn't much, but I imagine it makes a huge difference in mental health to wake up with the sun.

Because of the windows, there's enough light to see them in their beds. They're all still sleeping. Two have blond hair; can't be him. One is way too fat. That leaves two, one of whom is black. The other has the sheet pulled over his head, so we can't see his face, but it's gotta be him. I pull the ID card out of my pocket and press it against the black square. Green light and click.

Courtney and I look at each other for a long moment. His high forehead is creased, and he's frowning in nervous anticipation.

"You go first," he says. I notice that his hands are trembling.

I swallow and nod, pushing the door open gently. The figure under the sheets doesn't move.

I peer in cautiously. The room is about ten or eleven feet square. Contents are limited to the knee-high cot on which he's sleeping, a wooden footlocker, a metal chair that's bolted to the metal floor, and a little stainless-steel protrusion from the wall, which it takes me a moment to identify as a toilet. A few of the other inmates had posters or magazine clippings taped to the wall. Silas has nothing.

Through the window by the head of the bed I can see an empty basketball court beneath a grey sky. I flick on the lone switch beside the doorway, and my eyes adjust to the harsh light provided by the bulb hanging from the ceiling, protected by a mesh cage that presumably prevents patients from smashing it and using the glass as a weapon.

Courtney cautiously enters behind me and sets his pack down to keep the door propped open. We both stare at the lump hidden by the cot's thin green sheet. No snoring. No breathing. Courtney points to me: *This is all you.*

"Silas," I say softly.

Immediately the sheet flies off, and my chest constricts. Staring up at us from the cot is something barely recognizable as human; an emaciated face with sunken cheekbones sits upon a withering skeleton shrouded in hospital whites. The only relation this pitiful specimen bears to the newspaper clippings in Greta's folder and the cell-phone video is the tattoos.

I can't stop staring at them.

They're much brighter and more intricate than I'd imagined; wild swirls of deep reds, royal purples and stretches of black as dark as coal cover every surface of his face and bare scalp. Most of them are faces, I realize. Faces etched into skin. Though most prominent is a tattoo wrapped around the circumference of his bare head. A dark black, sinewy line. Two snakes, one eating the other's tail in the center of his forehead. Or is it one snake that wraps all the way around and is consuming itself?

Silas's little black eyes are fixed on Courtney and me. His body is rigid, like a rat frozen by a streetlight. I take a step toward him, and he just keeps staring at us, his face stone, impossible to decipher. I sit down on top of the footlocker and gesture to Courtney to sit in the lone chair behind me.

It's hard to picture this scrawny creature in the cabin basement wrapping a plastic bag around Savannah Kanter's head. He still hasn't budged.

I lean in and say again, "Silas—"

He jerks away from me, pins himself against the wall and bares his teeth, breathing hard. His fingernails are long and yellow, his teeth brown and dry. His eyes are tiny holes, sunken craters in the colorful maze painted on his face.

"Who are you?" he rasps. His voice is dry and hoarse.

"Doesn't matter," I say.

"Who sent you?" he croaks, his lips quivering.

"We don't want to hurt you," I assure him, but this appears to provide him little comfort.

"Demons," he whispers to himself and brings his left hand to his mouth to chew on the tips of his fingernails. His hands are red and peeling from eczema.

Courtney and I exchange a quick look.

"Silas," I try again. "We need your help. We're looking for something."

"Who sent you?" he asks again. "Who sent you?"

"We're looking for a tape," I say.

His eyes widen in fear, and he appears to stop breathing for a moment.

"I don't have it!" he finally whispers. "I told you I don't have it! Leave me, demons. Leave me be!"

Then he drops back into a fetal position on his cot, throws the green sheet over his head. Cries over and over, "Leave me be!"

I look over my shoulder at Courtney, who still appears to be shocked by Silas's appearance.

Turning back to the lump on the bed, I wring my hands. It's clear I won't be able to beat anything out of this specimen. He's too far gone, wires completely fried. No way I'll be able to frighten him as much as whatever's inside his head. Similarly, logical reasoning is probably off the table. And interrogation without using fear or reasoning is like golfing without arms. How do I approach this?

I stare at his form whimpering beneath his sheet.

Courtney taps me on the knee, his eyes wide.

"Frank," he whispers and connotes urgency with his hands: *we can't stay for long.* Then he points to the bag and pantomimes a stabbing motion: *maybe threaten him with the knife?*

I shake my head at Courtney: *no.*

Courtney points at him and makes a choking motion. *It's okay to hurt him. He strangled a girl.*

I shake my head again, more adamantly. The figure continues to writhe and moan beneath the green sheet. I exhale deeply, a possible approach for dealing with this creature starting to come to me. One thing we definitely know about him: He had issues with Mommy and Daddy, enough to bash their heads in.

I stand up and rip the sheet off of him. "We don't have time for this, Silas," I say sternly, in the same voice I use to force Sadie to stop watching TV and do her homework. "Silas!" I repeat. He shrivels beneath me like a bug, looking up at me through glassy black eyes. "I don't have time for these games. Please tell me where the tape is before I really lose my temper."

He wheezes like he's having a panic attack, then startles me by suddenly sitting up straight and jabbing a finger at my nose.

"I'll never say a word," he spits with a phlegmy laugh. "Do what you want to me, but you'll never find it. Never."

Disgusted by his rancid scent—like rotting onions and moldy fruit—I put a gentle hand on his shoulder to try to put him at ease, but he recoils, tries to push me away. I'm shocked by how weak he is despite his height. He flails, trying to get away from me, backing into the corner and shrieking. "You'll never find it! You can kill me, you'll never find it!"

Courtney's looking on, scratching his cheeks. We lock eyes and I say, "Court. Could you check out that footlocker?"

Courtney gets out of his chair, bends over Silas's unlocked trunk—the only place he could possibly hide anything in this room. But when Silas hears it click open, he suddenly leaps from the bed and lunges at Courtney with astounding speed, teeth bared, hands outstretched like claws. Before he can touch Courtney though I have his collar in a firm hold. The withered man twists and turns wildly in my grip, like a fish on a line, trying to keep Courtney from his secrets.

I try to breathe through my mouth; his smell is absolutely devastating. The back of his bald head is right in front of my face. It's covered in colorful faces; most appear to be moaning or crying out. And from this angle I can confirm that the black snake wraps its way all around his head before meeting to eat its own tail on his forehead.

"Those are my things!" he cries as Courtney flips open the top. "My private things!"

I glance out in the hallway, hoping this isn't waking up any of the other Western Wing inmates.

"Have something interesting in there, Silas?" I say in his ear.

He shrieks as Courtney dumps the crate upside down and sifts through its contents. It is filled with paper.

"No tape," Courtney says, on his knees, combing through papers.

"Stop! Stop!" Silas sobs, hardly even struggling anymore.

"What are they?" I ask Courtney, dodging one of Silas's pointy elbows.

"Letters, I think," he says, sorting through the torn envelopes and Hallmark cards on the cold floor.

Silas whimpers like a puppy. If he hadn't killed a girl a few years ago, I might even be moved to pity.

"Nothing but letters," Courtney says, standing up and kicking a few in frustration.

"Letters from who?" I ask as Silas's energy wanes and his unwashed body goes progressively limp in my arms. Courtney picks one up at random and reads it out loud:

"'My love, last night I dreamed you were here. We walked around a lake poured by moonlight'—that doesn't even make sense—'and you held my hand. When I awoke I touched myself thinking of you, as you asked. I will wait forever for you.'" He throws the letter down in disgust and picks up another one.

"Same nonsense," Courtney mutters.

Courtney turns to Silas, still restrained by me.

"Who sent these?" he asks.

Silas perks up his head. "Women," he hisses to Courtney. "Hundreds, thousands of them. They want to *fuck* me."

I crinkle my nose.

"Trust me, nobody wants to fuck you," I say, then toss him back onto his thin mattress, mostly because I can't bear to smell the back of his bald head for another second. I sit down beside him and lean in close enough that I can make out the individual needle pricks of color on his face. Startling craftsmanship, I can't help but notice. And the exact same designs I saw on the full glossies of Savannah's corpse.

"Silas," I say, "we are in a *very* big hurry and are becoming *very* disappointed that you don't want to help us. Could you please tell us where the tape is? And then we'll be right on our way."

He stares at me defiantly. It takes all the willpower I have not to hit him, but I know it would do nothing but send him into convulsions of self-pity.

"Where's the tape?" I ask again, looking straight into the black pits of his eyes. His face shares the same expression as many of the tattoos adorning it: wide mouth, high eyebrows; somewhere between unbridled terror and utter confusion.

"Where's the tape?" I ask again, gripping his emaciated shoulders firmly, ignoring the nauseous smell of his rotting breath. "Tell us and we'll go, Silas. Is it still at the cabin? Did you bury it somewhere? Did you destroy it? Did you give it to Dr. Nancy?"

He's blubbering a bit, choking sobs.

"Kill me," he cries. "Kill me."

"What's on the tape? What does it say?"

I fixate briefly on a yellow, quarter-sized tattoo of a face that rests on his chin. As Silas's face contorts, the miniature one runs a gambit of emotions as its mouth, cheeks and eyes stretch in different directions.

"I don't know where it is," he heaves.

"What do you mean, you don't know? Don't lie to me, Silas," I say sternly. I see Courtney out the corner of my eye fidgeting helplessly.

"I don't know, I swear!" he pleads.

"Why did you tattoo her, Silas?" I say.

He smiles weakly through his tears.

"They told me to do it. So they wouldn't recognize her," he says with a weird hint of pride.

"Who?"

"The angels."

I grip his shoulders even harder. My rising blood pressure

is causing the wound in my ankle to pulse with pain, and each breath makes my chest feel like it's going to burst.

"Where's the fucking tape!" I shout.

He grins. "You think you frighten me? Nothing in this world can frighten me anymore."

I smack him across the cheek. Not particularly hard, but still I immediately curse myself for losing control. I exhale hard and wait for him to just withdraw into sobs, but instead the fact that I've resorted to physical violence seems to empower him.

"You're only hurting my body, demon," he cackles. "I don't care about this sack of skin anymore. Do what you want to it."

"Where is it?" I demand, heart pounding in my ears.

"You're fools. Both of you," he gasps. "Leave the tape. It will only lead to madness. It's cursed."

"What do you mean?" Courtney butts in as he sticks his head over my shoulder. "What do you mean it's cursed?"

"It can never be unheard," he wheezes.

"Then what does it *say*?" I ask.

"I don't know . . ." He suddenly breaks down into sobs again, tries to squirm out of my grasp. "Demons! Leave me, leave me be!"

He's limp as a rag doll in my hands, just sputtering. I try to picture this pathetic man murdering Savannah Kanter, pulling the bag tight over her head until she stops moving.

"Frank," Courtney whispers in my ear. "They're up." He's pointing outside the open cell door. Indeed, behind the other cells that I can see from this angle, the other Western Wing psychos are awake and pounding against the insides of their cells. They're making a lot of noise. Fuck.

I turn back to Silas, take a deep breath to try to compose myself, get in character. "Silas," I say seriously, but he's doubled over on the bed, body flabby, crying to himself, hardly listening. "Don't you see how upset I am? How upset your dishonesty is making *you*? Think about how proud I'll be—and how happy you'll be—when you tell me what I want to know."

"I'm . . . ready, demon," he says, then unfolds his form and lies stomach up on his cot like he's surrendering. "I knew you'd come. Take me."

I stand up at Courtney and shake my head somberly. Behind him, the rising din of rapists and killers as they pound on their cell doors.

"No chance."

Courtney looks down at Silas, thinking, I'm sure, that if we walk out of here without any new info, we're pretty much sunk. "We have to try—"

"Try what?" I say. "Squeezing it out through his ears? It's not like he's even resisting me. He's just totally fried."

On cue, Silas stirs, half here, half somewhere else. Sobbing gently, "I'm ready, demons . . ."

"Courtney"—I put a hand on his shoulder—"we gotta make sure we get out of here. I have a kid."

Courtney takes a second, then nods. "Yeah," he says, then is on his knees shoving the letters back into the footlocker. "Just let me straighten up. Don't want to give them any reason to review security tape of this area too."

I realize my ankle is bleeding again, the stain in my scrubs spreading like a low, dark cloud. There are a few bloodstains on the floor, and Courtney is wiping them up with the sleeve of his white smock.

Silas is lying faceup with his hands across his chest like a corpse. He's totally settled down, almost like he's fallen back asleep.

I limp back into the circular chamber. The other inmates' shrieking and banging is rising in intensity, echoing around the circular room like we're the middle of some primitive ritual. All this risk, and all we're walking away with is a medical folder.

I suddenly want to rush back in there and smack Silas, send his gangly body sprawling to the floor. Punish him for not talking. It's not fair, that these secrets are gone forever, buried in his vault of insanity, and there's no key on earth that will make him focus enough to release them. Instead I close my eyes and breathe. Try to think about Sadie, think about walking her to school, holding her hand. Think about Sadie reading a book or how happy the Bronx Zoo makes her.

My pulse settles ever so slightly. I hear the door to Silas's cell slam closed and then Courtney is beside me. He looks into my eyes. Why is he smirking?

"What?" I say over the banging, though the inmates seem to be tiring themselves out. "C'mon, let's get out of here."

I start toward the door that will take us back up to the employee lounge, then down to the hallway that will lead us out of here. But Courtney grabs my shoulder and turns me back around. He's holding one of the torn envelopes from Silas's footlocker.

"Patience," he says theatrically, shaking the envelope as if this paper itself embodies this virtue. "Can't overlook patience and attention to detail."

"What?" I say, glancing down at it. "Half an empty envelope from some stripper named Candy. Great."

"Where did she live, Frank?" Courtney asks, grinning.

I force my eyes to focus on the return address.

"Beulah," I read. "Beulah, Colorado."

PART THREE:

Fast Forward

MY BARE FEET are so cold. I carefully grope down the staircase in the darkness, until reaching the dirt floor. A chilly wind, like the cold breath of God.

A metal table on which lies cold metal tools. Needles. A few Sony cassette tapes, still in their individual plastic wrapping.

I sense something behind me. Swivel around, and there's Savannah, sitting in a low wooden chair, her legs tied together and anchored to something in the damp earth.

"Savannah," I whisper and step toward her.

She stares at me, face frozen in fear. Opens her mouth and warbles something I can't understand.

"I can't understand you," I say delicately. "I'm sorry."

Tears of frustration run down her soft cheeks. I'm at her side, hand on her shoulder to comfort her. She tries again, pleading with me, and I can only hug her. Feel her freezing tears against my cheek.

"I'm sorry, I don't understand," I murmur.

She suddenly shoves me away and tries more adamantly to make herself understood, gesturing wildly from her seat, pointing at me and shouting, her strange cries echoing in this low space.

"Are you trying to tell me where the tape is?" I ask helplessly.

She shakes her head furiously: *no*. Points at her face, which is not yet tattooed, as I've come to think of her thanks to the pictures in the folder, laid out on the slab.

"Your tattoos went away?" I try. "That's what you want to tell me?"

Shakes her head. Crying in reverse now, droplets flying up from the dirt and lodging themselves in her watery eyes.

A frigid wind whips through the cellar, prickling the hairs on my neck. For an instant, it picks up Savannah's long blond hair and carries it into a glowing yellow crown. I suddenly understand.

"Have I made a mistake?" I ask.

Her face tightens and she nods, *yes.*

"I've made a big mistake, haven't I?"

Her eyes start welling again, filling with cold tears, as she nods again.

"What is it?" I say. "*Tell me.*"

She opens her mouth and a stream of senseless, *screaming* syllables tumbles out, a river bursting through her lips.

But suddenly it's not Savannah sitting in the chair. It's her sister, Greta. Sharp eyes the color of bitter melon, tender, wet lips. She stands up, unencumbered by the chains that bound her sister to the dirt floor. She approaches me, breathing deeply, leans into me and lets her body snake around mine. Her hand finds the small of my back, her breasts push up against my chest. As her thigh starts grinding into my crotch, she whispers in my ear:

"Find it, and you will have me."

COURTNEY GRABS MY arm and shakes. It takes me a second to internalize my surroundings. Airplane. Strapped into an economy-class seat between Courtney and a septuagenarian nun. Cold, recycled air blasts my face from a nozzle in the ceiling. I've been sleeping on the shoulder of Courtney's raggedy shearling coat, and now my face smells like mothballs and his weird all-natural lavender deodorant. I rub some sleep out of my eyes.

"Frank," he says urgently, "we're landing in twenty minutes."

I glare at him. "Then why the fuck did you wake me up?"

It's been three days since Sachar. Escaping was as easy as flashing our ID cards to the guy at the front gate and showing him my ankle wound, explaining urgently that one of the prisoners got at me with a rake. Security guard was too baffled, too worried about fucking up, to ask any more questions. Just opened the gate, and we were out.

They'll probably review the security footage that shows us breaking into Dr. Nancy's office and Silas's cell. But even if they do, chance of them IDing us based on that footage is approximately nil. First, they'll assume it was one of their own and work through all hundred actual orderlies to see if any fit the grainy video. But even on the off chance they spot us shimmying down the wall on closed circuit, what are they gonna do? Once they do a prisoner count and nobody is missing, and they find there's no property damage save a ruined keyhole, hopefully it won't even be worth their time to follow up.

I feel my ankle. Nicely cleaned and bandaged. Courtney gave me a hydrogen peroxide bath back in the motel that stung with the fury of a thousand raging suns, but now the pain isn't too bad. My ribs are still hurting, but there's nothing to do about that but wait for them to heal.

I called Sadie from the motel bed as the peroxide worked its bubbly magic on my ankle wound, Nick at Nite on mute on the twenty-year-old motel TV.

And then I collapsed and slept for days while Courtney booked tickets to Denver International and delved into Silas's psychiatric file, plus anything he could find about the Beulah Twelve.

The old nun in the airplane seat on my right is staring at me. Her face is like a rotting peach, wrinkled and pink beneath her wimple. She's not mad. Her expression is closer to pity. Why?

"I apologize for my friend's coarse language," Courtney says.

Oh.

"Sorry," I mutter.

Slowly, her face melts into a smile. She leans in a little. Her voice is brittle and croaky.

"If that's the worst thing you do today, you're doing alright." She laughs a little.

I force a smile, thinking that's the end of our exchange. But then something occurs to me, and I turn back to her.

"May I ask you something, Sister?" I say. "About your faith?"

She shrugs. "Alright."

Courtney looks aghast, already starting to apologize to the nun for what he assumes will be something brusque and offensive. I lean forward in my seat to kind of box him out.

"You're Catholic, right?"

She glances down and inspects her outfit, then looks back up and nods. "Looks like it."

I smirk. Old bird has a sense of humor. Good thing she's saving herself for Jesus; they're gonna have a hoot together.

"What do you believe happens when we die?"

She looks momentarily taken aback.

"Sister, I'm so sorry—" Courtney starts in. I smack him softly on the thigh.

"That's quite alright," she responds, then looks me square in the eyes. "When we pass, the soul departs our body. The body remains behind, and having served its function, it withers away and is reclaimed by the earth. The soul, however, ascends and is judged by the Lord. It is then sent to either eternal damnation or eternal salvation. There is also a third option, for those who may not deserve eternal damnation but still have some marks on their record"—she smiles ever so slightly, as if to imply that I probably fall into this category—"and that's what we call purgatory. A temporary punishment that cleanses you of your sins, after which you are admitted to heaven." She eyes me suspiciously. "But it's never too late for anyone. You can always repent and confess."

I chortle. "You misunderstand. I'm not asking for myself . . ."

"Of course," she smiles knowingly.

Courtney chimes in over my shoulder. "We're very sorry to have bothered you, Sister—"

"It's fine," she says to him, then turns back to me. "What else did you want to ask me?"

The pilot interrupts over the PA with the usual spiel: *"We'll be landing in fifteen, might be bumpy because of light snow. Seats and tray tables upright and locked. Thanks for flying American."*

The whole time the nun keeps her kind eyes on me. Makes me a little uncomfortable, honestly. Nobody should be this patient. When the pilot finishes up, I ask:

"So how sure are you about all that?"

She frowns. "I'm not sure I follow."

"I mean, you just said all that like it was fact. But obviously you can't *know* these things. You just believe them. Feel very strongly about them being the truth. Admittedly, strong enough to live your life according to those beliefs. But still. Surely you must have . . . doubts?"

The nun nods slowly. "Of course. Everyone has doubts, I think. And anyone who denies that is probably not being honest with either you or herself. But that's the nature of this world. If we *knew*, and didn't have to *believe*, then it would all be easy. Everyone would follow the word of God. There would be no choice. No free will."

My stomach drops as we begin our initial descent into Denver International. The captain wasn't messing around. This is getting seriously bumpy.

"What would it take for you to know?" I ask, clinging to the arms of my seat like I'm on a bucking bronco. "Imagine for whatever reason, God wanted to prove his existence to you. What would it take, you think?"

"It's happened before," she responds thoughtfully, seemingly unaffected by the increasing turbulence. Unlike Courtney, who's going a little green and has beads of cold sweat forming on his forehead. "That's what prophets are. The Lord reveals himself to a select few via prophecy. Usually in the form of very vivid dreams."

"*Ladies and Gentlemen, I apologize for the turbulence. We're just getting some strong headwinds here. Please keep your seat belts fastened. We should be on the ground shortly.*"

I try to ignore something bad happening in my stomach.

"Are there prophets today, you think?"

She shakes her head. "No. Not anymore."

"What if someone claimed he was a prophet today? And that he had all the answers, straight from the source? Would you just think he was crazy?"

She mulls this over as the plane finally shudders to the ground, the passengers releasing a collective sigh of relief.

"I'd like to think I'd keep an open mind." She smiles as we shuttle to the gate. "But yes, I'd probably just write him off as crazy, to be honest."

I nod, satisfied. "So, to sum up: If you *believe*, you're a good person. And the more you believe, the better you are. Until you *know*, and then you're a psycho."

"I've never thought of it that way," she admits. "That's certainly an oversimplification, but I can't argue with you."

Then she bends over in her seat, combs through a shopping

bag and sits up, holding a small, shrink-wrapped Bible. The kind nut-job ministers hand out in Times Square. She hands it to me.

"You're curious, which is good. It's healthy. Read this over. It should answer some of your questions about what I *believe*."

I accept the book, thinking this might be the first time I've ever actually touched a Bible. Then on a whim I whip out my wallet and hand her one of my cards.

"And if you ever meet anyone who claims to *know*, give me a call," I say. "I'd like to ask them a few questions."

COURTNEY'S GETTING EXCITED as we blast down I-25 in our latest rental: a stupid blue PT Cruiser that smells like a whole pine forest was melted down and shoved in the glove compartment. There was light snow on the drive from Denver down to Colorado Springs, where I stopped for a coffee and a bathroom break. Courtney sat pat in the passenger seat, eyeing me like my physical callings are a sign of weakness.

Now we're chugging down to a city called Pueblo, the closest thing to Beulah that even resembles a metropolitan area. I'm cutting around a seemingly endless supply of eighteen-wheelers as Courtney's trying to make sense of a mess of papers spread on his lap. Farmland on our left, rocky hills on our right, the latter punctuated with gas stations, a racing track, a driving school. Unbelievable how much empty land there still is in this country. Everything between New York and California is like a blank canvas of grass, with just a few splotches of civilization and highway dribbled randomly by some stoned avant-garde artist.

"Silas tried to strangle himself three years ago, Frank," Courtney says. "That's how he did it. Stuffed the end of his sheet in his mouth, wrapped the rest around his head and nose, tried to suffocate himself. Succeeded only in giving himself a mild seizure. Was found frothing from the mouth on the floor of his cell at breakfast time."

"The GPS says it's another two hours," I say. "I'm aiming for an hour and a half. Those estimates are for pussies."

"Suffocation, Frank. Think about it. That's how he killed Savannah too. Interesting, right?"

"This fucker thinks she's the only one on the road? Hey, pull over and let me pass, granny."

"What if we find out that the Beulah Twelve *strangled* that kid?" Courtney's eyes are wide. He strokes his sporadic stubble like he's trying to start a fire. "Or what if, wait, Frank, what if this girl Candy was one of them? They were all men, that's what it said in the papers, but what if they were wrong?"

"Settle down, chief." I rev up to 90 and shoot past a truck emblazoned with some cartoon vegetables. "Patience, thoughtfulness and subtlety, right?"

"Of course, of course." He nods. His leg is shaking with furious nervous energy. "You gonna try to call Greta again?"

"It can wait till we get to Beulah," I say. "But my phone is in my pack in the backseat if you wanna try yourself. I think I owe Orange a call, too, if you feel up to it. He called while we were on the plane."

Courtney shakes his head adamantly. "I'll wait for you."

"How much should we tell her, you think?"

"Umm." Courtney taps his long fingers on the dashboard. He's been in quite a mood ever since we left the airport. Maybe it's the thin air. But probably it's the thrill of actually having a lead on this thing. "Enough to make it clear we're working our asses off, but holding back enough to make sure we still have some facts to spread out over the next week if we don't find anything new. You know, and stay vague enough that she doesn't feel like she can just boot us off the case and go find it herself."

"You mean sound like I still have no idea exactly what's going on? That shouldn't take much imagination."

"Ha." Courtney returns to his maze of photographed medical files and newspaper clippings. "You and me both, Frank. But we're getting close to something big. I can feel it."

"I thought I could feel it, too, about an hour ago, but then it turned out I just needed to drop a deuce."

Courtney glares at me.

SOUTHERN COLORADO MAKES rural Maine look like a metropolis. Beulah is only a three-and-a-half-hour drive from Denver International but feels like a different world. Hell, it doesn't even seem possible that the steelworking city of Pueblo is forty-five minutes away. The vegetarian Mexican restaurant we found there is a distant memory as the hybrid cruises down a single-lane highway bordered only by desolate, endless fields on either side. To the west, eventually, are the foothills and then the Rockies. The east stretches out to an infinity of rolling hills covered in dead brown.

But the actual town of Beulah is somehow even more desolate than the empty landscape. Wikipedia puts the population at five hundred, but that seems generous. Nearly all the residents seem to live in cabins that line Main Street—what highway 70 is called for a half mile. Smoke rises from most of the chimneys.

Courtney pulls off the road in front of a brick building that appears to double as a tavern and someone's private residence.

We step out of the car, and I breathe in deep. Crisp, dry air. So clean and pure it almost tastes sweet on the back of my throat. On the front porch of the house is a middle-aged woman with curly brown hair. She's wearing a thick down jacket and sitting on a wooden swing anchored by two rusty chains. No book, no computer, no phone. Just sitting. She smiles pleasantly as we step out of the car and walk up the steps, but she doesn't leave her swing.

"Not open for dinner 'til six," she announces. "But you're welcome to help yourself to a coffee inside."

"We actually could use some help," Courtney says and removes a notepad from his shearling coat. "We're looking for a woman named Candy Robinson. Used to live at 27 Main Street."

The woman's round face falls. "Still does," she says, a slight edge to her voice now. I think I can see Courtney's pulse quicken. "What you want with that poor girl?"

"Just would like to ask her a few questions," I say.

A few snowflakes fall tentatively from the sky, like they were the only ones to escape. The woman shakes her curly mop of hair.

"Leave the car here, you can just walk. Not more than five minutes down Main Street, across from the Ritz. She'll be outside, I'm sure. Always is. But I don't think she'll be of much help to you two, whatever you're after."

I jam my hands into the pockets of my jacket. Really need to buy gloves.

"Why do you say that?" Courtney asks.

"What are you two, cops?" She glares at us. Her cheeks have the pink flush of someone who's never warm.

"Kinda," I say.

She nods knowingly and tightens her mouth. "I'm not saying another word."

"Alright, thanks for your help," Courtney says, and we retreat down the steps.

Not many people on Main Street: two kids playing with action figures on a front lawn, an elderly woman carrying a plastic grocery bag, and a postman—hard to imagine that's a full-time job around here—on foot, depositing a rubber-banded bundle into a wooden mailbox, then lowering the flag. After living in the city for so long I'd forgotten real mailboxes existed.

The whole town is located either on or right off Main Street, like it's the major artery providing blood flow to every building. To our right—north—the houses are built right off the street. Each one in a totally different design and shape from the next, as if they were constructed during some sort of rural architectural competition. A flat, one-story house painted bright yellow; an unfinished wooden farmhouse the color of burned hair; a two-story relatively modern house with huge glass windows facing us. To our left—south and downhill—the town disperses somewhat. I think I hear the low purr of a running creek. Winding driveways of red dirt trail off, and I catch glimpses of structures behind the trees. I see one silver trailer hooked to a pickup truck.

"Gonna try Greta?" Courtney asks. We're walking slowly because of my ankle.

"I wonder if they even have cell service out here," I say. I check the bars on my phone. There is reception, but it's not great. I dial Greta. It rings three times and goes to voice mail. I hang up.

"Leave a message," Courtney says.

"Shut up."

"Tell her we have a lead, that we're in Colorado following up, and it's potentially very promising. I guarantee you she listens to her messages."

"When's the last time you owned a phone? It doesn't work like that anymore. She'll just see that she has a missed call from me and call back if she wants to."

Courtney frowns and tucks his mittened hands deeper into the folds of his shearling coat. He says, mostly to himself, "If someone didn't leave me a message, I'd assume they have nothing to talk about . . ."

I point to the postman. "Kinda funny to think about, isn't it, this woman Candy eagerly checking her mail every day to see if she got anything from her serial killer pen pal."

"Yeah," Courtney mutters. "Hilarious."

The Ritz appears to be the only other place to eat in Beulah. It's a faux-Victorian building on the south side of the street, with a pink and blue facade faded by weather. And directly across is a large white house with a pitched roof and overgrown front lawn. Vines and weeds climb up the dirty, white-painted shingles, some reaching as high as the dusty second-floor windows. No smoke rising from this chimney.

As we cross the street I notice that the house is built strangely. It bulges where it shouldn't. It's tall in places and short in others, like it was a perfect cube, and then jagged pieces were plucked out at random. It reminds me of a pale hand jutting up from the dirt, reaching for the sky.

Then we spot what might be Candy in the front yard, sitting hunched over in a rocking chair, staring at her feet. She's in the middle of a small garden filled with dead plants, surrounded by a knee-high fence coated in peeling white paint.

"Candace?" Courtney asks as we step onto the property. She's about ten feet away but doesn't look up. "Candace, we were wondering if we could speak to you?"

We take a few steps forward through high weeds. She doesn't budge. We're about to step over the garden fence, when my stomach falls.

"Wait, Courtney," I say and grab his shoulder. "Look."

I point to her ankle, around which is tied a thick piece of twine. The other end is wrapped around a round peg hammered into the ground. I immediately think of my dream: Savannah chained to the cold dirt in the cabin basement.

"What the fuck?" I whisper.

"Candace?" Courtney tries again. "Candy?"

She doesn't move. Just stares at her feet, shoulders hunched, face covered by dry black hair. She's wrapped in a thick wool blanket. A few stray snowflakes settle on the crown of her head. Stuck in the dirt around her are several miniature clay statues of the Virgin, arranged in a semicircle—a protective perimeter. Under a web of long-dead flowers is a welcome mat that reads, *God Bless This House.*

"Candy?" I whisper and step over the fence. I lay my hand on her shoulder, and she finally reacts. She looks up at me, and an involuntary cry escapes my lips.

Her eyes are totally dead, glazed over. I can tell as she looks at me that nothing is getting through. And the side of her head is horribly malformed. Caved in, almost like someone went at it with an ice cream scoop. Beneath the hair on the mauled side is dull red scar tissue.

"Candy?" I say weakly.

She's probably around thirty-two, but I could be off by ten years on either end. She tries to open her mouth but succeeds only in slightly raising the corner of a purple lip. She makes a raspy sound, her dead eyes looking through me.

"Jesus," Courtney says. "Why doesn't anybody do anything? She'll die out here from cold." He drops to his knees and goes at the twine with his pocketknife, but jerks up when we hear the front door of the house slam open. A tiny woman with wild white hair that sticks straight up like a troll doll appears on the porch steps, leaning on a cane with one hand, wielding a polished shotgun with the other.

"Don't touch her!" she says, taking wobbly aim at Courtney's head. She's a little imp of a woman. Would barely make it to my belly button. She's wearing a fraying blue sweater over what I think is a white nightgown that hangs all the way to her ankles. Plastic glasses with huge frames give her face an owl-like quality. Loose skin hangs from her chin, and her face is Valentine's Day pink with anger.

Courtney slowly rises to his feet and puts his hands behind his head. I do the same.

"She's going to die out here," he says delicately. "From cold."

"She's just fine," the woman says slowly, her voice—like many old women's—sounding a bit like it's being filtered through a chicken gullet. "You don't know anything. Now get off my land."

"We were just trying—"

"You've done *enough*," she says, her withered face going cherry red, eyes blazing lumps of black coal. "You people have done *enough*." She eases down the porch steps, cane first, somehow managing to keep the gun pointed at Courtney's head. She carefully lowers herself onto the cold ground and approaches, house slippers crunching frozen undergrowth, her right hand shaking on the butt of the gun.

"I don't know who you think we are, but—" I say slowly.

"I know who you are. You cops are all the same. You think she's going to talk to you. But it's over. What's done is done. Unless you have a warrant, just go. Leave her alone."

"We're not police, ma'am, I assure you," Courtney says, thin hands clasped behind his head. "We're private investigators from New York. We just came here to ask Candace a few questions."

I think I see a hint of surprise or confusion in the old woman's eyes, but she quickly resumes her hard line.

"Well go on then. Try. Ask her whatever you want," she says. Her hands are shaky. My eyes are glued to her trigger finger, praying it doesn't slip and end Courtney's career as a human. "Go on ahead. Ask her."

"Please," Courtney says. "We don't want to hurt anyone. We just want to talk. Maybe you can help us. Maybe . . . maybe we can help you. And your . . . daughter?"

The white-haired woman clenches her jaw. Behind us, we hear a boy's voice.

"You need help, Ms. Anderson?" he asks.

"I got this under control," she mutters. "Thank you."

My fingers are getting numb behind my head. The butt of Ms. Anderson's plastic cane has dug into the cold dirt, and she seems content to keep standing there leaning on it, keeping her shotgun trained on Courtney until we decide to leave. Her snow-white, Don King hairdo, oversized ears and prune face make her look like a little gnome.

"We—" I croak. She seems to notice me for the first time, and the muzzle of her weapon swivels to my chest. "We're looking for something. A tape."

It takes her a moment to process what I said. Creasing her pink forehead, she keeps staring at me down the barrel of what looks like a cheap Harrington pump-action.

"What did you say?" she says slowly.

I glance sideways at Courtney.

"A tape," I repeat.

I can hear her nasal breathing from here. She's so small. Not much taller than Sadie, and she's positively swimming in her loose blue sweater. Her eyes dart quickly to the crumpled girl behind us, then back, first to me, then Courtney.

"Do you two have weapons?"

"I have a knife," I say. Had to mail my Magnum to my East Broadway address before getting on the plane.

"Take it out slowly and lay it at your feet. I swear on my husband's grave, you try anything I'll fire."

I oblige, and then she finally lowers her shotgun. I exhale.

"She's not my daughter, she's my niece," Ms. Anderson says.

"What happened to her?" Courtney asks.

She sizes us up warily, leaning forward so she can see over the tops of her glasses.

"Come inside," she finally says. "But if you two are taking advantage of me—"

"I know." I nod. "We get it."

She stares at me, tight-lipped, then turns and shuffles back toward the house. She moves slowly up the porch steps, taking her time to steady herself with her cane. When Courtney offers her his elbow to grab, she rejects it.

"I'm fine," she says.

We follow her through the swinging screen door, leaving Candy tied up in the garden. The door opens into a dreary hallway with cream-colored wallpaper and a ceiling so low that Courtney has to slouch to avoid hitting his head.

"Get chairs," she says, motioning to a closet down the hall. She stays back and hangs her shotgun on a rack by the door, then shuffles out of sight. It's freezing in here; seems even colder than outside.

We squeeze down the tight hallway—single file—to the closet, and the hallway is so narrow that there's barely room to open the closet door. It's filled mostly with men's clothing on hangers, all wrapped in plastic. Smells like mothballs. Beneath the clothes we find two metal folding chairs.

"What's going on?" I whisper to Courtney as I pull out the chairs and close the closet door. "What's with that girl?"

"Seriously, Frank? How would I know?"

I notice that his jaw is chattering slightly and his eyes are darting around in his head.

"Are you alright?" I ask.

"I don't like tight spaces," he says.

We move back toward the door, Courtney first, in a hurry to get out of this hall.

"I'm in here," we hear our host shout.

We follow the sound of her voice through an open doorway and find her in the kitchen. Immediately Courtney straightens his back and seems to relax. In here, the ceiling is impossibly high, perhaps fifteen feet. This room is shaped like an elevator. I look back at the cramped hallway to try to reconcile the two spaces and my brain feels like it's going to explode. This house seems to exist in a space exempt from the physical laws that govern the outside world.

The ceiling creates the illusion of spaciousness, but in terms of square footage the kitchen is quite small and cluttered. Half the room is a countertop kitchenette: sink filled with dirty dishes; two-burner gas stove; a few very old-looking pots and pans piled in the corner. Against the far wall of the kitchen are dozens of taped-up cardboard boxes stacked precariously on top of one another, reaching nearly to the cathedral ceiling. I gaze up their height and still can't quite figure what the hell is going on with the architecture in here. Whoever designed this place must have been dropping some serious acid.

Ms. Anderson is sitting in a velvet upholstered chair, elbows on an Ikea-esque card table, looking out the kitchen window. She's partially draped in a puffy down coat that envelops both her and the back of the chair. The window she's looking through provides a view of Candy, sitting still in the garden.

We unfold the chairs and sit on either side of her at the table. In front of her on the table is an illustrated almanac, which I guess she was reading when she saw us walk up. The only other item on the tabletop is a glass jar filled with NutraSweet packets.

"I'm the one who tied her up out there," she sighs, clearly relieved to be sitting. "I had no choice. She's wandered off twice. She nearly fell in a stream and drowned the last time. I had to tie her up for her own protection. Lord knows I can't sit and watch her *all* day."

"Why don't you bring her inside?" Courtney asks.

Ms. Anderson's eyes are wet and distant as she stares at the creature in her garden. She's definitely over eighty but seems pretty with it. Her skin sags like it's trying to escape from her face. She smells of baby wipes and bacon.

"She wants to be outside when it's light. She'll fight me tooth and nail if I try to bring her in before nightfall. She doesn't mind the cold."

I glance around at the kitchen. Everything is old and crummy in here. Shitty fridge, tile floor and peeling yellow wallpaper stained brown from water damage. Everything except the high ceiling, which—though it could be some trick of the light—looks to be a white so clean and new that it's almost sparkling. Through a doorway opposite the hallway I see what must be the living room, carpeted in puke-green shag. A wooden crucifix hangs over a muted TV, local news anchor discussing something seriously. The walls of the living room appear to be curved, like the whole room is a cylinder. I've never bought any of that feng shui bullshit, but if it's possible to convey bad vibes through interior space, this house has nailed it.

"What happened to her?" I ask.

Ms. Anderson ignores my question, or maybe just doesn't hear me. "You said you're looking for a tape."

I flinch as I hear a rustling behind me. Turn just in time to see a mouse dive into a trashcan overflowing with egg cartons and empty sausage wrappers. I turn back to Ms. Anderson, who hasn't taken her eyes off the window.

"That's right," I say. Courtney keeps stealing glances out the window at Candy's stooped form.

"What kind of tape?" she asks.

"We're not sure, exactly," I answer.

"Why are you two here?" she says.

Courtney and I exchange a look, and he makes a little show of reluctance as he pulls the torn envelope out of his canvas bag, no doubt trying to earn her trust by confiding in her. He shows her the return address.

"That's her, isn't it? Your niece?"

Ms. Anderson turns away from the window and looks over the top of her glasses to squint at the writing.

"Yes. Where did you get this?"

"The man who made the tape. Candy was corresponding with him by post."

Ms. Anderson says nothing. Coughs and clears her throat.

"So you've heard about this tape?" I ask.

She glares at me, her wrinkled fingers affectionately stroking the cane that leans against the arm of her chair. Outside a truck rumbles down Main Street, leaving behind a thick silence.

"What's your name?" she asks me.

"Frank Lamb."

"Am I making a mistake trusting you, Frank?" Ms. Anderson says, staring at me with eyes that, even through her thick glasses, convey a life filled with unimaginable pain. "We just want peace and privacy, Candy and I. We don't want you to write about us and we don't want any more reporters to come."

I shake my head. "We don't want anything like that, Ms. Anderson. I'm being truthful with you. All we care about is finding this tape."

She turns to Courtney. "And who are you?"

"Courtney Lavagnino."

"Courtney? Isn't that a girl's name?"

"That's what they tell me."

She breathes through her nose. "My name is Paula Anderson," she says carefully. "I want to believe you two. You have good souls, I think. Can I trust you?"

"We'll never write about you," Courtney says, "You have my word."

"And no photographs?" she asks.

"Absolutely not."

Ms. Anderson looks at him like she's x-raying him with her eyes, trying to read his thoughts. And it seems to work:

"Would you like some tea?" she asks.

Courtney's eyes light up. "Yes please," he says.

With great effort, she grasps her cane and pushes herself out of her chair. Both Courtney and I rush up to help her, but she motions with her palm that she's fine.

"You boys won't be here tomorrow to help," she says. "And if I take one day off, I might never be able to do it again." She walks to the sink, fills up a pot with water and puts it on the propane burner.

I look out the window and see that Candy hasn't moved. She's hunched over, staring at the hard ground, each of her breaths a sad puff of steam. Looking at her makes me feel even colder.

"My father, rest in peace, grew up on a farm," Ms. Anderson says, watching the water heat up. "And *his* father told him, 'If you want to be the strongest man alive, take a newborn calf, put it on your shoulders and carry him around all sides of the farm every morning. Never take a day off, and soon you'll be carrying a cow.'" She exhales. "That's the important thing. Never take a day off."

She seems to lose herself for a moment in the depths of the pot, then turns to us and says, "One of the neighbors called me at my house in Trinidad the night Candace got hurt. This was a few years ago. He found my number on my little brother's fridge."

"Your little brother is—was—Candace's father?"

"Yes." Ms. Anderson nods. "This was back when I still drove. I got in the car and to the hospital as soon as I could. She was in Memorial Hospital in Pueblo. They were trying to stitch her up. She was losing so much blood and had already had three or four strokes. With each one a little more of her left. I was never really that close to her, to tell you the truth. My little brother and I talked rarely— there was thirteen years between us—and I hadn't seen Candace since she was probably fourteen, at my husband's funeral. But still I expected her to recognize me. She had no idea who I was. I'm not sure if she knew what anything was. I could see her brain."

Courtney sucks his teeth.

"I'm sorry," he says.

She doesn't seem to hear him. "She could still speak by the time I got there, but it was nonsense. Word salad, is what they called it. The cops were trying to get her to tell them what happened, but there was no chance. But I remember one word that kept coming up. *Tape.* She said it a few times. She couldn't even control her limbs; they were flailing around while they tried to stitch her head. They had to tie her down to the gurney. But she said that a few times. She said *tape.* And I never really thought much of it, to tell you the truth. Figured it was nonsense. Hardly thought about it since then. Until today, when you showed up here asking about it."

The water starts boiling, and she takes the pot off the fire. She finds two mugs in the cupboard and distributes the water between them. Manages to carry both over to the table in one hand, using the other for her cane. Hands us each a steaming cup and a tea bag. Mango dream, it says. I watch the steam from my tea swirl all the way up to the ceiling, the mango's spirit finally released from his tea-bag prison.

"You said years," Courtney says. "How many?"

Ms. Anderson sits back down. "About three years ago, now, I guess."

"What happened?" I ask. "How did she get hurt?"

Ms. Anderson looks out the window, as if to make sure nothing has changed since she left.

"It was the same night they killed the Olson boy, then disappeared. The town was overrun by press and cops. Most of the articles don't mention her, because I wouldn't let them into the hospital room. But twelve men killing a child and disappearing into thin air is big news on its own."

"Wait," I say. "Candy was hurt the same night the Beulah Twelve killed the kid and disappeared?"

Ms. Anderson nods.

"So then they're related?" I ask.

"Of course." She laughs lightly. "Those twelve men used to meet in this house. In the attic. Lincoln—her father, my brother—started the whole group. The police think Candace was trying to stop them from killing the boy, and that's when one of them hit her."

Courtney swallows. "I didn't read anything about this," he says.

Ms. Anderson sniffs proudly and pushes her round glasses up on her nose. "I didn't press charges on Candace's behalf, and I kept the press out as best I could. I kept Candace in the hospital, and then a home, until everything died down. It seemed like the best thing I could do for her. Give her some privacy."

"So her father—your brother—did this?"

"A doctor told me in the hospital he thought she was hit with the sharp side of a shovel. The police found the shovel a few days after they left town, in the corner of the attic under some cardboard boxes. The edge was still sticky."

Courtney flinches. "Were you surprised? That Lincoln would do that to his own daughter?"

She sighs. I imagine I can see the wear of the last few years, caring for her vegetating niece, in every crag of Ms. Anderson's sunken forehead and chin.

"I was surprised that he and eleven others killed that boy. After that, I guess all bets are off, as they say."

Courtney scratches his stubbly cheeks.

"So the detectives and all them, when this happened," I stammer, "they knew all about Candace?"

"Of course." Ms. Anderson nods. "But what's the difference to them? It's not as if they needed another reason to find those men—and there was no question it was them. Everyone told me they heard the twelve of them up in that attic at ungodly hours for weeks before the murder. I had no idea any of this was going on. Lived miles away and hardly spoke to Lincoln. But the next-door neighbor, Harry Everette is his name, told the police that when he came over that night after hearing screams, the boy was already dead, and Candace was bleeding on the stairs. The men and their trucks were gone. And you must know the story after that. No trace of them, except they later discovered some credit card activity in Chicago. I sold my house in Trinidad after that and moved in here to take care of Candace. Been here ever since."

Courtney sips on his tea, visibly disturbed. I wrap my hands around the cup to warm them.

"So what is this tape?" she asks. "And why was my niece talking about it before she lost the ability to speak?"

I inhale. Maybe I'll just let Courtney handle this. But he's looking at me like *go ahead,* probably thinking along similar lines.

"We were hired to find it," I say. "The man who your niece was corresponding with was a killer. He made this tape. It supposedly contains the dying words of one of his victims. A young woman."

Ms. Anderson raises a white eyebrow. "Why would anybody care enough about that to hire you?"

I crack my neck to either side. "We're not exactly sure." It's not a lie, precisely. More of a lack of truth. "But it seems increasingly clear to me that for some reason, this man mailed the tape to your niece. And that it was somehow what instigated this boy's murder, as well as Candace's injury."

Courtney nods at me, like he's telling me he agrees with my on-the-spot deduction. He turns back to Ms. Anderson. "Essentially, it seems clear that finding this tape, and what it contains, will also help clear up exactly what happened to your niece. I assume this is something you'd like to resolve as well?"

Ms. Anderson nods. Gazes out the window. "Yes."

"So," I say. "Don't take this the wrong way, obviously anyone would be surprised that their brother could do this, but . . . had you ever seen him exhibit any behaviors at all that maybe, looking back, make this whole thing make a little more sense?"

Ms. Anderson shakes her head slowly. "I've asked myself the same thing many times. No. We weren't close, didn't really see eye to eye, and I don't even know if I'd consider him a particularly nice person. But this wasn't him. He was solid. Simple. A little boring. Liked trucks, beer and football."

"So then you agree that something drastic must have happened. Something must have come into his life—like this tape. Then he's starting a cult, killing a kid, hitting his daughter and disappearing."

The back of her chair creaks as she reclines and rests her veiny hands on her lap. The snow picks up outside. It could be my imagination, but I think Candy is looking at the sky, like she's searching for where the snow comes from.

"I don't know anything about this tape," Ms. Anderson says. "But I've come to the conclusion that there's only one explanation for why my brother could do that."

Courtney polishes off his tea. "And what is that explanation?" he asks.

"He was possessed."

I grind my teeth. "What do you mean?" I ask.

"Lincoln couldn't have killed a child. He wasn't crazy or sick or evil. He must have been possessed by the devil."

Courtney is frowning and stroking his cheeks on maximum throttle. He's obviously come to the same conclusion I have: This would be too much of a coincidence. Girl corresponds with Silas and then a cult starts up in her house, ending with a boy dead and her a vegetable, talking about the tape with her last cognizant breaths. So Silas mails her the tape . . . why? Because he loved her? And how does a tape turn someone into a killer?

I fiddle with my empty cup. "I don't believe in the devil," I say.

"Neither did I," Ms. Anderson responds. "But when you see what's in the attic, I think you'll reconsider."

WE FOLLOW Ms. Anderson through the living room. I was right, the room is completely circular, with a ceiling just as high as the kitchen's. A tall cylinder. Dull afternoon light creeps in through a pair of filthy windows that curve along the concave walls. It's like someone tried to design a hypermodern house on a tiny budget and also had terrible taste.

Through the windows I see snow falling quietly on a fenced-in backyard that looks like it used to be a vegetable garden.

The TV flickers silently as we walk past, the only sound the dull thud of Ms. Anderson's rubber-bottomed cane hitting the carpet. I get the feeling the TV never goes off; keeps her company. Wallpaper the sickly color of curdling cream. Conspicuously missing are any photos on the walls or resting on the TV. The only decorative pieces are a pair of pink porcelain angels resting on a wooden cabinet and a three-foot crucifix mounted on the wall.

Like the kitchen, most of the room is devoted to storing taped-up cardboard boxes. Maybe Lincoln's old stuff?

Ms. Anderson shuffles into a dark dining room of unremark-able proportions. The table is covered in dusty plastic, hasn't been used for years. As if reading my mind, she says, "I usually feed Candace when she's in bed. It's easier. And no reason to sit at the big table by myself."

She stops and leans on a windowsill. Looks out at the snow for a moment, and when she looks back, her face is cast in shadow. She points to a dark brown door at the far end of the dining room.

"Go on up," she says. "I'll be waiting in the kitchen. The stairs are too hard for me, but I wouldn't go up there anyways. Nobody's been up for years. I hope the lights still work."

As Courtney and I approach the door, she turns and walks back through the living room, like she doesn't even want to be around when we open it. Courtney breathes into his hands to warm them up. Looks at me, like he expects me to go first. I grimace and pull open the attic door.

A whiff of cold, moldy air. I reach up for a beaded metal chain and a bulb tentatively flickers on, illuminating a narrow, unfin-ished staircase.

"Think the tape is up there?" I ask Courtney.

He shakes his head. "Doubt it."

"Why?"

"Just a hunch. One thing we're certain of: This tape is valuable to people. It was valuable to Candy and the guys up there." He juts his chin up the dark stairway. "People don't leave things like that behind. And neither do cops. Any real evidence will be gone."

"But you think it was here at one point?"

Courtney nods.

"Yeah." He rubs his hands together. "I think we're getting close. Might wanna start thinking about how Greta's gonna pay us."

I smirk. "Patience."

I go first up the stairs. Have my phone out for supplementary light. Courtney has to crouch, and I can hear him struggling behind me, bitching to himself about how the Beulah Twelve must have been little people. I grip the shaky railing, haul myself up, not wanting to put too much weight on my bad ankle. Feels like we're in a mine shaft. Floor covered in grime and old sawdust. I wonder if Lincoln built this house himself. There's no heat in here, and it feels like there are open windows upstairs.

"Kind of a bummer Silas couldn't have mailed that tape to someone in Malibu, eh?" I say as I pivot around a bend in the stairway.

"This may sound crazy," Courtney says from behind me, "but I'm getting a strange feeling that it had to be this way, somehow. That the tape was always meant to come here. And so were we. Sort of a destiny feeling, you know."

I turn around and shine my phone in Courtney's green eyes. "Don't start with that shit. Keep your head screwed on."

Courtney puts up a hand to block the light. "Why, because it scares you?"

"At least I'm not scared of the dark," I say and huff my way up the last couple of stairs.

"It's not the dark; it's just these tight spaces that make me uneasy."

At the top is a thin plywood door with a rusty gold knob. Have to put my shoulder into it to get it open. And then I step into the attic, Courtney a few seconds behind me. There's a lot of natural light in here; windows on each of the four walls. Some of the windowpanes are busted, and it's about the same temperature in here that it is outside. The ceiling is the inside of the slanted roof. Dark brown wooden beams run between the tops of the walls.

Looks like the place was pretty well cleared out by the cops. But they left the centerpiece: an enormous stone table that looks like it must weigh a literal ton.

"Don't touch anything. We don't have gloves," Courtney says as I approach the monolith.

It comes up to about waist height. I shine the flashlight on it, and my stomach curdles. The flat surface is coated in what I immediately recognize as very old blood. I'm suddenly grateful for the ventilation in here. There are four leather straps hewn into the surface, screwed down into chiseled holes. Doesn't take much imagination: two for ankles, two for wrists. Spaced out just right for a kid.

"It's an altar," Courtney whispers, taking my phone from me and kneeling to inspect the sides of the stone. Beckons me to look closely. Dark, sticky droplets of old blood. "Cops didn't want to scrub too hard, were worried about damaging evidence."

"Did the articles say if they just left the kid here? Strapped down?"

Courtney nods grimly.

"Rape?" I ask, my voice a little squeaky.

"No," Courtney responds. "But they made a real ritual out of it."

Feeling a little queasy, I shift my attention away from the altar. Arranged so they face the altar are two rows of wooden pews that look ripped straight from a church. I'm thinking, enough to sit ten, while the other two put on a show. On the wall behind the pews is a rack for hanging tools, empty. Undoubtedly confiscated and wrapped in plastic, buried deep in some evidence room. Could take months to locate them, just to confirm the obvious: sharp, lightly used, sticky with blood. Would like to see the shovel someone hit Candy with for myself though, just to confirm what Ms. Anderson told us.

"I don't understand how they got this in here," Courtney says, mostly to himself, still fixated on the altar. "You'd need a crane or something. And even if you could lift it, no way it would squeeze up that staircase."

I break away from the tool rack. Not much else in here. Gaze out the broken window that faces Candy, still sitting rigid in the garden. An old woman walks slowly down Main Street and stops to rest on the steps of the Ritz. Beyond the dirty blue and pink of the old Victorian are just pine trees for fucking ever.

I turn around. Courtney's still crouched at the altar. My gaze drifts up to the skylight and freezes.

"Courtney. Let me see my phone," I say and grab it from him before he can hand it to me. I shine it on the beams that wrap around the room where the walls meet the ceiling. The beams are of a different consistency than either; polished, more expensive looking, like they were brought in special.

Stretching around the room, carved into the beams, is a flowing dark line. I dash to one of the pews and climb up, lean in close enough to see the etching. It's highly detailed, textured. I follow it around the perimeter of the room until I reach the spot right above the window from which you can see Candy and the Ritz. A chill shoots down my spine.

"Look, Courtney."

"What is it?"

"That line all around is a snake. And here," I whisper, indicating the crux of the carving, "he's devouring his own tail." I gulp. "I've seen this before."

"Where?" asks Courtney.

My pulse picks up. Prickles on my forearms.

"Silas had the same thing tattooed around the circumference of his head," I say.

Courtney and I stare hard at each other, then turn back to the image. The line melts into an oversized, bulbous serpent's head, jaw wide, baring sharp teeth, only inches away from the tip of his own tail.

"There's more," Courtney says, pointing above the drawing. I was so enraptured with the snake that I missed the board hanging above it, coated in shadow, clearly made of the same wood as this polished snake board. Etched into the board are two lines:

It is better to never have been born.
Nrob neeb evah reven ot retteb si ti.

"Jesus," I whisper, suddenly feeling like I might throw up.

"It's a palind—"

"Yeah. I got that. Thanks."

I stagger to one of the pews and take a seat, vision starting to swim a little. I need a drink. Bad. Can feel the evil in this place. In this very bench beneath me, I can feel something unholy. The altar, caked in dried blood. A little boy strapped to it—

I keel over from the pew and vomit all over the old floorboards. Probably better off without that vegetarian Mexican food anyways.

"Oh shit, Frank." Courtney is at my side. "What a mess. Wait here, I'll go ask Ms. Anderson for a towel."

"No," I wheeze, climbing to my wobbly feet and groping to the staircase. "I'm outta here."

"Frank—" Courtney starts.

"Nothing else to see here, you know that." I open the door and begin a tentative descent down the narrow staircase. "I'll be across the street drinking. Come over when you're done."

THE SUSTAINED EXISTENCE of the Ritz Tavern in Beulah, Colorado, is nothing short of a miracle. The six-table dining room is half full for dinnertime, and I get the feeling this is a relative bustle for the family operation. Decorations are old-timey and cutesy: stuffed deer heads mounted on the walls, black-and-white photos of this place a hundred years ago—not much has changed. First floor is a restaurant/bar, second and third floors are rooms.

Courtney cautiously probes a steaming plate of fajitas with his fork, then sits back, looks at me with a grimace. "I'm not hungry either."

My untouched burger is growing cold in front of me. Thought maybe once I saw the food I'd want it. I was wrong. Wish there was somewhere else to eat and sleep in this "city"—somewhere that wasn't right across the fucking street from Candy, Paula Anderson and that evil house. That attic.

I flag the waiter over, a thin boy with long hair, swimming in his white button-down. Looks like he can't wait to get off his shift and get stoned. Don't blame him. What else do you do in this town?

Human sacrifice, I guess.

"Get me another double bourbon, kid. No ice."

I catch the boy glancing at our untouched food, then he nods and shuffles to the next table. I rest my head in my hands. Feels heavy. Don't even like closing my eyes because of what I see when I do.

"This is all fucked, Courtney," I say.

I see him bobbing his long head in agreement. "Yeah."

"What now?" I ask. We might as well talk about it, because I can't think about anything else.

"You try calling Greta again?"

"Twenty minutes ago."

"You leave a message?"

I pick my head up and glare at him. "No I didn't leave a god-damn message, because this isn't nineteen-ninety-fucking-five. I texted her that this was my new number. She can see me calling her. If she wants to talk, she'll call back."

Boy arrives with my drink.

"This is a double?" I stare at him.

"Think so," he says.

"Better go get me another one," I growl, raising the glass to my lips and letting the shitty house whiskey shoot down my throat, imagining it's burning off some of the vile spiritual shit I can feel inside of me.

"Frank . . ." Courtney's giving me a sad, maternal look.

"What?" I say. "You want one?"

He crosses his arms. "You know I don't drink."

"If you want my professional opinion, you should start to-night."

I'm feeling a little warmer now. A thin haze is starting to build between the tavern room and the house across the street. It's dark now, so Candy has probably gone inside. Maybe Ms. Anderson helped her take a bath. I imagine what Candy must look like naked in the tub; eighty pounds of emaciated flesh. Can't even talk. Those empty fucking eyes. While upstairs, still in the attic over their heads, is a goddamn *sacrificial altar*.

"So the tape was here," I say, gesturing vaguely in the direction of Main Street.

"Yeah."

"Silas mailed it to her from Sachar."

"Yeah."

"They'd let him mail something like that, you think?"

Courtney shrugs. "Don't see why not. Just a tape, as far as they knew."

"Then her dad got his hands on it, and some nasty shit went down."

"That's what it looks like," Courtney agrees.

The boy returns with another bourbon, hands it to me carefully, like I'm a hyena and he's feeding me raw red meat.

"Anything else?" he asks.

"Could you make me a black tea? With lemon?" Courtney asks.

"Uh, yeah." The boy wipes some shaggy hair out of his eyes, then goes.

I pick up my next full shot and look Courtney squarely in the eyes as I pound it, then slam the empty glass down on the paper tablecloth.

"Why?" I ask, feeling suddenly angry at something I can't define. "Why would Silas mail her the tape? This was his prize, right?"

"And why would he wait until he was in the loony bin for two years to do it?" Courtney adds, swirling fajitas around with his fork. I watch for a second, mesmerized. There's something graceful about the way the greasy peppers and onions centrifuge around his tines.

"Something happened," I say slowly. "It all happened at about the same time. Two years into his sentence. He tried to kill himself, withdrew into his room, and mailed the tape to Candy." I look up at Courtney. "Something happened. What happened? Anything in the file?"

He stops spinning the fork.

"I'm only halfway through. There's a lot in there, Frank. Five years' worth of appointments. But so far, nothing stands out. I've read about the suicide attempt and the withdrawal, but nothing particular that seems to have precipitated it."

Booze is working its magic. I'd like another one, but I'm already getting a little woozy, and I don't wanna be hung over tomorrow. Besides, it's only seven at night. Jesus. Time feels different in a shit hole like Beulah.

"Where did the tape go?" I say.

Courtney sighs. "It seems to me, unfortunately, that in all likelihood, wherever the Beulah Twelve disappeared to, the tape went with them."

I click my tongue. "And that's something that a whole shitload of dudes smarter than us, with a significantly larger budget, couldn't figure for shit. Just left it as unsolved after eight months, right?"

"A year. They gave up after a year."

I start chuckling, and then I'm flat out laughing. "Great. So now in order to find the tape, we gotta solve the crime of the decade. How the fuck we gonna do that?"

I'm half aware that I'm talking loudly. A few parents at adjacent tables are staring daggers at me.

"Well." Courtney scratches his forehead. "We *do* know something they didn't. About the connection to Silas and the tape."

212 E. Z. RINSKY

I snort, which then turns into a round of hiccups. "Great."

"And we have our three weapons, Frank: thoughtfulness, subtlety and patience."

I roll my eyes and snap my fingers in the air. "*Garçon!*"

"Frank . . ."

The poor boy meanders back to our table, like a prisoner to the gallows.

"Another double shot please. This night is over as far as I'm concerned."

"Uh, you sure—" he starts, looking at Courtney for help.

I pull two of the hundreds Greta gave me out of my pocket, waggle them in his face.

"Don't worry, kid, we're gonna take care of you, okay?" My words are slurring. I don't care.

"Frank . . ." Courtney tries again.

"Shuddup," I say to him. "I'm a grown man." To the kid: "Make that two double shots, okay? This fucker here is gonna take one with me."

The boy nods nearly imperceptibly and backs away cautiously. Courtney is looking at me with disgust.

"I'm not taking a shot, Frank."

I grin. "I know."

I'M DEEP IN what is, by default, the best sleep I've had in a week—no dreams, just straight black—when Courtney shakes me urgently. Eyes flit open. I'm still drunk.

"Frank! I found it."

"The tape?" I jerk up.

"Oh." Courtney frowns. "No, not that."

"What time is it?" I ask.

"Three."

"Jesus," I groan, let my head sink back into the pillow. "We'll talk in the morning."

"No, Frank." Courtney smacks me lightly on the cheek. "You gotta see this. This is serious shit."

The word *shit* sounds weird coming out of his mouth. I take a few seconds to collect myself, then sit up, roll my legs onto the faux Oriental rug. Rub some sleep out of my eyes.

"Talk to me."

Courtney sits down on his own bed, across from me. Papers are scattered all over his blanket. He hasn't slept at all tonight.

"You said yourself at dinner, something must have happened two years into Silas's sentence, right? He sends the tape to Candy, then tries to kill himself, and withdraws. That can't be a coincidence, all those things just happening together, right?"

"I guess."

"So I read all the notes that Dr. Nancy took during that period. And there was nothing I could figure. It was just like, same old, then *bam*, he tries to asphyxiate himself. As far as she could tell, it was spontaneous, I think."

"Okay, so what did you find?" I ask.

"A copy of his visitor log was near the back of his file. At first I didn't think much of it. A few dozen women, girls like Candy that thought they loved him. But *look*." In an instant, Courtney is at my side, jabbing at the bottom of the list. "Look who his last visitor was, Frank. Three days before he tried to kill himself. Last visitor he ever agreed to speak to."

My blood goes cold.

Last name on the list is Greta Kanter.

I look up at Courtney. "Maybe it wasn't really her, you know."

"It had to be her. They record these officially. Take your ID and stuff. They don't just let you sign yourself in."

"Christ." I rub my temples. "So what does this mean, Court?"

"It's not entirely unsurprising that she would go there herself and try to find the tape. What is, well, *infuriating,* and more than a little *disconcerting,* is that she didn't tell us that she'd ever been there."

"Fuck," I groan, the import of this sinking in. *What else don't we know about her?*

"Plus," Courtney adds, "why did her visit disturb him so much, so much that it prompted him to mail the tape to Cand—"

"*Shit!*" I grab a wastebasket and hurl it against the wall. "That fucking bitch. We could have been arrested or *killed* breaking into that place!"

"Believe me, I'm as upset as you are—"

"*Fuck.*" I punch Courtney's mattress as hard as I can. "Fucking *bitch!*"

"Okay, but the important thing is to think about how we're going to proceed now, in light of this development."

"I'll tell you how we're gonna proceed." I snatch my cell phone off the nightstand. "Gonna give that bitch a piece of my mind."

"Frank, let's talk about this, please."

I ignore him, key in Greta's cell number. Four rings and then, big surprise, it goes to her message machine.

"Greta," I growl into the phone. "It's Frank Lamb. I am very perturbed by some information that has recently been brought to my attention. It seems that you visited Silas at the Berkley Clinic a few years ago, yet for some reason, you conveniently *neglected* to share this critical *fucking information* with us before we *broke into the goddamn place for you*! I suppose it didn't occur to you that this might be helpful? Useful to know? We could have been arrested. Five years in the can. If you don't call me back by noon, it's over. We're keeping the fifteen grand and billing you another fifteen for ten days of wasted time. Have a great fucking evening."

I hang up and nearly throw the cell phone against the wall in frustration, but I stop myself with what little is left of my clear thinking. I feel drunk again. Breathing heavily. I can feel my face flushing.

Courtney is looking at me. "We should have talked that over. That's not a decision you make unilaterally. We're partners."

"Well I'm the one she hired. So we're partners, but not *equal* partners, capiche?"

Courtney shakes his head sadly. "Whatever you say."

I snort. "What. You're not gonna rub it in my face? How I would have gotten nowhere without you? How you're the brains of this operation, and I'm the fucking idiot just tagging along because I'm the one whose number she got from Orange?"

Courtney's face falls. "That's really how you feel, Frank?"

I collapse on the bed. "It's not how I feel. It's how it is. You know it, I know it. Let's just leave it."

Courtney sits back down on his bed. "I don't feel that way at all. I think you have a lot to offer. Really. You're good at this."

"Shut up," I groan, feeling a little physically ill, bile rising in my throat again. Can't believe I have any left. "Just shut up. It's fucked. Everything is fucked."

I switch off the bedside lamp. Hear Courtney shuffling papers in darkness, making some space to sleep. A little glow from the moon seeping in through a slit in the curtains. There's no way I'm gonna sleep another wink tonight. I stretch my imagination, but it's hard to conceive of tomorrow bringing anything but more bad news.

BREAKFAST IN THE dining room. Place smells like roasting meat and smoke around the clock. I force some eggs down my throat. Objectively, they are some of the freshest eggs I've ever eaten. But they taste stale and drab in my cotton mouth.

Courtney gingerly peels an apple—worried it's not organic probably—then cuts it up into little bite-sized pieces.

My cell phone rests on the table between us. It's a little after nine. It occurred to me sometime around dawn that I didn't specify whether I meant noon eastern time or mountain. Don't get the feeling it's gonna make much difference.

"I had to give her that ultimatum," I tell Courtney. "We can't keep going on this if we don't get some more assurance that she's gonna pay us."

Courtney nods silently. Sagging blue bags under his wide eyes. Guess he didn't sleep much last night either.

"We've only spent three grand," I say. "So really, six grand each for ten days of work isn't *awful*."

Courtney shoots me a quick look, then returns to the apple on his plate. I've never seen anyone cut an apple up with a knife and fork before.

I'm pretty sure I know what he's thinking: Even if Greta bails on us, he wants to keep looking. He wants that tape. I do, too, I guess, but I've got Sadie waiting back at home and a healthy dose of skepticism regarding our prospects of finding the Beulah Twelve. Part of me would be ecstatic to just wash my hands of all this shit. I don't like the way following this trail is making me feel. I feel like every day, I'm seeing shit that can never be unseen, no matter how much I drink. And what Courtney said yesterday about us not having a choice, about us being carried here by some kind of cosmic force, I sort of feel that too. And I don't like it.

My phone buzzes. I snatch it. Unknown number.

"It's her," I tell Courtney, heart thumping. "Taking it outside."

I dash out past the reception desk—little more than a wall of keys and lockbox—out into the frigid Colorado morning. Answer it on the porch.

"Hello?" My voice is trembling. With rage, or fear? I try to control it.

It's snowing lightly, and there's a faint, dry breeze that cuts through my jeans, but it feels refreshing.

"Where are you?" she says. Her voice makes me shiver. I'm staring at Paula Anderson's Escherian house across the street. Candy is back in her chair again. Twine wrapped around her ankle, little porcelain statues of Mary gathered around, facing her like it's story time.

"Colorado."

"Why?"

"None of your goddamn business," I snap.

"I received your message," she says. "You've been dreaming about me, haven't you?"

My vision goes a little crooked as a bunch of dreams I've had of her—and forgotten—return to me. There's been a lot of them, and if memory serves, they've all taken place in that cold cellar, and all involved a certain indecent proposal.

"Excuse me?" I say weakly.

Long pause. I'm sweating despite the cold. Candy sitting as still as the statues around her feet. A beat-up Volvo slowly drives down Main Street.

Greta finally breathes hard into the phone and says, "Do you have it?"

"No, but we're close," I lie. The cold stings my eyes but seems to help me focus.

An image from a dream flashes through my head: Greta heaving on top of me, firm breasts rising and falling. The memory evokes a strange kind of terror.

"You've made a big mistake, Lamb," she says. I clench my jaw. I realize Courtney is beside me, staring at me imploringly, like *what's she saying?*

"You lied to us—" I say.

"You broke our deal first," she says. "You talked to Orange. I specifically requested discretion."

A dead moment on the air. A woman walks past me down Main Street, a child bundled to her chest. Those scrambled eggs already want out. My face must look pretty bad, because Courtney looks horrified.

"How could you not tell us that you visited Silas?" I gasp. "What happened during that visit?"

A pregnant silence. Her voice finally crackles over the phone, an ice pick chipping away at my heart.

"You broke our agreement by speaking to Orange. So I'm perfectly within my rights to restructure our arrangement."

"What the fuck are you talking about?" I try to force some oomph into my voice.

Courtney's scratching his cheeks frantically, intuiting things going south.

Another brooding silence on the other end. I dance back and forth to get some blood going in my legs. *Jesus. Please say something, anything.* Terrified curiosity on Courtney's face.

Her sudden baritone cuts deep and makes the skin on the back of my neck tingle.

"Your daughter, Sadie, attends P.S. 134 on the Lower East Side, on East Broadway. She carries a blue lunch box with horses on it.

She was dropped off outside the school this morning, but if you call the school, you'll confirm that she was marked absent today."

It takes me a second to process this, and then the ground falls out from under me. I stagger to a freezing metal railing and throw my weight against it.

"Is . . ." I gasp. "How dare you," I whisper. "How dare—"

"I haven't hurt her. You have until Sunday evening to get me the tape," she says. "Don't call the police. Don't come back to the city without it. If you do either, I'll kill her. Don't do anything stupid, Lamb. Bring me the tape and this all goes away."

"You're lying," I wheeze. "You don't know—"

"500 Grand Street, apartment 3B. That's where she was staying. She has a little discoloration on the big toe on her right foot. She said it's from when you dropped a couch on her foot. Don't call me until you have the tape."

She hangs up.

"Frank? Frank!"

I'm on my knees, Courtney standing over me. It takes me a moment to remember who, where I am. I feel like I just got kicked hard in the stomach.

"Frank, what the hell just happened?"

"She . . ." Hot tears running down my cheeks. "She has Sadie."

Courtney looks like he was just stung with a cattle prod. His face frozen mid-gasp.

"What?" He can hardly speak. "What do you mean she has Sadie?"

I hear my mouth talking, but I'm somewhere else. Somewhere very dark.

"She says she got her on the way to school. We have a week to get her the tape."

"Oh no." Courtney shakes his head. "Oh no. Oh god. Oh no."

"How did I let this happen?" Blood pumps through my temples. Nonsensical scenes of violence flash then disappear in my mind's eye.

"Okay, okay." Courtney is trying to calm himself down. "Give me your phone, I'll call the family she was staying with, have them check with the school. If she's really missing, we'll go straight to Denver to fly back, I'll call some old cop friends—"

"She said not to call the cops," I say. "Said not to come back to the city without the tape. She means it. You can hear it in her voice. She'll do anything for this thing. It's all that matters to her."

"Just give me your phone, Frank. You're not thinking straight—"

"You're not calling the fucking cops," I snap. "She means it."

An older couple leaving the Ritz stares at us, me on my knees spitting out phlegm, Courtney tugging anxiously on his thin hair.

"I'll call the Feinsods in a sec," I say.

I roll onto my side. An emptiness in my stomach, a black hole sucking all feeling out of me, leaving only dread. I pull my knees to my chest, shivering, body quaking, convulsing, my ribs hurting each time I breathe. Through the railing of the porch fence I see Candy, unmoving. Those dead eyes. She can see, but she can't process anything. It must be like staring into bright light all the time. I envy that. My eyes flit to the broken window of the attic above her. I think there are indeed moments so painful that it would have been better to have never been born.

AN HOUR LATER, sitting on my hotel bed, blanket pulled over my head, *actual* double shot in hand, second of the day. Popped three aspirin too. Eyes puffy. Throat raw. I barely managed to keep it together long enough to tell Tammy Feinsod that there was a family emergency, and Sadie's aunt picked her up from school. That she'd come back next week to pick up her stuff.

Keep thinking about this time a couple years ago when Sadie and I were in some park on the Lower East Side, and she tripped, and I heard a horrible crack as her head collided with the cement. She was fine, as little kids usually are, but in that split second when she was on the ground I felt something I'd never felt before. It was the most awful feeling of helplessness, so potent that it actually manifested itself physically—as a burning pain in my stomach and groin. A million times worse than actually getting hurt myself.

I hear Courtney enter, gently close the door, sit down on his bed across from me.

I rip off the blanket and with my eyes ask him the only question there is to ask.

Courtney bites his lip. "She's not at school."

I shoot down the rest of the shot and pull the blanket back over my head.

"If Greta touches her," I say, "I'll kill her. I mean it. I'll kill her."

Courtney touches my knee. "I won't pretend to know how this feels, Frank."

"I actually appreciate that."

Courtney rips the blanket off my head. His face is way too close to mine.

"I'm gonna help you with this."

I nod, tight-lipped. "Thanks."

"So." I can smell Courtney's breath. Better than most; I attribute it to tea over coffee. "So what are we gonna do, Frank? Your call. You say we don't call the cops, we don't call the cops."

I wipe my eyes with the back of my hand. "I don't know."

"Well, I'll tell you the first thing you need to do," Courtney says evenly. "You need to stop getting drunk. That's not helping anything."

I return his level gaze.

"Fine," I say, dropping the empty glass onto the floor.

"Okay then." Courtney nods, satisfied. Sits back down across from me. "This is hard to hear, but emotion is the enemy right now. We need to be logical. Patient, thoughtful and subtle."

These are mantras I could get behind right about now. Easier said than done.

"First, we need to find out who we're really dealing with here," I say. "Who knows how much of what she told us is lies? One thing is for sure"—I swallow—"she definitely lied about why she wants the tape. And maybe if we can figure out the real reason, we'll be able to get inside her head."

Courtney expresses approval with a puffed-out lower lip. "Sounds good."

"Give me my phone back," I say. Courtney obliges, though he gives me a wary look, like *you're not going to do anything stupid, are you?*

I ignore him and dial Helen Langdon.

Please pick up . . . Please . . .

Five rings. Then my prayers are answered.

"Helen Langdon," she answers.

"Helen." The relief in my voice must be tangible; I'm vaguely aware of how crazed I sound. "Listen, it's Frank again. Please don't hang up. I'm begging you."

An eternal silence.

"Frank. I'm at work. What do you want?"

"Helen," I say. "I'm in deep. Real deep. And I really need you to run a way wider check on that woman. Greta Kanter. I need the real shit. Credit card and phone bills, all associations from the last five yea—"

"Christ, Frank. Settle down. What the hell is going on?"

I'm trying not to sound too hysterical. I can't tell her. If I tell her, she'll be legally obliged to start the manhunt, and if Greta gets a whiff of that, she'll kill my daughter. I know it. I could hear it in her voice.

"I made a big mistake, that's the bottom line. I fucked everything up, and now . . ." I lose it, choking on sobs. "And I need to know about her."

"Frank, get a grip. What the hell is going on?"

I bite my lip. "I can't tell you. I can't get the cops or feds involved."

Helen kind of half laughs. "A criminal told you not to call the cops? Buddy, that's what they all say. What is this, blackmail? Kidnapping? You can't—"

"Helen, I heard it in her voice. I know she means it. *I know.* I feel like I'm risking so much even by telling you."

Another deep breath.

"Her? This Greta woman is the perp?"

Goddamn it. I've said way too much. Or maybe Helen is just way too sharp.

"I know what I'm asking you to do is illegal without a warrant," I say. "I'm begging you. I need your help." I sigh and pull out my last card. "It's my daughter."

Dead air.

"I have a daughter now. It's just me."

Heart in my throat.

"Oh, Frank . . ." Helen finally says, whispering into the phone. "You have to tell me what the hell is going on. This is serious."

"I *know* it's fucking *serious*," I pant, then force myself to take it down a notch. Courtney can hardly contain himself. "Helen, just trust me. I know what I'm dealing with here. She's been ahead of me at every step. And if she finds out I've involved the NYPD, she has nothing to lose. She's not stupid, she just doesn't care."

The mother of all sighs.

"Did she give you a deadline?"

"Sunday."

Dead air. She must be chewing the hell out of her pen.

"Okay, listen. How about this: You know that most manhunts resolve in forty-eight hours or don't resolve at all. I'll try to find you what you want, and then you get until Thursday at midnight. It's now Monday afternoon, so that's close to fifty-fifty. If you haven't figured out whatever you need to by then though, I'm taking over, okay? You'll tell me everything you know, and I'll go after your daughter, doing my best to keep it quiet. Deal?"

I click my tongue idly. I'm finding it a little tough to actually think anything over right now.

"Okay," I say.

"Give me until tonight to dig into this. I'll wait for most of the office to clear out."

Tears of relief. "Thank you. Thank you so much. You don't even—"

"It's fine. And Frank? I'm sorry this is happening to you, okay? Really. I'm sorry."

I hang up with shaky hands. I can taste cold salt on my lips.

"She'll help?" Courtney asks.

I nod.

"Good."

I stand up and wipe the tears away. Take a few deep breaths, try to focus on standing up straight.

"That was the easy part," I say. "Now we have to find that fucking tape."

WE SPEND THE rest of the day trying to suck any droplet of knowledge about the Beulah Twelve out of this town, talking to everyone in sight. Anyone who's willing.

Helen calls that night, says she needs another night to get me the info, there's a lot to comb through. I guess that's good?

So the next day—Tuesday—I roll out of bed after a largely sleepless night in the zone. Determined not to waste a moment of time. Sadie's time. I don't dare call Greta until I can leave her the message I need to: We have it.

After forcing down some coffee and fruit, we cross the street and convince Ms. Anderson to let us go through Candy's old room, which is off that cramped hallway, past the closet with the men's clothing.

It appears to be untouched since being scoped by the cops the night after the accident; Candy now sleeps across the hall in a crib-like thing beside Ms. Anderson's bed. It's weird to see how Candy decorated her room, because that person is essentially dead, replaced by whatever she is now. Posters of heavy metal bands hang on the brick walls (brick for interior walls?), and there's a little vanity with mirror and half-filled tubes of nail polish and lipstick, clothes stuffed in the dresser that are mostly black. No windows in here, and the ceiling—painted gloomy grey—isn't level; instead it slants, so that when you walk into the room you have to duck, but back by the closet I can't touch the ceiling even if I jump.

Courtney insists that I not interfere while he probes every corner, wearing latex gloves and the kind of binocular-like eyewear that dentists sometimes use, complete with a built-in light.

"No offense, Frank," he says, dusting the top of the dresser—for prints? "I just have a method."

"Fine by me." I sit on Candy's bare mattress and watch Courtney slave away. "What are you looking for?"

"Heh. Well, wouldn't mind finding the tape in here, for starters."

My eyelids are heavy from exhaustion. Courtney's method seems about as scientific as dowsing for water. He brushes areas and just stares at them.

"What are you doing?" I ask blearily. "Cops already turned the place over. Probably already wiped away prints."

"Ah." Courtney turns to me and grins, the weird illuminated binocular glasses and long, eager fingers making him look like a giant insect. "Indeed. I'm not looking for prints. People leave other indications when they touch areas more frequently than others. Oils, extremely fine erosion . . . classic example is a numerical keypad. Always easy to figure out which numbers are being pushed most often, and sometimes you can even figure out the order by the direction of the oil swirls."

I leave the house to start canvassing neighbors, asking about the night Candy was hurt and the boy who was killed. When I return two hours later, Courtney has finally worked his way around the room to the brick wall behind the bed.

The metal posters are rolled up on the floor, and he's inspecting the wall brick by brick, brushing and examining with the utmost care. I stand off to the side, not wanting to disturb him for a few minutes. Then he leans away from the wall and takes off his goggles.

"Find anything?" he asks.

"There's one woman who said she'd talk to me, said to come back tonight. You find anything?"

"There's one brick . . ." Courtney searches, then points to a red brick near the head of the bed, where he made a tiny scratch with chalk. "I thought I saw some buildup. Was waiting for you to come back to check it out."

"A brick she'd been touching a lot?" I ask.

"Her or someone else. Probably her."

"Check if it's loose yet?"

Courtney shakes his head solemnly. "Didn't want to without you here. Didn't feel right. Just in case, you know, it's in there."

"Well I'm here now." I take a deep breath, feel compelled to offer a silent prayer, but am not sure to whom I should address it. "Go for it."

Courtney grips the edges of the brick with his latex-gloved hands and carefully, delicately pulls. The brick moves. It slides out.

Immediately Courtney drops it on the bed and we're shoulder to shoulder, looking inside with the aid of Courtney's head lamp. There's some stuff rubber-banded together, which I eagerly pull out—before Courtney can chastise me for getting my prints all over it—and drop on the bed.

I tear off the rubber band. No tape. But banded together are letters from Silas and some diaries kept in soft-cover notebooks.

"Guess I can't argue with your method, Court," I say, sifting through the papers, arranging them on the bare mattress. "My technique would have been to get drunk and kick everything."

We spend most of the afternoon going through the contents of Candy's hiding spot. Between the diaries, letters and her personal belongings, we can paint a rough portrait of her before her dad took a shovel to her head: twenty-seven years old, commuted to Pueblo every day for a job in an auto parts store. Wore goth clothes, painted her nails black. Listened to heavy metal. Had some rage issues. A virgin by choice; never felt she met a man she could trust enough to let him bed her. Read about Silas's trial on the internet and simply had to write him, felt she'd finally found the man she could trust—a man who shared her fascination with death. Didn't take long for her to ask what she could do to please him: tattoo herself? *Hurt* herself?

Big surprise: He was more interested in nude pictures. Asked her to touch herself and think about him. According to her diary, she agreed on both counts. She had plans to visit him; was saving up enough money for what would have been one surreal fucking conjugal visit.

His letters are all typed. Courtney recalls Dr. Nancy saying he had some sort of learning disability, dyslexia or something. So we figure he probably had a friend help type them up for him.

They corresponded for about a year. Then he sent her his last letter, written in a totally different tone than the preceding ones. Before, he seemed collected, confident. This one oozes panic, desperation. Plus it seems he typed it himself, aided only with a bad spell check. Probably didn't feel he could trust anyone, even a fellow resident, with the content:

> *My dearest candy firstly dove of my hearts please don't recall*
> *me from thesis words of mien I am never to be culpable of*
> *giving in such a feeling as is in me from words wich is my*
> *needing to be seeing you in face and brushing eachothers skin*
> *but no I reef you are not to approach such me I amen't in such*
> *disfortune that quite danger is near and feering four you the*
> *dove of hearts so your hearing forth tender Silas nearly ends*

*my hearts and hands and feers grow week and no seeing you in
face and brushing eachothers skin no longer but alac I leaf your
tender heart not emptiness as inclosed a pears such tender item
as I express yet bad as knife on yourskin.*

*Mydearestcandy take such tender item to dirtand put it as
deeply down as can believe it is a knife that cuts hearts and
need be hidden in dirt MYDEARSETCANDYDONTLITNES
MDYEARSTCAᴅNYDNTOTILNES
MDARESCAᴅONTSITNEL YMEARDETSᴅNCON*

Courtney carefully folds the letter up with his latex-gloved
hands and puts it in a Ziploc bag.

" 'My dearest Candy, don't listen,' " he murmurs. "No question
now. The tape was here."

"But she did, probably, right?" I ask. "Listen?"

"Wouldn't you?" he asks grimly.

It's confirmed in her diary. A week after she describes her confusion and sadness at Silas saying he'll never write again, something starts happening to the way she writes. First she only does it
for a few words, but within two weeks of the date she received the
tape, she's writing a full mirror image—a palindrome—of each
diary entry on the page opposite.

"What about the guy who wrote the same way at Orange's?" I
ask. "So he heard the tape somehow, somewhere—"

"Good Frank! Yes! Wait . . ." Courtney suddenly digs into his
backpack for his notebook, flipping back to the day he wrote about
meeting with Orange. "Okay, well, that guy came in to see Orange
two months after the murder here. And Candy's accident. And
mentioned the Beulah Twelve. Which means . . ." He jerks the

ends of his mustache growth so hard it looks like he might pull it out, pushing his frown down as far as it will go. It's like he's on coke but really not enjoying it. "Which means that *probably,* as we guessed, the Beulah Twelve took the tape with them wherever they went. And somehow this guy ended up hearing it."

"Or he really was one of them, as he seemed to be implying when he confessed to killing that boy." I shake my head. "How do twelve men just disappear when the whole country is looking for them?"

Courtney nods slowly, then sits back down on Candy's old bed.

"So . . ." I ask. "Can we take this stuff? I mean, seems like it sort of belongs to Ms. Anderson, right?"

Courtney frowns. "It would cause her nothing but distress to see all this . . ." He sighs. "But I suppose you're right. I'll photograph it all, and then we'll put it back."

He takes his spy camera out of his bag but hesitates before starting his documentation.

"I just had a thought," I say, staring at the letter sitting on the bed. "Remember how Silas told us that he didn't know what was on the tape? Like he never heard it?"

"Right. Spewing nonsense."

I suck on my teeth. "Yeah, except, when you read this letter, don't you kind of believe him?"

"Kinda," Courtney nods almost imperceptibly. "Yes."

"And Greta scared the shit out of him. He sent the tape right after her visit, right before he tried to kill himself. It's almost like he was trying to keep it away from *her.*"

WE'RE THE ONLY ones in the Ritz tonight besides the help. Different waiter: a portly, middle-aged man who seems to genuinely enjoy this work. I think he's either one of the owners or a relative. I get a burger, am determined to eat. I need my strength. Do it for Sadie.

Courtney gets the nachos—hold the cheese—which as far as I'm concerned is like getting a glass of wine, hold the wine.

We split up after leaving Ms. Anderson's house at around six. I spoke with two people: Harry something, the neighbor who heard the screams the night of the murder—plus weird sounds coming from the attic for a few weeks prior—and a girl, Ashley Potter, now fourteen, who was friends with the boy they sacrificed on that altar.

Courtney spoke to Linda Jones, wife—widow?—of Walter Jones, one of the members of the Beulah Twelve.

Courtney pores over my notes. He won't find anything surprising, I assure him, but I know the day he takes my word on that is the day he hangs up the old PI license. Harry the neighbor basically recounted what Ms. Anderson told us. The girl, Ashley, only recalled that Todd was a nice boy, and she had no idea why they chose him as their victim.

I listen to the recordings of Courtney's interview with Linda.

Walter Jones sounds like he was a pretty normal dude before the tape fell into Lincoln Anderson's lap. He was hardly even friends with Lincoln—insofar as two people who have lived in this town for decades could not be friends. Walter was a doctor in Pueblo. Pediatrician. Lincoln was a logger. Not much in common there. Walter had three kids and a loving wife in Linda. Lincoln was a light drunk with a messed-up emo daughter who everyone correctly figured would end up in trouble eventually. Then Lincoln stopped by Walter's house one night, asked Walter to come over for a "guy's night"—have some beers, play some cards—and Walter was a little surprised but agreed.

For those ten days, between the offer and the murder, Linda didn't see much of her husband. First couple days he went over to Lincoln's right after work and didn't come home until she was asleep. Then he called in sick to the office for a week (she only found this out after); didn't even leave town. Just lived at Lincoln's. Sure, Linda was worried and confused, but what could she do? There were other men in town doing the same thing. She talked to their wives or girlfriends. They were getting ready to either barge into Lincoln's house or call the cops when they woke up and their men—along with a few trucks—were gone forever.

I listen closely to her conversation with Courtney through my headphones as I munch on the burger.

"Did you see Lincoln when he came over that first night to invite over Walter?"

"Briefly. I was in the living room, I walked over to see who Walter was talking to at the door, make sure everything was alright. He assured me it was. I only caught a quick glimpse of Lincoln."

"How did he look? Notice anything unusual?"

"I . . . I'm not sure if at the time I really thought about it. Only after Walter . . . left. I thought back on that night. So I don't know if it was real, or my imagination, but I have a memory of Lincoln's hands shaking so badly that he put them in his pockets. And he looked really, really tired, I think."

"Tired?"

"Yeah. His speech was sort of slurring like it gets when you're really tired."

"When was the last time you saw your husband?"

"The last time I saw him . . . It was three nights after Lincoln came over. Walter came home around three in the morning. I was in bed already. His footsteps coming up the stairs woke me up. I didn't

think it was him at first. We'd been married fifteen years. I knew his footsteps. And something was different. Slower maybe. He came into the room. He smelled funny—"

"Like alcohol?"

"No. Definitely not. Maybe like, spices of some kind? I remember thinking he smelled a little like cinnamon, only it wasn't cinnamon..."

"Incense, maybe?"

"Could be."

"So he came into your room."

"Yes."

"And then what?"

"I..."

"Please, Linda. Anything can help—"

"I've never ... I've really never talked about this ever. I knew the police would never find them. I could feel it. It felt wrong. But you, I want to believe you so badly. I want to tell you everything, it's just so..."

"It's okay. It's okay, Linda."

"I'm going to try."

"Alright. When you're ready."

[Long pause]

"He ... came in. And I turned over. I was awake. I asked him, 'Walter, where have you been?' I wasn't mad, exactly. But he didn't answer. He just started taking off his clothes. The smell I described earlier, it grew stronger as he took off his clothes, like it was clinging to his bare skin. I asked again. Nothing. I reached over to turn on the bedside lamp, but he grabbed my wrist to stop me. Hard. Harder than he'd ever touched me. He held onto my wrist as he pulled off the rest of his clothes. I said, 'Stop,' I think, or 'Let go of

me,' but he didn't respond. It wasn't Walter. I mean, it was him, but it's like there was someone else inside of his head, controlling him. He grabbed my other wrist, too, and pinned me to the bed, then . . ."

"It's okay, Linda . . ."

"He, he . . . I didn't want to. But he did anyways. I was trying to push him off of me. I was crying. It hurt. I stopped struggling eventually, I lost my strength. He kept going and going, silently, like he wasn't even enjoying it. Just purely mechanical. He did that for over an hour—"

"An hour?"

"Yes. And in the end, he didn't even, you know. Finish. He just decided to stop and rolled over and instantly fell into a silent sleep. I was so upset I didn't know what to do. I went downstairs to sleep on the couch. When I woke up in the morning he was gone. I thought he went to work. He didn't. Someone told me later they saw him walking into Lincoln's house holding a bag of groceries. But that . . . that was the last time I saw him."

"And you never told anybody?"

"I . . . I swear I was going to. I really was. I needed time to work up the courage. But before I could, he was gone."

"You didn't tell the cops?"

"I . . . No. Maybe this sounds silly, but I didn't want to tarnish what people thought of him once he was gone. Especially the kids. I don't want them to think of their father like that. I know what the men did . . . to the boy, Todd . . . but he was my husband, you have to understand. I loved him. And he was a good father. And I think of the man who did that to me, and the man who helped hurt that boy, that was someone else. Maybe that's weak of me. Maybe that's how I deal with it. But that's how I feel."

I pull off my headphones. Snap my fingers to get Courtney's

attention. He looks up from his papers, a cheeseless nacho—a chip—in his mouth.

"I'm not gonna lie, I'm glad I wasn't there with you to talk to this woman."

Courtney chews slowly. "Yup. That was tough."

My phone vibrates against my leg. I jerk it out frantically. Helen Langdon. I answer after one ring.

"Helen."

"Frank. Get a pen and sit down."

I'VE GOT HER on speaker up in the room so Courtney can hear. My chest is like a strong hand crushing the soda can that is my heart.

"Frank, I have to report this and go after her right away. This is deep."

"Tell me what you have," I say.

"She's not Greta Kanter," Helen says. "At least, not the sister of the girl who was killed."

I'm surprised to find that I was expecting this once I saw her name on that visitation log. Judging by Courtney's grim nod, he did as well.

"The sister of Savannah is married and changed her last name to Green. Greta Green. She also moved—along with her husband and child—to California a year after the murder."

"Christ." I rub my temples. Think about that beautiful woman who sat across from me in my apartment. Never took her gloves off. The woman I think I may have dreamed about again last night but can't quite recall. Think about that woman keeping Sadie tied up in some shed behind the house. "So who is she?"

"I'm not sure. I combed through all the basic stuff, and I swear, at first, just like a few days ago, everything looked totally normal. Social Security number is linked to her name, ditto credit rating. And no criminal record. It was only after a few hours of digging that I found a hole: This was her first driver's license. Got it three years ago. No license before that. Red flag. So I keep looking, and she also had no credit card activity before three years ago."

"Identity theft?" I ask.

"No," Helen replies. "Not theft. *Creation*. She made Greta Kanter up. She might have even legally changed her name and bought a Social from an immigrant. *This* Greta Kanter has only existed for three years. And I've tried, but there's no way to find what her name was before. Point is, whoever this woman is, she knows what she's doing. This is not some kind of side act gone awry. This is her life. How exactly did you say you got involved with this woman again?"

"I didn't," I reply. "But basically, she wants us to find something for her."

"What?"

"I can't tell you."

"Frank. Listen carefully to me. I assumed we were dealing with some low-level nut, that's why I figured forty-eight hours would be plenty for me to find her. But this woman is some kind of professional. She's created an almost flawless identity cover, so she'll have also made herself nearly impossible to find. And every hour we wait to move on this, the less likely it is we'll get your daughter back safely. You have to turn this over to me and let me do my thing."

I exchange a look with Courtney, ask with my eyes if he agrees. He deliberates for a moment, then puts palms to the sky like he doesn't know. I keep pushing images of Sadie out of my head, try to concentrate, think clearly, objectively.

"Listen, Helen. You said it yourself. Impossible to find. This woman is obsessed. The only way out of this is for me to get her what she wants. Let's stick with Thursday night. If I don't have anything by then, I'll tell you everything, fly back to NYC, and we can figure out how to . . . I don't know . . . negotiate with her or something. But I already know there will be no deal. It's either get her what she wants, or nothing. I swear. Every cell in my body is telling me that."

I picture Helen on the other end, massaging her temples and chewing on her pen.

"Thursday."

"Thursday night."

"You know we want the same thing here, Frank."

"I know."

"This woman is a real nutter. This is not an isolated incident. She's probably kidnapped before, or worse."

"Or worse, probably. Just . . . Thursday night. Midnight."

"Your call."

"I really can't thank you enough."

"Don't mention it. Really, don't. I could lose my job."

"I, um—" I shoot Courtney a look, like *get outta here*. He reluctantly saunters into the bathroom and closes the door. I take the phone off speaker. "I just, I wanted to tell you, also . . . I still think about you sometimes."

Silence.

"I'd like to take you out to dinner to thank you for your help. After I get my daughter back. She'll come along. You'll love her."

She's probably destroying a pen on the other end.

"I'll talk to you Thursday night, Frank. I hope you find what you're looking for."

I SLEEP MAYBE two hours that night.

I'm awakened around four by doubt. Sit up in bed, then toss my feet onto the carpet. Grope my way to the bathroom and flip the light on, shut the door. Splash my face with cold water, let it drip down my stubbly chin. Reflected in the circular mirror over the sink is a portrait of weariness: puffy blue bags under my eyes, complexion only a few shades north of corpse. Gaunt cheeks. I've aged five years in a week.

I turn on the valve for hot water, but it never gets past tepid.

I glare at myself again. Doubt.

I can't do this, even with Courtney's help. There's not enough time, we're not smart enough. Or maybe it's impossible. Maybe the Beulah Twelve and the tape are just simply *gone,* vanished off the face of the earth. I think about the destruction and pain that this tape has left in its wake. First Savannah. Then the man at Orange's—"Egnaro"—and Silas, Candy, Paula, Todd, Linda. And now me and Sadie. That's what happens. The tape comes into your life and tears it apart.

I stare deeper into my own brown eyes.

"Please," I whisper to my own reflection. "Don't punish Sadie. She's done nothing. Punish me, or punish Courtney, I guess. Anyone but her. If Greta lays a hand on her, I won't be able to live with myself. I mean that. I won't be able to live knowing what I've done."

I notice a corner of the shrink-wrapped Bible from the airplane nun poking out of my dopp kit, which is resting on the sink. I don't remember putting it in there. I pull it out with a hand trembling from exhaustion. I think, *Just like Lincoln, the night he invited over Walter.*

I pull off the shrink wrapping and sit down on the edge of the tub. Open it up, realize I don't know the first thing about the Bible. Do you just start at the beginning? First couple pages are vaguely familiar. The Lord makes light, darkness, birds, bees . . . A hundred pages later Joseph is in Egypt. Toward the second half there's stuff about Jesus and his disciples. That's right. Old Testament and New Testament. I'm not a complete ignoramus.

I flip backwards, and the Bible falls open somewhere in the middle. I read.

And Elijah came unto all the people, and said, How long halt ye between two opinions? if the LORD *[be] God, follow him: but if Baal, [then] follow him. And the people answered him not a word. Then said Elijah unto the people, Only I remain a prophet of the* LORD; *but Baal's prophets [are] four hundred and fifty men. Let them therefore give us two bullocks; and let them choose one bullock for themselves, and cut it in pieces, and lay [it] on wood, and put no fire [under:] and I will dress the other bullock, and lay [it] on wood, and put no fire [under:] And call ye on the name of your gods, and I will call on the name of the* LORD: *and the God that answereth by fire, let him be God. And all the people answered and said, It is well spoken. And Elijah said unto the prophets of Baal, Choose you one bullock for yourselves, and dress [it] first; for ye [are] many; and call on the name of your gods, but put no fire [under.] And they took the bullock which was given them, and they dressed [it,] and called on the name of Baal from morning even until noon, saying, O Baal, hear us. But [there was] no voice, nor any that answered. And they leaped upon the altar which was made. {18:27} And it came to pass at noon, that Elijah mocked them, and said, Cry aloud: for he*

[is] a god; either he is talking, or he is pursuing, or he is in a
journey, [or] peradventure he sleepeth, and must be awaked.
{18:28} And they cried aloud, and cut themselves after their
manner with knives and lancets until the blood gushed out
upon them.

I smirk sadly. Proof. Guess wanting some proof is nothing new.
I close the book and walk out of the bathroom. Flip on the lights.
Courtney's eyes are already open.

"Let's go," I say.

WE DON'T STOP for seventeen hours. Five in the morning through
ten at night. Begging people to talk to us about the Beulah Twelve.
Most slam the doors on us. A few have heard that Ms. Anderson
and Linda opened up to us and therefore feel obligated to do the
same.

We sit beside Candy for an hour in a light snow, gently asking
again and again what happened to the tape. Nothing but an occasional empty stare.

We decide to show Ms. Anderson the loose brick in the room
and the diaries and letters. Ask if we can show them to her niece,
see if they muster some sort of visceral reaction. This she agrees
to, but it's for naught. The diaries mean as little to Candy as our
questions do.

Back at the Ritz, Courtney reads his collection of articles on
the Beulah Twelve for the twentieth time while I pace up and
down Main Street like a caged tiger, waiting for the proverbial
lightbulb to flick on.

Tammy Feinsod calls, asks if Sadie's doing alright at her aunt's.
I say yes, thanks for thinking of us. I wander aimlessly, ending

up in the Beulah General Store, where I walk the aisles, not at all hungry, finally buying some beef jerky on pure autopilot.

Outside, I sit down on a wet lunch table and chew on a piece of dried meat. I can't stop thinking about the woman who calls herself Greta Kanter. My rage for her seems to intensify with every passing hour. I have visions of hurting her, humiliating her, punishing her for doing—

Makes me sick to wonder where Sadie is right now. What's happening to her.

My body is proving to have an endless supply of adrenaline and cortisol; it's been locked in a whole-body flinch all day. I half hope some punk will walk up to me here at the bench and give me a reason to beat his ass to a pulp. My eyes are twitching, and there's a cold buried beneath my jacket that has nothing to do with the dry winter air.

Part of my anger becomes directed at this Midwestern shantytown. Who could live in a place like this? Two restaurants, one general store that also serves as a post office and pharmacy and that's *it*. You want to buy a book? See a doctor? Buy *gas*? Gotta drive forty-five minutes into Pueblo. If there's a blizzard here, forget it. No wonder those guys wanted to get the hell out of here.

I throw away the jerky and walk up the short driveway back to Main Street. Stare in the direction opposite where Courtney and I arrived, follow it as far as I can with my eyes until it snakes around a tight corner, is lost behind pine trees. And then turn to face the direction from where we came. No real turnoffs on the highway before Pueblo. Which direction did those twelve guys go? Were they fleeing the scene of the crime? Just trying to escape the law? That seems unlikely, somehow. I imagine these guys—like Silas, like Greta—didn't really care what happened to them. They had some sort of deeper purpose in mind, crazy though it might have been. But they already *had* the tape. They weren't looking for anything. Why did they go to Chicago and max out their credit cards?

I wander back to the Ritz. Mercifully, nobody tries to talk to me as I clomp through the dining room, past the black-and-white photos and stupid stuffed animal heads hanging on the walls, up the carpeted stairs to the third floor.

Our room is unlocked. Courtney is on the floor of our room on all fours—wearing a flannel I'm pretty sure he's had on since we flew into Denver—combing through a carpet of papers.

"Where did they shop in Chicago?" I ask him. "Does anyone know? They say they maxed out their credit cards there."

"Yeah," Courtney says without looking up. "They made two stops. One at a warehouse that sells industrial kitchen equipment, then they went to a place that sells wholesale materials to construction companies."

"What did they buy precisely though?"

"Umm . . ." Courtney isn't really listening to me.

"Hey." I wave a hand in front of his eyes, summoning him from his trance. "What did they buy?"

"Oh, um, I don't know. I know the places. We might be able to go there and go deep into their records, or get them from the formal police report, but we don't have time for either."

"Well, isn't that probably relevant—"

"Of *course*!" Courtney groans. "Of course it's relevant. But we don't have time, so it doesn't matter."

I sit down on the floor next to him. "And they combed Chicago, right?"

"Yeah. Feds were ordered to stop any vehicles fitting the description of the seven trucks within two hundred miles of downtown Chicago. Nothing. But of course, they didn't find the credit card activity until a few days after the fact, so it's no surprise they didn't find them driving around, really."

"They kill a kid here, send a girl to the hospital," I muse to myself, "then book it to *Chicago*, buy a bunch of some kind of industrial equipment there, then are never seen again."

"Yes, yes." Courtney nods impatiently.

"You know what the hardest part of that whole thing to explain is? *Chicago*. So they're nuts, and they need all this equipment or whatever. Why not just go to Denver?"

Courtney shakes his head. "I don't know. *I don't know*."

I leave him to his research, pad down to the dining room. For a moment I have a horrible vision of Sadie in a cage, her little hands handcuffed behind her back, tape over her mouth . . . But how do I know she's even still alive? I push it from my mind. If I go down that rabbit hole, I'll have no chance of getting anything done.

I walk through the lobby, across Main Street, back over to Candy. Squat down beside her, along with the porcelain statues of the Virgin Mary. Paula is sitting behind her usual window. I wave at her, and she returns a sad wave. Then I return to Candy's dead eyes.

"You know the answers, don't you, Candy? You definitely know what's on that tape, that's for sure."

She doesn't budge. Snowflakes collect in her wispy, tangled hair.

"I know you probably can't hear me, but if you could help me, it could help save my daughter's life."

For a moment, I imagine I see her eyes flitting to me, maybe some hint of cognizance behind the glaze. But then it's gone. I lean in close, whisper in her ear. She smells like baby shampoo and spoiled milk.

"What's on the tape, Candy? I'm begging you. Tell me what's on that tape. Tell me where they took it."

I pull back, stare into her eyes, looking for any trace of a reaction. Snow lands on her nose and melts. She doesn't notice.

I turn away, realize I'm crying.

I AWAKE THURSDAY with tingling dread in my belly. Unsure if I slept at all, between fantasies of hurting Greta, of her hurting Sadie, of me hurting myself. Because if this doesn't work out, there's no doubt that I will. Hurt myself.

Can't get down a thing at breakfast besides coffee. I've never felt this weary, and it's getting hard to remember a time when I didn't feel like I was on the verge of collapsing. Courtney looks like shit too. He's gotten paler and lost a few pounds he could ill afford to part with. Crow's-feet blossom from his wide eyes, and every time he talks his forehead wrinkles like a Chinese fan.

I haven't had a bowel movement since getting here, and I can tell I've lost muscle on my arms and chest.

Thursday.

"What's the plan, boss?" I ask weakly.

"We have sixteen hours until midnight."

"Fourteen. We're two hours behind New York," I say.

"Fourteen," Courtney repeats emptily. He shrugs. "I don't know what else to do."

"Don't say that." I shake my head. "Don't fucking say that, please. There has to be more to do. Tell me what to do."

He sighs. "Go back to the attic?" His suggestion is so half-hearted that just looking at him makes me want to cry.

"We could do that." I nod. "If Paula will let us."

I'm desperate here. Grasping at straws. Anything that makes

me feel like I'm moving this thing forward. Like I'm doing something to help Sadie. I feel infuriatingly helpless.

Courtney looks down at his papers, then up at me, blinks emptily.

"Maybe there are more people to talk to," he says.

"Maybe," I try to agree. Try not to think about how deep in mud and shit I am, how anything I do now feels like trying to climb out of a well, the walls made of shit, no grip, grasping at loose pieces of shit that keep giving way, me sliding right back down to the bottom.

"You know," Courtney says, wiping some fatigue from his eyes, "maybe we should try to relax a little. Odds are we're not gonna discover anything new today. Sometimes a little space, a little step back, is the best way to gain perspective."

I gape at him. "You're serious?"

"Yeah. You ever done yoga?"

I gaze levelly at him. And then just burst out laughing. The only other customers in the tavern, a young couple, stare at me. I'm in hysterics. Slam a fist on the table, laughing uncontrollably. It's mirthless, horrible, cosmic-joke laughing. I'm almost retching. Courtney's eyes are wide with concern. I'm thinking, *This is it. This is what it feels like to go crazy.* Not bad.

"Yoga," I gasp, clearing tears out of my eyes. "Yeah, I have some experience."

"I wasn't joking," he says.

"I know." I laugh. "I know you weren't. That's what's so goddamn funny. My daughter's been kidnapped by a psychopath and you think the best use of our time is *yoga.* And you know what the funniest part is? I can't even fucking argue with you. So, what, is there a fucking YMCA around here?" I can't stop giggling.

"Actually, I'm a certified instructor," Courtney says.

246 E. Z. RINSKY

"Of course you are!" I slam a fist on the table. "Of course you fucking are! Well what are we fucking *waiting* for?" I shoot to my feet. The waiter on duty for breakfast is the skater-looking boy from the other night. I point at him. "Hey! Champ, wanna go up-stairs and fucking *meditate*? We don't have a second to lose."

He's cowering behind the bar.

Courtney stands up and wraps an arm around my shoulder. Shoots a nonverbal apology to the other patrons and the little stoner.

"Let's go upstairs, Frank," he says in a therapist voice.

"Sure." I laugh as he leads me up the carpeted stairway. "All the answers are upstairs, right? Maybe that's where they hid it, Court! Upstairs!"

"JUST LET YOUR mind go blank," Courtney intones.

We're both on the carpeted floor in what Courtney calls child's pose. The shades are drawn. I'm in a filthy Rolling Stones T-shirt and boxers. Courtney is wearing only a spandex bottom. He's built like a lemur. He dumped all the papers in a recycling bin and set it on top of the TV, figuratively demonstrating that we've ab-sorbed all the information we're going to. The rest is processing it.

"It's not working. I keep imagining making people's faces bleed."

"Shut up, Frank. This has no chance if you don't give yourself over to it. Now, I want you to push up from the floor with your palms, rise into downward dog. Your knees can be bent. Push back with your hands, driving your toes into the carpet."

"Okay," I mumble.

"Now, slowly pick up your right leg and stretch it back toward the wall behind you. It's not about height, it's about distance."

I silently oblige. My mind still isn't blank though. *When is my fucking mind going to go blank?*

Courtney runs us through an hour-long progression, his voice like a metronome. He's more gentle and reasonable than the instructor at the class Sadie took me to. Feels a little less like bullshit. At the end I'm sweating profusely, and though the gag reflex is once again rearing his ugly head, I feel a little better than I did before. We lie down flat on the carpet, palms up.

"Now just imagine you're on top of a mountain," Courtney coos. "There's nobody else around. You're on the very, very top of the mountain alone. It's warm. The sun is shining on your face. There is nothing else but you, the mountain, the sun, and the warm grass beneath your hands. Can you feel the grass? I can. It feels wonderful. It feels like spring: like lemonade and squirrels and kissing girls by the tire swing. And you have no worries, Frank. You are just letting the sun's warmth wash over you. Your mind is . . . blank."

I'm on the mountain. I can feel the sun and the grass. I feel a peace I haven't in so long. I lie there for a very long time, and when I slowly open my eyes and sit up I'm not alone on the mountain. Savannah Kanter is sitting beside me, wearing an amber sundress, her pale shoulders freckly in the sun. We are sitting beside each other on a smooth boulder, our feet dangling, flirting with the top of a cool stream. I let clear water rush over my pair of filthy feet. Her feet are refracted by water, clean and pale an inch beneath the glassy surface.

We look at each other.

"Savannah," I say.

She nods.

"You were right. I made a mistake."

She nods again, smiling sadly.

"Is it too late? Or can I fix this? Can I save my daughter?"

She looks down at her feet, like she's considering my request, then shoots to her feet. She slips on a pair of sandals and urgently beckons me to stand as well. Then she starts walking backwards, like a tour guide, telling me with her eyes to follow her.

We follow the creek, which gushes down the rocky slope of the mountain. Yellow daisies and some purple wildflower I don't recognize sprout on its banks.

She's moving quickly. I have to hurry to keep up with her. She doesn't walk so much as skip backwards. Dance.

"Where are we going?" I ask her. She says something in response that I can't understand.

As we descend the mountain, the sky darkens, and the breeze grows colder. The trees start to gather snow. The flowers disappear. The rocks grow sharp. I'm wearing no shoes, I realize. And I'm struggling to keep Savannah in sight.

"Wait!" I call after her, racing down the steep path, cold wind whipping in my ears. Where is she? "Savannah!" I call. Nothing. I run faster, blood pumping in my ears, and then I think I glimpse her up ahead, at the edge of a clearing.

I slow to a halt as I reach her. We stand shoulder to shoulder and look out over the dead, snow-covered meadow before us. The stream ends in a murky swamp that gurgles off to our left. The scene is still, save a cold breeze that ruffles her light hair. A blackbird screams something and shoots across the sky, then the scene resumes its heavy stillness.

"Where are we going?"

She points ahead, across the clearing, toward a dark mound of trees. Something about this looks familiar.

"Where are we?" I ask.

She responds, but it's again the damn incomprehensible warbling.

"I can't understand," I say.

She tries again, nearly shouting, like it's the most obvious thing in the world, but it sounds like she's an adult in a Peanuts cartoon. I can only shake my head helplessly.

She takes my hand, sandwiches it between her two petite ones. Her hands are warm, and I can feel her pulse pumping through them.

"What is this?" I ask. "Are you a ghost or something?"

This amuses her. She laughs, low at first, and then laughs hard and squeezes my hand tightly. She gazes into my face, eyes tearing a little, and shrugs: *I don't know.*

And then she drops my hand and turns away. Retreats back up the mountain, back to where we started. I glance over my shoulder at the dark mound of trees she'd pointed to.

"Are you not coming with me?" I shout after her.

She turns and shakes her head adamantly, then points at me—"Frank!"

I open my eyes. I'm lying flat on my back in the hotel room. "It's seven at night!" Courtney says. "We slept all day."

I blink at him. "What?"

"It's seven. We only have three hours before Helen is taking over. What's with you? What's wrong?"

"I . . . I was dreaming, I guess. Savannah Kanter. She was showing me some place. There was a mountain and a field." I sit up and look at Courtney. The sleep has done my body good, that's for sure. And then my stomach falls out as I remember who I am, where I am, why I'm here.

"What else?" Courtney asks.

"I mean . . ." The pain in my ribs and cut-up ankle slowly return, and I sink back into a familiar whole-body sickness. "I guess I sort of felt like she was pointing to some trees. And I think . . . I think I knew that the tape was there, beyond those trees."

Courtney looks devastated. "And I woke you up. I'm so—"

"Forget it. It's all bullshit."

I stand up, look at my watch. Three hours.

"Let's call Helen now," I say. "Give her another few hours to work with."

Courtney looks pained. "We still have time. What if . . ." He stares at me. "It exists. It's *somewhere*. The clues are all in front of us, I feel it. I can *feel* it, Frank. It's so close . . ." His hands are clenched into fists.

"No, Courtney," I say, put a hand on his shoulder. "It's okay. We did what we could. But we have to do whatever gives Sadie the best chance."

Courtney nods, but I can tell how much this hurts him. I wonder if he's ever *not* solved a case.

"Go wait for me downstairs," I say. "I'm gonna call Helen. Then let's get out of this shit hole of a town."

WE CHECK OUT of the Ritz. I can't bear another minute in that goddamn place: the stuffed deer mounted on the walls, the tacky polished wood, red-checkered tablecloths.

The tiniest of weights lifts from my chest as we leave Beulah. It's like escaping the pull of a black hole. The whole town is mired in some kind of evil haze; I'm only able to see this as we speed away from Candy, Ms. Anderson, Linda. That house. The altar.

We don't say anything. There's nothing to talk about. The case is out of our hands. Courtney buys tickets to NYC on my phone while I drive.

I spilled my guts to Helen, told her every detail, down to those black leather gloves that "Greta" wore. Helen assured me that I was doing the right thing. Said I was giving my daughter the best chance of being safe by handing it over to her. Said she'd have a team mobilized within a few hours.

Assuming they haven't found her by the time I get back to NYC, I'm supposed to go to Helen's office. Then we'll have to talk options: negotiating alternatives with Greta or just lying to her about having the tape.

I admire Helen's cautious optimism, but I'm the only one who's met Greta face-to-face; I'm the only one who understands how serious she is. There will be no negotiating with her—money is meaningless to her—and there's no way she'll fall for any sort of trickery.

Headlights capture a sliver of yellow-lined asphalt, empty fields, shadows of mountains. I should have let Courtney drive, probably. I can feel a sort of apathy as I take each turn in the road a little too quickly, in the back of my head thinking that sliding off the road, flipping into a ditch and just burning up or getting my head bashed open . . . that might be easier than facing what's back in New York.

I turn on the radio. Led Zeppelin's "Kashmir."

"Great song," I mumble.

"Never heard it," Courtney replies. He's got his red duck-hunting hat back on. Starting the hard transition back to civilian. Guess he lost his ponytail for nothing.

"Let's get a drink," I say. "We'll sober up by early morning and drive to DIA for our flight."

Courtney doesn't say yes, but he doesn't say no.

I pull into the first place we pass as we enter Pueblo: Harry's Hole. In the parking lot, I step over a dead rat the size of a small squirrel. Kinda comforting. Little slice of home.

The bouncer doesn't ask for ID. Anybody as dreary looking as us deserves to get fucked up, regardless of age. Inside a heavy funk bass line is pumping out of the speakers. A couple hipsters sit around eating oysters and twirling their wax mustaches. Maybe in Colorado they're not called hipsters; they're just guys. A creepy, primitive-looking man is standing by the pool table in the back, holding a cue vertically like a fishing pole. He doesn't seem to be in the middle of a game. We squeeze into the bar between an old bald guy and a pair of giggling girls around Savanah's age. Or how old she was when she was killed.

The bartender is a heavily tattooed girl, her shiny black hair clipped into a bowl around her head.

I look at Courtney. "I tried your yoga. Now you try my therapy, alright?"

He nods wearily, resigning himself.

"Two PBRs," I tell the bartender.

"It's five dollars for a PBR and a shot," she offers.

"Fine. Two meal deals."

There's a TV mounted on the wall, but instead of sports it's showing some kind of vintage porn that looks to be a takeoff on Flash Gordon. Ah. *Flesh* Gordon.

The waitress gives us the beers and two shots of something vile. Yellow chemical color. Without hesitation, Courtney downs his shot and follows it with a healthy swig of beer.

"Whoa there, champ," I say. "This is your first time, right?"

"I had a beer once in high school. Didn't like the way it made me feel."

"Nobody likes the way it makes them feel." I chuckle. "It's just the lesser of two evils. Reality or drunk reality."

My shot burns all the way down, and the PBR doesn't do much to ease the pain.

"See, I like Pabst," I grumble, "but it's ridiculous. See this can? It's called Blue Ribbon because it won this award in 1893. Jesus. That's good and all, but what have you done for me lately, right?"

Courtney turns to the bartender. "Two more please, ma'am."

We down the shots, clink cans. This is irresponsible, sure. But I guess this is marginally better than spending time at the airport. Airport. Try not to think about what might be facing me when I get off the plane in NYC.

I chug the rest of the PBR.

"Who's Sadie's mom?" Courtney asks.

I gawk at him. He's totally serious.

"You really wanna hear about it?"

"Yeah," he says. "If you don't mind talking about it."

I swallow a lump in my throat, focus on the warm buzz starting in my head.

"Her name's Jennifer. I hardly knew her. One-night stand. I met her in a bar in Williamsburg and brought her home. Thought I wrapped up, but who knows. I was trashed. She called me two months later and told me. Wanted me to pay for half the abortion. I met up with her for coffee. Sweet girl. Young. When I saw her, I felt terrible about it all. She said her insurance wouldn't cover the operation, but she wanted to make sure she did it right. Two grand.

"But . . . I dunno. I'd never really given much thought to it before, but she was showing just a little bit. And I thought, hey, there's a person inside her. We're just going to, like, *end* this person? So I looked her straight in the eye and said, 'Jennifer, it's your body, and my fault, and if you want me to pay for the operation, I'll pay the whole fucking thing, no questions asked. But if you're willing, I would love if you have this baby. I'll do everything for you. I'll pay for everything. And after, I'll take her. I'll raise her myself. You never have to see her if you don't want to. And she said yes. Still can't believe it. It was a miracle."

Getting misty-eyed. Courtney's about to order another round when I stop him.

"Miss?" I say to the bartender. "How about something a little classier than PBR? Surprise us."

She smiles and goes to the tap. Hands us two glasses of dark brown lager.

"It's your first time getting wasted," I tell Courtney. "You shouldn't have to drink shit."

He smiles and sips the beer, thinks about it, then nods appreciatively. "Not bad. So Frank, if you don't mind me prodding . . . what led you to make her that offer?"

I shrug. "I don't know. That's the god-honest truth. I don't know. It was totally impulsive. I showed up to that coffee shop fully intending to just give her the money. But something came over me. Maybe I realized this was probably my only chance to have a kid."

Some good old New Orleans boogie jam comes on. Half the people in the place jump to their feet and start shimmying. We don't even consider it.

"You're a good guy, Frank. I've suspected this for a while. Even though you don't see it, way down deep, you're a good guy."

"Thanks, champ." I sigh, drain my beer. It's thick. Feels like drinking a loaf of rye bread. I wave my empty glass at Courtney, and he takes a deep breath and chugs his down as well.

"Two more of those, please." I wave at the bartender.

"Take it easy, fellas. The night is young." She winks.

"Yeah, but we aren't. And the jury is out on whether you can get fucked up after death."

A girl in skintight leopard print sits down next to Courtney.

"I like your hat," she coos.

"That's a very kind thing to say," he responds in monotone and sips on his beer.

"Do you have a cigarette?" she asks him.

"Nope."

She has long blond curls that keep getting in her eyes. In response, she throws her head back every few seconds to brush them away. Not a very effective system.

"Want to buy me a drink?" she asks. She looks like she's already knocked back more than her fair share tonight.

"Nope," Courtney says.

"Asshole," she says and leaves.

"She didn't ask *me*," I tell Courtney. "Maybe I would have."

"Mmm." Courtney's about halfway through his second dark beer. Something is shifting in his face. He must be one of those zero-to-sixty-type drunks.

The bartender smiles at us. "Doing alright, boys?"

"Not really, but you're doing your best," I reply. She laughs and moves onto someone else.

"Keep an eye on that bartender," Courtney says in a low voice. The switch has been flipped. "Make sure she doesn't put anything in our drinks. She's been looking at us funny all night."

"Uh-huh."

Courtney suddenly sniffs his beer warily.

"Think she's trying to date-rape you, Courtney?" I ask, then laugh a little too hard and smack the bar.

"Laugh away," he says seriously. "I'm a good-looking guy though. I have to watch my back—"

He stops suddenly.

"Give me your phone," he says.

I hand him my phone, and he goes at it like a man possessed. I realize he's checking his email.

"Is everything going okay?" I ask. My eyes are getting heavy. "Just tell me everything's going to be okay, Courtney."

"I was tentatively involved with a woman before we left, but I'm beginning to suspect she's getting nailed by someone else in her spinning class," he growls, fiddling with the ends of one of his few mustache hairs, slurring his words. "If she's even going to spinning classes at all. Great cover. Every evening I see her, she's sweating and pumped with endorphins. Her 'class' is probably getting it from behind in a Best Western."

"Why didn't you tell me you were seeing someone? We coulda had guy talk," I say, my head swimming pleasantly, vaguely surprised that he's not gay.

"Wasn't relevant to the case. Didn't want any distractions," he says demurely. Then hands me back my phone. "No word. Remember Frank, if it's too good to be true . . ." He jabs my chest with a boney index finger, then swivels back to the bartender. "Two more beers," he says slowly, then lowers his head onto the bar for a quick nap.

There's a cup of water on the bar that might be mine. I chug it. The girls next to me are braying like donkeys. A guy with a tattoo on his face appears to be threatening a much smaller man, but then they both smile and hug each other. The beers arrive. The bartender leaves Courtney's right in front of his nose and closed eyes.

"Hey," I say in his ear. "I don't know how much more we should drink. We gotta drive to the airport at some point."

He jerks up violently, fire in his eyes.

"Frank . . ." he says slowly. "Frank," he repeats, beckoning me to come close. I roll my eyes and oblige. "How do we know it wasn't a setup?"

I lean away from him, catching myself to prevent an embarrassing tumble onto the disgusting floor.

"Setup?" I ask, struggling to keep my eyes open. I grope on the bar blindly, hoping to summon another glass of water.

"What if Savannah isn't dead!" His eyes are frighteningly wide now, veins and blood vessels scurrying across his irises like roaches. He lowers his voice, presumably to prevent anyone in this bar from eavesdropping on his drunken ranting. "Have we seen the body? No. Supposedly buried six feet under. The pictures are all doctored! It's all a setup, don't you see?"

"Shut up."

He tries to flag down the tattooed bartender, not even aware of the untouched beer in front of him. I slap his hand out of the air. He eyes me suspiciously.

"What?" He's slurring badly now. "Why d-d-don't you want me to drink? You think I'm gonna fucking . . . fucking . . ."

"I'm gonna drive." I check my watch. "If I stop drinking now, I'll probably be sober enough by three or four in the morning."

"I like this beer," Courtney groans, reaching his glass to his lips with great deliberation. "Hey." He waves to the bartender. "What beer is this? I *like* it."

"Yeah, it's a doozy, isn't it?" She smiles. "Black Lab. Brewed up in Colorado Springs."

"Mmm." Courtney takes a gulp.

Something clicks in my mind. A flash. In an instant I'm half sober, my vision suddenly straight. I spring from my barstool, nearly grab the bartender.

"What did you say this beer is called?"

"Black Lab," she says, confused.

"It's a Colorado beer," I say slowly. "A local craft beer?"

"Uh-huh." She nods, looking around like *anyone else see this guy?*

"Small brewery, right? I've never seen this on the East Coast."

"Yeah, I guess."

"And there's a black dog on the bottle, right?"

"Um . . ." She takes a step back. "I think so."

I smack Courtney on the cheek. He looks up at me in a daze.

"Courtney. This beer we're drinking. *Black Lab.* Sound familiar?"

"It's . . . *delicious.*" He smiles.

"Courtney!" I squeak. "This is the beer that was stacked in the cabin. Outside Bangor. Silas's cabin."

This gets through to him. He sits up a little straighter.

"Are you sure?" he says groggily.

"Check your notes or pictures, but I'm almost positive." I lean in close. "The only way this beer ends up in Maine is if someone brings it. From Colorado."

Courtney's eyes are wide.

I continue in a whisper: "The Beulah Twelve. They knew what they liked to drink, so they brought it with them, all the way across the country. Stopping in Chicago first to pick up some supplies."

Courtney's pupils narrow. He's silent.

"And there were trucks back behind the cabin. Rusty skeletons of old pickup trucks."

"Jesus Christ, Frank." He's shaking his head. "So they . . . they went there . . . but we were already there. They weren't there. So where did they go from there?"

"We weren't thorough enough." I grimace. "They must still be there. In the cellar."

PART FOUR:

Rewind

WE CHANGE OUR tickets to Boston and get into rainy Logan at eleven in the morning on Friday, dash to the airport Hertz in a trance. I've got that jolting, manic, hungover energy. Courtney is just sick, his pallor the color of a dollar bill. Spent the first twenty minutes of our drive to Denver raving nonsense about Savannah and Silas and asking to see my phone to check his email. Then I think he blacked out for the rest.

Helen was incredulous when I called her from the parking lot of Harry's Hole in Pueblo. Called her cell three times before she picked up, swearing at me. I forgot it's two hours later on the East Coast. I could feel the unmitigated words pouring out of me, a river of conspiracy bursting through the dam. Knew I must have sounded nuts. Took me fifteen minutes to convince her we figured it out. We were gonna get Greta what she wanted. Probably.

"Have you started the search yet?" I demanded.

"I . . . I started making calls yeah, of course. Haven't briefed anyone yet though."

She only agreed to call off the troops once I leveled with her:

"It's my daughter, Helen. I wouldn't do this unless I was damn near sure. Because I realize, if I'm wrong, her blood is on my hands."

The words felt sort of empty when I said them. But she relented.

Words have to feel empty, because to really process them, the situation, would probably leave me in shock. So I pretend Courtney and I just have a series of tasks to complete, each devoid of importance or emotion. They are simply things that have to get done. Household chores. Mow the lawn, paint the fence, acquire water saw. Don't think about the endgame here. Just one foot in front of the other: smile to the lady at Hertz, pretend that we're not walking hangovers that reek of sweat and the smoked meat odor of the Ritz that seems to be permanently ingrained in all of our possessions.

I floor the minivan out of Logan, stopping only to pick up a dozen donuts and a lake-sized coffee. I feel like I'm driving a tank, but it's critical that we have plenty of room in the back.

It's about a four-hour drive to the cabin, but we have a crucial stop to make first. Courtney is on my phone trying to figure out where that stop is.

"Davis Brothers Metalworking," Courtney mutters. "Sounds promising." He keys in a number and shields his bloodshot eyes from the mist-clouded sun as the phone rings. "Hi, my name is Leonard Donavan. I'm calling from AquaTech. We're a producer of cutting-edge waterjet saws and were wondering if—Oh, I see. Well thank you very much for your time."

Hangs up.

"They don't use water. Have a huge conventional drill."

"Way too heavy for our purposes," I say. "Is there any place that like, rents these out?"

Courtney shakes his head. "No. I looked into that. This is the kind of thing that's a permanent fixture in a manufacturing warehouse. Maybe if we had more money and more time, but we're probably the first people in history that have needed to rent an industrial water saw for onetime use."

He makes eight more calls before we find a candidate.

"It's a textile manufacturer," Courtney explains to me. "Gonna have to go about an hour and a half into western Mass. But they have one. Take the next exit off this highway and pick up Route 90."

I try to arrange the upcoming hours in my head, which currently feels like a kernel of wheat being ground into powder.

"But we'll still get to the cabin tonight, right?"

Courtney nods. "We should. But it depends how long it takes us to get the saw."

I slurp down some coffee and take a bite of chocolate donut, spilling crumbs all over my lap.

"So what are you thinking?" Courtney asks. "We offer them three grand to borrow it for a few days and they'll just let us waltz out of there with it?"

"Honestly, I haven't thought that far ahead."

"The saws are worth about fifteen grand, based on what I saw online," he says, gazing emptily at the rain-splattered windshield.

"Then I guess that possibility seems unlikely, doesn't it?" The implications of this hang in the air for a moment. I say, "We're just going to have to take it."

Courtney throws his head back and rubs a hand through his stringy hair.

"How much do they weigh?" he asks.

"Don't know exactly. Few hundred pounds? Never actually seen one in person before. Just read an article about them in *Popular Mechanics* a few years ago."

Courtney stares at the sunroof. "So you don't even know if it will fit back there?" he sighs.

"It probably will."

Courtney rubs his hands together nervously, chest heaving. "And if it doesn't?"

"This is our only shot at getting into that basement," I reply, fully aware that I didn't really answer the question. "This isn't going to be a smooth, clean operation. You understand that, right? Things are going to get a little 'extralegal.' You're okay with that, right?"

This is just like before we busted in on those Italian forgers, the threat of imminent physical confrontation making Courtney bite his fingernails, twitch and blink rapidly.

"Yeah," he replies softly, lacking conviction.

"We can't leave this place without that saw."

WE PARK THE minivan in a strip mall across the street and each slip on a black balaclava. The rain has picked up and is splattering angrily on the windshield like God knows what we're about to do and isn't crazy about it. Three in the afternoon. Every time I check my watch, another little piece of me dies. Friday. We have till Sunday.

I keep waiting for an adrenaline rush, but it's like trying to rev up an engine without gas. Tank is just empty; been running on nothing but booze, coffee and donuts for over twenty-four hours. Still, I couldn't eat now to save my life.

"I'm gonna say some real nasty things," I say as Courtney slips on latex gloves, then hands me a pair. "I just want you to know, I don't really mean any of this. It's all about intimidation. Being in and out before they really realize what hit them. So don't, you know, think less of me."

"*That's* what you're worried about?"

I snap on the gloves and admire them. They create the temporary illusion that we're about to engage in a precise operation.

"It's been a while since I've tried anything like this." *Maybe ever.* But I gotta keep Courtney's confidence up. "Especially in broad daylight. Let's hope I've still got it, eh?"

"Can we just try this straight, like we did at Berkley?" Courtney pleads.

I shake my head. "We have no credentials, and we need that thing *now.*"

His face is bloodless, hands trembling. "Should we take some vitamins first?"

I shake my head. I don't want to draw this out or even give myself a chance to really mull over this "plan." Pretty sure I won't realize how stupid this is until some skinhead cellmate is making me his bitch.

"Let's just fucking go."

We jump out of the car, slam our doors shut, and march across the street to Fortin Fabrics, cold rain blasting our faces.

It's a dull, whitewashed box of a building. Size of a large restaurant. Shares a parking lot with a paint store, and only seven cars between them. So there won't be a lot of people here. Let's hope they're not big people.

I think I spot someone in the paint store window looking at us, probably confused as hell on account of the ski masks. I just stare at the wet asphalt, listen to Courtney's boots splashing behind me.

I put on sunglasses as we approach the entrance. Stop and turn to Courtney, indicate for him to do the same. With the ski mask, glasses, flannel and jeans, he looks like some kind of modern interpretation of a scarecrow. A soaked scarecrow.

"Are you sure you—" he starts.

I snap my fingers in front of his face. "Shut up. This is for my daughter. If we don't get this saw, my daughter dies. Simple. Just keep thinking about that."

The adrenaline finally fires up as we burst through the glass door. A small front office, the kind that never actually receives people besides employees. Just for administration. A sixty-year-old woman with pink cheeks and round glasses sits behind a desk, typing on a grey, boxy computer. Before she can even let out a gasp, I'm around the desk, have a gloved hand around her mouth, my ceramic knife at her neck.

"You have a waterjet saw inside, right?" I ask coolly, trying to emulate Courtney's yoga voice. Her eyes are wide, darting from him, back to me. He's not sure how to stand, so he awkwardly crosses his arms and tries to look menacing. I pray this woman doesn't faint. "Nod yes or no."

It takes a few seconds. She's confused as hell. But she eventually jerks her head up and down. Yes.

"I'm going to take my hand off your mouth in a moment, and when I do that, I'd like you to pick up your phone, call whichever department has that saw, and tell them that the manufacturers are here. That we've been getting some malfunctions on the model you have, and we're going to take it back with us today and service it. Try to fix it up. Do you understand?"

She nods fast this time, her eyes about to pop out of her head. Courtney flinches. I can see the guilt consuming him even through his disguise.

"If you say anything else into that phone, I'm going to stab you in the throat. You probably won't die—I'll avoid the jugular—but you will likely lose the ability to speak, and may well have to eat and drink intravenously for the rest of your life. You understand?"

She makes a sound like *mmm*, muffled by my latex-gloved hand. Courtney stares at the wet linoleum floor and shudders.

"Just nod yes if you're going to do what I'm asking of you as soon as I let go of your mouth. Just make that call and we're not going to have any problems. Got it?"

She nods, furious little nods. Tears streaming down her cheeks. Fuck. She's definitely somebody's grandma.

"Alright then," I say, deep and intense—even scarier than yelling. The voice I've used a handful of times to discipline Sadie. Sadie. *Sadie.* "Here we go."

I gently remove my gloved hand from her mouth but keep the tip of my blade under her neck. She takes a deep, panicked breath, gives me a quick look, then picks up the phone. Courtney watches her fingers.

"Keep it on speaker," I say. She obliges. Phone rings once, then a man picks up.

"Kerney," he says.

"H-h-hi, Patrick," she stammers. I wrinkle my nose. I think she pissed herself. "There are two gentlemen here from, um—"

"AquaTech," Courtney whispers reassuringly, leaning in over the desk. Good cop.

"From Aq . . . AquaTech. They want to take a look at our water saw."

"Um . . ." Patrick has a deep fucking voice. I clench my hands into fists imagining him as a husky ape in overalls. "Alright, I mean, I'm a little busy now, but send 'em in, I guess."

I clamp a hand over the woman's mouth again. Nod urgently to Courtney: *Talk to him.*

Courtney throws his palms up helplessly.

"Make him bring it to us," I whisper.

Courtney shivers, then leans into the phone. "Patrick?" His voice is warm and sultry. Salesman voice. For a second, I forget what we're doing and allow myself to just admire Courtney's composure and attention to detail. "This is Leonard Donovan from

AquaTech. We actually were hoping we could take the saw with us today. We brought the truck all the way over from Boston. There have been a few users who've been experiencing malfunctions, and since you're still under warranty, we thought we'd just take it back to the shop and fix it up for you."

"Uh . . ." Patrick sounds distracted. "I mean, I'll probably need it this afternoon—"

"Yeah, I know. Thing is, it's potentially dangerous. I'm not saying it's likely, but we need to check the pressure envelope to make sure it hasn't eroded. If it has, it's really a huge hazard. I really would be more comfortable if you'd let us take a look at it. We'll get it back to you by tomorrow morning."

"Um, shit. Alright fine. You want to take your truck around back to the loading dock?"

I grit my teeth. Loading dock is no good. Then he'll see we have a Hertz minivan and start asking questions. I lean over the desk.

I say, "Actually we're parked out front. Maybe you could just roll it around front for us?"

I look down at the terrified receptionist as Patrick mulls over this request. My hand's clamped over her mouth, knife point tickling her wrinkling neck.

"Goddammit," Patrick mutters into the phone. "Don't know why you guys didn't call first. Look, just take your truck around back to the loading dock. Gonna be way too heavy to just lift into your truck. Gotta back up to the dock."

Courtney and I look at each other. I shake my head. Courtney's body language says we have no choice.

"Okay, thanks, Patrick," I say. "We'll take the car around now."

I hang up the phone. Courtney takes a thousand dollars cash out of his pocket and puts it in front of the woman on her desk.

"Court, you got some twine in your backpack, right?" I ask.

"My name is *Leonard*." He sighs. "And yeah."

He tosses me some twine, which I use to bind the old woman's hands to the arms of her chair.

"You did everything we asked," Courtney says gently. "My pal is just going to tie you up so that you don't call anyone after we leave. Someone will find you and untie you once we're gone. And that money is yours. Thank you."

She's basically in shock. Doesn't even resist as I tighten her restraints.

"Thanks, ma'am," I mumble. "Sorry about everything."

We're back out of the door into the rain. Dash through parking lot puddles, across the street into the van. I fire up the ignition and rip off my balaclava.

"They'll be able to ID us," Courtney protests. "Why did we wear them before if—"

"If we roll up in ski masks, they're just gonna look at us like we're crazy. We won't even be able to get the van parked."

Courtney groans as he pulls off his own mask.

"This is a terrible plan, Frank."

"Honestly, calling it a 'plan' is probably a misnomer."

I pull the van out of the strip mall parking lot. Seems like it takes an eternity for the traffic to provide an opportunity to shoot across the street. Breathing hard as I drive through Fortin's parking lot, past the paint shop, pull through the narrow little driveway that winds around back. My heart feels like it's going to burst out of my chest.

There's a hairy man in a dirty T-shirt waiting for us just inside the shelter of an open hangar. It's clear I'm supposed to back up into it so we don't have to lift the machine, just roll it into the back.

"Get out and talk to him," I snap at Courtney. "Talk to him while I back up. Explain why we have a goddamn minivan."

Courtney pops out of the passenger door. I instinctively finger my knife as I watch Courtney wave to Patrick through the rain. They're talking. Looks amicable-ish.

Takes me three minutes to back the van properly into the loading dock garage. Mostly because I'm nervous as fuck. Then I'm out the door, keeping the engine running. I pop the trunk and walk around to where Courtney and Patrick are standing on the elevated platform. Cold water drips from my chin onto the cement dock. Patrick is about my height, wearing a white polo shirt that reads *Fortin* in yellow letters. He's standing beside the saw—a bright orange machine that looks like a squat beer keg resting on a rolling car. The whole thing is at about waist level. I'd be shocked if it weighs less than two hundred pounds. Patrick wears a look of wary confusion on his grizzled face.

Courtney is smiling at me as I approach, a smile I read as trouble. There are two other guys in the corner of the garage working on something else. An open doorway behind Patrick leads into a wide room filled with huge rolls of cloth and machines. I hear the clank of what I picture as man-sized looms, auto-weaving like mechanized spiders. Smells like fresh-cut lumber. I try not to favor my good ankle; don't want to give away any weakness.

"Hey, Ben?" Courtney says. "Little mix-up. Turns out they don't have an AquaTech model. It's a Ward."

I sidle up next to Courtney. Patrick smells a rat. The van, the fact that we're dressed like bums . . . The only thing stopping him from raising the alarm is the disbelief that someone would not only want to steal a waterjet saw but would go about it in this idiotic fashion.

"Oh, wow. Our mistake I guess," I say. Pulse pumping.

"Well, alright," Patrick shrugs. "Sorry about the mix-up, I guess. Though I don't really see how that—"

Gotta do it for Sadie. We're not leaving here without that saw. For Sadie.

My hand is a flash, bringing down the butt of my knife against Patrick's temple. He instantly goes limp and crumples to the oily floor. It takes the two other men in the garage a second to process what just happened. By then I already have the back of the van open, and Courtney is wheeling the saw around Patrick's comatose form.

"What the fuck?" They're charging toward us. It's gonna take both of us to shove the saw into the back, and they'll be on us in an instant. I brandish the knife. Courtney stays behind the saw, like it's his pillow fort.

"Stay back," I intone. "We don't want to hurt anyone."

The two men are both wiry. One is a little taller than Courtney, the other is about my height. Both wear identical white polo shirts.

"What the fuck do you think you're doing?" the short one asks, staring at his fallen comrade. The taller one takes a step toward me.

"We're taking the water saw," I state.

The taller one looks down at Patrick, then back up at us, his eyes screwed in consternation. "What the fuck?" he says, looking at my knife as he takes another step toward us. "You can't just—"

"If you try to stop us, I'll slice open your stomach and feed your friend your entrails."

This gives them pause.

"Here's what's going to happen," I say. "My friend and I are going to roll the water saw into the trunk and take it. Then you can report it stolen, collect insurance money and get a brand-new one."

Patrick groans at our feet. I kick him in the stomach, and he shuts up.

I keep talking, starting to feel really fucking alive, not sure where these words are coming from but loving it. "If you try to stop us, you'll still lose the saw, plus you're going to be shitting into a plastic bag for years. I fucking mean it. Don't make me prove it. You have no idea how desperate I am."

A three-second standoff. Everyone paralyzed. And then I clamp the knife between my teeth and back up slowly, until I'm in a position to help Courtney with the saw. Slowly, we roll it toward the trunk, keeping our eyes trained on the two baffled textile workers, feet rooted to the oil-slick floor.

It's heavy as fuck. We have to put our shoulders into it, basically body check it into the back. Then I close the trunk door. We stare at the two workers for a moment.

"Thanks, fellas," I say. Then the short one blinks, turns around and dashes away. I realize where he's going at the same instant as the tall one, who smirks: Shorty's gonna close the garage door.

I grab Courtney's sleeve, and we dash around to the front doors of the van. Glad I left it running. Before Courtney even has his door closed, I floor it. The guy just flipped the switch, and the metal grate starts creaking down. My tires squeak as we shoot out of the loading dock, under the closing door with a few feet to spare. I slam the wheel to the right, make a turn so sharp it feels like we might topple, and then we're down the driveway and cruising down the street. Sheets of rain smash against the windshield.

"I can't believe that worked!" I shout. I look at Courtney and shriek, "It worked! It fucking worked!"

Courtney is hyperventilating as he clicks in his seat belt. "Oh my god," he groans.

"We did it!" I scream. "I mean, mostly me. But you were good too."

"I can taste the beer from last night," he says, hand over his mouth. "Is that normal?"

"We got the saw!" I say. "Everything might be alright!"

"You threatened an old woman. And might have given a man a brain hemorrhage."

"Well, yeah . . ."

"Ugh." Courtney lowers his head into his lap. "My body has never felt this bad. Frank, is this what you feel like all the time?"

IT TAKES SIX hours to get to the cabin from Fortin Fabrics. We make three stops: first is behind an empty office park in western Mass, where we peel off the fake license plates and I take a whiz in some bushes. As the adrenaline rush wears off, the pain in my ribs returns, a throbbing ache that's become so familiar it's almost comforting. A few hours later, I pull into a gas station to fill up the tank and two additional gasoline canisters.

Maybe I should be nervous in the aftermath of the robbery, but I'm not. Theft of industrial equipment isn't the kind of thing that makes the news. And if it doesn't make news, there's a good chance cops do a cursory search and call it a day. Seriously doubt they'll devote the resources necessary to finding the van, linking it to Hertz, going through Hertz's records to find the fake names and credit card info we gave them . . .

Final stop is Sears for a gasoline-powered generator to run the saw. Puts us out eight hundred bucks, but we can't risk getting a shitty one that's going to die on us in the woods. Also pick up two twenty-liter water tanks and fill them up with a hose in the garden section.

By the time we pass the Maine, The Way Life Should Be sign, it's already dusk. I miss our exit twice; not exactly a lot of distinguishing landmarks in rural Maine. And then we spend an hour and a half driving up and down the same three-mile stretch of road trying to spot the tell-tale mailbox, again unable to rely on GPS in these backwoods. It all looks the same during the *day*. At night, forget about it: narrow, single-lane back roads bordered by the thick shadows of ghostly pines. To make it worse, there's a bit of a fog from today's rain, limiting our visibility to the stretch of road directly in front of us.

But we recognize the driveway around ten thirty and pull in. The headlights catch the faint white writing on the mailbox—*33 Rutgers Lane*—and evoke the near-tangible dread hanging over this place.

"That dog that was cut up, probably sacrificially," I say as I ease the minivan up the muddy, uneven driveway. Roots snap under our seats, wet mud makes a sound like a squid squeezed in a vice. I hear the saw in the back rolling around on its cart and clanging into stuff with each bump. "We should have made the connection earlier."

"No sense kicking ourselves," Courtney says, his voice soft, as if he's scared of disturbing spirits floating just outside the foggy windows.

Waiting until morning is not an option, even though the thought of doing this in the dark is making my blood curdle and we're both several shades beyond exhausted. Morning is Monday. Can't cut it that close.

I follow the dirt driveway that curves around the side of the cabin. My chest is fluttering with something between terror and excitement, maybe a little touch of hunger in there too.

"You ever been so tired you hallucinated?" I ask Courtney, mostly to break the silence.

"Not that I'm aware of," Courtney responds distantly. "Of course, maybe you wouldn't be sure if you're hallucinating or not. Sorta like asking if you've ever been crazy."

"Ask me that in a month," I say. "If I'm still sentient, the answer is going to be a resounding 'Yes, about a month ago.'"

I try to ignore the brooding outline of the crumbling cabin outside Courtney's window. Sip on my cold coffee—fourth of the day—as the minivan creaks over bumpy ground. Alignment on this thing is gonna be a mess, but I don't really care as long as an axle doesn't snap and leave us calling AAA out here. That thought is enough to make me shudder.

"Alright, stop the car," Courtney says when we're beside the cabin. I hesitate for a moment before turning off the transmission, not wanting to be sucked into the cold silence of this place.

When Courtney opens his door, a mist flutters into the car. I bite my tongue and try not to think about all the places I'd rather be at this moment.

I step out of the van, crunch of wet pine needles under my feet. A heavy, wet cold. My breath forms a cloud of steam that lingers for a moment, hovers in front of my face like a wispy ghost before disappearing into nothingness. I have a flashlight in my hand but don't turn it on yet, not really wanting to see my surroundings. The sky is nearly starless because of the fog, and the moon is visible only as a faint muddled streetlight.

"C'mon." Courtney beckons me toward the back of the house. All I can see of him is the dancing dot of his penlight.

I plod over to him, and we walk in silence to the rear of the cabin. In the darkness, the wet logs that comprise the back wall of the cabin kind of look like giant, warted lips.

Court stops and kneels, shines his flashlight on the cement-encased trapdoor to the cellar. Just like we left it. Courtney inspects the cement, rubs his fingers tenderly over it like it's an old family photo album, like he can discern what lies beneath it just by touch.

"We're gonna be able to blast it, right?" he asks.

"Think so." I know it's stupid to whisper, but I can't help it. I'm imagining slumbering creatures surrounding us in the dark woods, and any sound could stir them from their sleep.

I think I hear something. My ears prick up, and the hairs on the back of my neck stand up. I swivel away from the cabin, shine my flashlight into the black abyss of forest. Something's out there, humming in the darkness.

"That's just the solar generator, Frank," Courtney says. I feel my shoulders relax slightly. I walk over to the shed, carefully stepping over rusty appliances, shredded tires, coils of wire. Shine my light on the side of the shed, then put my bare hand on the wet, cool wood of its siding. I point the flashlight on the battery, red light still on, humming. How long has this thing been running for? Courtney appears at my side.

I scratch my cheek. Don't recognize the feel of my stubbly skin under my tingling fingers.

"So maybe *Silas* didn't put this generator in," I say. "*They* put this in, then sealed themselves down there under the cement."

"Perhaps."

"Why?" I whisper. "And how is it still running?"

I listen to Courtney's breathing.

I continue: "It's like, impossible, Courtney. Nobody has been here for years. This thing shouldn't keep running at night, should it?"

"No," he says.

A shiver runs down my back, down the backs of my legs. I'm suddenly aware of a third presence floating silently around the two of us, observing. A presence that I can't quite describe, that keeps eluding me, hovering just at the edge of my vision.

I inhale the pungent dirt, minty pine. I know this smell will forever remind me of death.

"This is the place, Court," I whisper. "They're down there. I know it."

"Yeah." Courtney nods slowly, his voice cracking. "Me too."

We trudge back to the minivan. I turn it on, relieved that it starts; some part of me was sure that it wouldn't. Courtney stands in front like a traffic cop, guiding me with his flashlight. I pull past the cellar door until the rear door is more or less even with it, then stop the car and climb out, this time leaving the key in the ignition so the interior lights stay on.

Courtney has the back of the van open, muttering to himself as he itemizes everything in his head. I pull my coat tighter around my chest.

Courtney pops the end of his penlight in his mouth and drags our own generator—still in a heavy cardboard box with a plywood base—out onto the soft ground.

"Kneef," he says.

"Huh?"

He pulls out the light and looks at me with impatient disbelief. *"Knife."*

"Oh. Sure."

I dig it out of my boot and hand it to him. As he cuts away the box he says, "Get one of the tanks of gas out."

I root around the trunk until my light catches red plastic. Haul it out and lay it beside Courtney, who has the generator out of the box, is reading the instruction manual. The generator kinda looks like a push lawn mower. Basically just a silver chrome engine suspended inside a metal cage, with wheels on the bottom. The side of the box advertises the generator's "splash lubrication" and "automatic low oil-level shutdown."

"Wow," I whistle. "I've always wanted those features on a generator."

"It actually appears to be a pretty simple machine," Courtney says, too in the zone to note my sarcasm.

He unscrews a red cap on the side of the generator—the fuel tank—and carefully fills it with the red gas canister. Then he grabs the pull cord, steps up on top of the generator's cage for leverage, and tries to jerk it into life. I watch him try and fail a few times before stepping in.

"My dad took me out on a motorboat a few times," I say, gripping the cord handle, gritting my teeth, and pulling so hard my shoulder nearly snaps out of place. But the engine catches, humming, and eventually settling on a soothing growl.

"Thanks," Courtney says, not nearly as emasculated as most men would be. Hops in the back of the van and returns with a floodlight he must have stuck in the Sears shopping cart. I didn't even think of that. He plugs it in, and instantly we have a twenty-foot radius of ghostly light that pierces the mist, everything now cast in either harsh yellow or dark shadow.

I reassess our surroundings. Lit up, the back of the cabin looks blue and steamy. Behind us a few yards is the generator shack, a pole shooting up from its center, solar panels not visible, but I know they're resting on top, level with the treetops. The familiar piles of junk. I look out past the shack into the wall of pine trees, now all the darker for the contrast.

I wonder why Silas chose this place.

And then how—assuming the Beulah Twelve are down there—they found this place, where the tape was made.

"Help me with the saw," Courtney says. It's in the back of the trunk—a girthy neon-orange barrel resting in a metal rolling cart. He's standing on the ground with his thin arms wrapped around its circumference like it's a giant teddy bear. I duck into the van through the backseat and get around the back of the thing.

"Careful," Courtney says. "We'll try to roll it and lower it down smoothly."

I push the cart, he pulls the cart, but the wheels are caught in the carpeting.

"Might have to put your weight into it," Courtney says. "One, two three!"

I put my shoulder into the saw like a linebacker bringing down a running back, and the saw rolls out of its cart. It tips over, teeters on the lip of the trunk for a moment, then crashes out onto the dirt, landing on its side as Courtney jumps backwards to avoid being crushed beneath it.

He looks up at me, face a mask of horror.

"Is it okay?" I ask, breathing hard. "It's not broken, is it?"

Courtney kneels and runs his hands over the saw's midsection, like it's an injured soldier. I hop out of the trunk and squat beside him.

"Is it broken? If it's broken . . ." he gasps.

Courtney wordlessly gestures for me to help him lift the behemoth upright, which we do in silence, save heavy breathing.

"It can't be broken," he says, staring at the neon-orange barrel.

I snap on a pair of hard plastic goggles and unroll the tube coiled around the tank. Just looks like a hose with a shiny metal nozzle at the end. Then I unwrap the power cord and plug it into the running generator.

"Shit," I say.

Courtney's face distends in disbelief. He's on the cusp of an aneurism, when I grin and point to a little black button on the side.

"That's the power switch," I say.

I flip it, and when a green light comes on and it makes a sound like a vacuum starting up, Courtney's shoulders relax.

"This thing looks pretty durable," I say. "Honestly, I was more worried about getting enough amperage from that engine. Okay, I'm gonna start. Tank can hold two liters of water at a time, so when you see it getting low, you just pour more in, alright?"

"Roger," he says, pulling one of the water tanks out of the trunk. He sets it on the cold ground beside the whirring saw and sits on it. The saw is working on pressurizing a tank of water so densely that it will cut through cement. I put a protective hand over my nuts.

"Gotta give it a few minutes to get warmed up," I explain, crossing my arms and staring intently at the tank as if willing it into action. Courtney's face is shrouded in dramatic shadows from the floodlight over his shoulder.

"You want a cigarette?" I ask.

"No."

"C'mon, I bought a pack of Camel unfiltereds at the last gas station," I say, pulling the squished pack out of the back pocket of my jeans and offering him one. "We might be about to crack a five-year-old murder case, Court. That's cause for celebration."

"And if we don't?"

I lick my chapped lips. "If this all goes to shit, cardiovascular health will be the least of our concerns."

He sighs. "You're just a regular connoisseur of all things vice, aren't you?" He carefully selects a Camel with his thin fingers and sticks it between his teeth, dangling it from the side of his mouth as I'm sure he's seen people do in movies. I light his for him, then light my own. Savor the rich smoke crawling down my throat.

"Thanks for helping with this," I say. "If you'd turned down this job—"

"Maybe Sadie would have never been kidnapped?"

I grimace. Don't respond. Picture her little face in my cloud of smoke. I see her brown eyes, her tiny hands . . .

We puff on our cigarettes. The generator's steady purring and the tank's pressurizing hum provide a little comfort out here in the woods. I stare up at the night sky. Still can't see any stars, and the fog makes the moon look like it's covered in Saran wrap. I still feel that third presence here with us, but I'm starting to wonder if it isn't a friendly presence. A guide of some kind.

Savannah?

The saw stops buzzing. I toss the half-smoked Camel onto the wet earth and stamp out the smoldering embers. Tighten the goggles over my eyes and wordlessly adjust the tip of the hose.

IT TAKES LONGER than I thought it would. I was kind of imagining the cement just instantly dissolving under the pressure of the saw. But turns out the stream is extremely fine, so you have to be patient to carve out a hole big enough for a man to fit through. Plus the cement is about eighteen inches thick, far more than I'd estimated. This thing was built to survive World War III. Whoever is down here really valued their privacy.

After my twenty-minute shift, I lie down in the back of the van and fade in and out of a restless half sleep while the water chips away at cement, whining like those electric toothbrushes they use at the dentist, a pitch you can feel in your bones.

Courtney burns through four liters of water in twenty minutes, and then he needs to wake me up. He's panting, sweat dripping off his pale forehead. "Your turn."

We keep swapping shifts. Finally a little after midnight, when I'm back on water tank duty and nodding off a little, Courtney turns off the saw and rouses me from an empty dream.

"Done," he says.

I stand up, crack my neck and approach the black crevice we've bored out of the cement. The hole is about the same diameter as Courtney. I'm only optimistic about the feasibility of squeezing through because I haven't really eaten in a few days. I light up another cigarette and shine my flashlight in the hole. A wooden plank below—must be a stair—is all that's visible through the foot and a half of cement. I stare down into the darkness. My heart feels weak and heavy.

"Let's go," I say.

Courtney sucks his teeth. Doesn't budge.

"I'm not going," he says quietly.

I turn to him. "What?"

He's staring at the ground. "I don't like confined spaces. I didn't really think it would be a problem, but now that I'm looking at it, I can't go down there. I just can't."

I throw my head back, stare at the sky, exasperated. "Jesus Christ. You think *I'm* crazy about going down there? You think I wouldn't rather be in a hot tub in Hawaii right now?"

"I'm really sorry Frank, truly." He shakes his head. "I just can't do it. You gotta go alone."

I suck down the rest of my Camel and flick it off into the darkness.

"You're such a fucker," I say, mad mostly because I know I really have no right to complain.

He peels off his goggles—he's got a red raccoon ring around his eyes—and rubs some bleariness out of his face.

"I'm really sor—" he starts.

"It's fine, really." I sigh and step into the hole. "About time I carried my weight." I sit down on the edge of the hole and lower my legs until I'm in up to my waist. Try not to think about rats or something nibbling at my defenseless, dangling feet. Before I can protest, Courtney pushes down on my shoulders, and I slide down a few more inches. My feet find purchase. I look up at him, cement around my midriff like an inner tube. "Really makes sense for the preternaturally skinny guy to stay up top to keep guard, eh?"

Courtney's face falls. "Frank, if there was any way—"

"I'm kidding, it's fine," I say. "I'm just a little worried about getting out."

"I could keep drilling while you're down there," he offers.

"No, no," I say, adamant. "Then I won't be able to talk to you while I'm inside. No, that's no good."

"Scared?" He frowns.

"Of course I'm fucking scared," I growl. "Give me another push."

Another few inches, and I can just let myself slide through

completely, landing on my ass. I flip on my flashlight. I'm leaning back, cramped, on a cold wooden staircase, the cement just inches over my head. Courtney's peering at me through the hole like I'm at the bottom of a well.

"What do you see?" he says, unable to contain his giddiness.

"Holy shit, fucking amazing," I say, scanning nothing but a narrow wooden staircase leading down into darkness. The scent of mildew is overpowering, but it's tinged with something else, a chemical smell I recognize but can't quite place.

"Don't joke around," Courtney says.

"It's stairs, man," I say, sliding a few down until I have room to stand up if I crouch. "Just stairs."

"Go slowly," Courtney's voice echoes down behind me. "Be careful."

"Thanks, Mom," I shout back.

Shine the light above me, more alloyed concrete lining the ceiling and walls. This place is reinforced like a nuclear bunker. Why?

I climb down fifteen stairs, the ceiling getting lower and lower. By the bottom I'm basically squatting to avoid hitting my head on grey cement. The staircase ends in a door. I rap a knuckle on it. Thick, cold, shiny steel. I flatten my palm against the door and shiver. It's like ice. Impossibly, supernaturally cold. I know what's on the other side. I saw it in the crime-scene photos. Dirt floor, flimsy wood chair where Savannah was bound. Maybe a metal-working table if nobody confiscated it for evidence.

But there wasn't cement overhead—or this door—in the pictures. These are new. They've been installed since the murder. And not by the cops.

There's a large handle on the door where a knob would be. I've seen doors like this before. When I was a bartender at a restaurant. This is the same kind of door they had for their walk-in freezer.

"What do you see?" Courtney's voice is distant, coming from another world.

"There's a door," I reply, mostly to myself. My fingers tremble as I grip the handle and try to twist. Doesn't move. No surprises there; this thing can't have been opened since that cement was poured. I stick the light between my teeth, Courtney-style, and curl both hands around the thick handle. Brace myself against a cement wall and jerk.

Three things happen at once: the door slides open, the flashlight falls out of my mouth and switches off as it clatters to the floor, and I'm suddenly blasted with a freezing mass of sterile air.

It's like being shot in the face with a snowblower. I drop to my knees and grope around for my flashlight, too scared to curse.

"Frank?" I hear Courtney's voice so quiet, so far away. I don't respond.

Where's the goddamn flashlight? I feel around on the cement floor. Nothing. Realize it must have rolled into the room. I crawl through what I think is the doorway, the darkness thickening to the point of being a tangible thing I'm swimming through. The floor isn't dirt, as I realized I'd been expecting. It's also cement. *Freezing* cement. I'm shivering horribly. It's much, much colder than it was outside. The air smells different too. It's harsh and chemical.

I'm breathing hard, I realize. Way too hard. Throbbing in my bruised ribs. My chest is pounding.

I stop crawling. For a moment I rest on my knees, still, just listening. There's my own raspy breathing, but there's something else, a few feet in front of me. A muffled, but unequivocal, buzzing sound. There's something down here with me. Christ.

I'm not alone in this room.

Is it my imagination, or is something forming in front of my eyes? Something emerging from the darkness. An animal? A black hole of endless, roaring emptiness, teeth of ice, steady rumbling as it closes in on me.

I look away and comb my hands desperately over the cement floor. Blood roars in my ears. I need the light to make sure I'm imagining all of this. There can't be something down here. *It's been sealed for years. Nothing could survive in here.*

My heart jackhammers in my chest. Oh god. I think I might be having a heart attack. Getting light-headed. I'm not imagining it: There's definitely a sound, a humming. Coming from a point a few feet ahead of me. I grope around the uneven floor for the flashlight, cold wind rushing up behind me, carrying me toward this hole in front of me.

"Please," I whisper. "Please don't hurt me."

I plant my forehead into the cold floor. Wind swirling around me, constant buzzing or humming just a few feet in front of me.

"Please . . ."

My fingers are so numb that it takes me a moment to realize that the flashlight has just rolled into my right hand. I'm shaking so bad that I have to turn on the switch with my teeth. I switch it on as quickly, desperately, as I've ever done anything. And the darkness is pierced by the faint beam of my lamp.

The humming was real. It's being produced by a refrigeration unit that's pumping icy air into the space. This *is* a walk-in freezer. Still on my knees, I scan up and down the fridge with my light. I stop halfway up the height of the fridge, keeping the beam trained on what looks like permanent marker on the side of the buzzing refrigeration unit.

In my shaking circle of red light, I read the same words we saw in the attic:

Better to have never been born.

I slowly rise to my feet, knees quaking. Move my flashlight beam off the fridge to scan the walls. It's not a huge room, big enough to fit maybe two minivans. The walls are the same grey, alloyed concrete. I take a step toward the wall to the left of the fridge, shift my light toward the floor, and involuntarily cry out, my voice echoing against the hard walls.

"*Courtney!*" I scream. "*Courtney!*"

I was right: I'm not alone in the room.

Sitting against the wall is a naked dead body.

And there's another beside it.

I twirl around the perimeter of the room and see that there are bodies stacked all around me. Some with hands crossed over their chests, some curled into fetal positions. All are bearded men, and all died looking very, very cold.

"*COURTNEY!!*" I scream. No response.

I keep turning, mouth dry, fingers numb. I count the forms. Eleven. Eleven men with blue faces, blue lips, frost around their eyes, mouths, fingers, genitals. I slowly approach one of the frozen corpses.

White flakes of frost in his beard, empty eyes frozen open, like he died staring at something that surprised him. He looks freezer burned, like a year-old pint of opened ice cream. He's sitting with his butt against the wall, legs sprawled, palms facing the ceiling. Totally naked. His penis looks like it almost completely retracted into his body as he died.

I tap one of his hands with the butt of my flashlight. Rock hard.

"Fuck, fuck," I whisper to myself, scampering back into the center of the room. I scan each of the men's faces. All died with unkempt beards. Some eyes are mercifully closed, but most pairs are wide and knowing, accompanied by open mouths. Probably they were gasping for breath or something, but I can't help imagining that they were protesting something as their blood froze and their hearts stopped, like they were trying to say something important as the icy shadow of death washed over them.

I count again. Eleven. No question. I stagger again around the perimeter of the room, triple checking. What a miserable way to die.

Unless . . .

A shiver of horror shoots up my spine. What if they aren't dead? What if they're waiting to be *thawed out*?

"Oh god." I'm crying, desperately wanting to leave but compelled to stay by some feeling of duty. Must do due diligence. Sadie. Sadie.

But there's nothing in here besides the bodies and the refrigeration unit, which I realize must be running from the generator outside. I scan the room three more times. Eleven naked, frozen men and an AC unit.

And finally the idea of being up above ground—warm and away from this place—is too much to resist. I rush to the door and am about to slam it shut when I turn and force myself to take one last look at the place. For Sadie. Don't want to have to come back down here again tonight. Or ever.

I shine the light on the ceiling for the first time. It's only about seven feet high, also coated in grey cement. The whole room has been converted into a heavily insulated freezer.

Carved into the cement ceiling is another picture of the black snake consuming his own tail, and in the same writing as in the attic, it says:

Nrob neeb reven evah ot retteb

And dangling from a piece of ribbon, which is bolted into the ceiling, rotating slowly in the draft produced by the AC unit, is a cassette tape inside a plastic case.

I SQUEEZE OUT of the hole in a daze and stumble to the passenger seat of the minivan, sitting numbly.

"Frank, what was it? What's down there? Did you take pictures?"

I can only shake my head slightly, gesture for him to start driving, rub a finger over the cold plastic case in my jacket pocket.

"Frank, I'm not trying to be a bitch here, but you gotta go back down there and take pictures. We gotta *document* this. What was it? Are they down there? Like you said?"

I barely even hear Courtney. I feel like the cold from down there followed me back to the surface. It latched onto me as I stood on the AC unit to cut the ribbon, then followed me through the doorway as I dashed up those stairs like a startled cat fleeing a gunshot. I wish Courtney would go down there himself, just to verify what I saw so I know I'm not completely mad and didn't imagine the whole thing. But there's this hard little rectangle in my pocket. That's real, right?

"Are you alright, bud?" he asks.

"D-d-d . . . drive."

My hands are shaking in my pockets, lips trembling and

purple. I'm so cold. I just need to be far away from this place. I can't even turn to look at Courtney. There's no fear left, because I've seen all there is to see down there. Fear is when you don't know what's coming. Afterwards there's only this: a feeling like there's a poisonous worm eating its way through your brain. Some things can't be unseen.

"Alright, I'm just gonna cover up the hole with a tarp, okay?" Courtney says. "We'll come back for photos later. I'll get you to a motel now, maybe you can take a hot bath or something and tell me all about it. How does that sound?"

I manage the slightest of shrugs, an automatic gesture. He can't hide his curiosity—or his disappointment at what he must assume was an empty trip.

"It will be alright, Frank," he assures me.

My mind is somewhere else. Still down there behind that freezer door. Those bodies. I close my eyes. Try to go to my happy place, realize I'm not sure such a place exists. Distantly, I perceive Courtney cleaning up the scene outside. Covering up the hole, leaving the saw because he can't lift it without me, slamming the trunk shut, climbing into the driver's seat and starting the engine.

He keeps glancing over at me every couple seconds, a little sympathy mixed with unbearable curiosity. Taking all the restraint he has not to press me. I rest my head in my palm, feeling damp, cold sweat on my forehead.

"Frank?" Courtney tries.

"Drive."

I zone out, maybe fall into a restless sleep for a few minutes, one that I wake up from more exhausted than I was before. I see those open, unseeing eyes, eyebrows kissed with frost.

"Pull over," I say. We're about twenty minutes south of the cabin.

Without hesitation, Courtney pulls onto the shoulder of the empty road. Technically a one-lane highway, but there's no traffic in either direction. Car clock reads 1:30. We sit quietly for a moment, the only sound between us the patient ticking of the van's turn signal.

"What's up?" Courtney asks.

My stomach coils into a knot as I reach into my jacket pocket for the plastic case. It's still there; I note this fact without emotion. I pull it out and wordlessly set it between us on the armrest.

Courtney's face freezes. He's speechless. Then he looks up at me. I find I'm avoiding his gaze, as if he'll be able to read everything in my face, and I want to spare him.

"Frank..." he whispers, unable to even formulate the question.

"The Beulah Twelve," I choke on the words. "They put in all the cement, built a freezer down there and are all ... dead. Frozen. In the basement."

"Are you sure?"

"No doubt. Wrote the same shit about not being born on the ceiling. The snake too."

Courtney is stunned for a moment. Gawks out the windshield, his frozen expression reminding me a little of Candy. Finally he thaws a bit.

"And this..." Courtney motions in the general direction of the tape, unable to bring himself to actually touch it.

"Dangling from the ceiling."

"You opened it yet?" he asks, tremor in his throat.

I shake my head.

Breathing hard, Courtney reaches into the back and finds a pair of latex gloves in his bag. By the dim interior light of the minivan, he carefully opens the plastic case.

It's just a plain, old Sony cassette. Written on it is simply:

Kanter, 07/08
33 Rutgers Lane.

There are tears in his eyes. "We did it, Frank," Courtney gasps. "Now we go get your daughter back."

I nod emptily. What he's saying makes sense, but instead of feeling light, liberated, I feel only dread. Courtney picks up the tape and examines it next to the interior light.

And then we both notice it at the same time: the minivan has a tape deck.

Courtney licks his lips and slowly lowers the tape, his gloved hand making for the dashboard's general direction. My hand shoots from my pocket, and I grip him hard around the wrist.

"No," I say.

What was a thin smile on his long face turns down into a slight frown. He feigns surprise.

"Frank . . . we're detectives. This is what we do. Besides, we have to verify—"

"I'm not listening, and neither are you."

My grip on his skinny wrist tightens. Our eyes are locked.

"Be reasonable—" he starts.

"I am," I snap. "Look what's happened to everyone who's listened."

Courtney's expression contorts into something between anger and intense frustration.

"You don't think they were already a little nuts, Frank? C'mon. It's us. It's just an audio recording."

"No it's not. You know that."

Courtney blinks but doesn't capitulate. I slowly bring my other hand to rest on the tape.

"Give it to me, Courtney," I say.

"Frank, please, just think about this."

"What you're holding in your hands is my daughter's life," I growl. "Give it to me."

His nostrils flare. "What if I refuse?"

I shake my head slowly. "Don't refuse, Court."

He bites his lip, then finally releases his grasp on the tape. Relieved, I take it and put it back in the case, put the case in my pocket.

"I'll hold onto this," I say, glaring at him warily. "We're never going to hear what's on this tape. Come to terms with that right now."

"I . . ." Courtney sighs exasperatedly. "Maybe, you know—"

"Never," I say, hoping I'm exuding more finality than I really believe.

Courtney shakes his head, flicks off the wholly unnecessary turn signal, and turns back onto the road.

"Pull into the first motel we pass," I say quietly. We don't talk the rest of the ride.

I CALL HELEN from the motel and leave a message, want to make sure she's still holding off on the old manhunt. Tell her I got what I was looking for. Then I sleep around a half hour before waking up in a cold sweat. First thing I do is check the pockets of the pants I'm sleeping in for the tape. Still there. Check the bedside clock: 3:30. I have to sleep. One of us has to drive us back to the city tomorrow, and I don't know about Courtney, but I wouldn't feel comfortable taking a tricycle around the block in my current state.

I listen for a moment and am pretty sure I hear Courtney emitting sleeplike breathing patterns. Thank God. He can drive.

I lie flat on top of the sweat-stained motel blanket. Can't remember the last time I showered. There's really no good excuse for that.

My eyelids are both twitching, and my vision is watery. Hard to imagine my body feeling any worse than it does right now. What if I'm dying? I laugh silently to myself. That would be fucking poetic.

I wonder if the tape in my pocket still works. Must have been hanging there for years, with cold air blowing on it. It was in a case though. And is cold even bad for film—or tape—whatever that black stuff is called? If it still works, it's entirely conceivable that I have $350K tucked about three inches away from my sweaty, unwashed balls.

So what does it say? What could it *possibly* say that would drive twelve men to kill a child, and then themselves?

Eleven. There were only eleven down there.

Which actually makes sense.

One had to close the door, seal them in with cement, and then turn on the generator. That was probably the guy that ended up at Orange's a month later. *Egnaro.* Little doubt that he ran off and killed himself after that rant in Orange's office.

Suicide. I'm the closest I've ever been to understanding it now. I'd give almost anything not to feel the way I feel right now. No question that feeling *nothing* would be an improvement.

Better to have never been born . . .

God, she better not have touched a hair on Sadie's head. If she has, I won't be able to contain myself. How do you negotiate reasonably with someone who has hurt your daughter?

Who is she—and why does she want the tape—if she's not Savannah's sister?

If she's not Savannah's sister, the whole story about speaking to Silas at the trial was probably bullshit, so how does she even know about it? Maybe she just saw that grainy video online? Because it was certainly never in her possession: Silas turned himself in with it, then sent it to Candy, then Candy's father got it and carried it back to the cabin for what must have been a weird couple hours, communally freezing themselves to death.

"Greta" fabricated an identity and visited Silas in prison before he sent it to Candy, which is a lot of dedication for someone who's only seen a twenty second video clip. In fact, nothing makes sense if she's never heard the tape herself, and knows for sure that it exists.

Could she have heard it between when Silas killed Savannah and turned himself in ten days later?

That seems like the only possibility.

I think about that first dream I had of Savannah in the motel room, where she was pleading incomprehensibly. Then imagine her leading me down the mountain, stopping at the edge of the meadow and pointing. I know she has more to tell me. She has the answers to all these questions. I close my eyes and hope she'll reappear, to guide me to the end of this. But no sleep and no Savannah. Just those eleven naked frozen figures, sitting stiff on cold cement, where I suppose they'll remain indefinitely.

I remembered to close the freezer door, right?

FROSTY DAWN. COURTNEY drives. I call Helen to tell her she can expect us in a few hours. I'm relieved to hear that I preempted the manhunt. Maybe I'll actually be able to pull this exchange off smoothly. She instructs me to meet her at her apartment on the Upper West Side and to not call Greta until we get there so that she can help me work out a swap.

I promise to hold off, then hang up.

It's felt like I've been in a bad dream for a while now. And not a lucid one. A dream that's carrying Courtney and me like leaves atop a white-water creek, hurling us downstream faster than we're able to understand what's happening. And I certainly haven't had the strength to resist for days. Wonder if I ever will again.

Courtney's face is hard, his motions at the wheel mechanical. I wonder what he's thinking but am scared to break the silence. I glare at my phone. The thought of calling Greta twists my balls in a knot. What if she tells me it's too late? What if she just doesn't pick up and I never hear from her—or Sadie—again?

Courtney, prescient, talks to me for the first time today, without taking his eyes off the road. "Think she'll keep her word?"

I sigh in falsetto, tremolo in my chest.

"I want to say yes." My voice sounds like a squeeze-toy getting mauled by a puppy. "What good does Sadie do her?"

Courtney nods. "Right," he says metallically.

I'm glad I can't see what's going on in his head right now. Bad enough I have to see what's in my own.

No words for another hour. I just stare at my phone, getting more and more nervous as we approach the city. Images of the woman who calls herself Greta floating in my mind's eye. Seeing her beauty in my head is like drinking a sickeningly sweet syrup. Picture Sadie drowning in that syrup.

Break the silence when I see the Bronx Bridge rising to our right. "Helen lives on 86th and Amsterdam," I say.

"Mmk."

"You thinking about taking me to a back alley and killing me?" I ask wearily. "Taking the tape?"

Courtney frowns and says, "Shut up."

I laugh mirthlessly.

"If I was going to kill you and take the tape, I would have just smothered you last night in the motel room. If you have a choice, you don't kill someone in the city. I'd much rather have the Bangor, Maine PD on my tail."

He picks up Broadway, takes us past block after block of Bronx: auto-repair shops, redbrick projects, kids sitting laughing on benches, pizza joints, ninety-nine-cent shops. Press my face against the cold window, try to reconcile faces of people on the street with the heavy cassette tape in my jacket pocket, the pale blue faces of the corpses sitting below the cabin.

I do want to hear it. No doubt. If it wasn't for Sadie, I would have popped it right in. So who exactly is saving who?

The streets move into double digits. Projects turn to high-rise luxury apartments. Garages turn to boutiques, Hispanic kids in beanies turn to white women in heels and waistcoats. In two and a half weeks I forgot how crowded New York is. The humanity is disgusting; thousands of maggots swarming atop the rotting corpse of this city, all trying to get their bite. Pouring from subway stops, from upscale delis, sitting in the sea of taxis around us.

I stare down helplessly at my phone. Chest empty.

Courtney turns off Broadway at 86th.

Pulls into a parking garage, takes a ticket, and slides the minivan into the first available spot. Turns the ignition off and looks at me.

"You totally trust her, right?"

"Totally," I say.

"Because if you don't, you could leave the tape here. In the car."

"No way," I say and pop out the door.

Take a sharp breath of Manhattan parking garage stink. I follow Courtney out of the garage, thinking, *Let the stream do its thing.* Who knows. Maybe it will lead somewhere okay. Maybe somebody up there likes me and just has a real dark sense of humor.

My heart flutters as I ring her bell. She lives on the fourth floor of a walk-up, and it's embarrassing how out of breath both Courtney and I are from the steps. Haven't been taking great care of ourselves the last week. Cut-up ankle pulses beneath the bandage Courtney hasn't changed for two days. It's getting pretty rank down there. In fact—I sniff the armpit of my Pink Floyd T-shirt to confirm—I'm pretty rank everywhere. I'm considering fleeing down to the drugstore to pick up some deodorant, when the door swings in.

Helen sizes me up in an instant. The first thing she says to my face after ten years is "You look like total shit."

"Good to see you too," I say.

I don't wait for an invitation, just limp straight past her into the apartment and collapse on a black leather couch. Rub my tender ribs. Courtney is still standing on the threshold. He extends a clammy hand to Helen, who's staring at him with trepidation. I can't blame her. I've gotten used to Courtney's appearance, having spent nearly every waking moment with him since embarking on this thing. But objectively . . . he is pale and sickly looking, hair unkempt, long face unshaven and prickly with stubble, eyes turning yellow from sleep deprivation.

"Helen." I sigh. "This is my partner, Courtney Lavagnino. Courtney, allow me to introduce NYPD Detective Second Grade and former paramour, Helen Langdon."

Helen glares at me, gives Courtney a perfunctory handshake and forces a smile.

"Welcome," she says. "Come in and sit down on the couch. Gonna have to get that thing steam-cleaned now anyways."

She strides into the kitchen and returns with a chair, two bottles of water and two cork coasters. Sets the coasters on the glass coffee table in front of us, the bottles on the coasters. Then she sits down facing us, hunched, with her elbows on her thighs.

She says, "Alright. Let's hear it."

Helen is still very pretty. She's aged, obviously, but the few additional lines on her face and strings of grey hair look right on her. Some people were born to be middle-aged, and it breaks my heart a little to see that Helen is one of them.

I try to keep my emotions in check as I steal looks at her face. She never wore makeup when we were together, but now she's wearing just a touch of blue eyeliner beneath her wide brown eyes. Her cheeks have tightened a little, as if she's spent the better part of the last decade exasperated, but they still have that pink flush of youth I always loved. And her nose is, of course, still perfect. She has the best nose I've ever seen. A delicate, tender nose. After Helen, every nose I look at is just a two-holed smelling beak. Crude, crooked.

I pull the plastic case that contains the tape out of my jacket pocket and place it on the glass coffee table between us.

"This is it. This is what she wants."

Helen raises an eyebrow. Courtney sits beside me, arms crossed, still not entirely sold on Helen's trustworthiness. Keeps covertly glancing around the contents of Helen's living room, as if to uncover hidden cameras. Looks pretty innocuous though: sparkling white floors; sleek, hypermodern lights; flat-screen TV; every surface pristine and clear of clutter. Modern, minimalist, efficient. I can easily picture Helen laboring over every square inch with a baby wipe, like she used to do in the much smaller apartment she lived in when we dated. She's the first to admit that she's obsessive about cleanliness but used to argue that taking it out on her living space helped keep her anality out of the other parts of her life.

"That's the tape?" she says.

"That's it," I reply. "Not much to look at, I know. That's the nature of audio devices."

She looks first at me, then at Courtney. "What does it say?"

"We don't know," Courtney responds in an exasperated drawl, rolling his eyes. "We haven't *listened*."

"Well I could probably scrounge up a tape player some—"

"We're not listening to it," I interrupt firmly. I think I catch Courtney tightening in my peripheral vision.

Helen looks at me, confused. "What?"

I rub a hand through my hair—feels thinner than I remember—and just shake my head in response.

Helen claps her palms to her cheeks and summons a look that under different circumstances I might interpret as semi-flirtatious.

"We have to listen, Frank. Otherwise you're risking giving this woman the wrong thing. She won't be happy about that. What is it? Evidence or something?"

I shake my head adamantly. "It's nothing like that. And this is the right tape. Trust me."

Helen gives me the once-over, then Courtney, maybe questioning for the first time if we're both just heroin addicts that have totally lost it. I swallow, looking at Courtney desperately scratching at his pointy chin. I rub my forehead and exhale.

"What is this thing?" she asks. "Where did you find it?"

I laugh to myself, shake my head. No way to not come off nuts with this whole thing.

"I found it . . . with the Beulah Twelve."

She stares at me. Takes her a second to process the name, recall the details. "I—what? What the hell are you talking about? Don't fuck with me, Frankie."

"I'm not. We'll take you to them first thing, once we get this straightened out."

She looks to Courtney, as if to verify what I'm saying, but then seems to remember that there's no reason to believe that this Italian scarecrow is any more coherent than I am.

"You're saying that you . . . that you found the *Beulah Twelve*?"

We both nod.

"And . . . dead?" she asks.

"Oh yeah," I say. "Very, very dead. Okay, but let's get this show on the road—"

Helen interrupts with a glare, leans in closer, like she'll be able to better assess my verity with the aid of another few inches. Pulls an already mauled pen out of some crevice of her blue jeans and sticks the business end in her mouth, chews intently as she stares at us.

"I'm gonna help you with this situation, Frank, but you have to tell me exactly what the fuck is going on here. You didn't mention all of this on the phone."

I check my watch. Ten twenty in the morning.

"I need to call her," I say.

"You can spare fifteen minutes. Spill. Don't leave anything out," she says. "I want to hear it all."

"Jesus." I rub my eyes, sigh, and then launch into a feverish explanation of everything since I got that phone call in Washington Square Park, rehashing what I'd already explained, and now adding the events of the last two days. Helen's face becomes harder and harder to read as I go on. Courtney bites his nails as I describe stealing the drill, then he chimes in to assure her that though admittedly we just left it out in the woods, we have every intention of returning it. When I'm done, she purses her lips and stares first at me, then Courtney, then back at me.

"I would think that you're lying," she sighs, "except for two things: First, you don't want to lie to me when your daughter's life is on the line, assuming, of course, that you're not lying about that, too, for some deranged reason. And second, that's an *elaborate* fucking lie. That's some *Beautiful Mind* shit right there," she says. "So you're telling me those bodies are still sitting right where you left them? Frozen? The crime of the decade solved by you two sad sacks." She laughs to herself. "I wouldn't hire you two to pick me up a sandwich from the corner deli right now."

"Helen, every word is true," I say. "I swear." I point to the tape. "And all the proof is right there."

"But you won't let me listen." She smirks.

I shake my head in disbelief, look first at her, then at Courtney. "Weren't you listening to me? Don't you see what that thing does to you? It drove twelve perfectly normal men to murder and suicide!"

Helen raises an eyebrow, then says calmly, like she's talking to a child, "Even if everything you said is true, I don't see what could possibly be on a *cassette* tape that would spontaneously turn men into *murderers*, Frank."

She gives me a kind, belittling look. I must look even worse than I thought.

"Propose something, Frank," she says gently but firmly. "Propose *anything* that could be on this little tape here that would turn me into a killer or drive me mad if I heard it."

I turn helplessly to Courtney, who shrugs like *I'm kinda curious to hear your answer too.*

"We think it's a palindrome," I say weakly. "Same played backwards as forwards."

Helen shrugs. "So?"

"I mean, that's weird, right? You know, physically impossible?"

"If only there were some really simple way to settle this . . ." Courtney mutters to himself.

"Maybe," Helen says. "But I don't think that would make me brain my daughter with a shovel."

"I . . . I . . ." I shake my head helplessly, then snatch the tape off the table and stuff it back in my pocket. "Doesn't matter. My daughter, my tape, my rules. Now let's call this bitch," I say, fiddling with my phone, fingers trembling. "So what's the plan? I'll just call and say I have what she wants and ask where to meet her, right?"

"Well," Helen says softly, thoughtfully, pursing her chapped lips. She has that hippy look. Looks natural with a fifty-liter pack on her back and a bandana around her head. Time has only enhanced that. "Remember that you have some leverage here. Not much, because you want your daughter back unharmed, and she knows that, but from what I understand—Courtney, I'm sorry, but please keep that bottle on the coaster—this woman is just as serious about getting her hands on this thing. A broken deal would also be devastating for her, right?"

"Right." I nod. Courtney's leg is fidgeting. I turn to him, irritated. "You alright? You wanna go get some fresh air or something? You don't really need to be here."

"I'm fine," he grunts, scratches his stubbly chin. I wonder what Helen thinks of him. I wonder what *I* think of him.

"The most important thing," Helen says, "and the reason I wanted to make sure I was next to you when you called, is to stay calm. Do *not* show any anger, impatience . . . don't rush her, don't make *demands*."

I hiss some air out between my teeth.

Courtney mumbles, "You want me to just talk to her?"

"Shut up, Courtney."

"Just saying, thoughtfulness, patience—"

"Shut *up*, Courtney!" I snap.

Helen raises an eyebrow. "So how long have you two been married?"

I grunt in response. Stare down at my phone. "Okay, I'm gonna call now, alright? I really can't wait on this."

"Alright," Helen says. "But put it on speaker so I can help you through it, and talk *slowly* so you have time to think things over. Keep calm, keep in control."

I bite my lip, pull up Greta's number and hit dial. I turn on speakerphone and set the cell phone on the coffee table. Four rings, five rings. Voice mail.

"*Fuck*," I groan, hanging up and dropping my head into my hands.

"What's the matter with you," Courtney cries. "Leave a message!"

"I'm not leaving a goddamn—"

"You probably should have, Frank," Helen says as gently as she can manage. "You know, so—"

We all go silent as my phone starts vibrating. I take a deep breath, look at Helen. She smiles at me. Goddamn, I miss her. Being around her makes me feel safer than I have in a while.

"Hello?" I answer. Courtney and Helen lean in close.

"You have it?" The deep voice makes me shiver. Helen flinches. But I feel a flood of relief. She hasn't disappeared. I have what she needs. This might all work out.

"Let me talk to my daughter," I say.

Heavy, expectant breathing.

"Do you have it?" she repeats with more edge to her voice. I look up at Helen, who nods.

"Yes," I say. "I have it."

"Describe it."

Again Helen nods. I take it out of my jacket pocket, open the case and turn it over in my hands.

"It's a Sony," I say. "Beneath *Sony* it says, *Type normal position.* On the other side it says, *CHF60* on it, I guess that's the model number. And in the spot where you write a description it just says, *Kanter, 07/08. 33 Rutgers Lane.*"

Silence on the other end. For a second my heart screams, thinking she's hung up, it's the wrong tape.

"Hello?" I say.

"Where are you?" the voice asks, now with a totally different edge. Now alive, tinged with tortured desperation.

"Let me speak to my daughter," I say.

Ten seconds of silence. I look from Helen to Courtney; eyes wide, they both give me looks: *calm down, you're doing fine.* I hear something muffled, a scratching sound, and then:

"Dad?"

I lose it. Slap a hand over my mouth to hold in the sobs. Choking on tears. Courtney wraps his arm around my back, trying to comfort me.

"S-S-S . . . Sadie?" I gasp. "Sadie, it's Dad."

My fingers are practically ripping out my hair.

"Hi, Dad."

"Sadie." My heart feels like it's going to burst out of my chest, my lungs are going to collapse. "Tell me, are you okay? Have you been hurt?"

"I'm okay—" she starts, and then the phone is ripped away from her.

"Where are you?" Greta demands.

My hands are clenched into tight, shaking fists, my face burning with blood. *I'll kill her. I'll kill her.* Gnashing my teeth, body wound tight, eyes pulsing.

Helen is out of her chair, hand on my shoulder, whispering in my ear, "It's fine, Frank. It's going to be okay. It's okay. Tell her you're in the city."

"I . . ." I stammer into the phone. "I'm in Manhattan."

"Where?"

I swallow a stream of curses. Helen squeezes my shoulder tightly. My voice comes out warbled. "Doesn't matter. Let's meet tonight."

Long pause. Blood screaming in my eardrums. I think I can hear her muttering, debating to herself, then she finally says, "Tomorrow night. That was the arrangement. At nine. I'll call you a half hour before to tell you where."

"Tonight!" I shout, slamming my fist on the table, but she's hung up. I close my eyes. I taste blood, realize my nose is bleeding. Helen has a paper towel up to my nostrils.

"Lean your head back," she instructs.

"I can't wait any more, Helen," I whimper. "I can't."

"If it makes you feel better," she sighs as she dabs at my nose, "she hasn't hurt Sadie. If she had, she wouldn't have let you talk to her."

"Don't patronize me. You can't know that."

"Psychologically speaking, it's a near certainty. I've read about it several times. The worse they treat the victim, the more under wraps they keep them because they're scared of the deal falling through."

"Helen," I say. "Does this woman sound like the kind of person who's scared of *anything*?"

ABOUT TWENTY MINUTES later, as I stomp around Helen's apartment trying to compose myself, Courtney involuntarily passes out on the couch. Helen suggests we let him sleep and go eat something at the diner around the corner. We leave him a note.

We're seated in a red leather booth. Without consulting me, Helen orders coffee for both of us, two broccoli feta omelets and an order of pancakes to share.

"You gotta eat," she says.

I rub my temples and try to block out the ambient noise of this place: clatter of silverware on cheap ceramic, laughs, screaming babies, brain-dead eighties music.

"I know," I say. Look up at her. "You live alone, don't you? You couldn't keep the place that clean if you lived with a man."

She doesn't answer. That's a yes.

"You dating anyone?" I ask.

"Ha." She ties her long brown hair up into a bun with a rubber band. "Not right now." Then she adds, "I'm divorced."

"Oh." I nod, not sure whether this is good news or not. "Kids?"

"No."

I take a long drink of ice water. "It's good to see you, Helen, even under such unpleasant circumstances. I mean that."

"I–"

I hold up a hand. "Don't humor me. I know this is an unwelcome intrusion. Nobody could be happy having smelly Courtney passed out on their couch."

She smiles a little.

I tap the tile tabletop, look around the restaurant for a moment just to collect myself, then turn back to her. "Aren't you going to ask if *I'm* dating anyone?"

She rolls her eyes. "Are you dating anyone, Frank?"

"No, I'm not actually. Thanks for asking."

She cocks her head. Her voice gets a little too pleasant. "We're not going to date again, Frank. I'm sorry. It took a little while, but now I realize that we weren't really right for each other. That whole little mess was for the best."

I look at the table and nod, like I was expecting this. "Sure, sure . . ."

The waiter interrupts just in time. Refills the coffee and delivers platters of steaming food with a smile. I can't stomach the omelet, but being around Helen actually stimulates my appetite enough for me to choke down a few bites of pancake smothered in syrup.

"I'm pretty sure I loved you, you know." I throw it out there, like an unbaited hook. *Who knows, maybe one of these days you'll catch something with it.*

She laughs sadly. "No you didn't. You're misremembering. You're just being nostalgic."

I sigh. She's probably right.

"Can I sleep over tonight?" I ask. "I'll sleep on the couch. I just don't wanna go home. It will feel too empty. Without . . . you know."

She waits till she finishes a bite of omelet before answering. "Fine."

"Scoot over."

I look up, and Courtney's standing beside our table, frowning intensely, massaging his temples.

"What the fuck, man?"

"Scoot over," he repeats. I roll my eyes and oblige. I think Helen is actually pleased with the interruption, even if it comes in this dour form. He sidles in next to me, gives Helen a cursory smile, then turns to me.

"How could you let me sleep?" he asks. "There's no time."

"What are you—"

"We gotta go," he says.

"What the fuck are you talking about?" I snort.

He lowers his voice. "Our deal with Orange, remember? We have to bring it to him before you give it to Greta. He said he'd let his girls go."

I laugh. "No way, man. No fucking way. You think we're just gonna march in there, let him listen once, and then just march out of there with all our extremities? I've got to be alive to get my daughter back."

"Frank, it's not just that. Think about it. We made a deal with Orange, and how did Greta find us in the first place? Through Orange. What if he hears that she got her tape back without him getting his listen? You think he's going to be pleased? Or do you think he might feel like hunting us down and feeding us our own testicles? We simply have to take care of this or we're going to be in some seriously hot water. You're right: You have to be alive to get

Sadie back. So give it to me and I'll do it alone." His boney hand starts toward my jacket pocket.

"No, Courtney." I slap away his hands. "C'mon, no chance. If we lose that tape, we lose Sadie. Think reasonably about it."

"I told you, I'd make *sure*—"

"Knock it off, both of you," interrupts Helen, sipping on her coffee. "This is the guy you mentioned who runs the sex den out of the gym?"

We both nod dumbly.

"Why don't you idiots just make a copy of it?"

Courtney and I look at each other.

"That's not bad," I say.

"Yeah." Courtney scratches his flaking scalp. "That's not bad."

TAKES AN HOUR to find a machine that can copy cassette tapes. Finally a pawnbroker in K-town cracks up when we tell him what we need but says he's pretty sure he has something like that deep in the back. Sells us the machine plus a sealed pack of six tapes for a hundred fifty bucks.

"It's an antique," he chuckles. "Collector's item."

Take a cab back to Helen's, pick up AA batteries in a CVS for the tape deck, and try to keep up with Courtney as he storms up the four flights to her place.

"This thing makes me feel old," Helen says as we sit around her stainless-steel kitchen table. The kitchen has a killer view of another apartment building, a redbrick monstrosity. From just the right angle you can glimpse a sliver of Central Park.

I crack open an orange-flavored energy drink and throw our supplies on the table. Courtney eagerly tears one tape out of the packaging and shoves it into the second tape deck, the one on the right.

I pull out the original, carefully open the case, and slide it into the left tape deck.

Courtney's fingers hover over the play/record button. I smack them away.

"I'm gonna put it in Helen's bedroom, close the door, and let it copy," I say. Then I take three packages of earplugs I bought from CVS along with the batteries out of the plastic bag on the table. "And we're each wearing these, to be safe."

"Frank . . ." Helen starts.

"It's either my way, or we don't do it at all," I say and put in my own earplugs. Courtney puts in his, and Helen rolls her eyes but eventually relents.

"And for me, who will be the only one going in there," I say, digging back into the plastic bag and removing a thirty-dollar set of headphones, which I slap over my budded-ears and plug into my phone. Choose a heavy Nine Inch Nails song—which until now I'd only listened to during my monthly gym expeditions— and crank it up until it's unpleasantly loud, screaming into my ears: "*You let me desecrate you . . .*"

Courtney mouths something I can't decipher. Perfect. I give them both a thumbs-up and somberly pick up the tape deck.

I carry it into Helen's room and close the door behind me. Smells the same as her room did back when we dated: same fruity shampoo, same laundry detergent. A woman of habit. There are no frills in here: made bed with white comforter, desk and lamp from Ikea. It could be mistaken for a man's room if it weren't for a bra cup I see protruding from the top drawer of her dresser. I think it looks like the room of a woman who's lonely, but maybe that's just wishful thinking.

As I place the tape recorder on her blanket, I can't hear anything but Trent Reznor describing what he'd like to do to me. I crank the music up one more level just to be safe—it now actually feels like it's making my ears bleed, even through the earplugs—turn down the volume on the tape deck, and hit play/record, ready to immediately dash out of the room and close the door.

But my feet don't move. Instead I watch, transfixed by the white plastic gears in the middle of the tape, spinning slowly through the transparent cover of the machine. Music and blood pounding in my ears.

All I have to do is take off these headphones for a split second and I'll know why the Beulah Twelve killed a kid, then drove to Maine and froze themselves. I'll know what three-minute sound could possibly be worth $350K to the woman who calls herself Greta Kanter. I'll know something I was never supposed to know. Something forbidden but delicious.

I feel my hands reaching for my headphones, as if on their own accord.

Just a few seconds, then I'll slip them right back on. It's just a tape. Helen was right; it can't hurt you.

Deep breaths. This feels right. I feel warm. Reminds me of just before the first time I had sex; the excited deep breathing, the blood flow tingling my fingers.

The headphones begin to slip off my ears. My body feels light, like it's about to surrender. My vision is going white.

And then, though they were never closed, I have the sensation of opening my eyes. The headphones are still on, barely. The music is screaming but sounds distant, like it's coming from the bottom of a well.

Savannah Kanter and I are face-to-face, her delicate hands over mine, preventing me from pulling off the headphones.

This is the first time I've seen her this close. She's so young, her hair so light. Wearing the same amber sundress she was murdered in, the same one she was wearing when she led me down beside that mountain stream. Her eyes are deep and wide, connoting wordlessly the depth of emotion behind them.

She whispers in my ear. A warm, glowing voice that makes me think of fresh-cut grass. I can't understand the words, but I get the general thrust: *Don't listen. You don't want to hear it.*

I lean into her, feel her aura around me. I can feel her body, hear her breathing over the distant thumping of music. I breathe in deep, want to swallow her, but she has no smell.

"What does it say?" I ask into her pink ear.

She doesn't respond.

"Is Sadie going to be okay?" I ask. She pulls away from me and smiles. I think she nods slightly, yes.

And I'm back in Helen's bedroom, hands on my headphones. I can't have been standing here long, because Trent is still singing. I'm breathing hard. My ankle burns. The tapes are still spinning, thin black film rolling gently like a low tide. I rush out of Helen's room and shut the door hard behind me. Courtney and Helen are staring at me. Their earplugs are still in. Courtney's face is stretched into a serious frown. He regards me with dubious eyes, like I'm some kind of unpredictable animal that might attack. Helen just looks concerned.

Courtney mimes a question, pointing to his ear, then at me: *Did you listen?*

I exhale and shake my head.

He sizes me up, trying to tell if I'm lying. I flip him off, which actually seems to put him at ease.

I join them at the table and we sit in silence for fifteen minutes, occasionally giving each other largely meaningless eyebrow raises. Finally I turn on another song in my headphones, dash into Helen's room and hit pause. Carry the tape player back into the kitchen and set it on the table. We all pull out our earplugs.

"Why were you in there so long before?" Courtney immediately demands.

"It wasn't that long."

"How long does it take to hit record?"

I glare at him. "I didn't listen, okay?"

I open the slot with the copied tape and hand it to him. "Here you go. You can bring this one to Orange."

Courtney holds it up to the kitchen light, as if he can absorb its contents visually. Then squints and says, "It's broken."

Helen says, "What do you mean?"

"Look." Courtney points. "The film is snapped in half. It won't play now. The little gear things will just spin emptily."

I lean in to inspect the duplicate. Indeed, the film snapped cleanly.

"Was it spinning in there?" Helen asks me. "When you hit record?"

"I . . . I'm pretty sure, yeah."

Courtney sets it back down on the table.

"Well, this one is worthless." He looks at me. "Let's try again. We have five more blank tapes."

I look at Helen. "What do you think?" I ask, my mouth suddenly dry.

"Why not?" she says. "You want me to do it?"

"No," I say, putting my earplugs back in. "I'll do it."

We all inspect the next blank tape, verify that it appears to be totally fine. I repeat the process, the second time managing to exit Helen's bedroom immediately after hitting record.

But when I retrieve our second attempt at a copy, same deal. Film snapped cleanly, right at the spot that would contain the audio from the original.

Helen is clearly on edge when she sees this second one. Courtney goes quiet.

"I don't understand." She shakes her head.

I rub my jaw.

"I'll try one more?" I ask the two of them. They stare blankly at me for a moment, perhaps considering the implications of it happening a third time, if they really want to witness such a thing. What they'll be forced to accept.

"Okay," Courtney whispers hoarsely.

"Yeah. One more," Helen reluctantly agrees, chewing on the end of a ballpoint.

Fifteen minutes later, another flawless film is snapped cleanly in two.

Helen is pale. Courtney vigorously strokes his cheeks.

"Well . . ." I say.

They both nod slowly. Helen rises from her chair and wordlessly starts rubbing at the sides of her already sparkling sink with a sponge.

Courtney clicks his tongue. "So, but . . . what should I bring to Orange's?" Courtney asks slowly. "A blank?"

"Can't you wait until after tomorrow to deal with this?" Helen asks. "Once Frank has his daughter back?"

Courtney shakes his head. "I'm sure he's already pissed that we haven't been returning his calls. I have to see Orange before you see Greta."

I let my head slip down into my hands.

"What a fucking mess," I groan. "This tape, man. Brings nothing but trouble."

"It's after seven, Courtney," Helen says. Indeed, I notice for the first time the sun glowing bloodred out her window. "At least sleep on it. No offense, but I can tell how exhausted you are just by looking at you. You don't even have a plan. You're just going to barge in there and get yourself killed."

Courtney's face looks even longer than usual as he considers this.

"Okay, so you can't bring the original," I say quietly. "That's clear . . ." I tap a finger on the tabletop. "How about this, go in there empty-handed. Tell him you have the tape in your car outside, and if he wants to hear it, he'll have to go out there alone."

"So what," Courtney asks, wiping his wet eyes. "Then I flip on the tape for him and it's blank? That's really going to please him. You have to let me borrow the real thing."

"Fuck," I mutter. Stand up and walk to the window, look down on Helen's view of Amsterdam Avenue. Whole scene's flushed in the hazy pink of dusk. Courtney's right: We have to deal with Orange. He fancies himself a man of his word and isn't thrilled when others renege. I breathe onto the glass, letting it steam up. The weariness has sunk so deeply into my bones I wonder if it will ever leave. I close my eyes and let my forehead rest on the glass.

Orange must be taken care of.

"Helen," I say into the glass, "you and I have to go with Courtney. Otherwise Orange will just take the real thing. Or, if Courtney brings a fake, he'll just kill him."

I turn around and face them with a grim smile. "We'll wait until early tomorrow morning. When Orange is low staffed enough that he won't want to bring many goons along with him and leave his place unattended. I have to go in with Courtney because Orange hates him. But he likes and trusts me and might actually follow me to the van. And you"—I point to Helen—"will be waiting in the backseat. To shoot him. And whoever he brings along."

Helen flinches.

"Or just pepper spray and arrest him," I suggest. "Whichever."

"I can't just *arrest* him, Frank. You know that."

"Sure you could. Just plant some drugs on him. Or book him for un-permitted weapons." I smile. "He is a fucking criminal, after all. You'll find no shortage of drugs and prostitutes in the club. Don't tell me you've never broken procedure to get some guys you knew were nasty?"

She shakes her head slowly. "Guess I'm calling in sick again tomorrow, huh?"

NINE IN THE morning. Sunday.

Gonna be a big day, one way or another.

Courtney looks approximately 10 percent more awful than he did last night as he pulls the minivan into a parking garage two blocks from Orange's place on 59th Street.

Guard in the booth asks for his parking permit, and Courtney slides him two hundreds. Guard blinks, then lifts the bar for us.

Courtney wordlessly pulls into a spot three stories up. The garage is packed full of cars, but there's little foot traffic at this hour. He shuts off the ignition.

In the backseat, Helen's got a picnic spread of police tools beside her. The implements of apprehension: handcuffs, pepper spray, baton, Taser.

"Taser might work well," I muse.

"Just . . . really try to get him alone," she responds with a deadpan stare.

"If we're gone more than a half hour and haven't texted, it's probably gone to shit," I say. "Don't come in. Return the van, take my phone and the tape, and meet Greta tonight to get Sadie back. I don't think she ultimately cares who delivers it."

Helen purses her lips. Shakes her head slowly like she can't believe what she's gotten caught up in.

"Helen," I say. "Promise me. If we don't get back, answer Greta's call, tell her you have it, and make the swap. I have to take care of this Orange situation, or else even if I get back Sadie we're going to have to go into witness protection."

She nods grimly. "I'll do it."

"You'll like her," I say. Look deeper into her eyes than I have since showing up at her door yesterday morning, hoping I'm connoting something vaguely romantic.

"I'm sure I will," she says. "But I'm sure she'd strongly prefer *you* picking her up from Greta in one piece. Don't screw up."

"Just get that Taser ready."

Courtney and I step out of the van. I take a deep breath of Manhattan parking garage air: notes of gasoline, exhaust and general malaise.

"Leave your knife," Courtney instructs. "They'll just take it from us anyways."

"I know. I'm not an idiot."

I wave good-bye to Helen through the window and follow him

out onto 57th. Squint. Billboards, people listening to headphones, honking cabs. I hate this fucking city.

Two blocks to Orange's. Our boots clomp over cold, pigeon-shit-splattered cement. The thought of descending below ground again so soon after the cellar is stirring up something nasty in my gut. I could use a cigarette.

We arrive at the heavy metal grate. To our right, a Chinese Laundromat, on our left the dirty Polish restaurant advertising specials that don't sound like food. Feels like months since we last stood here. I hit the buzzer, and we stand shoulder to shoulder, expectant as two grooms waiting at the altar. Seconds pass, a minute. I pull up my pants and tighten my belt a notch. I've lost at least eight pounds since we were last here. I buzz again. Nothing.

"Maybe they're not open this early?" Courtney muses.

I shake my head. "Twenty-four/seven operation. Lust never sleeps."

I buzz again, then kick the door in frustration. Am surprised to see it swing open. This door is never left ajar. I look at Courtney with concern.

"Something's wrong."

Courtney smirks. "Hope Orange is okay."

We plunge through the gate, clank down the metal staircase. Air is still.

At the base of the stairs, we turn into the corridor lined by the whores' rooms. The lights are all on, and the doors are all open. That's a first. My neck hairs prick up. This place is dead.

I peer into the first room on our right. Bare mattress draped in fluid-resistant plastic, huge mirror on the ceiling, all illuminated by lights on the floor that emit a low, frosted, ostensibly erotic glow. Enough empty pegs on the wall to hold two men's outfits at a time. Spray can of Febreze beside the mattress. I'll bet Orange buys that shit wholesale.

Courtney looks over my shoulder.

"Think everyone's out at brunch?" he asks.

"Let's go," I say, continuing down the hallway.

But it's only once I see that the glass doors leading to the front desk and gym are agape—and there's nobody inside—that I'm sure something has seriously gone awry.

Courtney steps in to the front desk to look at the CC TVs and emits a mouselike squeak. I rush to his side. The guy with the crew cut who was managing the front desk last time we were here is slumped on the floor faceup. There's a bullet wound in the middle of his forehead and a trail of dried blood leading down the side of his face, terminating in a sticky, wine-colored lake surrounding his head.

"It's been a few days at least," Courtney wheezes, trying to appear unfazed. I wonder when the last time he saw a dead body was. After the freezer, I've got a little more filler for the old stiff resumé than I'd like. "You can tell from the smell."

"Christ," I say. Were I compelled to find a silver lining in even the most sordid of situations, I'd admit that at least in that cellar the corpses didn't smell.

Courtney jerks up from the corpse and scans the dimly lit gym like an eagle.

"Drug deal gone bad? Robbery? Assassination?" I ask.

"Don't know," he replies.

"Hello?" I cup my hands over my mouth and yell. Courtney freezes, as if expecting a vicious criminal to suddenly pop out of the woodwork. But only silence. He relaxes and frowns at me.

"That wasn't very thoughtful."

"C'mon, let's look around."

"Text Helen," he commands. "It's a proper crime scene now."

"No," I say, "she's staying outside. You have latex gloves with you?"

Courtney summons two pairs from his acrylic bag. I snap one on and pick up Crew Cut's weapon. It's empty, but there's a magazine nearby on his desk. Look over my shoulder at the entranceway and try to imagine what happened.

"Someone got buzzed in," I say. "Pulled their gun and shot this guy before he could load his weapon."

"So it wasn't a robbery," Courtney muses. "Shot him before even asking him to open the cash box."

I pack the magazine into Crew's old weapon and flip off the safety.

"Guess we might as well inspect the scope of damage," I say, heading for the door marked Supplies. Courtney stands behind me as I turn the knob, put my shoulder into the door, and burst through, gun up high, ready to shoot.

No bodies, alive or otherwise.

I relax and lower my gun. There was a scrum here of some kind: spilled drinks everywhere, poker table overturned. A lone high heel lies sadly on the red carpet, perhaps abandoned in the chaos. Only the leather-bound books in the cases stretching to the high ceiling look as untouched as ever.

A smashed tumbler lies on Orange's leather chaise, drops of whiskey pooled in chunks of broken glass. Courtney looks up at the ceiling.

"There's a broken bulb in the chandelier," he says, and I follow his finger as he points to the far wall. "And bullet holes over there.

They came in here and fired warning shots. Then let everyone flee."

"Not a pistol . . ." I say.

"No. Some sort of automatic weapon."

"So they weren't after money," I say, clicking my tongue. "And they didn't just want to kill people. So . . ."

"Looking for Orange, maybe?" Courtney says.

We move wordlessly through the wreckage. Wading through cards, chips and cash. Coats still sit on the backs of chairs. I nearly step in a half-eaten tuna sub. Bullet holes on the walls, but they start around seven feet up; not meant to hit anyone.

I push aside the beaded curtain that Orange led us through last time. A dark, narrow hallway that leads to the kitchen and the stairway up to his office. Air was stale in the salon, but even worse back here. Bad ventilation system.

I grip my gun as I ascend to Orange's office, Courtney close behind. We can see the door at the top is ajar. Not sure why I'm ready to shoot—odds of finding someone alive in there are dubious—but Courtney and I both stay silent, as if to surprise whatever is waiting in there for us.

I kick the door wide open and scan the office. No bodies. But definitely evidence of foul play.

All of Orange's desk drawers are pulled out, and his papers are strewn angrily all over the floor. You can practically feel the desperation, feverishness of the search. His file cabinets are knocked over and their contents similarly dispersed.

"Robbery. Or attempted robbery, anyways," I say.

"The tape?" Courtney says.

"Wouldn't surprise me."

We retreat down the stairs. As my adrenaline tapers off I check my watch. It's been only fifteen minutes since we walked through the metal grate but feels much longer. I text Helen: *All good. For us, anyway. See you in a few w/o Orange.*

"What happened to Orange?" I say as we exit back into the salon.

Courtney rubs his cheeks, doesn't respond.

"And looks like the girls ended up getting out of here anyways, eh?" I add.

Courtney grunts. "I mean, allowed up onto the surface, perhaps. But without enough cash to get home and being addicted to drugs, they'll probably just find a new pimp."

As we pass back through the salon, I pick up a few fifties that must have been on the poker table when the shooting started. Courtney notices, raises an eyebrow, but lets it go.

Out in the front gym area, the whole sad room smells a little like Crew rotting behind the front desk.

"Let's get out of here," Courtney says, heading for the glass doors.

"Wait," I say, still standing in the center of the room. I point to the locker room, my gut experiencing a visceral reaction at the memory of that hairy communal shower. "We didn't look in there."

"Looked for what?" Courtney asks. "We have the tape already."

"Orange," I say. I take Crew's gun out of the back of my jeans. "We still have to make sure he doesn't come after us."

Courtney nods in reluctant agreement. Holding the gun out in front of me, I lead the way. Wet tile floor that reeks of mildew. Not that this place was exactly an exemplar of cleanliness, but a few days without any sort of maintenance has noticeably magnified the smell. We turn the corner into the changing area lined with shitty wood lockers. Empty.

I peer into the shower. Empty.

"Okay," I say. "Let's go."

"Just one more place to check," Courtney says, walking through the shower, around the corner, toward the telltale hiss of steam.

I follow him, find him with his nose against the steamed-up glass, squinting, trying to discern any gorillas in the mist.

"You really think Orange is just chilling here, *shvitzing*?" I laugh and grab the handle to pull open the door. It doesn't budge.

"What the fuck?" I say. Tug again. Then I see why: A metal hook has been bored into the base of the door, and another is screwed into the wall beside it. A slice of black ribbon is strung between them, effectively locking the door from the outside.

Courtney kneels with me to inspect it. Adrenaline picks up again as I consider the very limited number of reasons why someone would lock a steam-room door in this fashion. I untie the ribbon and fling the door open, getting blasted in the face with rancid steam.

I throw my sleeved arm over my mouth and cough. The hot steam carries the worst smell I've ever experienced. It's like powerful mold mixed with sewage. Courtney also is coughing uncontrollably; my eyes are watering.

"Oh god," I moan as the steam pours out, dissipating into the locker room way too slowly. "What is that smell?"

Courtney steels himself and takes a step into the *shvitz*, momentarily disappearing into the white cloud. Then he reappears, face the color of milk. Rushes past me into the shower room and pukes his guts out.

My disgust at the smell, at seeing the bile pouring from Courtney, is surpassed only by morbid curiosity. I take a deep breath and plunge into the steam. The smell intensifies, but for a moment I look around and see nothing. I step in it before I see it, my boot sinking into something the texture of rotting melon.

It's not immediately identifiable as a body. It's contorted and bloated beyond belief, an order of magnitude far beyond even Orange's living proportions. The form on the ground is like an enormous pink grape that was dried, left out in the sun to wrinkle into a raisin, and then puffed up with some sulfuric gas.

His arms, now inflated with moisture, are like two tubular pink pillows groping for the door, his sausage-link fingers frozen in his pathetic last gasp of strength. His stomach is a huge bubble of flesh that looks like I could pop it with a pin and his liquefied innards would come gushing out.

The smell is pure death, and I'm dry heaving within moments as I drop to my knees. I want only to get as far from this as I can but am getting light-headed and weak.

But it's only when I'm on my knees, once I'm close enough to what used to be Orange's face to see it through the steam, that I grasp the true import of what's happened here.

His eyes are oversized, bloated by steam and literally bulging from their sockets in what looks like an exaggerated mask of terror. His lips are puffed up so thick that it looks like he couldn't really open his mouth by the end. But these are secondary.

Orange's face and shaved head are covered in a colorful tattoo. A bright painting that covers every surface, from his chin, up through his cheeks, wide forehead, the entirety of his scalp. Faces, all of them, bright faces. And a black snake wrapped around the circumference of his head, from his temples past his ears. A black snake eating its own tail.

BACK IN HELEN's apartment. Five in the afternoon. Just a few hours until Greta is supposed to call. I sit on the floor of the shower, let the warm water dribble down what's turning into a beard and pour down my back.

I stare at my phone resting on the sink, turned to maximum ring volume. Beside it is the tape, still in the case I found it in.

I crack my knuckles and lean against the white porcelain siding, run through the path of destruction again in my head. Savannah, Silas, Candy, Lincoln and the rest of the Beulah Twelve, Orange . . . Where does Greta fit into this?

I feel small and weak. I want to give up. Why can't I just fucking surrender? I don't want anything from anybody, except my daughter back. Greta must understand that. I don't want anything more from her. I wouldn't dare bring the cops despite Helen subtly but firmly implying that *of course* I have to tell her where I'm going to meet Greta. What if something happens to me? What if the handoff is botched?

But Helen doesn't understand Greta. Neither does Courtney. They can't. Without meeting her face-to-face it's impossible to understand the way she seemed powered by a bronze steam engine in her chest, the hunger in her green eyes, her otherworldly affect, the way her presence seemed to make the temperature in the room drop.

I look up at the showerhead and let it sprinkle my cheeks.

A knock on the door, Helen's voice: "Frank? You okay? Been in there for like a half hour."

"I'm fine," I groan.

"Okay, well when you come out, Courtney and I might have figured something out."

I snort under my breath. Nothing is ever figured out. The only thing to understand about the past three weeks is that the tape leads you down a dark, cold hole that never ends. False bottom after false bottom; just when I think it's done, there's another trap-door and I tumble into deeper, thicker darkness.

What if I just destroyed the tape?

It would be idiocy, obviously, since I need it to get back Sadie, but there's a part of me that is certain that as soon as it ceases to exist, so will all my problems. That everything will be undone, like that Superman movie where he reverses the Earth's rotation and makes time go backwards. The last three weeks will all be a bad dream. Hands still trembling from yoga, I'll be watching Sadie eat ice cream in Washington Square Park, when my phone rings. But this time I don't pick up.

Hot water is running out. I take my time standing up, imagining the sad irony of making it this far only to slip and die in the fucking shower a few hours before the meet-up. Turn off the water and gingerly step out of the shower. I hold my face in one of Helen's fuzzy towels for a long moment, exhaling into it, then dry off my hair and wrap a different towel around my waist. Grab the tape and phone and walk out.

Helen and Courtney are sitting side by side on the black leather couch. Helen has her laptop out, looking at the pictures Courtney insisted on snapping of Orange's corpse once the steam cleared.

"Frank," Courtney says. At first I think he's half smiling, but that's not quite right. Weird expression. Painful bewilderment, perhaps. "We are idiots."

"Why, Courtney," I sigh, pulling a chair in from the kitchen and sitting to face them, not even self-conscious about the wretched state of my physique or the possibility of them catching a glimpse of my genitals under my towel—they've both seen it all before.

Feels like my body has become something external to me, simply a burden that I must drag along with my consciousness.

"Not just you," Helen adds. "Everyone on the case."

"What case?" I ask, setting my phone and the tape on the coffee table.

"Silas Graham's murder case."

I raise an eyebrow. "Go on."

"I don't think Silas killed Savannah," Courtney says. "Or at the very least, he didn't do it alone. It should have been obvious all along, but it didn't click until I saw what happened to Orange."

I cross my arms. Helen is giving me a look like *your friend is pretty sharp.*

"Explain," I say.

"Silas's tattoos are exactly the same as Savannah's, right? Based on the pictures," Courtney says. "Not similar, *exact*. And then Orange's are the same, too, which was what made it click. If Silas had tattooed Savannah, then he couldn't have also tattooed himself. At least, certainly not in the *exact same way.* Think about it. A barber can't cut his hair the exact same way he cuts yours, right? At the very least, maybe it would be a mirror image. But no. Exactly the same images. And the same person who tattooed Savannah also tattooed Silas and, presumably, Orange."

I mull this over, listening to the traffic down on the street.

"Greta?" I ask.

"Would make sense," Helen says. "Explains how she knew about the tape, why she went to visit Silas in prison. Maybe they were partners, he took it, and she wanted it back."

I nod slowly.

"Yes," I say, biting my lip. "And think about why Savannah was tattooed . . . it was like, sacrificial, right? So why would her killer put the same tattoos on himself? Doesn't make sense."

"So maybe Silas was going to be the next victim," Courtney says, excitement edging into his voice. "So he stole the tape and turned himself in. To avoid being murdered."

"Christ," I mutter.

"Think about it. He became terrified after Greta's visit! That's when the transformation happened. He probably felt safe in that institution until she showed up. Found him. Now he lives in fear of her returning."

"Oh man," I say, lowering my head into my hands. "But Orange? Why tattoo Orange?"

"Maybe she's afraid she won't get the tape back. Tried to make a new one."

This makes too much sense. I laugh.

"Of course, Court. Of course the only person who would be this desperate to get the tape would be the person who was willing, who was *crazy*, enough, to try to make it in the first place."

"We got played real bad, Frank." Courtney shakes his head. "Worse than we even realized."

All I can do is shake my head and stare at the floor.

"It always gets worse," I whisper.

The three of us stare at each other in silence. I should be colder, just wearing a towel. Maybe I'm just used to feeling like overall shit. My shit receptors are fried.

"Fucking hell," I mutter. I can't believe how gullible I was. I should have figured this out the second "Greta" told me her story and showed me the police report. "Fucking shit." I smack myself in the forehead a few times with my open palm.

Finally Helen says softly, "So, Frank. Seems that this woman

you're supposed to rendezvous with this evening is, in all likelihood, a serial killer—"

"*Fuck!*" I stand up and kick my chair over, towel almost slipping off. "Fucking *fuck!*"

"If we don't catch her tonight," Courtney says delicately, "she'll
disappear. Probably to kill again."

"This goddamn . . ." I kick at the chair, grab the closest object to
me—a bottle of wine sitting in a rack on top of Helen's bookshelf—
and hurl it against the wall over the TV. It smashes into a dozen
pieces. Glass and wine fly everywhere.

"Fuck!" I scream, dropping back into my chair and clasping
my hands over my eyes to catch hot tears of frustration.

"It's my fault," I whimper. "Sadie getting taken . . . it's my fault
for getting involved with this woman. How did I not see this . . ."

Courtney is behind me, his lanky hands on my shoulders.

"Listen . . ." he says. "It's not just you. I didn't see it either.
Nobody made the connection—"

I shove him off me and storm into Helen's room. Throw off my
towel and pull on a pair of jeans, T-shirt, and my jacket, which is
stiff with sweat. Shove the pistol from Orange's into the back of
my jeans.

I tear back into the living room, huffing, face burning.

Courtney is seated back on the couch beside Helen, and they're
both eyeing me with something between sympathy and fear.

"I'm sorry about the wine," I say, noticing the crime-scene-
esque stain dripping onto the TV. "I'll clean it up when I'm back."

"Where are you going?" Helen says warily.

"I'm going to get my daughter back," I say and look down to
the tabletop, where I left my phone and the tape. Neither remains.

Slowly I look back up at the two of them. Courtney is rubbing his cheek with one hand, the other hand is covering a familiar-looking lump in the pocket of his blue jeans. He's avoiding my gaze. Helen's face is a mask of seriousness.

"Courtney . . ." I say slowly, trying to keep my voice level, under control. "Give them to me."

"Frank," Helen says in her all-business voice. The kind she uses around the office to make it clear she's not looking for a conversation. "This woman is a deranged *serial* killer. I can't allow you to go after her like a vigilante and get you or your daughter killed. I'll have a professional hostage negotiator talk to her, we'll make the swap with a dozen armed officers stationed in a three-hundred-foot radius, waiting to take her down once your daughter's back—"

"You said—" My voice cracks. "You told me if we found what she wanted, you'd help us do it ourselves."

"That was before I knew she's a *murderer,* which makes it infinitely more likely that she'll simply kill both you and your daughter as soon as she has what she wants if she thinks she'll get away with it."

I force myself to breathe. A film of red is slowly descending over my vision; my hands are quaking in rage.

"You don't understand," I gasp to Helen. Courtney chews on his pinky and inspects the leather grain of his armrest. "It has to be *her way* or it's *over.* Now give me the tape and my phone, and let me go get my daughter back!"

Neither budges. I feel a vein popping out above my right eyebrow. My chest feels like it's squeezing my heart up through my neck.

"*Courtney!*" I plead. "You know what I mean. You've heard Greta. She's not human. If she thinks the police are involved, it's over! *It's OVER!*"

Courtney fidgets beside Helen on the couch. His hand squeezes the rectangular bulge in his pocket. He looks at Helen, then back to me.

"I think . . ." he practically whispers. "I think she might be right, Frank."

My pulse is spiking, a low bass-drum sound track thumping through a vein in my neck. I feel this slipping out of my control.

"Don't bullshit me," I say. "You want to listen to it yourself. You know if I walk out with this you'll never hear it. That's all you care about, admit it. You care more about that fucking tape than you do about Sadie!"

"No, Frank." He shakes his head, eyes getting wet. "I really think Helen's choice gives Sadie the best chance. And if we let you walk out and something happens to either of you, that blood is on our hands."

I rub my eyes. Getting light-headed. Hard to think clearly, knees quivering, entire body feeling like it's going to explode.

Helen and Courtney sitting calmly on the couch. Are they right? I can't think. Helen slowly reaches for her cell phone, which is resting on the bookcase just below the wine stain on the wall.

"So," she says gently, fucking patronizing me. "I'm just going to call my office—"

"Put down your phone," I say. My hand works on its own accord, grabbing the pistol out of the back of my jeans. And before I can think it through, I'm pointing it first at Helen, then at Courtney.

Helen opens her mouth but doesn't say anything. Courtney's eyes are wide.

"Frank," he says.

"I'm sorry." I'm choking on my own words. "You have to give me my phone and the tape. I'm so sorry, but give them to me."

"Fr—" Helen starts.

"You don't have children," I say, gun shaking in my hand, salty tears on my lips. "Neither of you. You'd do the same in my position. I have to. You don't understand Greta . . . She has some kind of power. It's like she's in my head. She knows everything about me."

Courtney stares at me in disbelief.

"Give me the tape."

Shaking his head, he pulls first my phone, then the tape, out of his pocket and sets them on the glass coffee table. I grab them both and scoop them into the side pocket of my jacket, then lower the gun, tuck it back into my waistband.

"Now the blood's not on your hands," I say softly. "I forced you. Both of you." I wipe my nose with my sleeve. "This case fell into my lap, not either of yours. And I'm genuinely sorry for bringing all of this fucked-up madness into your lives. But you're done now. Both of you. You've helped me as much as you can. You're relieved. I have to go finish this now, alone."

They stare at me.

To Helen I say, "I'm not going to tie you up, but I hope you have the sense to wait until tomorrow to go after Greta. Once I have my daughter back."

Helen doesn't respond. Stares at me like she doesn't know who I am.

"I'm sorry," I say again to both of them. Give a tight-lipped nod and step out into the hall, letting the door slam behind me. I stomp down the stairs, mind replaying what just happened on a loop. I burst out onto 86th Street, still unable—or unwilling—to process the last five minutes of my life. Instead I grip the bulge in my jacket pocket and focus on the feel of the hard plastic beneath my fingers.

QUARTER TO SEVEN. It's dark outside. An automated man's voice over scratchy PA informs patrons that the museum will be closing in fifteen minutes, prompting cries of protest from every kid in sight.

I sit motionless on a stiff bench, staring at the prehistoric skeleton of what looks like an eight-foot-tall beaver with claws and fangs. Check my phone for the fiftieth time in the past half hour, just in case I missed her call.

Ended up in this room, on the top floor of the Museum of Natural History, without even thinking about it. Feet just carried me over the cold sidewalks on autopilot. I think I suspected I'd find the dinosaur skeletons comforting; used to be one of my favorite spots in the whole city when I was a kid.

Scaffolding of enormous, flesh-eating creatures, with jaws big enough to snap me in half used to evoke a sense of wonder; these things were once *real*. This whole island was covered in foliage and reptilian predators. That's a *fact*.

But there's no wonder tonight. The skeletons just make me sad. Make me imagine my own skeleton someday being displayed in a museum for field trips of giggling fifth-graders.

"*This is a relic from the turn of the twenty-first century, kids: Pathetic Man.*"

Maybe some little fat kid with a shit-eating grin will point and laugh at my bones.

"*I wouldn't want to be that guy!*"

Mousey librarian-esque teacher takes him seriously.

"*That's right, Toby. Do you see the way his lower vertebrae are ground down? That's from years of horrible posture, likely due to fruitless, joyless toil. If you look closely at his skull, you can almost see how unhappy he still is. Do you see it?*"

"Didn't they have yoga back then, miss?"

"They did, Toby. But he probably was too lazy or jaded or stubborn to give it a chance."

Then the teacher leads her kids on to the next exhibit: successful, happy man. Walks upright, thick bones because he works out regularly, and some of his teeth are even still there because he sees the dentist four times a year. Field trips come and go all day, comparing the motionless forms of first me, then my proud companion. Finally at the end of the day the kids file out and the lights go dim. Just the two of us alone in the dark, save the night janitor coming to buff the floors a few times a week.

A uniformed guard breaks my reverie.

"Museum closing. Time to go, pal," he says.

"Thanks," I say, rise up from the bench and stretch a little, then walk out past the rest of the skeletons, follow the flow of exiting patrons. Hands in my jacket pockets. Left on the phone, right on the tape. Get a little comfort each time I confirm that both are still there. Get a little more each time I feel the cold butt of my pistol jabbing my right butt cheek.

If there's one takeaway from the last half hour, it's that museum security really isn't up to snuff.

I pull my collar tight around my neck as the revolving door casts me out into the wet night. I buy a scarf from a street peddler, using one of my last hundreds. When he eyes me suspiciously, I tell him to just keep it.

Laugh to myself as I walk off, thinking that for all I know, the whole $15K was counterfeit. Walk south for a while, then duck into a crowded Starbucks, order the biggest bucket of medicine I can, and squeeze into a counter between an older Hispanic woman and a pretty young college student working on her laptop.

It's starting to snow a little. I watch Columbus Circle pedestrians progressively note this and open up their umbrellas, like a choreographed dance.

Between the street and me floats the hideous, pale specter of my own reflection in the window. My eyes are like buoys floating on pits of tar. Can hardly even bear to study it. Pull the lid off my coffee so I can chug it faster.

Check my phone. A little after eight. No missed calls.

Feeling surprisingly relaxed, not sure why. Check to make sure the tape is still in my other pocket. Have a sudden craving for a cigarette. Polish off my coffee and toss the cup, head out into the light snow. It's only once I'm outside that I remember I don't have any cash for a pack of American Spirits. Think about going back into Starbucks when I feel my phone vibrate.

Pull it out. Blocked number. It's her.

"You're calling early," I say, shielding the speaker from the wind.

"Are you alone?"

"Yes."

"If you're lying, you'll never see her."

"I'm alone."

"Come to the lobby of the New York Palace hotel on Madison," she says. "In fifteen minutes, I'll call you to tell you where to go from there. You try anything, Lamb, the whole thing is off."

"I don't know if I believe you," I say, ducking into a pay phone kiosk so I can hear her better, heart pounding, but feeling strangely alive for the first time in a while. "This tape is your life's work, isn't it? You probably want it as badly as I want my daughter back. I saw what you did to Orange's place and to him. You're as desperate as I am. How about this: You bring my daughter to the island in the middle of Columbus Circle. We'll do the handoff right there, in public."

Feeling a weird jubilance. Empowered. Not taking any more of her shit.

"Orange was a waste of ink," she says slowly. I bite my lip.

"You can't replicate what happened with Savannah, can you?" I say. "I'll bet you've been trying for years. And you finally came to me when you realized you couldn't. You had to get back the origi- nal. What I have in my pocket is one of a kind, and you know it."

Extended silence. Did she hang up?

"It's true that the procedure has never worked again," she fi- nally says. "But I'm hopeful. Your daughter is very vibrant, and I've never tried with a child. New York Palace hotel on 88th, just east of the park. I'll call in fifteen minutes. If you walk into the lobby with a friend or a weapon, you'll never see me or your daughter again."

"Give me a half hour—" I try. Too late.

SLOWEST CAB RIDE of my life. Goddamn driver laughing into his headset in Arabic. Cab lurches forward for thirty feet then he slams the brakes, like the bus in front of us just materialized out of thin air. Make it halfway through the park on 86th, herking and jerking, making impossibly little progress, when I can't take it anymore. I jump out of the cab without paying and just run.

I start regretting my decision after half a minute. Haven't really tried to run since bruising my ribs or cutting my ankle. I push myself forward through the light snow, actually moving faster than the bumper-to-bumper beside me, having to force each painful step. Check my phone without slowing down: another five minutes. Try to convince myself she'll have to give me some leeway on that. For all she knew I could be coming from Staten Island.

Yeah Frank. Greta has shown herself to be nothing but reasonable during this whole ordeal.

Crew's gun is poking me in the ass with every stride. I consider pulling it out and tossing it into the darkness, thinking its presence might encourage me to do something stupid, but I can't bring myself to part with its cold, empowering comfort just yet.

Have to stop for a moment to catch my breath, my lungs on fire, can feel my pulse in my ankle where the wound is rubbing against the inside of my boot. Rest my hands on my knees and just gasp, spit up some phlegm. Check my phone: nothing. Move to confirm the tape is still in my pocket, then realize my left hand has been gripping it tightly since before I got in the cab.

I pick myself up and keep going. Try to remember how many blocks over Madison is once I'm out of the park. Just one?

Phone vibrates. I stop and lean against a cement wall, watching the traffic relent and the taxi that used to be mine shoot past. My chest's heaving and pumping like a rusty accordion.

"I'm not there yet," I say between breaths. "Five minutes away."

"I've changed my mind," she says. "Different hotel. Tower, on Park and 72nd."

I put my hand over the receiver while I emit a stream of curses into the night air. Take a deep breath, wince as my chest expands and contracts.

"Okay," I say. "Gimme fifteen minutes. I'll get there."

"Ten minutes. Walk into the lobby alone, or it's over."

I hang up and get my bearings. I consider hailing another cab, but the traffic has once again halted to a standstill. It will take at least fifteen minutes to get there running, considering my physical

PALINDROME 341

condition. But she must be full of shit, right? Nobody would call this off over five minutes. I have to give her credit: no time to call Courtney or Helen to meet me at the Tower, even if I wanted to.

I take a couple of deep breaths, then pick up my jog, limping badly. Barely even a sidewalk here; I'm hauling myself down an asphalt shoulder, past rows of cabs that might as well be parked. I'm just starting to wonder what the deal is with all the traffic tonight—nine on a weeknight isn't exactly rush hour—when I pass the accident.

No room for traffic to pass. A crying couple being comforted by a paramedic beside one of the ambulances.

I shuffle past, thinking maybe I'm supposed to be taking some kind of weird cosmic solace in the fact that someone is having an even worse day than me.

In a pathetic half jog, half hobble now, I push past a group of tourists in front of the stairs to the Met, nearly get an eye poked out by one of their umbrellas. Hardly even snowing here, people, tough it out.

Dash across 80th Street, narrowly avoiding getting clipped by the side of a speeding van. The maze of people on the sidewalk is mercifully thin on account of the weather; the only cap on my speed here is the pitiful state of my body.

Phone vibrating. I don't slow down as I answer.

"I'm three blocks away," I plead over the honking of taxis and shrieking of sirens, my voice hoarse.

I'm rewarded with some heavy breathing and then again she just hangs up. Christ. Really can't wait to get a nice, easy client next time. Maybe snap some pictures of an adulterous liaison and call it a day. Or, maybe, might be time to start thinking about changing career paths. Maybe Courtney and I—

A stab in my chest as I remember Courtney and Helen. Surely they understand what I did, what I *had* to do . . .

Bust through the revolving doors into the lobby of the Tower hotel. Can hardly breathe. Rip off my jacket, grab my knees and pant. Totally aware I'm getting some stares. Think I see a concierge moving my way. I force a warm smile to connote that *yes, I'm a fucking guest,* despite my torn jeans, T-shirt garnished with healthy yellow pit stains, and a face that could probably melt plastic right now.

Force myself to act like I belong. Saunter to a long velour couch and collapse, each laborious breath escaping my lips sounding muffled and throaty, what people on respirators sound like. Across from me, on an identical couch, a businessman looks up quickly from his laptop, raises a fleeting eyebrow, then returns to his shit.

Beautiful lobby, beautiful hotel, but I'm not in much of a mood to appreciate the fountain with stone-carved angelic faces spewing airy streams of water, or the grand, glittering chandeliers, rich velvet carpeting, grand piano, marble counters.

It's not the Ritz Tavern, but it does the job.

I stare at my phone, and my stomach twists: one missed call from a blocked number.

I missed her fucking call.

I try to call back, but of course my phone can't because it doesn't know the number. I scan the lobby, hoping to spot her. Nothing. Check my watch: It's been twenty-two minutes since our last talk. I'm seven minutes late.

I wipe a film of cold sweat off my forehead with the corner of my jacket. My nose is running from a healthy combination of cold, general malaise, ten days of substituting heavy drinking for sleep, and inhuman stress levels.

Climbing up walls of slippery shit.

When my phone rings again, I pick up instantly.

"I'm here," I say. Can't believe how bad my voice sounds, like a dying cat's. "Lobby of the Tower. I don't see you."

"Does anybody know you're here?" The anticipation in her voice is unmistakable. I look around, trying to spot her. Is she in disguise?

"No, I swear."

"You have it on your person?"

I rub my eyes. Think maybe that was stupid. Should have stashed it in a gym locker or PO box or something. Now she can just kill me and grab it.

"Yes," I say.

I hear her raspy, expectant breathing.

"Lamb," she says, "I'm a reasonable person. I'm not crazy. When I make deals, I keep them—"

"You lied about who you were," I whisper harshly into the phone, "and you kidnapped my daughter."

"You broke our deal first. If you'd never gone to Orange, I wouldn't have had to resort to this. But I couldn't be sure that you wouldn't sell him the tape."

I'm sweating again. "Fine." I want to sound like I'm driving a hard bargain, but my voice is falling apart. "So what?"

"I'm reasonable. And I want you to be reasonable. If you don't try anything stupid, this will work out well for both of us. Are you armed?"

I grope around my ass for the butt of my gun, rub it like a talisman. "No."

"I am. I have a gun. If you're lying to me, I'll kill you as soon as you walk in the door."

344   E. Z. RINSKY

"How would you even—"

"I'm in room 3206. Top floor. Your daughter is untouched, but she's not here with me. Come straight up. Knock four times."

I STARE AT myself in the elevator as it shoots up to the thirty-second floor; mirrors on parallel walls so I see an army of Frank Lambs stretching to infinity on either side. Every movement I make is imitated by my clones, reverberates all the way down the line.

I close my eyes to make them go away. Kenny G's saxophone hums distantly from somewhere over my head. I try to control my breathing; I'm still panting from my run, plus sweating uncontrollably. Awful cotton mouth. Ankle protests vehemently every time my right foot touches the floor.

A soft tone, and the elevator smoothly ends its ascent. Doors open like the yawning jaws of a demon. I warily step off onto the beige carpet, hands trembling. Faint Muzak's still buzzing from somewhere impossible to pin down. Drop of sweat trickles down the back of my shirt, making me shudder. The recycled air is still, foreboding.

I'm in a hallway, with my back to a wall of three elevators and an endless parade of doors to either side of me. I nearly jump out of my skin as a door slams on my left and a man in a suit exits, walking toward me, giving me an obligatory smile, which I try in vain to return as he brushes past me.

I turn to my right, headed for 3206, but stop when I pass an inlet with a coke and ice machine. An idea starts forming. I'm in no state to assess its judiciousness, so I act on instinct.

I enter the closet-sized space, pull the tape out of my pocket, and stash it between the wall and the vending machine. Stop to think for a moment. That makes sense, right? I try to concentrate, think what Courtney would do here, but I feel feverish, and my heart is screaming and my stomach feels like someone with cruel intentions is tightening it with a wrench.

Then I pull the gun out of the back pocket of my jeans, look at it lovingly, and tuck it in with the tape. Vaguely thinking, *She frisks me, we negotiate, then I leave to get the tape, come back and shoot her in the forehead.*

Can hardly feel my hands as I walk back into the hall. Turn right and limp down the corridor. Numbers going down from 3242, 3240 . . .

Is this a trap? Am I walking into the lion's mouth?

I notice a security camera, disguised in a corner of the ceiling as a mirror. Smile grimly and wave as I pass, thinking this might be the last anyone ever sees of me.

3210

3208

3206

I stop in front of the featureless white door. I swallow, close my eyes, and knock four times.

Open my eyes and smile for the peephole. She's probably inspecting every square inch of me through that thing. Or maybe I'm giving myself too much credit. She's never given any indication that she fears me in any way.

I knock again, four times.

Nothing.

I check my phone. No missed calls. Only been four minutes since we talked.

I hop anxiously from foot to foot. I have to pee really bad all of a sudden, and it feels like it might start dribbling out on its own if I don't—

I jump and turn as I sense something behind me. The door to 3207, directly across the hall, is open, and the woman who calls herself Greta Kanter is standing in silence.

More gorgeous than I remember. Somehow even more phenomenal in person than she'd been in my dreams: a few inches taller than my five foot ten; very short, shiny brown hair; breathtaking cheeks with just a gentle twinge of pink; deep green eyes that are fixed on me, seem to be boring through my chest like an ice pick. Potently, overwhelmingly, frighteningly gorgeous.

She's dressed entirely in some kind of black spandex that extends from the ankles of her black leather boots up to the top of her neck. Almost looks like a yoga outfit, although the silenced pistol she's holding in her gloved hand sort of spoils that vibe.

"Unarmed," she says.

I nod, flummoxed, tongue stuck.

Something blazes in her eyes.

"Come in," she says, stepping backwards into near darkness.

I follow her into 3207, letting the door slam behind me. A luxury hotel room lit only by a green reading lamp resting on a small table next to the window. A California king bed to my left adorned with plush pillows and a leopard skin throw blanket. Floor is rich cherrywood. The gold tasseled curtains are pulled open, and I glimpse the Manhattan nightscape spreading out beneath us like a carpet of Christmas lights.

She sits down at the table by the window, facing me and the door. Sets her pistol casually onto the tabletop—so polished I can see her reflection in it—then purses her lips and almost, *almost* smiles at me; shows me just a sliver of her snow-colored teeth. But then her face quickly reverts to an emotionless mask.

She locks her leather-gloved hands together on top of the table.

I remain standing, unable to really come to terms with her physical presence. Yet even in my terror, I'm unable to ignore her beauty. The green reading lamp illuminates half her face in soft, smooth yellow light. Every contour of her body is visible beneath the tight black shirt, her breasts like round, supple pears. The spandex squeezes her body like a fist and doesn't leave a trace of skin visible below her chin. Her radiance—in light of what a monster I now know her to be—only adds to the unreality of this moment.

"You can sit down, Lamb," she says.

It takes me a moment, but I pull out the chair opposite her at the table and gently ease myself in. I force myself to face her but can only look into her face for a moment before flinching, turning away from her burning intensity as if it would blind me. But for a split second our eyes are locked, and I feel I understand her:

She is entirely and utterly consumed by desire, by hunger. Every breath she takes is tortured. She wants, she *needs*. She is, in some ways, a pathetic creature, and what I first mistook for the glow of sensuality is perhaps only the emanation of the burning, unbridled lust for the tape that informs her every movement.

And now that she senses it's so close, it's all she can do to contain herself. Her body language is no longer cold and rigid, unaffected, as it was in my apartment; it's tense and coiled, expectant, almost—if I'm reading her right—giddy.

"So," she says, and yes, under her voice is something that's been waiting to burst free for quite some time. "As I said, I can be very reasonable about this. You give it to me, and I return your daughter to you."

Greta removes a pink stick of gum from some fold of her pants and—with a gloved hand—tucks it into her cheek. Smell of cinnamon wafts over to me as she masticates mechanically. Doesn't offer me any.

I take a deep breath. Try to assume control of this situation. Looking past her, out the window at the glowing skyscrapers, I say, "I'll give it back to you once I have my daughter. And if you're thinking about shooting me and taking it, it's not on my person."

A twinge of rage crosses her face.

"You *lied*," she says, rearing up slightly in her chair, like a cobra preparing to strike.

"No. I did have it on the phone," I say. Can't believe I sound apologetic. "I hid it on the way up here. I'll go get it for you as soon as I see my daughter."

"She's safe," she says. "I give you my word."

"I think you'll understand if I don't find your promise to be very reassuring," I say.

I hear hot air hiss from her nostrils. Glance quickly at her, then back out the window. I change my mind: She has an even better nose than Helen.

Try not to look at her, Frank. Her beauty is a weapon, and she knows it. Remember what she did to you! She took Sadie.

"I've told you"—a smoldering bitterness in her voice—"I *keep* my promises."

She stands and picks up the gun, and I jump back, thinking she's about to empty it into my chest. But she holds it by her side and dashes for the dresser behind me. She rips open a drawer and pulls out a grey duffel bag, throws it to me, and I catch it like it's a bomb.

"Open it," she says.

"*What is it, a poisonous snake?*"

"*Open it!*" she shrieks.

I warily, delicately unzip it, steeling myself for something horrible, but am startled when I understand. Cash. I take out a packet of hundreds and ruffle through it like a flip-book. Best I can tell, totally real.

"Three hundred fifty thousand, Lamb," she says, her pistol hand shaking at her side. Her teeth are chattering. "I don't break my word." Her voice is much more terrible when it's soft.

"You said you were Greta Kanter," I counter. "Your whole life is a lie. I don't even know your real name."

She glares at me, and I can see the hunger pumping beneath her breasts.

"Hannah," she says.

I zip the duffel bag back up.

"Last name?" I ask.

She shakes her head. "Give me the tape," she whispers. "I've waited long enough."

"I want assurance that my daughter is unharmed."

She flushes, reaches into the chest of her turtleneck and removes a cell phone, a crappy model I haven't seen in a decade. She pulls up a number, and it starts ringing on speakerphone. It looks like the anticipation is going to rip her apart from the inside.

"Hello?"

It's Sadie's voice. Greta motions to me not to speak.

"Hello dear," Greta says.

"Oh, hi."

Tears of relief stream down my face. She sounds okay.

"How are you doing," Greta says emptily. "How are the cartoons?"

"The cartoons are fine."

"Please do me a favor. In the bathroom there is a wrapped bar of soap and several small bottles of shampoo. Could you please tell me what's written on their labels?"

"Uh . . . okay. Is my dad still coming to pick me up today?"

"Yes. Just read the soap bar, please."

I hear static, then Sadie reading, "Um, it says . . . Tower."

Greta—Hannah—hangs up, stares at me. She's close to hitting a breaking point.

"See? She's in another room in this hotel. Unharmed," she hisses. "Where is *the tape*?"

I nod, rise to my feet, tears running down my cheeks.

"I'll go get it."

"No, no." She shakes her head feverishly, pointing her pistol at my chest. "You'll stay right here if you ever want to see her again. Tell me where it is."

She breathes a throaty breath, and I catch an involuntary sigh escaping her lips. It's like she's losing control of herself.

"I put—"

"If you're lying to me, Lamb, and you don't have it, it would be in your best interest to tell me now. I might consider killing you quickly." She licks her flawless lips, her face now cherry red. "If you lead me on any more, only to disappoint me, I will make what I did to Orange look like a day at the park. You will watch me kill your daughter, and then I'll let you live long enough to fully internalize the pain, the loss, before I . . ."

She trails off, unable to form words, breathing heavily, chest heaving.

"Turn left out the door," I say. "It's between the Coke machine and the wall. There's also a gun there. I'll understand if you just want to leave that or throw it out."

She looks at me for a moment, then jams her pistol into some fold of her pants, turns and is out the door, letting it clunk closed behind her.

I sigh with relief. Simply not having her in the same room as me makes me feel relatively relaxed. My mind seems to clear up instantly, like her presence was drowning me and I just now am gasping at fresh air.

But wait a second. What if she just walks back in and shoots me in the head?

Suddenly that scenario seems eminently plausible. She gets what she wants, and then I'm the only loose end to tie up. She puts a bullet through my brain and walks out of this hotel carefree.

Fuck. Fuck. I thought I'd handled this well, but I'm about to get played yet again. Of course she shows me the money. Then kills me and takes it back. Am I even sure that girl on the phone was Sadie? I mean, it certainly sounded like her, but I also wanted that to be her more than anything—

The lock clicks, and the door opens. My heart stops, and I stare, frozen, as Greta enters. Her face is totally blank, unreadable. In her right hand she holds the tape.

She lets the door click closed behind her. I close my eyes, waiting for the bullet, but hear only the clatter as she sets her pistol down on the dresser. Opens the same drawer that held my money and pulls out a clunky grey machine, the likes of which I haven't seen for at least twenty years: a Walkman with a pair of sleek white earbuds wrapped around it. She sits back down across from me. Opens the Walkman and inserts the tape, sticks in the earbuds.

Our eyes are locked as she hits play. My heart seizes as I realize that if it's broken—from the freezer or something—she's going to think I tried to fool her. Bite my lip. Try to read her face: *Is it working?*

Anguished seconds drip past. She left the gun on top of the dresser, behind me, but it seems like she did it intentionally, as if daring me to make a move for it. Instead I sit glued across from her as inside the Sony Walkman the two little gears revolve, the smaller gear reeling in black film from the larger, like there's a little game of tug-of-war that he's winning.

Greta—Hannah—suddenly jerks up straight in her chair. Her eyes rivet to some point over my right shoulder, staring fixedly at something that I know isn't there. Her lower jaw opens slightly, and I hear a wisp of breath escape her lips.

Color shoots to her face, her cheeks glow deep orange. Her face—normally preternaturally stoic—alights with a kind of infantile wonder. Her breasts pulse beneath her black turtleneck. The tips of her gloved fingers try to dig into the wood tabletop, her hands clenched like claws. Her eyes are aflame with green, her face connoting an ambiguous emotion that is readable only as pure intensity, as if she is on the cusp of a furious orgasm.

My nose picks something up, and for a moment I think I'm imagining it, but then the scent becomes stronger until there's no doubt: I can smell her. The sickeningly sweet scent of arousal. An intoxicating, meaty perfume.

And then what appeared to be an expression of ecstasy shifts. Her eyes darken.

Again I consider whether I could make a move for the pistol. I turn slightly in my chair, readying myself for a dash. I'm about to shoot up from my seat when Greta makes a sound that gives me pause.

She's sort of cowering now, whatever she's listening to clearly unpleasant. She emits a gasp of anguish, then tears out her earbuds and slams the pause button, breathing like she just finished a sprint.

Takes a moment to recover, then looks up at me.

"That's it, right?" I say. "Give her back."

Greta is visibly transformed. Shaken. Frightened, perhaps. She grabs the Walkman and stands up. Strides over to the window, Walkman still in her right hand, and gazes out on the city, then back to me. I think she seems almost melancholy. I still think I could probably make a run for the gun and grab it before she could react, but I'm thrown off by her indifference to this possibility. It also appears that this whole thing might just end up going smoothly, and I don't want to ruin that.

"Which room is my daughter in?" I say.

Softly to the window, she says, "We're not quite done here, Lamb."

I watch as her left hand—the one not holding the Walkman—moves to her mouth. She bites, then wrenches off the glove with her teeth, lets it fall gently to the ground like an autumn leaf. Then she reaches that hand back to where her turtleneck meets the nape of her neck, and slowly starts tearing. One of her fingernails is cut sharp enough to tear straight from her neck to her tailbone, and then the shirt simply falls off.

I stiffen as she grabs the waist of her pants and effortlessly pushes them to the floor. Steps out of them delicately, as if from a shallow puddle, still shrouded in shadow.

She's wearing nothing now but the glove on her right hand, still holding the Walkman. She keeps staring out the window. Her shapely contours catch a fleeting bar of light from outside, illuminating a slit of her flesh for only a moment.

"What . . ." I ask.

Then she turns to me, finally, and steps into the light of the reading lamp.

My jaw goes limp.

The entire front of her body, from the neck down to her toes, is tattooed. A beautiful, brightly colored mural. Stripes of sun orange, dandelion yellow, earthy red, royal purple, sky blue. The intricacy and craftsmanship are astounding. There appears to be dozens of layers, as if she never stopped adding them, burying old pictures and words beneath newer, fresher ink.

I'm lost in them, absolutely mesmerized. It's so beautiful I could cry. Her body is a perfect work of art painted on a flawlessly maintained canvas. I look up at her face. She's standing over me, her cold green eyes staring down at me, my heart pounding, blood rushing everywhere, her smell . . .

I jerk up from the chair and stumble backwards.

"What are you doing?" I say. "I gave you what you wanted. Tell me where my daughter is."

"Don't you recall the final condition of our agreement, Lamb?"

She steps toward me, and her naked hips move into the light of the reading lamp. I see that a black snake is tattooed around her waist like a belt, the mouth and tail both terminating in the fold of her groin.

"I don't . . . I just want . . ."

"Of course you want this," she says. "You've been dreaming about it, haven't you?"

She moves closer, her scent dizzying, and suddenly grabs me by my hair and jerks my ear to her lips. Whispers, "You don't think I need a gun to kill you, do you, Lamb?"

Then with astonishing force, she pushes down on my scalp, forcing me to my knees. She grips either side of my head and pushes my nose into her groin. My face is buried in her, and I'm overwhelmed by the smell, by the smooth skin of her thighs on my cheeks.

"Finish the job, Lamb." I hear her above me, in vibrato. Her thumbs push on my temples with such force that it's clear she could simply crush my skull. I suddenly remember Linda's story about her husband, Walter, clomping up the steps, climbing into bed and gripping her wrist harder than he ever had before.

She tightens the pressure on my forehead. My teeth mash together.

"Do it!" she screams, then forces my face all the way into her.

Not seeing a choice, I lick whatever is directly in front of my face, and immediately she relaxes her hands and emits a deep, guttural groan that makes my heart flutter. I dig deeper with my tongue and she entrenches her nails in my back, drawing blood. She moans horribly, almost like she's in pain.

And then she pulls my face out, jerks me to my feet by my armpits—absolutely manhandles me—and throws me onto the California king bed. My heart's screaming in my throat. In the dim light, she crawls up onto the bed and sits on me, squeezing my hips with her knees.

Some garbled words of protest leave my lips as she cuts down the middle of my shirt with her sharpened index fingernail, then rips my jeans clean off with such force that she tears a hole in one of the knees.

My boxer briefs are torn to shreds in a ravenous flurry, and then her ungloved hand is gripping my flaccid member tightly.

She looks in my eyes.

"Don't resist, Lamb," she says, her voice throaty like a wolf's, full breasts perked and expectant, as if they're ready to burst. "It's too late for us. We've heard the tape. We know what's coming. We've made mistakes that will be echoed back and forth for eternity. But let's make someone new. Someone perfect."

Before I have time to respond she forces me into her, sits back and gasps.

She wants to . . . conceive?

In the shadows I can barely see her face. I can only hear her raspy, heightened breathing; feel her back arching; her hips quivering; smell her growing more fragrant by the second, to the point that her scent seems to be something thick and dense swirling around us.

There are no words, only sounds. The snapping of the mattress with every rise and fall; her breathing, my own breathing. I close my eyes and listen to the pleasure crescendoing in the back of her throat.

Greta's hips grind desperately. Darkness seeps over my eyes, and I feel myself sinking deeper, like she's an endless abyss that's sucking me into her world. And I'm getting closer to letting go.

Greta's shadowy form is writhing, nearing a point of finality. I catch glimpses of the colorful faces painted on her body as they slip in and out of the scant light of the reading lamp. They, too, seem to be screaming for release, begging their host to speed up, which she does. I'm feeling the first tingling tremors in my own loins. Greta emits an ear-shattering groan that sends shivers down my spine. She grabs her hair with one hand and screams again, an inhuman wail that sounds more like anguish than pleasure.

"I need . . ." she gasps and leans over me, her breasts dropping on my face. She's stopped grinding, but I'm still pulsing inside of her. She's fidgeting with something in the darkness that I can't see.

And when she pulls up again, I see that her gloved hand is still holding the Walkman.

She resumes her grinding, but somehow with an even more fervent intensity as she does something with her hands. I'm losing control, nearly impossible to focus, but I think that between the flails and screams, she is fiddling with the device. Putting her earbuds in.

She plunges me into her as deeply as I can go, without abandon, and through a shimmer of light from the window, I catch the terrified ecstasy on her face, the dreadful anticipation. My body is shivering, I feel almost feverish.

A click as Greta hits play. My fingers dig into the sheet beneath me. Unbearable pressure welling up inside of me.

Greta lets loose a howl that reverberates inside the room, a sound so tremulous and jarring that I have a quick moment of clarity in my mind's eye. Sadie sitting somewhere alone, waiting for me, while I do this with her kidnapper. A killer.

Oh god. Did she tattoo Sadie?

"Ergh!" I scream and sit up with all my power, swiping the tape player out of her hands. Her earbuds rip out, and I hear a small crack as the Walkman slams into the window.

In the sudden silence that follows, she stares at me, stunned. We listen for a moment to the distant honking of traffic, sirens. She's still breathing hard; it's clear by the tension on her face that she hasn't quite reached where she wanted to go. For a second, I'm positive she's going to kill me with her bare hands.

Instead she shoots off me and lunges for the Walkman. I watch her fumble with the earbuds and growl in displeasure. The earbuds are broken, cord ripped.

Now is my moment. I roll off the bed, naked, and half stumble to the dresser. Grab the pistol and point it at Greta, who's still crouched on the floor with the Walkman. I see the glimmer of flying tape. She's rewinding. *Rewinding?*

"Where's my daughter," I say. She hardly even seems to hear

me. The Walkman clicks and stops. Done rewinding. She hits a button, and the tape starts to play again. She unplugs the earbuds from the headphone jack. It's some kind of professional model; there are built-in speakers.

It starts from the beginning.

"Stop," I say, voice and pistol shaking. "Turn it off."

She doesn't. Just looks up at me. I'm frozen. Listening.

From the Walkman I hear Greta's muffled but unmistakable voice saying:

"You tell me."

Then comes the sound of crinkling plastic. Plastic bag. A struggle. Horrible gasping. A high-pitched half cry stifled by the bag. Flailing. Last strained twitch against the bag. Then nothing. A pregnant silence from the tape player for a few seconds during which Greta's—Hannah's—and my eyes meet again. I could end this. Could shoot her in the head and pause the tape. Instead my sneakers remain rooted to the slick wood floor. The cassette player continues to whirr.

And then my chest goes cold as a sound suddenly bursts into the air of the hotel room, emanating from the Walkman, a still, thin cry. Not a cry . . . a note. Singing.

I see Savannah sitting in the dirty cellar, face wrapped tightly by a plastic bag, singing a single, glorious note. Beautiful. Like a choir of pink-cheeked cherubs, except it's all coming from one mouth. My eyes water. The note is bliss. It's light, warmth. The note is exactly the way I felt when Sadie was born. The same awe, the same inexplicable gratitude to something, *someone,* bigger than me. Though the sound from her throat is loud, there is no echo—as if the sound is being absorbed by the walls.

But in a moment that feeling—and the sound—disappear,

leaving Greta sitting beside Savannah's limp form in a damp basement. I hear the pitter-patter of rain outside. Savannah's bagged head hangs loose as a rag doll's. The cellar, which was just filled with this beautiful song, now feels horribly barren. Greta—stunned—is about to stop recording when Savannah's head suddenly jerks up again, and from somewhere under the tight plastic comes a new sound: a low, droning bass note, loud and terrible, like an airplane engine.

The frequency shatters the lone lightbulb in the basement, and we're immersed in thick ink with her rumbling groan. And then from the cloudy darkness—perhaps from Savannah's bagged throat—sneaks a form: a black snake, his yellow eyes illuminating the two women as he slithers in the air between them, forked tongue flickering at me. He almost smiles at me, then turns away, displaying to me his hovering, lengthwise form. Spiraled around his body is a strip of tiny glittering scales, a million mirrors. I take a step toward his body to examine them more closely and realize each of the tiny mirrors contains my face. But not my reflection; rather still images from my life. One of me in a lecture in law school, nodding off. There's a picture of me on one of my early cases, tearing my hair out with stress. In another I see myself drunk, laughing uproariously at something filthy . . . my stomach churns as I recognize this night. The night I cheated on Helen.

I tear myself away and shift down the snake's length. The images turn brighter as I move toward his mouth. A day at the swimming pool in the summer before ninth grade, in the lifeguard shed. I'm offered a flask and take a sip. My first drink. I don't want to watch this either. I move closer to the mouth, finally hitting some pleasant images. Me as a smiling, deliriously happy toddler, an infant, a newborn . . .

The pictures start to ripple and fade. The snake is moving. He turns to look at me with a toothy grin, and then his head floats past my chest, dragging his thick form in the direction of his tail. He's spiraling in on himself, curving inwardly in an almost sensual motion, searching for his own tail. And I want him to devour it, to devour himself fully. And once he does, the tape will end and I'll simply flip back to the start of the tape and listen to the sweet beginning again, and again, and again . . .

Behind the snake Savannah looks at me, her face clear again of tattoos, the bag evaporated, and whispers, "*Stop, Frank.*"

My first shot opens a hole directly beneath Greta's bare collarbone. The rest are aimed at the Walkman, and the fifth connects, jarring the machine's primitive mechanism enough to stop the gears midspin, plunging the hotel room into blissful silence.

Greta—Hannah—looks first at her wound and then at me. She's on her knees, glistening blood streaming down her tattooed torso.

"Which room is my daughter in?" I ask. Unclear if the question registered. She's losing blood very fast. "*Which room is Sadie in?*" I scream, still keeping the pistol trained on her even though the chamber is empty.

"723," she gurgles.

"Where's the key card?"

"Under the . . . money."

"Did you hurt her?" I demand. She doesn't respond. Her eyelids flicker. "Did you *hurt her?*"

Greta bares bloodstained teeth. I see her gloved hand fumbling weakly with the dented Walkman. "The end. The snake," she says.

Then her eyes roll back and she topples over onto the cherrywood floor face-first, blood fountaining from the exit wound on her back, sprinkling the tapestry of faces. I heave the money bag onto my shoulder, sift through the bills frantically until I find the key card. Pull on my shirt and jeans, leaving my shredded boxer shorts, and rush out the door, not turning around for another look at her draining body.

I think, *Doesn't get much less professional than that.*

I throw the pistol into the duffel bag as I sprint toward the elevators, imagining, praying that Sadie is sitting calmly in front of a TV on the seventh floor. Frantically slam my fist against the down button and pull out my phone to call Helen.

Epilogue

I SINK DEEPER into my plastic lounge chair, chug the rest of my piña colada, then woozily wave my empty glass in the air until a bronzed Sicilian twenty-something in a spanking white uniform materializes to take it from me.

"Keep 'em coming," I say, but before I can hand her a twenty-euro bill, she takes an already prepared refill off her tray and hands it to me.

"*Grazie,*" I say.

"*Prego.*" She smiles, and only then does she pluck the bill from my outstretched fingers. Been staying at this place for about two months now; guess it's about time they got the idea.

Through my green-tinted aviators, I watch the waitress hurry back to the poolside bar. Take a long slurp of frozen slush and set the glass down on the scorching cement.

Around the pool is a perimeter of vacationers—mostly European—being pampered by over-the-top-polite resort staff, the kind you can spit on and they'll still serve you with a smile. White stone steps lead off the side of the pool area down to the private beach: white sand, no dogs, girls in bikinis, cool blue salt water that licks your ankles as you stare off to the horizon, struggling to remember what it's like to be broke.

Behind me the glorious coral hotel stretches toward the cloudless sky.

"Dad!" Sadie is clinging to the side of the pool, about ten feet away. She's wearing a goofy pair of goggles. "Come swim!"

"Gimme a few minutes," I say.

"If you just sit in the sun all day, you're going to get fat and burned."

"Too late on both counts, sweetie."

Sadie rolls her eyes and drops off the wall. Doggy-paddles away to the other side of the pool. Splashes around in the shallow end with a chunky Spanish boy she's made friends with this week.

A shirtless bear of a man a few seats down from me roars in laughter and shouts something in what I think is Russian. I light up an Italian brand cigarette and close my eyes for a second. Feel the Mediterranean sun tickle my belly, luxury tobacco snake out through my nostrils. Try tuning out the ambient noise. Haven't been sleeping well again. But maybe if I just—

The cigarette is suddenly plucked from my mouth. I open my eyes and jerk up in my lounge chair to behold what I initially assume is a mirage: Courtney standing over me, clad only in a wide-brimmed sombrero and a saggy black swimsuit, grinding out my cigarette in the ashtray beside me.

"It's one thing to smoke when you're on the job," Courtney mutters, pulling up another chair and easing his cricketlike body into it.

I rub my eyes. "Took your sweet time. Wasn't sure you got my email."

Courtney blinks. "It's not carrier pigeon, Frank. Emails have a remarkable delivery success rate."

"You know what I mean. Thought maybe you wouldn't remember the name Ben Donovan."

"How could I forget. I was up all night making those fake FBI badges." Courtney laughs lightly. "I just had to wait until some of the heat dropped off." His lanky stick-frame is as pale as ever, almost looks like a translucent jellyfish under the bright sunlight. He has white splotches on his cheeks where he failed to rub in his sunscreen all the way. Not that he really needs it—no light is piercing that thick sombrero.

"So . . . Are they still looking for me?"

"Yes, but they're winding down," he says, looking around the pool area. "I mean, they've known you killed Greta from the start. But the more they uncover about her, the more they figure it was some kind of drug-deal-gone-bad-type situation. Not the senseless hotel room slaughter the *Post* reported."

I chew on my lower lip.

"This could all have been avoided. I could have cleaned up the room, wiped my prints . . . was just in such a hurry to make sure Sadie was downstairs. Been cursing myself every day since."

"Understandable. A drop of fear can poison a gallon of patience, thoughtfulness and subtlety," Courtney says.

I stare up at the electric-blue sky, resist the urge to smack him.

"And what about Helen?"

Courtney grimaces. "She didn't clear your name, but she's also not giving them any really pertinent info. Her story is that you were an ex-lover gone mad who showed up and threatened her. You can't blame her—you were gonna get tied back to her. She had to protect herself."

"Naturally." I pick my melting piña colada off the ground and chug it down. I wave my empty glass in the air, and when nobody immediately appears, I say, "Well, let's go on inside and I'll get you your money. And then you can be on your way."

I start to stand up, but Courtney stays seated. He looks hurt.

"You think I came just for the money?"

I raise an eyebrow and sit back down. I keep my eyes on him even as the Sicilian waitress finally shows up to swap my empty glass out for a full one.

"I mean . . . I just . . ."

"I came, first and foremost, to apologize."

I look at him. "For what?"

"I should have never put you in that situation. Forced you to threaten us like that."

I stare into his long, pale face, eyes grey in the shade afforded by his hat. Then I grin.

"Bullshit."

Courtney feigns being taken aback. "What?"

"You came here to apologize for *me* pulling a gun on *you*?" I laugh. "It's alright, Court. I know what you want. Besides the money."

Courtney wrings his hands.

"Frank, I—"

"Just ask."

Courtney frowns dourly. Claws at the inside of his ear for a second, then taps his lips and says, "Well, I mean, did you . . . you know. Did you hear it?"

I light up another cigarette.

"Just the first few seconds. But I think I've got it figured out. Want a drink?"

Courtney shakes his head adamantly. Every second I keep him waiting is pure torture.

"Her name was Hannah," I say. "And after making a few phone calls, I'm all but sure that her last name was Graham."

Courtney's eyes go wide. "Silas's . . ."

"Older sister. I don't have much to do with myself these days. So I started making calls, just hoping to learn a little more about Silas. Finally got ahold of his elementary school in Alabama—you know, where he grew up before he killed his parents. Was talking to one of his teachers, who mentioned that Silas was always a little weird, but what really creeped her out was his *sister*, who would pick him up after school. Looked like a full-grown woman at four-teen, inordinately fascinated with death and self-mutilation, spent a *lot* of time hanging around the local church . . . until it burned down. Gorgeous. Teacher didn't remember her name off the top of her head. I asked, 'Hannah?' and she said that sounded right."

Perhaps in a subconscious reaction to the story, Courtney forms a steeple with his hands.

"So, I have no way of verifying this, Court, because any men-tion of a big sister is totally absent from Silas's police report. But here's what I figure: *Hannah* killed her and Silas's parents with a ball-peen hammer and buried them in the garbage dump. Or maybe she made Silas help her. After all—it was always a little suspect that an eleven-year-old kid would be able to do that alone, right? Silas is shipped off to a foster home, Greta—Hannah—is sent somewhere else. Maybe the same spot. Who knows. Any-ways, once she gets this idea to tape people as they die she recruits her old assistant: her little brother. Remember how that doctor told us Silas kept saying he was 'told' to do all this stuff? What if he meant it literally?"

Courtney is very still. His face is embroiled in some type of inner conflict.

"Hmmm," he says. "And then, like you thought before, after killing Savannah, Silas got scared—"

"She tattooed his face. Hundred percent. She's the artist—only the front of her body, the parts she could reach herself, are tattooed. She did it after making the tape, that I now know," I say and shudder, picturing the black snake curling in on itself.

"How can you be sure?" Courtney asks.

"I just . . . Leave that for now. But anyways, it makes sense that Silas freaked out and tried to escape from her. Steals the tape, as that's the source of his fear. In his mind, it's the reason she tattooed him. Marked him. Maybe he was going to be next. To replicate her success with Savannah. So he turns himself in so that she can't get to him. And there's no reason for them to look into his sister—he confesses to killing both Savannah and his parents himself."

Courtney strokes one of his eyebrows, glaring at me. Can tell I'm holding out on him but doesn't want to push me too hard.

"Okay. But then so . . . what about—"

"Okay, so then, as we'd already figured, once his big sister finally gets in to see him at Sachar, he freaks out and mails the tape to his snail-mail paramour in Beulah, and—"

"Frank," Courtney interrupts, "this is all secondary. You said you heard the first few seconds . . . What happened in that hotel room?"

I sigh, grind out the end of my cigarette and watch Sadie splashing around in the pool. She hasn't spotted Courtney yet. Or maybe she just doesn't recognize him without his winter clothes.

The last two months here at the resort—and the weeks before

that, moving to a different city every other night, initially scared to stop moving—have been tainted by memories of that night in the hotel room. Even now, sitting here thousands of miles away, I can't seem to get her scent off of me. Can't stop feeling her clawlike hands on the sides of my face, keep picturing the look on her face immediately before I shot her.

But mostly I keep thinking about the tape. The snake. What Greta said:

"We've made mistakes that will be echoed back and forth for eternity."

I didn't hear the whole tape, but as I've stared at the ceiling at three, four in the morning these past months, replaying the images the snake showed me, I've come to suspect (or fear) that it's not the cassette itself that's a palindrome, it's *everything.* Like, once you die, the system just hits stop, then rewind, and you go backwards—your mistakes being echoed back, replayed—until starting at the beginning again. A train slowly chugging to a halt, and then the engineer cranking it into reverse for another ride backwards, down the same tracks. That life and death are the snake consuming his own tail. Was that what Savannah was when she visited me? An echo coming back the other direction?

I only saw the start of this process. I'm still guessing about this stuff. But if I'm right, that this is what the end of the tape makes explicit, I figure the Beulah Twelve saw that they were stuck in an infinite loop and lost their marbles. Because who's lived a life so well that they want to live it again and again forever? First they killed a kid, thinking it was an act of mercy, to spare *him.* Better to have never been born, or to never grow up, than to get stuck in that loop, right? And then, perhaps exacerbated by the realization that the murder itself would be part of their endless film reel, they attempted what appeared to be the only escape. They couldn't just kill themselves, knowing what they knew. The only way out was to keep themselves suspended, somewhere in between life and death. Frozen. That was the only way to get some peace. Some rest. What they must not have realized is that cryogenically freezing oneself is somewhat complicated.

I polish off the colada in my hand, savoring the cold rum on the back of my throat.

"Frank?" Courtney is leaning in close, looking desperate. "So?"

But because I didn't hear the whole cassette, nothing was *proven* to me, as it was to Greta and the Beulah Twelve and ostensibly Candy. There's still a skeptical—or hopeful—part of me that's sure the snake hallucination was some kind of self-induced placebo effect, like speaking in tongues. All the images I saw of myself are obviously things my subconscious could have summoned on its own. And so I'm fortunate, in a way, to be struggling in the nether zone that nun on the plane described. A place of belief, just short of knowing.

Still, it's kept me from a good night's sleep ever since I put a bullet in Hannah Graham (admittedly, fleeing the country hasn't helped either): I can't shake the thought that one day, I'll echo back this way, then back again. Every moment repeated and analyzed forever. It's too much pressure to live with. I wish with every cell in my body that Greta hadn't let me hear that thing. I keep thinking about those divine first few seconds, and then the low bass note. The snake. Some things can never be unheard.

"Frank?"

Before I can think about how to answer, we're interrupted by Sadie emerging from the pool. She patters over to us, dripping on the polished stone.

"Courtney!" she says.

"Hello." He gives her a weird smile as I wrap a green towel around her shoulders.

"Are you staying here with us?" she asks.

Courtney looks around, as if considering whether this resort is up to his lofty standards.

"I certainly wouldn't be opposed to checking in here for a week or so if your father doesn't mind the company."

"Wanna go swimming?" she asks Courtney.

"I . . ." Courtney looks longingly at me. "Maybe a bit later, Sadie."

"Then why are you wearing a swimsuit? Come on."

"Go on, Court." I grin. "We can talk later. Live a little."

"Yes, live, like you're doing." Courtney rises to his feet. Gives me a look of disapproval. "Live with skin cancer and liver failure."

"Courtney. Come on!" Sadie tugs at his hand.

Courtney sighs, takes Sadie by the hand and leads her back to the pool. Removes her green towel and sets it carefully on the edge of the cement. She jumps in, trying to tuck in her knees for a cannonball, but fails miserably. Courtney tentatively sits down on the edge and dips in his feet.

I watch Sadie paddle over to him and splash him, prompting him to flail spastically and try to escape, but Sadie is suddenly clinging to his leg, trying to pull him in with her. I laugh a little, watching him try to extricate himself from her puny grip without hurting her. I set down my empty glass and stagger to my feet, head swooning a bit. Gaze up at the clear azure sky and breathe deep, then walk over to the edge of the pool and push him in from behind.

He disappears under the water for a moment, leaving his sombrero hovering on the water, and then he surfaces, gasping.

Sadie splashes him again, and he tries to shield himself from her, using his ruined sombrero.

There's only one thing I can't even start to figure out. And it's nagging at me more than any other, because I know even *Hannah* didn't know the answer: Why did this process "work"—do whatever Hannah wanted it to—that time with Savannah, and not with anyone else? Savannah probably wasn't the first attempt, and Hannah surely tried to replicate the process many times afterwards—she intended to with Silas, and actually did with Orange. This is the most tempting reason to tell Courtney exactly what I saw—the possibility that he'll be able to help me figure this out.

I put my sunglasses on Sadie's towel and prepare to join the two of them in the pool. Sadie spots me and gives Courtney a respite.

"Do a cannonball!" she says.

Courtney looks concerned as I teeter at the lip of the pool.

"You really shouldn't swim when you're this drunk, Frank. Go sleep it off—"

"No, no," Sadie screams over Courtney. "Cannonball!"

I shrug. "You only live once, Court."

I leap into the air, simultaneously grinning at Courtney and clumsily trying to tuck in my knees. Just moments before executing a flawless belly flop, I realize that the kindest thing I can do for my friend is to tell him nothing about what happened in that hotel room. And I certainly won't mention that the tape—undamaged—is upstairs in my bag, tucked into a dirty sock.

Acknowledgments

My AGENT, ELIZABETH Copps, is an absolute pleasure to work with in every capacity—without her guidance, wisdom and patience, none of this would have happened. Additionally, everyone else at MCA including: Maria Carvainis, Martha Guzman and Sam Brody.

Everybody at Witness Impulse, particularly my editor, Chloe Moffett, whose enthusiasm, brilliant sensibilities and humor have made this whole process a delight.

Maxx Loup—without his support I likely would have stopped writing years before *Palindrome* was even born. He's nurtured my writing career as a gifted editor, sounding board and dear friend. Every artist should have someone this interesting to talk to in their lives.

My brother and writing partner, Noah Rinsky, an incredibly talented reader, whose prose, company and music have influenced me far more than he realizes.

Chelsey Emmelhainz now at SkyHorse, the first editor to champion this manuscript.

12 Corners coffee shop on East Broadway, where I wrote almost all of this book.

Eric Alterman, J. P. Medved and "Uncle" Mark Rinsky, who have been giving me astoundingly thoughtful notes since I started writing.

Asking Jonah Bromwich, Avishay Naamat and Lori Ungemah to read early drafts of this is among the best decisions I've ever made, and their fingerprints are all over this book.

Robert McGuill, Steve "Mr." Schriener, Carly Silver at Harlequin, Daniel Millenson, Shira Schindel, Jacob Hartz and Laura Rogers all helped my career at critical junctures, sometimes unwittingly.

And Mom and Dad, my biggest fans.

About the Author

E.Z. RINSKY has worked as a statistics professor, copywriter and—for one misguided year—a street musician. He currently lives in Tel Aviv. More at ezrinsky.com.

Discover great authors, exclusive offers, and more at hc.com.